THE WOLF

OF

116TH STREET

THE WOLF

OF

116TH STREET

A NEW YORK STORY

by

BRUCE WIGGINS

Picture Credits:
Cover design: Irene Smid
Photos: back cover photos by the author. Real people, real dogs, fictional story.

ISBN: 979-8-218-21710-5 paperback
979-8-218-21711-2 e-Book

First Edition
Printed in the United States of America

Acknowledgements

I begin with a full-throated thank you to my wife, Marti, for being my first reader and constant support.

Thank you too to my small group of readers, without whose advice and support I would have blundered all too often: Marg Moss, Pam Barkentin, Rosemary Didear, and Paula Shapiro.

My deepest gratitude to my editor, Peter Kelman, who treated me kindly when he should have thrown in the towel—his willingness to call it like he saw it saved the book from being even more tedious.

"If the person you are talking to doesn't appear to be listening, be patient. It may simply be that he has a small piece of fluff in his ear."

A.A. Milne, Winnie the Pooh

The story you are about to read is true. Only the plot and the names have been changed to protect the innocent. New York, however, remains as it was in 1978—unmolested by the author.

Contents

-1-

The Capture

Manhattan
Washington Heights

February 1978

An Arctic wind screamed uphill from the Hudson River, scattering trashcan lids across 158th Street like the shields of a vanquished army. Debris from the open cans spiraled into the air providing early risers in upper-floor apartments with a glimpse of yesterday's headlines to enjoy with their toast and jam.

It was the third day of ten-degree daytime highs. The blinding blizzard of previous days had finally abated, with only occasional flakes fluttering in the gusts. Pedestrians exiting the subway at Broadway and 157th Street snugged their hats and scarves, squinting painfully into the wind. It was Sunday and vendors of roasted chestnuts and hot pretzels paused long over their breakfast tea while only those unlucky enough to have strong reason to leave home trudged through the fresh snow toward their destinations.

The entrance to and exit from the West Side Highway (aka Henry Hudson Parkway) at 158th Street lies at the bottom of a deep canyon bordered on each side by cliffs of monotonous brown brick and a checkerboard of apartment windows, shimmering like mercury in the winter light. When viewing from an angle, denizens of the upper stories could enjoy a glimpse of the crenelated Palisades of New Jersey or the occasional passage of a tug pushing a barge along the Hudson.

There are sidewalks on either side of the street, but they do not encourage pedestrians. The crosscurrents of the highway and the river provide only the deadest of ends. Foot traffic is limited to grim-faced building custodians, trundling galvanized trash cans through the heavy metal doors of their castle keep. If pedestrians were to appear, they were apt to be regarded with suspicion by both custodians and police—the former standing firmly by their trash cans, deflecting miscreants into the street, the latter easing their cruisers beside these dubious souls, hurrying them along like stray sheep.

At the confluence of East Riverside Drive and 158th Street, a dog and her man braced against the wind's cold burn. The dog was a brown German shepherd with a thick winter coat. The man on her leash was tall and wore a padded military-style coat; a wool-knit hat pulled low over the ears; blue jeans; and high leather boots with snow-caked laces. His tightly trimmed beard did little to protect him from the wind. His cheeks were chafed, and bits of ice clung to his mustache.

Of the few cars that moved cautiously along the Westside Highway or up and down Broadway, none dared challenge the pitch of 158th Street.

Dog and man had paused in their walk, focusing their attention on the bottom of the hill where the snow swirled like Kansas, and a shadowy figure moved searchingly among the uncapped trash cans. The man thought it might be a child, and the dog thought it must be a dog. Both were right.

As dog and man stepped cautiously down the hill, the forager came more clearly into view. It was indeed a dog, standing on hind legs, its head partially buried inside a can. The shepherd gave a low growl and strained against her leash.

"It's okay, Isa," said the man, moving forward and tightening his grip.

As they approached, a head emerged from the can and turned to look. From its coloring and the texture of its fur, the man considered it might be a husky or a malamute. As they sized one another up, the wagging tail of the derelict dispelled any likelihood of danger. Man, dogs, and leash relaxed so that the dogs could get acquainted in their fashion.

It was clear from body language that the shepherd was the alpha dog, and the playful subservience of the other revealed both the temperament and snowshoe size of a half-grown male puppy with the markings of an Alaskan malamute.

Perhaps a rush of frozen air flung from the narrow centrifuge of the Arctic Circle had swept over teams of Inuit wolfdogs, herds of moose, elk, and caribou and, gathering their scent, cut a wide swath through Canada and the upper Midwest, guzzling moisture from the mists of the Great Lakes and the broad watershed of the Hudson River Valley until, unable to hold its crystalline load for one more mile, dumped it on the iron-hard streets of Manhattan, igniting the yet unkindled DNA of this now forsaken whelp, propelling him out into the street to whirl and bound until only exhaustion brought both hunger and the realization that he'd lost his way. Or, in a more likely scenario, he'd tumbled to the street at the end of a boot, leaving in his wake the entrails of shredded cushions, gnawed chair spindles, and a bounty of other gratuitous gifts.

But this was not the time to speculate or judge. It was time for a decision: rescue or abandon. The vagrant wore a plain leather collar with no tags, so while the dogs feigned bloodshed with gnashing of teeth and low growls, the man slipped the loop of his leash under the cub's collar and, binding the two dogs together, turned their backs to the wind and shambled up the hill toward the warmth and security of home.

-2-

A Kosher Solution

By mid-morning, the snow had started up again in earnest. Just a few miles downriver, sustained gusts squalled across the Hudson and up the wind tunnel of 116th Street. Accelerating uphill from Riverside Drive toward Broadway, flakes had morphed into the arrows of a medieval siege. College students from Columbia and Barnard, trudging downhill, leaned into the wind with all the daring of Nordic ski jumpers in mid-flight.

Wind and snow continued their uphill assault, cresting on Broadway, sweeping unabridged through the ornamental gates of the university onto College Walk, channeling the interstices between buildings and, finally, unrestrained, diffusing into the anarchy of motion that filled the campus quad. Snow piled deep on the grass and granite, filled the basins of fountains, and accumulated on stairs and in angular drifts against the hedges that lined the walkways. The bronze statue of *Alma Mater* sat windswept on her throne before the Romanesque columns of the old library, her arms widespread in a welcoming gesture of static grace that belied the kinetic frenzy surrounding her.

On the east side of the campus, College Walk again narrows between buildings. There, wind and snow sluice across Amsterdam Avenue to make their mad dash down the final block of 116th Street, where they explode over the ramparts of Morningside Park and the flatlands of Harlem that lie below, covered in a white mockery of the Heights that look down upon them.

Natural drifts and tall berms from the plows had buried the cars parked along the uptown side of 116th, revealing only their wind-scrubbed rooftops, strung in a muted line like the beads of a rosary. Alternate side of the street parking resulted in deep banks of snow piled along the downtown curb and sidewalk, leaving only a footpath of cleared snow for pedestrian travel. At this moment, just two travelers dared to brave the elements: a boy and his small dog.

*

A little less than a year previous, on a cold Saturday morning in mid-February, Blair Kennedy slipped unnoticed from her apartment at 425 West 116th Street, carrying a large hatbox. It was a "need to know" mission, which only she and Ian Kennedy, the titular head of the Kennedy clan, needed to know. Arriving with her hatbox and a hot cup of coffee at Bideawee Animal Shelter on East 38th Street, Blair had plenty of time to compare spots and splotches, the tilt of ears, and the quality of wag, all before management closed the doors at noon. It was a heart-wrenching task, as there were many qualified candidates, but one pup, born and nurtured in-house over the last eight weeks, engaged her like no other: a black-and-white female rat terrier mix, weighing slightly more than a cheesecake. A deal was struck, and she was carried home in the hatbox, now tied with a ribbon.

Blair's return home was anything but stealthy. She rang the doorbell in rapid succession to draw the family together. When the door opened, she stepped inside the foyer and, extending the box at arm's length, exclaimed, "Happy Valentine's Day!"

Ian feigned surprise while Maxwell and his sister Logan, ages ten and twelve, looked on excitedly.

"Take it," pleaded Blair, "my arms are getting tired." Ian took the box and placed it rumbling on the foyer's hardwood floor.

"Here," he said to the children, dropping to one knee and tugging gently on the loose ends of the bow, "on the count of three, each take an end and pull. One (pause), two (longer pause), three!"

The moment the pressure eased, the lid popped open, the box tumbled to one side, and a wobbly-legged puppy skidded onto the floor. Its clumsy scrambling electrified the family.

"Does she have a name?" asked Logan, desperately hoping she didn't.

"Not yet," answered her mother, shaking her head.

They all moved to the living room to get acquainted, the new arrival slipping on the hardwood, trying to keep up. Sitting in a circle in the center of the room, they passed their lively guest from lap to lap. Amid the licking of hands and nipping of fingers, suggestions for names erupted.

"How about Valentine?" suggested Logan.

"Or Kitty," offered Max, with his usual wry humor.

"Or Blithe," said Mom, stroking the soft head with the tips of her fingers.

Offerings continued to snap and pop for some time before Ian offered this bit of reasoning: "We have here a New York dog, born on the East Side," he said, in his best news-anchor voice, "and she should have a distinctly New York name. What name would make her unquestionably a New Yorker?"

The children, being seasoned urbanites, poured forth a flurry of ideas. First came the foods: pasta, cheesecake, pretzel, chestnut, and wiener (good try); then the boroughs: Brooklyn, Bronx, Queens (all rejected for xenophobic reasons); then, famous places: Schwarz (F.A.O.), Saks, Bergdorf, Macy, Broadway, SoHo (possibles, but not probables); local fauna: pigeon, rat, roach (again, Max-humor); teams: Mets, Knicks, Jets (all too plural); and, finally, back to food: pickle, matzah, knish, blintz (now we're getting somewhere); until, ultimately, it kneaded down to a duel between Bagel and Bialy.

A heated discussion ensued, comparing their unique qualities. All agreed that they both looked and tasted similar. Blair offered the following from her culinary expertise: "A bagel is boiled before baking and is made with unbleached bread flour, sugar, and malt (which converts to sugar in the oven—yum). A bialy is just baked and uses gluten flour, no malt or sugar, so it is lower in carbs and higher in protein (marginally better for you). A bagel is round with a hole in the middle, while a bialy is flatter with no hole, just a slight depression filled with caramelized onions."

It seemed there was no way out of this conundrum, as it was a tie based on taste. It was time for Blair Kennedy, arbiter of all things domestic, to bring this discussion to a truly kosher conclusion.

"The bialy is not known worldwide," she said with certainty. "Outside of New York and Bialystok, Poland, it is hardly known at all, while the only places you will *not* find a bagel are in Kathmandu, Kandahar, or even in New Delhi, despite the confusion associated with that name."

Although this argument was a bit arcane for the kids, mama's imprimatur closed the book on the dispute and the name of the new, brown-eyed, tippy-eared puppy was to be, now and forever, Bagel.

Back on the icy sidewalk of 116th Street a year later, strong winds and pelting snow made dog walking a struggle for the mighty Max. After spending nearly five frozen minutes finding the right spot to place her stain, Bagel continued moving eastward along her carefully measured fiefdom to discern what interloper had dared to leave its mark.

Being an official, tag-carrying, New York dog and part rat terrier to boot, Bagel followed the "dig we must" pronouncements of Con Edison, Manhattan's keeper of the cables, and started to dig.

Snow flew in a crescent as she honed in on her target until, with a quick 90-degree shift, she placed three perfect droplets of her own exactly where she wanted them, effectively purging her domain of any trace of invasive species.

Bagel looked smugly at Max and kicked some loose snow over her deposit. It was time to go home.

-3-

The Trojan Horse

Inside the Kennedy apartment, a late breakfast was underway. The smells of bacon, eggs, toast, and coffee filled the air with the ambrosia of a Sunday morning. Sections of the *New York Times* lay open and scattered about the living room: *Arts & Leisure* on Ian's chair, the *Book Review* on Blair's blanketed corner of the couch, while others lay well-rummaged on the coffee table.

Despite the near-blizzard conditions of the previous night, Ian Kennedy had donned his winter wear and leaned into the headwinds to plod across campus to the newsstand on Broadway. Every Saturday night at about 11:00 p.m., trucks tossed the early edition of the Sunday *Times* beside newsstands around Manhattan. On this raw night, they arrived like Nebraska hay bales, the scent of fresh ink calling the newshounds in from the fields.

Ian approached his apartment building with a Sunday paper the size of a Christmas turkey snugged under his arm. Images from Dickens provided him with some spiritual warmth as he fancied himself a kindly Scrooge bringing joy to the Cratchit family. Entering his apartment, he called out, "God bless us, everyone!"

Only Bagel clicked down the hallway into the foyer. Seeing Ian trying to pull off a boot while still holding the newspaper under his arm was not compelling, and she trotted off.

The following day, as Mom plated the breakfast, Max asked, "Do I have to eat eggs?"

"You can do your usual," said Mom. Max's "usual" consisted of smothering his scrambled eggs (the only way he'd eat them) under a thick shroud of ketchup—his red badge of courage.

When food was being prepared or served, Bagel would walk about the kitchen or alongside the dining table on her hind legs like a circus performer. The added height gave her nose a deeper appreciation of the menu and occasionally put her slender jaws within striking distance of an errant piece of bacon.

With all plates and bodies settled, eating and the usual rambling dialogue of Sunday breakfast commenced. Bagel sat under the table between the legs of Max and Logan, primed for any miscalculations from above deck.

"Max, did you rinse the salt from Bagel's paws when you came in?" Mom asked.

"Uh-huh," he answered, pounding the base of the ketchup bottle.

"Is it still snowing hard?" asked Dad.

"Uh-huh," Max said, whose efforts to cover the offending yellow mash on his plate resulted in a sudden burp of ketchup, arching drops onto the tablecloth and the rim of Logan's plate.

"Max!" cried Blair and Logan in a dissonant duet. Max looked sheepish, but as a flow had started, he continued patting the bottle to achieve his required density.

"Shall we try and get tickets to the *Pirates of Penzance*?" asked Ian. "It's opening next month at the Uris on 51st."

"That would be fun," Blairs said with mild interest. "A revival of Virginia Wolf is coming in a month or so, too."

"I've had more than a decade of nightmares since first seeing the film. I think I'll pass," said Ian as he watched Max commence his scrambled egg-eating ritual. It was furtive and reptilian, with sudden snaps and gulps, executed with checked breath to avoid any hint of what Max called "the flavor of the unborn." Full-grown chickens, however, whether roasted, stewed, sliced, or ground into sausage, were welcomed with gushing glands. On the other hand, Logan had the beatific look of someone savoring the coalescence of salt, fat, and flesh that was the essence of bacon. Perhaps she shared his view, mused Ian, that bacon was even better than chocolate—excluding, of course, that cut labeled "Canadian," which was not bacon at all but ham.

Suddenly, Ian burst into song:

> "I am the very model of a modern Major-General
> "I've information vegetable, animal, and mineral
> "I know the kings of England, and I quote the fights historical
> "From Marathon to Waterloo, in order categorical."

The children looked up from their plates, and Blair clapped silently with the tips of her fingers.

"One more time, please, Dad?" begged Logan.

"Only if you insist," he replied with feigned indifference, and just as he was about to launch into "matters mathematical," the doorbell rang.

It was not just any ring. It was *dit-da, dit-dit-dit, dit-dit-dit; dit-dah, dit-dit-dit dit-dit-dit.* Or, in the vernacular, A-S-S; A-S-S; A-S-S.

"It's Uncle Mike," shrieked the kids simultaneously as they knew his signature ring, which gave them a reason to jump up from the table and run to the front door—Bagel barking and keeping pace. Uncle Mike rarely arrived without a gift.

Michael Kennedy had a flair for languages that included Morse code—a skill he'd learned from a radio operator *en route* to Italy on a Yugoslav freighter. When announcing himself electronically, Michael demonstrated his antique talent using one of three distinctive rings: "S-O-S" or "A-S-S," and, on occasion, "N-I-C-E A-S-S." The first two were easiest for doorbell ringing, while he could whistle the latter as a compliment when necessary.

Michael had always been a rebel. His blue eyes and curly orange hair should have augured eccentricities, as there were no known pink-skinned, blue-eyed, freckle-faced carrot-tops perched in the boughs of his family tree. Moreover, his eleven-year-old daughter had brown eyes and auburn hair, which showed no inclination to wax red. Ian was blond growing up but was gradually morphing brown. Logan and Max were blond and brown-haired, respectively, with brown eyes and sporting freckles only in the summer. However, both paternal and maternal pedigrees attributed a possible influence to marauding Vikings, who spread their mutant DNA throughout Scotland like the pox, not necessarily to contributions from the milkman.

The door to apartment 1F was located at the back of the first-floor lobby next to the elevator. In front of that door stood a man in snow-covered combat boots and a combination of military and civilian winter clothes. He wore no hat, only a black ski mask with a red maple leaf sewn above the eye holes.

Bagel continued barking, and Max grabbed her by the collar as Logan opened the door to a masked man and a large, gray dog—turning Bagel's frantic barking into a low growl.

Logan, confused by the unfamiliar canine, said, "Uncle Mike, is that you?"

"*Naturalmente*, my little chickadee," Mike replied, pulling off his ski mask and shaking its snow onto the lobby floor.

Max reached his hand out for the dog to sniff. "Did you get a new dog? It looks like a husky."

Logan turned her head and called down the hallway, "Mom, Dad, it's Uncle Mike. He's got a new dog!"

"He does resemble a husky, Max," replied Uncle Mike, "but this is a malamute. No blue eyes. He's just a pup but already bigger than a husky."

Blair and Ian joined the group at the front door. "Hello, Michael," said Blair, using the full form of his proper name, something she often did when questioning the motives behind some of Uncle Mike's eccentric behaviors.

"Good morrow, Nanook," Ian said in his best Elizabethan English. "I am sorry, but there are no walruses here."

"Alas!" said Mike. "My intrepid companion and I trekked down from the tundra in the hope of nourishment or, in lieu of that, a dram of whiskey would suffice."

They all laughed, except Bagel, who was still growling and giving Max a hard time.

"Why don't you put Bagel in your room, Max," said his mother. "We'll let her out when we know she can get along."

Max picked her up and carried her off.

"So, Nanook, would you and your trusty sidekick like to come in," asked Ian, opening the door a bit wider, "or must you hurry back to the Iditarod?"

"There is nowhere to park, so I left the van running in the street," answered Mike. "I'd better get out there before a plow dumps it into Morningside Park. The fact is," he continued in a more serious tone, "I have brought this beautiful creature here to talk about adoption."

As no one responded, Uncle Mike pushed forward with his explanation. "When I walked Isa this morning, I found the pup rummaging in the trashcans behind our apartment building. I think he's about six or seven months old and possibly a purebred malamute. He's amiable, but I think he's been abandoned."

"He looks like a raccoon," offered Max, who had returned to the group.

"He is beautiful, Michael, Blair said. "He seems to be almost smiling," she added, smiling herself. "But why don't you and Lizanne keep him?"

"Isa is going into heat soon, and we're committed to breeding her with a shepherd. It would be impossible to keep this guy contained. Liz is fine with a few days, but she doesn't want him permanently."

"I can't imagine someone just abandoning him," said Blair, offering her hand to the dog for a sniff, receiving a lick and a wag in return.

"He's so handsome," said Logan. "Bagel is spayed, so no problem there," she added like the adult she wasn't.

Mike sensed the resistance of his brother and Blair. "I can take him home and put up a few 'lost dog' notices by the subway and the bus stops. Someone may claim him. If not, I can take him to Baideawee." The mention of Baideawee turned the conversation.

"Why don't we give him a chance," Blair said, turning to her family. "We can introduce Bagel to him and see how it goes for a day or two while Mike checks the 'lost dog' angle."

There was general agreement, followed by a short discussion about how they should proceed. Mike said he'd brought a new bag of dog food in the car, "just in case," but he needed to keep the leash for Isa. "There's some rope in the bus you can use for now," he said.

As Mike unhooked the leash, Ian took the dog by the collar and pulled him into the foyer, and the undocumented transfer of parenthood was done.

Ian put on his coat, hat, and boots; Mike donned his ski mask, and they walked out to the van. It was doubled-parked, its flashers still blinking, but the engine had stopped, and ice was collecting on the windshield.

As Mike slid open the door to retrieve the bag of dog food, Ian inspected the vehicle. The minivan had been in Mike's possession for more than ten years. In its halcyon days, under Mike's pilotage, it had traveled from New York to Miami, then to Dallas, Mexico City, Acapulco, and back to New York. Although an upgrade was long since affordable, this 1963, cream-colored, split-window, hippy bus—top speed 70 mph (downhill), remained Mike's favored choice for transportation.

Ian was relieved to see that there were chains on the rear wheels. "How did you manage the chains?"

"The plows had packed me in. I had to dig out to chain up," answered Mike. "Fortunately, there was almost no traffic on Broadway. The toughest spot was the hill rising from 125th, but I had a good head of steam before I got there. It'll be the same going back." Mike was referring to the drop into the valley that veed sharply at 125th Street and then shot up again for another ten blocks before leveling off.

Ian admired his brother's thirst for adventure. It must have taken him an hour to dig out and chain up.

Mike handed over the bag of dried food and said optimistically, "Let's see if she starts." He climbed into the driver's seat, closed the door, and rolled down the window. After a tense display of gastritis, the van started.

"Oh, I almost forgot," he said, reaching to the seat beside him and picking up a long length of nylon rope wound in a circle, "this should do until you can get proper gear."

Mike handed Ian the rope through the window, then banged his gloved hand against the side of the van. "My faithful steed," he said to Ian. "I'll cut over to Broadway at 114th and then make the toboggan run."

Turning the van around, he shouted across the street to Ian, who was watching the van's departure with some concern. "Hi Ho Silver, away!" The van pushed into the wind, turned left on Amsterdam Avenue, and, flashers flashing, rolled away.

Meanwhile, inside the apartment, introductions were underway.

-4-

Name-dropping

The foyer seemed the safest location for initial greetings: no lamps, no vases, just a coat rack and four bicycles—two against each wall. As Bagel had stopped barking, she had been released from exile in Max's bedroom and allowed to join the family in the foyer, where she treated the playful overtures of her new housemate with icy indifference.

As Ian came in carrying the bag of dog food and length of rope, he was pelted with questions before he could even take off his hat and hang up his coat.

"Dad, what should we name him?" Logan asked. "I think we should call him Bialy. We'd have Bagel and Bialy. Wouldn't it be perfect?" Ian struggled with his boots, placing a hand against a wall to keep from falling.

"What about Big Foot or Sasquatch?" suggested Max in his usual way.

"How about Sergeant or King?" offered Blair, channeling names from a favorite childhood TV show.

Ian shrugged off his boots and, holding up his hands in defense, suggested they retire to the living room and calmly discuss the naming. Ian went to his wingback chair; Mom and the kids took the couch. Bagel proceeded to her usual roost on Blair's lap. Seeing he was the only one not seated, the guest leaped to the couch, taking up residence on Logan's lap like a temple-gate lion. This unexpected motion caused considerable confusion and a reshuffling of positions, with their visitor decamping to the rug and adopting the expression of a prisoner in the dock.

"Remember," said Ian, "this dog may already have a name and a family."

"Aw, Dad," whined Logan, "we can't just call him 'dog.' It's too unfriendly. Dogs need a name, just like we do."

Blair and Max concurred, and the naming continued:

"Sylvester" (Max),
"Eeyore" (Logan),
"Mr. Darcy" (Blair).

Ian suggested they consider the dog's ethnicity, but no one knew any Eskimo names other than Nanook, which seemed inappropriate. Max said his eyes looked Asian. Logan said there was a Chinese boy in her class at school named "Oscar." Max suggested "Grasshopper" after the hero in the TV series *Kung Fu*, but neither rang with enough authenticity.

"Dad, you must know some Chinese names," said Logan, with a hint of desperation.

At this point, the reason for Logan's entreaty deserves a bit of explication.

Chinatown was a favorite family destination for fried rice, boiled dumplings, and Hong Kong-produced kung-fu movies. Despite their swordplay and spraying blood, the special effects of these films were primitive enough that it was easy to suspend both disbelief and belief and render these films "child-safe," on the order of John Wayne westerns.

The heroes and heroines of these films did not tote Winchesters or pearl-handled six-shooters. Instead, their weapons consisted of knives, swords, spears, and throwing stars. But most importantly, they possessed special powers, such as lifting teapots from across the room and vanquishing dozens of armed attackers with bare hands and slippered feet. They could also flutter, near-weightless, through trees and across rooftops.

The venue for such films was the Music Palace, a decaying fifty-year-old 600-seat theater located along the curve of Hester and Bowery Streets—technically not Chinatown, but close enough. Serving mostly Hong Kong immigrants, the Palace was a refuge for those needing a place to sleep out of the rain or snow or for families whose adults sought a few hours of reprieve from the drudgery of working in Chinatown's restaurants or sweatshops.

A visit to this theater resembled a picnic in Central Park or flying China Airlines: kids running freely; people talking, drinking, and smoking; babies crying; and family dinners unfolding from plastic bags filling the air with the scent of garlic, pepper oil, fried chicken, and fish; and all under the worrisome whine of a projector on its last legs.

Following the example of other theater patrons, the Kennedys brought their food. Blair, a meticulous planner, knew the protocol for a double feature: a shopping bag containing egg salad sandwiches wrapped in Saran, salted pretzels (bought at an underground stand next to the Times Square shuttle), potato chips, four cans of Coke, and a can opener. If they purchased anything at the theater, it was a giant-sized box of chocolate mints to be shared by all. However, even with these provisions, they were pikers compared to the natives.

Kung Fu films such as the Shaw Brothers' *Come Drink with Me, One-Armed Swordsman,* or *Challenge of the Masters* were family favorites. Still, nothing inspired the clan to climb onto the subway and zigzag their way from the Westside to the Eastside and down to Canal Street like a Japanese *Zatoichi* film.

Except for the *Zatoichi* series, Japanese samurai-style fighting films were not part of the Music Palace fare. This kind of cinematic racism was partly due to the language barrier but was more the result of a lingering wartime animus for anything Japanese. However, despite the conflicts of a deep cultural divide, Zatoichi, the eponymous hero of these films, with his uniquely flawed but beguiling character, seemed to have bridged the gap of national enmity through his swordplay and his earthy but sympathetic persona. Japanese dialogue was first translated into Mandarin, then into a sublayer of English. It was sometimes arduous to follow, but somehow, it worked—even for young Max.

The Kennedys had seen only a handful of *Zatoichi* films, but from the very first, they were captivated. The stories are set in feudal times. Their hero is a blind masseur traveling on foot from village to village. He is somewhat tragic, living by his wits, gambling, and incomparable skills with the *shikomi-zue*—a sword secreted in a walking stick. Central to the character is his compassion for the innocent and defense of anyone suffering injustice. He loves but cannot endure love. Like Alan Ladd in the movie *Shane*, he rights the wrongs of the vulnerable and moves on, leaving in his wake one or more distressed damsels (Come back, Shane! Come back!) His character is coarse but empathetic and, when necessary, ruthless. In short, he is lovable—even to the Nipponophobes of Chinatown.

Once the name "Zatoichi" was presented to the group, there was unanimous and immediate approval.

Logan's insistence that her father "must know some Chinese names" was predicated on the fact that he had studied Chinese language at Columbia University for seven years, gaining both a BA and an MA in Asian Studies. In the early 1960s, China/US relations were uniformly hostile, and China's economy struggled in the deadly vortex of the failed policies of Mao's "Great Leap Forward" and a devastating famine. Studying in China was out of the question for Americans, so budding Sinophiles went either to Taiwan or Hong Kong. Ian did both, spending a year in Taipei and six months in Hong Kong working on his master's thesis, during which he became fluent in Mandarin and developed a deep appreciation for dim sum, chicken feet, pot stickers, and kung-fu films.

Blair Kensington favored the films of Bergman, Truffaut, and Kurosawa, but she quickly caught kung-fu fever when Ian took her to Chinatown on their second date. By the time Ian had returned from studying in Taiwan, Blair was a senior at Barnard, majoring in Russian language and literature. In the fall of 1965, a small student protest concerning CIA recruitment on the Columbia campus brought them together. Over beers in the West End Bar, they discovered they also shared some misgivings about the university's fledgling chapter of Students for a Democratic Society (SDS). Both agreed with the cause, but Ian bristled at the Marxist rhetoric, and Blair felt the leadership misogynistic. Six months later, they were engaged and, within a year, married.

After finishing his Master's degree, Ian found work at the Parker School—a progressive girls' school located on West 81st Street. Parker was among the first of New York's elite private schools to offer its students classes in Asian history (China, Japan, India) and Chinese language, but was not quite progressive enough to hire a native speaker for those duties. Ian applied for and won this position at just the right moment.

Blair had similar good fortune when a month before graduation, she heard from a friend that Mildred Harrison, the long-term administrative secretary of the Russian Institute, was retiring. Bravely, Blair introduced herself to Mildred and inquired how she might apply for the position. It turned out that retirement was three years away, but Mildred needed an assistant, and Blair landed the job. Over the following three years, she proved herself indispensable and the right choice to succeed her mentor in that position. As a parting gift, Mildred secured Blair's young family—Logan having arrived a year before—a ground-floor, five-room apartment in Columbia housing opposite the law school on West 116th Street, thus providing a considerable upgrade from their five-story walk-up on Columbus Avenue.

With the arbitration of the dog's name complete, a reconfiguration of the duty roster became necessary. All agreed to take turns walking the probationer and picking up his deposits, which would no doubt be a different order of magnitude than those presented by Bagel. Zatoichi's crew would consist of Max and Ian on one day, followed by Logan and Blair on the next. Ian was not sure Max was up to handling Zato (pron. like Otto; his name now shortened for convenience), so they agreed to work together for a few days as a test run. Blair and Ian could walk both dogs at the same time, but the kids would only be allowed to shepherd one.

The best-laid plans…

-5-

A Walk in the Park

Zato's first excursion onto 116th Street happened late that afternoon. The wind and snow had stopped; a gray light velveted the university campus; buildings and cars stood dull and frozen; and the iridescent reds and greens of the traffic lights blinked their messages to no one.

Max and his father had bundled up appropriately and elected to execute Zato's initial walk without Bagel. Ian knotted his brother's rope through a metal loop on Zato's collar, handed it to Max, and opened the apartment door.

Considering this his cue, Zato rushed into the lobby, pulling Max behind him like a windless kite. Already, this appeared to be a questionable match.

"I think you'd better let me take him out, Max," suggested Ian as they stood looking through the door pane to the sidewalk and street.

"I can do it. I want to," implored Max.

"Okay, but if he starts to pull away from you, pass me the rope."

Ian slowly cracked open the lobby door. No sooner did the cold air rush in than Zato pushed his nose and body through the crack, bouncing Max off the door jamb as he exited and dashed to the edge of the deep snow berm left by plows along the length of 116th Street. The dog lifted his left hind leg, instinctively aiming for the tree surrounded by snow which was well out of striking distance. Ian and Max looked on, amazed at the capacity of the young canine's bladder.

Returning to all fours, Zato offered what appeared to be a slight bow for his performance. After a few seconds of reflection, he leaped into the depths of the berm and began to porpoise his way toward Morningside Drive. His powerful hind legs provided considerable spring, even in the deep snow, and his pace quickened as he mastered the mechanics of forward motion. Max ran alongside on the icy sidewalk but was quickly out of his depth and solved the problem by giving his charge more and more rope. Ian tried to keep up but lost his footing and found himself a seated observer to Max diving into the berm with the rope sliding from his gloved hands.

Sensing a release of constraints, Zato put more spring into his bounds and quickly reached Morningside Drive, which runs parallel to Morningside Park. On a regular day, this stretch of road is filled with moving cars and people with their dogs, but even on this muffled afternoon, it was no place for an unleashed and untutored canine of questionable deportment.

Ian raised himself gingerly and hurried to assist Max, breast-stroking through deep snow toward the sidewalk. "I'm sorry," he panted, "I just couldn't keep up."

"I'm sure I couldn't have either," replied his father as he pulled Max safely to shore. "I think Zato went into the park, but he may have turned right onto Morningside. We'll get him, don't worry."

They began walking as fast as the slippery sidewalk allowed, but at the corner of Morningside Drive, there was no sign of the runaway.

"You stay here, and I'll check out the park," Ian said as he crossed the street and started down the stairs. "Call me if you see him."

As Max scanned the windblown street for signs, the escapee emerged onto the sidewalk from between parked cars where some intrepid adventurer had shoveled his vehicle out from the curbside. For a moment, the dog stood still, tail wagging. Max patted his thighs in encouragement, and, taking the hint, Zato bolted toward him but was yanked to a tumbling stop when his rope caught beneath an exposed tire.

"Dad, Zato is up here!" Max yelled over the parapet. "I think he's stuck!"

"Okay, I'm coming!" His father shouted from below. "Don't move!"

Ian scrambled up the icy steps, and Max pointed to their quarry, who had just righted himself twenty yards away. The dog backed up a few steps, taking some tension off his leash, and looked over his shoulder.

"Pretend you are not interested in him," instructed Ian. "We're just out for a walk. No big deal. Easy does it."

The pair approached the dog cautiously, chatting indifferently about the weather. Zato wagged his tail, looked over his shoulder, then back at the approaching figures. Ian sensed the game was still afoot. Suddenly, Zato turned and sprang in the opposite direction, freeing his leash from the tire.

Father and son looked on as the animal gained speed, but just as it seemed Zato was off to the Yukon, the rope snagged again, toppling him to the ground. This time, he lay still, panting, as his captors approached. Ian rebuked the dog for his misbehavior, which produced a look of feigned remorse. They completed the walk with Ian at the reins: no further roadside distractions, no attempts at a jailbreak. It was clear that walking Zato was an adult responsibility.

As the trio entered the apartment, Bagel trotted into the foyer. She looked them over disdainfully, registering obvious disappointment that the beast was still in tow.

Blair was in the kitchen preparing dinner when "the boys" (as she called them) walked in. "How was your walk?" she asked. Max looked at his dad.

"Zato is an adult responsibility," answered Ian. "He's like a kid whose parents never said 'no' to him. He loves the deep snow, but he needs adult control. And," he added with emphasis, "a strong collar and leash."

Suspecting more to the story, Blair looked at Ian and then at Max, who looked back at Ian. "Did something happen?"

Sensing Max's hesitation, Ian replied, "The first surprise was how long he could stand on three legs. It took forever, didn't it, Max?" Max nodded. "It was worse than waiting for your number at the DMV. I pity any trees in the neighborhood."

"Is that it?" Blair asked, knowing it wasn't.

"Well," said Ian, cracking open the door to the confessional, "Zato jumped into the snow piled along the sidewalk and started vaulting toward Morningside Drive, picking up speed as he went. Max gave it a valiant effort, but there was no way he could keep up—Zato pulled the rope right out of his hands."

Ian placed his hand affectionately on his son's shoulder and, looking at Zato, who sat virtuously in the middle of the kitchen, said, "In the immortal words of George Washington and Richard Nixon, 'I cannot tell a lie.' The dog ran off. Fortunately, the rope caught under a tire, enabling us to corral him. I gave him a stern talking to."

Blair looked at the boys doubtfully, then at Zato, certain he was grinning.

-6-

Gratuitous Gifts

Malamutes love people, and people love them. That evening Zato was the center of attention. He loved to be scratched: behind the ears, chest, tummy, the base of his tail, even his cheeks. He would lay on his back, legs splayed, and assume that someone would scratch his tummy—a habit likely learned at his last residence, one that Logan and Max were happy to indulge.

Ian and Blair assumed, both from the dog's playfulness and the trust he displayed in his new benefactors, that there had been no previous abuse, which augmented the likelihood that the actual owners of this peripatetic pup might be hunting desperately for him at that very moment.

But what of Bagel? How was she dealing with this foundling in their midst? What had been *her* family was now to be shared with a bore who boldly displayed his privates without a hint of shame. She enjoyed a good tummy rub, too, but modestly, on a lap, cradled in the nook of Blair's arm. How could she live with this beast who had brushed her aside in the hallway with the indifference of a bus barreling down Amsterdam Avenue?

She knew that there was nothing she could do, physically, to push him off stage. For the moment, he was a novelty, cute and cuddly, despite his exhibitionism. Her advantage would come from her guile, her urbanity, maturity, and the nobility that comes with her role as the Kennedy family's minister without portfolio.

Before bed that night, Ian took Zato and Bagel out for a quick walk. As Zato, unbeknownst to others, had been lapping a good deal of water from the toilet bowl, his time at the berm was Wagnerian. Afterward, Blair and Ian closed the doors to the living room, the kids' bedrooms, and the bathroom, leaving only the kitchen and their bedroom door ajar. They decided to sleep "with one ear open," lest their guest require midnight shepherding. As an added precaution, Bagel, the family Cerberus, stood sentinel at the foot of their bed.

Across the city, light snow fell. There was no wind blowing, no traffic moving, only the flutter of snow silently drifting through triangles of light along the streets and boulevards, row after row, softly deepening.

The next morning Logan was first up, readying herself for school. She had only cracked her door when responding to the rustle of bedclothes, a nose poked in, followed by the bulk of a wagging malamute. Hopping onto Logan's bed, he lay down and looked at her expectantly.

"Good morning, Zato," she said, sitting next to him and patting his head. "I'm not sure you should be up here. Maybe just this once, but don't make a habit of it."

She scratched behind his ears, which softened in response.

"I've got to shower and get ready for school, so you need to get down. I don't want to leave you in here unchaperoned."

Logan stood up and backed into the hall. "Come on!" she said, clapping her hands together in the language of command that all dogs instinctively understand. Zato stood up and, with a spring of his hind legs, launched himself from her bed, raising the bedclothes into a rumpled pile and banging the bed frame hard against the wall.

As Logan turned to walk down the hall to the bathroom, her buoyant mood dissolved abruptly, as the sight and odor of a sizable deposit of steaming excrement, assailed her senses.

Zato stood by Logan's side, looking on with self-conscious innocence.

"Zato! You are a bad dog!"

Folding back his ears and dropping his shoulders, Zato looked at his front paws as if they might be responsible for Logan's upset. "Who's going to clean this up? Not me, I can assure you. Mom and Dad are not going to be happy with you."

Her parents were sitting up in bed when Logan entered their room. "What was that about?" asked her mother.

"Zato pooped in the hall. It's big, and it stinks."

"Where is he now?"

"In the foyer, being a bad dog."

"Okay," said Blair, getting out of bed and putting on her robe, "You wake Max and get ready for school. We'll take care of it."

Ian, Blair, and Bagel walked into the hall. Zato's deposit was indeed sizable, loose, and foul-smelling. They walked to the foyer and found the culprit curled up against the front door to the apartment: muzzle on the floor, ears back, sad-eyed, his tail tucked between his hind legs.

"Zato, come here; you've got to look at this," said Ian, roughly.

As there was no response, Ian took the dog by the collar and attempted to pull him upright, but he remained leaden. Ian dragged him across the wooden floor for a close look at the still-smoldering evidence.

"This is not acceptable. This is bad dog! When you need to pee or poop, you go outside! Do you get it?"

Zato gave his best "guilty-dog-filled-with-repentance" performance, impressing no one.

"I think you'd better take him out," Blair said. "I'll handle this."

As Ian got dressed, Zato returned to the foyer and reassumed his penitent posture. From the hallway, Bagel looked at him without comment, then trotted into the bedroom with a spring in her step.

The kids got ready for breakfast and school as Blair cleaned the mess, and Ian walked the dogs. The skies were clear and blue, and a few inches of fresh snow blanketed 116th Street. Zato lifted his leg in the direction of the tree while Ian and Bagel stood by. Afterward, it was Bagel's turn and, in what appeared to be a statement of defiance and strategy, she slowly and carefully inspected the berm, never looking at Zato, leaving only a few scrupulously placed drops as if she were laying mines for an unsuspecting enemy.

-7-

Fire & Ice

With the breakfast dishes washed and put away, the family readied themselves for work and school. The French doors to the living room, along with doors to the bedrooms and the bathroom, were all shut. Only the kitchen was left open, with a pair of water bowls placed side-by-side on the linoleum floor. The lockdown of the apartment was based solely on the unpredictability of Zato. Bagel, accustomed to spending much of her day curled up on the living room couch, was treated as an unwitting accessory to the morning's crime and with the same disrespect as this hulking Hun from the street.

As the group trooped off in various directions toward school and work, the dogs stood in the foyer like concerned family members waving goodbye to relatives aboard the Lusitania.

Left to their own devices, with only the foyer, hallway, and kitchen to explore, it was inevitable that the two might try to outmaneuver each other in a land grab. The first skirmish occurred almost immediately. As the door to the apartment closed, Bagel turned and walked to the kitchen—Zato following in her wake. She went to her metal bowl and began drinking, Zato following suit at a ceramic pot and, with considerable splashing, quickly emptied it. Observing water in his neighbor's bowl, he placed his muzzle next to Bagel's and began drinking with the giddy abandon of an elephant calf at a watering hole. As he nudged Bagel aside, she growled, trying to maintain her position and dignity. Neither prevailed. To Zato, her threats were no more than the buzzing of a housefly. Finally, Bagel stepped away, leaving her water bowl and the kitchen to the barbarian.

Zato lapped the bowl dry and went looking for a good time. He sauntered down the hallway and peeked into the foyer: empty. Continuing to the end of the hall, he found his diffident housemate around the corner, curled against the bathroom door. Throwing caution to the wind, he crouched forward with his elbows on the ground, rear in the air, tail wagging. It was a sudden movement, but despite its call to play, it caused Bagel to raise her head quickly and growl, displaying her low tolerance of oafs.

Continuing the same playful attitude, Zato sprang from side to side, inviting his housemate for a romp. Bagel remained unmoved, but realizing that the antics of this galumphing hair-bag were not threatening, she ceased to growl. Failing in his entreaties, Zato retired to the foyer, wondering if this small creature might not be a dog, after all. A few minutes later, Bagel entered the foyer and slid quietly behind two bicycles that were angled against the wall, successfully surrounding herself with a metal cage. From behind the spokes, she could safely keep mental notes of her neighbor's growing catalog of eccentricities.

It was Blair's habit to come home for lunch and walk Bagel before returning to work, and it was agreed that she would be responsible for the additional duty of giving Zato a short walk. Hearing the key in the door lock, Zato got up and waited expectantly, while Bagel remained behind bars. Blair opened the door to a happily wagging plume.

"Hi, Zato," she said affectionately. Then, noticing Bagel behind the bicycles, she added, "And what's up with you, Bagel? Are you on strike?" In response, she received only the mournful look of the disenfranchised.

Blair pulled off her boots and hung her coat on the rack. "Come on," she said, walking down the hall, "maybe there is a treat for you in the kitchen." Zato followed along happily while Bagel remained in place, quietly telegraphing her displeasure.

Blair arranged four bowls, two-by-two, for water and food. She portioned out the dogs' meals according to the prescriptions on their bags, then filled their water bowls, noting that Zato's had spillage from earlier in the day. As Bagel was a no-show, Blair walked down the hall, calling her name, finding her still stationed behind the bicycles in self-assigned exile.

"Are you pouting?" she asked, sensing a standoff. Bagel put her head between her paws, lowered her eyelids, and oozed a toxic indictment.

"Okay, I get the message. What's been going on?" she asked, while moving the bikes away from the wall. "Come on, that's enough. Come out, and we'll talk." As Bagel slinked out from behind the tires, Blair picked her up, cradling her in her arms.

"So, has Zato been pushing you around? Is he a bully? Or do you just not like competition?" No response. "Okay, but you may have to get used to it." She put Bagel down and returned to the kitchen.

Zato had already inhaled his meal, leaving a swamp around his water bowl, and, as Bagel had shown no interest in her lunch, he was happily crunching the last of her kibbles. "Zato, that is Bagel's food! You are being a pig!" He looked up, bewildered, his long, pink tongue licking powdery remnants from his lips.

"If you are going to be a member of this family, you need to learn manners," she said, now on all fours, mopping the floor with paper towels. "You can't be a slob and treat others like they don't exist."

She continued to scold him as she finished cleaning up. Zato listened soberly, ears back, the timbre of Blair's voice stirring echoes from his past. In such circumstances, it seemed prudent to lie on the kitchen floor and wait for instructions. Meanwhile, Bagel stood quietly by her bowls.

"Okay," Blair admitted to Bagel, "I *really* get it now, you don't have to gloat." She put another half cup of food in Bagel's bowl. "I'll stand guard while you eat." She made herself a sandwich and heated some soup while keeping an eye on Bagel, who was taking her time getting through her meal. There was no question, this was a "slowdown" and management was going to have to ride it out.

-8-

Newton's Law

After lunch, a short walk went off without a hitch; both dogs executed their duty without misadventure. Despite the icy conditions, Blair managed to pick up their deposits in plastic bags and dump them in a city trash barrel; however, it was clear that Zato would require a strong leash and proper collar, as with just a rope tether, he was a handful. Longer walks were going to be Ian's responsibility. As if on cue, when Ian returned home for dinner, he was bearing gifts: for Zato, a choke collar; a thick, leather leash; and a rubber dinosaur to gnaw on. For Bagel, it was a rubber mouse that squeaked.

Ian had visited the pet store on Broadway next to Zabar's delicatessen, and, based on the size and weight of the dog in question, the clerk recommended a Gothic looking expedient, called a *pinch* or *prong* collar.

"When pulled," he explained with the solemnity of an exodontist, "it provides even pressure around the neck that does not pinch the windpipe and is especially good for teaching obedience to naughty or vigorous dogs."

To Ian, it resembled a medieval restraint that might adorn the necks of hapless dungeon dwellers awaiting their turn on the rack. The clerk's touting that the collar was "made in Germany" did little to ease his qualms.

Later, in preparation for the evening walk, Zato willingly slipped his head through the new collar—Bagel looking on approvingly. Ian donned his winter apparel and leashed up the dogs. They were ready to weather the elements.

As the outside temperature was still in single digits, the evening walk was constrained to a quick out-and-in. Once outside, Zato assumed a position some distance from the tree while Bagel placed her marks to his left and right. Having relieved himself, Zato suddenly sprang toward the deep snow, causing the prongs of his collar to jolt him to a stop. It functioned as advertised, so Ian eased on the leash, allowing Zato to rollick in the berm.

The chill of breast-high snow instantly animated the dog, and he sprang toward Morningside Drive. Disinterested in a replay of hide-and-seek, Ian pulled hard on the leash, annulling the dog's progress but simultaneously initiating Newton's third law of motion: a reactive bulge of tendons that popped the collar like a champaign cork.

The dog, however, was slow to realize his freedom, allowing his chaperone just enough time to release Bagel's leash, dive into the berm, and bring the dog down with the grace of a rodeo cowboy bulldogging a steer. Wrapping the leash around the dissident's neck, Ian pulled it tight through the handle loop. Zato stood up, shook the snow from his fur, and looked at Ian: *Round 2* to the bipeds. Bagel watched the spectacle from the sidewalk, mentally adding another line to Zato's litany of misdemeanors.

The next morning, Logan was again the first to tentatively open her bedroom door. Zato wagged her a greeting, and with it, a fetid message wafted in from the hall, followed by the now-familiar reprimand, "Bad dog!"

The family gathered to inspect the latest offering—all but Zato in attendance. "Fortunately, this is not loose like yesterday," said Blair with a sense of relief. Then to Ian she said, "It appears, however, that your pet store purchases have not succumbed to Zato's digestive juices," as nestled at the top of the pile was the serrated tail of a rubber dinosaur and the metal squeaker of a mouse.

-9-

Good Dog

Winter had pulled back to the Arctic and tucked itself in for the next eight months, allowing spring to slip gently into the city. The sensitive ears of bats, cats, and dogs pulsed to the sound of new buds bursting through the thin-skinned ginkgos that lined 116th Street. A few warm days had melted the berms, and April rains had washed away the accumulations of soot and mud from the sidewalks and gutters. Students in light-weight sweaters carrying book bags strolled along College Walk or ate their lunches on the steps in front of Low Library, and people of the neighborhood peacefully walked their dogs.

Dog walking for the common man or woman is a personal thing. It has set times and routes, even set rituals. The former are created by the walker; the latter is the purview of the dogs. It is a time of reflection for the walker, a time to let the mind dwell on a movie seen or a book read, and a time to get some effortless exercise. However, there are also time limits; walkers have things to do, and often the nose that gets involved in pursuits of its own, can stretch the patience of those who wear watches.

The rituals involve many things: strategic urination to dominate the scent of interlopers; relieving the bowels on that perfect square of dirt or grass; and lingering long at the pheromones of quadrupeds who have left their mark. There are also social rituals that involve correct etiquette when meeting another of their species: inhaling the aromas of the anogenital regions, offering to play, displaying indifference to advances, or making modulated sounds of aggression. There are crude behaviors as well, but it is recommended that those interested refer to the literature on canine misbehavior for particulars. Seasoned walkers know the rituals and allow for them with caution, as it can be difficult to predict when a pleasantry might turn sour.

Since leaving the confines of her birthplace, Bagel had been schooled in the etiquette of sidewalk encounters and proper behavior in canine play areas. She understood her position regarding her species, large or small. At times she enjoyed play, but it never included the self-abasement she often observed in others of her kind. No amount of cajoling or biscuits could tempt her to lower her standards to include the repetitive chasing of sticks, balls, or Frisbees. It was obvious, such games were for grovelers and bootlickers: infantile minds who would sell their souls for a biscuit.

If a Rat Terrier was going to get exercise and show her stuff, it would be done as a Rat Terrier, not in imitation of a toad-eating retriever in a hypnotic trance, and not at the command of a biscuit-carrying biped. If run she must, the apartment building provided an abundance of opportunity. The random mouse scampering across the living room rug or basement floor was worthy of chase. And, if released from leash out of doors, the manicured lawns of the university would call her to action, running and digging with great speed and vigor—much to the consternation of university gardeners. But the full athleticism of this small dog was saved for the occasional trip to the countryside when the family would borrow Uncle Mike's van and travel to Connecticut to visit relatives. There she would have the run of an expansive lawn and a small patch of woods. If a rabbit, squirrel, or mouse were to flash its porcelain incisors, Bagel would leap into action. A stone wall or running brook was never an obstacle, as they were each taken in stride like a thoroughbred in a steeplechase. In pursuit of burrowing prey, she would dig into the earth or mud, inserting her muzzle deep into the rodent's tunnel, effectively preventing the opening of her jaws. Not to be thwarted, she resorted to deep inhales, attempting to vacuum her prey from its sanctuary. Such efforts inevitably produced only a billow of freshly turned earth and a bout of uncontrolled coughing. Finally, at the end of a day's hunt, she was hosed, toweled, and invited in for a treat and a well-earned nap.

In sum, the family considered Bagel a "good dog," provided the kitchen waste bin was securely fastened, and there were no low-lying comestibles for her to inhale. She was content with her calling as household guardian and keeper of Blair's lap. She loved well and was well-loved in return. An outsider might consider that she was a bit spoiled, but such is the bounty of a good dog with few eccentricities, who generally followed the rules. But what should be the bounty of the rule breaker, the rebel, the wanton defecator, the libertine?

-10-

Bad Dog

As Uncle Mike's efforts to discover the provenance of the wayward malamute had evoked no response, the "lost dog" posts came down from the bus stops and subway walls after two weeks. It was finally time for the family to hold a ceremony formally adopting Zato as an official clan member (with one abstention). In celebration, the newly minted Kennedy was awarded a small metal tag etched with his name and contact information to wear proudly on his collar. But here, the word "collar" needs a few words of explanation, as this was not a singular collar possessed by more common breeds, but a trifecta of collars, each of the same pinch and grasp construction whose solo version had proved insufficient.

"There is strength in numbers," asserted brother Mike, who, on hearing Ian's growing litany of dog-walking woes, presented him with a trio of the same German-made grappling hooks as a gift, thereby annulling Newton's third law of motion.

As Zato was still an untutored pre-teen, the task of his training fell to Ian. Lessons began immediately that winter and continued into spring. The intention was to impart basic manners so that Zato could be allowed more freedom for social intercourse and become easier to walk. Such refinements included the capacity to heel, sit, stay, drop it, wait, come, greet other dogs and people politely, and, of course, do one's business only out of doors. Zato had been working on these feats of self-control and making good progress—indoors.

During practice in the hallway, Zato would perform like a gentleman. He would heel and sit, then stay when ordered, allowing Ian to walk to the end of the hall, moving only on command. He was the quintessential "good dog." However, once outside, when the scents of Manhattan blew in from the Hudson or up from the plains of Harlem, Zato was a dog possessed. He would oblige with perfunctory obedience to a few practiced commands, but by the time they reached the first street corner, he was feral.

By early April, Ian had evolved an itinerary where his charge could practice deportment with minimal canine interruptions. They would cross Morningside Drive at 116th Street and continue south along the park's edge, Ian strolling the sidewalk, Zato sniffing the grass, or doing his business next to vehicles parked along the curb. He also displayed a curious habit of thrusting his nose beneath the chassis of cars like a garage mechanic in search of oil leaks.

Ian was puzzled by the dog's automotive interests, but early one morning, with a light frost still on the ground, the mystery was solved. Zato emerged from a muffler inspection with a large alley cat in his mouth. While being snapped like a dishrag from side to side, the cat protested loudly, trying desperately to gouge the eyes of its attacker.

As the command "Drop it" produced no effect, Ian employed a move that came to be known as the "block and tackle," which was hoisting the dog up as high as he could by the leash, allowing the trifecta of choke collars to do their work. When the hound's back feet were barely touching the ground, he opened his jaws to gulp some air, only then responding to the command, "Drop it!" Fortunately, this back-fence feline possessed a layer of loose fur and ran off to tell her friends that the mufflers of cars parked along Morningside Drive were no longer a haven for a warm nap.

*

Walking Zato required vigilance; this was not a time to think idle thoughts or ponder the pitching problems of the Mets—a slight dispersal of attention could have dire consequences. Being a handsome young male with a broad chest, powerful haunches, and an enviable tail, Zato was attractive to and attracted by female dogs of all shapes and sizes. He treated them with courtesy, and they, in turn, allowed him to savor their unique perfumes. Ian relaxed on the leash during these introductions and chitchatted with the walkers. However, encounters with males of the species were not so laissez-faire. Unlike Ian, Zato could discern a male from some distance, and his agitation increased as they closed quarters. This faculty benefited Ian, as he could stop walking and pull Zato tight against his leg, allowing the dogs to safely exchange unpleasantries as they crossed paths.

The flaw in this system was that Ian depended on Zato's power of long-distance gender discernment, and any lapse in alertness could result in a clash challenging to untangle. As the weeks went by, Zato's attitude toward male dogs of any size or stripe became more aggressive, at which times Ian resorted to winding the dog's leash around the wrought-iron spires that protruded from the length of the stone parapet above Morningside Park. This maneuver pinned Zato against the wall stones, allowing him to roar and spit foam at his would-be opponents while minimizing the likelihood of physical contact.

One morning, however, when man and dog were blithely walking along 116th Street toward the safety of the iron fence still many yards away, a mutt and his mistress slithered up from behind, unannounced. Before Ian could weld Zato's head to a leg or against a signpost, the jaws of death had clasped around the neck of that mottled bit of mange. Again, the thrashing back and forth began, and the offended dog walker, a lady of considerable years, started screaming in distress. Ian employed the "block and tackle" and, lifting Zato with both hands completely off the ground, the jaws relaxed, and the mutt released. A torrent of unladylike words ensued from a safe distance. Ian apologized profusely, offering his phone number for any veterinary needs. Taking a notepad and pencil from her shoulder bag, the lady wrote it down with the force of a stonemason chiseling the Code of Hammurabi. Then, hurrying off, she flung another spate of epithets into the air, her rant slowly fading as she passed around the corner of Morningside Drive.

Reports of such encounters were delivered to the family with trepidation, as Zato was now a beloved member of the Kennedy clan (sans one). Still, his ill manners and aggressive behavior tested management's patience. Thus, after a long conference with their veterinarian, it was decided it would be best to have Zato neutered before he became fully mature.

Ian and Blair were provided with literature that made the case for this operation:

"Most male animals (stallions, bulls, boars, rams, dogs, and tomcats) that are kept for companionship, work, or food production are neutered (castrated) unless they are intended to be used as breeding stock. This is a common practice to prevent unacceptable sexual behavior, reduce aggressiveness, and prevent accidental or indiscriminate breeding."

"We wouldn't want 'indiscriminate breeding,'" Blair said to Zato that evening after dinner, "and you have been quite aggressive when you're outside meeting other dogs. You don't even try to control your temper and have hurt some of our neighbor's pets. This behavior cannot go on." She looked to Ian for support.

"I'm afraid, Zato," Ian said, employing his best bedside manner, "that we are going to have to..." he looked at Blair, "be cruel to be kind. The doctor feels—with this operation—you would become friendlier to other dogs and much easier to manage outside. We love you and want to be able to keep you in the family, but continued recklessness might have dire results, and no one wants that."

Zato had been lying on the living room rug, head between his paws, quietly listening to the murmurings of his benefactors.

"You may not be aware of it, but Bagel is spayed," continued Ian, hoping this fact would somehow make the talk of castration more palatable, but Zato remained indifferent to the revelation.

"I prefer saying *neutered* to *castrated*," Ian commented to Blair. "*Castrated* sounds so Medieval. I hope it produces the advertised result. I don't want him to become a pothead like Colbert [pronounced like a French cheese]," he said, referring to their neighbor's Golden Retriever, who had been neutered and now walked the earth as though anesthetized.

They broke the news to the kids before bed that night, and by referencing Bagel's spaying, they attempted to place Zato's fate in a similar context. Ian explained the benefits of the operation and read to them from the vet's flier.

Logan looked anguished. “Can’t he be used for breeding?”

“It would be cute to see a litter of little Zatos running about, but don’t you think New York City has enough trouble with just one?” Logan nodded in stoic agreement.

Before turning in for the night, the kids spent some extra time scratching and stroking their childlike friend, who responded by lying on his back for a tummy rub, oblivious to the sword of Damocles that swung invisibly and inexorably overhead.

-11-

The Zoomies

A week later, Ian walked Zato across the campus to meet his brother at Watson's Bookstore, a university staple on Broadway and 115th Street since the mid-1940s. After a two-year walkabout in Italy, where he learned Italian, a proper veneration for Bacchus, and the correct rituals for the exorcism of unwanted house ghosts, brother Mike had returned to New York. There he found employment at Watson's and later married the daughter of a prominent New York psychiatrist—giving the disconsolate doctor much to chew on.

For the next twelve years, Mike had worked for Ward and Roberta Watson, starting as a clerk, then store manager, and finally, when they retired, taking over as owner. Watson's had a reputation for organized chaos, and, there was magic about the place. It was a magnet for bibliophiles from all over Manhattan, with people of every age and stamp browsing among its shelves, like prospectors sifting sand for gold.

Mike always drove to work. Arriving early, he would park his van in front of the store and feed the meter throughout the day. Working Saturday mornings was usual for him, and, as Ian had managed to get an appointment for Zato's operation on a Saturday, Mike had volunteered to drive him and dog to the vets on 91st Street and West End Avenue.

Over the years, Mike had had many dogs: a Boston Terrier called Asparagus, a Bullmastiff that drooled incessantly and from whose tail no glass was safe; and back-to-back German shepherds—one of which was partial to onions (by the bag). Mike assured Ian that he, too, had dealt with the neutering of a male dog, and he shouldn't worry. However, such assurances did little to mitigate the images of palace eunuchs or operatic castrati from slipping through Ian's mental defenses.

The operation went off without misadventure, and an hour later, a groggy Zato was carried to the van and returned home. He was lethargic but vigorously licked and nipped at his bandages when not asleep.

Blair encouraged the kids not to gush sympathy but to be strong for him. She was worried that giving him too much attention might push Bagel back behind the bicycles. But, unexpectedly, Bagel showed that she also had a heart, as while Zato was sleeping, she curled up against his underbelly and napped. Max documented the moment by taking pictures with his small camera.

*

From that day on, a détente existed between the two dogs. Bagel was more tolerant of her flatmate and spent less time behind the bikes. On walks, she would stand on her hind legs, using Zato as a prop to lean on, thus providing her with enough altitude to look over his back and observe what was not visible from four legs. For his part, Zato often allowed food to remain unmolested in Bagel's bowl for hours. As this was a noticeable improvement, both dogs were congratulated on their newly found equanimity and awarded new rawhide chews and biscuits.

Zato's recovery was supposed to take two weeks, but the constant licking of his wound made short work of his bandages, and by the end of the first week, he had removed his stitches. As he was allowed only short walks to relieve himself, it soon became apparent that Zato was losing patience with confinement. He was sulky and irritable. Finally, on the tenth day of his recovery, he was declared healed and offered a bath.

He was bathed in the tub with a shower hose and dog shampoo, during which he would show his enthusiasm by drenching his stylists in bursts of swirling water. Zato loved the process, especially grooming with a fine-tined wire brush. A complete blow-dry and brushing took about thirty minutes and could fill as many as three large grocery bags with soft, gray fleece. No matter how many bags were filled, there was always more to do, and the end of a session was determined only by a groomer's muscle fatigue.

The bath and grooming had removed any residual effects of Zato's convalescence, and he quivered with energy. When the bathroom door opened, he shot out of the blocks and tore down the hardwood at top speed. A few yards before reaching the end of the hallway, he began a slightly modified flip-turn, much like those perfected by Olympic swimmers.

Instinctively, he knew when to start into the turn and reverse position with his hind legs tucked under him as he hit the wall, enabling him to spring from the baseboard and propel himself in the other direction, reaching warp speed as he flew past Logan's room.

Ian and Blair watched from the bathroom door, Max and Logan from the foyer. As there was no reduction in speed when he passed by the children, all were certain that he would crash headfirst into the wall; instead, he veered off course and plunged into the master bedroom. Launching himself into the air, Zato improvised almost a complete *volte-face*, hitting the bed hard, propelling it with a thud into the wall. With blankets and pillows sailing, he sprang from the bed, barreling back down the hallway while Ian quickly shut the bedroom door. At the far end of the hall, Bagel had taken up a position in the kitchen doorway. As Zato's muzzle appeared in the door frame, she leaped out and bit him on the cheek, taking some loose fur away in her teeth. Unperturbed, he delivered a flawless turn and tore back in the other direction. As the path to the bedroom was blocked, he performed a perfect one-eighty and raced the other way, receiving another snap on the cheek for ignoring the speed limit. Finally, running out of steam, he pushed off the wall with a little less force and, panting heavily, eased into a cool down.

"Wonderful Zato!"

"Amazing!"

"Another Mark Spitz!"

"Wow!"

Zato lumbered to the winner's circle, awash with affection and praise.

"That was quite a display," Blair said. "I've never seen anything like it."

"It's called the 'zoomies,'" reported Max, "I read it in my book." Max had been studying dog breeds from his well-worn copy of *The Complete Book of Dogs*.

"Sometimes dogs become frantic when cooped up too long or after a bath. He's definitely got the zoomies," stated Max in the manner of a country doctor making a bedside pronouncement.

These explosions of energy happened about once each month thereafter. Once started, all doors were shut to prevent any off-road adventures. The family would race to their viewing stations, and Bagel would assume her role as traffic cop. It was the perfect family entertainment: no bumps, bruises, or screams from fleeing pedestrians clutching their wounded.

-12-

Dreamons

Before the arrival of the foundling, Bagel had unrestricted access to all the comforts of the apartment. She would curl up on a cushion or a bed pillow when the family was away. But, in the wake of her flatmate's misbehavior, these freedoms evaporated overnight. Now regarded as a guileless accessory to the likelihood of further crimes, the doors to such comforts were barred—leaving her boney elbows to rest on the hardwood.

This condition continued for some weeks before Blair insisted that Ian pay another visit to the pet store and purchase beds to comfort the dogs during their long hours of idleness. Each received a soft berth, differentiated by color and size. A red one for Zato, and a blue one for Bagel, were placed on opposite sides of the foyer.

Sleeping and dreaming are common to mammals, perhaps even fish. The renowned marine biologist and documentarian Jacques-Yves Cousteau may have proved the latter when doing a deep dive with fellow waterdogs off the Florida Keys. While probing the seabed for specimens under a battery of floodlights, they came upon a grouper of enormous size and weight, floating a few feet above the mud as if drugged. Lit up like a night game at Yankee Stadium, it registered no awareness of being the center of attention. When poked with a pole, there was no response, only the continuous twitching of a fin. Cousteau devotees have posited that this zeppelin of a sea bass was traveling in deep-dream space, wholly withdrawn from sensory perception, imagining itself a colossus of humpback size, scooping up crabs, lobsters, and sea turtles—cracking their shells like walnuts. Only when repeatedly probed with a pole did this quiescent aquanaut drift slowly back to wakefulness, acknowledging the presence of voyeurs with a detached shrug and a swipe of its tail, engulfing them in a cloud of sediment.

The dream "tell" of dogs is far more visible than that of the grouper. They writhe, groan, whimper, yelp, growl, and twitch their legs. Their cries suggest stressful encounters: street fights, blood drawn, a chase. With all his street bravado, Zato growls and twitches as he grapples with neighborhood toughs but then cries like a helpless newborn. Bagel envisions herself as a 70-pound Staffordshire terrier with hide like a rhino, roped with sinew and muscle; she is tough, self-assured, and stealthy but shrinks in fear of fictive fangs and chomping jaws.

One Friday afternoon, Blair returned home for lunch at her usual time, and as she removed the house key from her purse, muffled cries of anguish slipped from beneath the door. She stopped and listened. High and low-pitched moans continued, and she realized that the dogs were in the foyer, fast asleep, dreaming. Softly inserting her key, she opened the door wide enough to slide through and close it quietly behind her.

She watched the dogs struggling with their adversaries and wondered if Zato was dealing with canine or possibly human foes and if Bagel was on the run: her forelegs lunging forward in short spasms. Their bouts with the subconscious reminded her that she, too, had a few recurring nightmares, which she called her *dreamons*. In one, she was a young Indian woman, perhaps a teenager, living on the plains with other members of her race. She'd fallen in love with a man from a rival tribe—caught in a forbidden embrace. Her father threw him from a cliff, where buffalo had been driven to their death. She watched him fall; then, she, too, was pushed over the edge.

In another frequent dream, she exits an elevator and passes into a crowded restaurant at the top of a city skyscraper. Windows as tall and thin as young pines look out over a jeweled city—one opens, and the wind sweeps in, rippling the tablecloths and burnishing the crystal into a symphony of bells. Then, softly, it catches her, lifting her through the window to fall like a dinner plate into nothingness. Blair always awoke breathless before these dreams reached their inexorable end.

The murmur of these phantoms unsettled her, and she knelt to wake the pair with a gentle pat on the head: first Zato, then Bagel—startling each, in turn, with her magical appearance.

"Hello, sleepy heads," she soothed. "After battling with your dreamons, you must be hungry. Are you ready for lunch?" Zato responded with wags and Bagel with small leaps as they followed her down the hallway. Upon entering the breakfast nook adjacent to the kitchen, Blair observed that two spindles from a wooden bar stool were chewed through, rendering it unusable.

"Oh, Zato, you are such a bad dog."

Blair ate her lunch, walked the dogs, moved the bar stools to the countertop, and returned to work early. The office was quiet: no faculty working behind closed doors, no students trembling in the hall. She sat at her desk and started typing a proposal to fund a visiting professor from the Moscow State Institute of International Relations: a former diplomat and historian who had seen his share of adversity for airing opinions outside established boundaries. Approval from the budget committee was probable, but disapproval from Moscow's political overlords was inevitable. She paused, and her thoughts drifted to the sharp polarities of politics and the fragile lives of people living under the pounding of the Soviet hammer and the slashing of its sickle. In recent years at the institute, Blair had met a few defectors whose stories had moved her deeply.

She was drifting into melancholy and so attempted to type herself out of it, although she soon paused again, realizing that her low mood had started in the apartment. It wasn't the chewed spindles—yes, that was exasperating—it had started earlier, in the foyer. Watching the dogs battling their phantoms had ignited her own dark rumblings, always so vivid: the wind surging through the open window, the hum of the crystal—the falling; the weight of leather on her shoulders, the smell of horses, her father's anger and the anguish of her mother; the loss, and terrifying fear—the falling. These hauntings, whether in sleep or wakeful reverie, were more real to her than the day when she'd spun the family Ford on black ice, landing just a hair's breadth from the racing Delaware River.

With her fingertips paused on the keys, Blair refuted the theories of Freud and Jung. She didn't believe her dreamons were the spawn of the collective unconscious any more than that they implied a death wish. Instead, she posited a different theory, that these were *her* memories, floating in the timestream like dormant megalodons, connected to the present by tenuous threads where a word, a sigh, a scent, could wake and reel them to the surface in a spellbinding replay. The recurrence of such scenes was not worrying, as they suggested the existence of an infinite future. With these thoughts, she felt lighter, relieved.

"Dobryy den' Missis Kennedi. Kak u vas segodnya dela?" A man of advanced years and stately bearing entered the reception room like a lord returning to the manor house.

"I'm doing well, Professor Zaritsky," Blair answered in Russian. "Will you be having office hours this afternoon?"

Though in his early seventies, Vanya Zaritsky carried himself like a young Lincoln. He was tall and trim, with a broad forehead, narrow jaw, strong cheekbones, and clear, berylline eyes. His hair was white and unkempt; in contrast, he sported an impeccable Richelieu goatee. Always packaged in a dark suit with a crisp, white shirt, the only compromise to this uninflected palette was a bowtie. The professor's choice of ties covered the spectrum of visible light and would act as a barometer of his moods. The higher frequency blues and violets forecast a day of peevishness and reclusion, while lower frequency oranges and reds augured sociability and charitable pronouncements. Graduate students read these signs as if semaphore, scheduling their meetings accordingly.

Professor Zaritsky had been lecturing at the institute for a quarter-century, serving as its director for over a decade; in recent years, his office hours were irregular as he often worked at home. His specialty was pre-revolutionary and revolutionary Russia—he'd lived through both, but his parents had not. He also taught Russian political culture and literature when the institute's needs arose.

His relationship with Blair was formal, but a kind and caring man lay beneath the old-world posture and honorifics. A decade earlier, when Blair first took over the institute's administration from Mildred Harrison,

Professor Zaritsky had doubts about the transition. Blair was smart and spoke Russian like a Muscovite but was only in her mid-twenties: unlikely she could handle both the administrative work and the diverse personalities of a multi-disciplinary and multi-ethnic faculty. He had once commented to his peers that Mildred Harrison would have been UN Secretary-General if she hadn't chosen to preside over the institute and weave a tapestry from a patchwork quilt. He considered her a peer, not a minion. Mildred, however, was adamant: Blair was the right pick—the *only* pick.

After a year at the administrative helm, Blair had surprised and impressed the gray ladies and graybeards of the institute. She had yet to develop the diplomatic skills of her predecessor, but she proved competent and worked fast. Faculty trust came in the form of her overly full in-basket. Her success at Columbia, however, would have been no surprise to classmates or the faculty of New Hope-Solebury high school. Blair's senior page in the yearbook summed her up as follows:

Blair Kensington
Most Likely to Succeed

Speaks French like Simone Signoret
Conducts French Club like Toscanini
Captains field hockey like Napoleon

Favorite film: *Les Enfants du Paradis* (foreign), *Duck Soup* (American)
Favorite book: Tolstoy, *Anna Karenina* [who knew? -- the editors]
Favorite pastime: Watching foreign films at the Strand; 5000-piece puzzles
Favorite place: Bucks County, Pa.

Favorite experience: New ice; the smell of a fresh pipe
Pet peeve: High heels

In her last year of high school, Blair's literary affections morphed from the French romantics to the Russian: Tolstoy, Turgenev, Pasternack, Chekov—all of whom she read in translation and determined that wherever she went to college it must have a top-level Russian department. Barnard College granted her wish.

During her junior year at Barnard, she discovered a cache of reel-to-reel tapes in the catacombs of Columbia's Butler Library that contained readings in Russian of some of her favorite novels and poetry. In a cubicle reserved for sequestered work, she listened to many and, following along in her copy of the Russian text, she would stop and drill a sentence or paragraph over and over to perfect her accent and cadence. It was a game to play, as Barnard had no field hockey team.

Twelve years after assuming Mildred Harrison's duties, Blair finally tired of being a spectator watching students come and go from the institute. She enjoyed her job but felt only partially fulfilled. So, she applied and was accepted into the institute's Master of Arts in Regional Studies program—an opportunity gifted to only ten worthies each year.

The admissions committee selected her for her natural ability and because they considered her a good investment. As a university administrator, she was entitled to attend classes at no cost, which suited her pocketbook, and to take her required classes at a less intense pace (three years instead of two), thus permitting her to study, work, and fulfill her familial responsibilities.

"I have two appointments with students this afternoon," answered the professor, continuing their conversation in Russian, "the first at two and another at three. How is your paper coming?"

"I should have this done by the end of the day, barring interruptions."

"No, not that. There is no great rush; tomorrow is soon enough. I was referring to your *thesis*." He said the last word in English.

"It is coming along. I should have it ready before the winter break." She hoped this was true, but it was far from a certainty.

"What is the topic, again?"

"Anna Dostoevskaya."

"Ah, the stenographer who saved Fyodor from ruin. And the proposition?"

"That Fyodor could not have been Fyodor without her," she said glibly, instantly regretting it.

"As Professor Belgrade has approved your thesis topic, I am presuming you have something new to add," he said as a statement, not a question.

"I hope so," she responded, rushing to her own defense. "I am fascinated how an ingenue of twenty-three years could skillfully handle her husband's compulsive gambling, his debts, his illness, and the banging of begging bowls at their front door. She arrived in his life at the breaking point, never hesitating to dive into the trenches to expose the plots of schemers. Fyodor should have converted to her religion rather than she to his. He would never have referred to her arrival in his life as Fate, but he might have called it a miracle." Finally, Blair took a long breath, realizing that she had not yet answered his question and had failed to notice the presence of a high-frequency bowtie.

"Yes, a miracle," the professor agreed, slowly voicing each word in measured tones. "I very much believe in miracles." He remained silent for a moment, pinching the point of his goatee and looking through the window behind Blair's desk. She'd seen these lost eyes before, usually during winter snows.

"When Professor Belgrade has passed judgment on your paper, I hope you will allow me to read it," he said in a gentler voice. "I'm interested in this topic and look forward to your insights."

After Uncle Vanya (a name she used only at home) retreated to his office, Blair felt the gristmill of self-doubt begin to grind.

She had been gnawing on her thesis subject for nearly a year and felt she had drawn new marrow from well-picked bones. She firmly believed that what passed for scholarship of this kind was mortared together by subjective conjecture, and she considered herself a skilled mason when it came to substantiating her opinions. She felt her ideas were fresh; however, these were big league players at the institute, and they would not take kindly to specious reasoning offered as fact.

Looking at the paper in the carriage of her typewriter, she realized there had been no progress since returning from lunch, and she had typed the same word three times in succession. Smiling, she pictured herself a trembling St. George, sword in hand, slaying the dragons sent forth by the dogs, by Anna and Fyodor, Professor Belgrade and Uncle Vanya, and by this irritating spasm of self-doubt.

From behind the door of his sanctum sanctorum, Uncle Vanya fine-tuned his radio to a favorite station, conjuring Beethoven's "Ode to Joy" in mid-crescendo. The volume was louder than usual. The music ebbed and flowed, the bows scudding on their strings, the brass rejoicing, while a hundred voices rang and the kettle drums thundered; but, like the great maestro, Uncle Vanya heard it not, as he was in deep converse with his God, petitioning Him to stop skimping on miracles.

-13-

The Latin Ploy

Two weeks before the end of classes and the start of summer vacation, Max announced to the family that the following Monday was show-and-tell, and he would like to bring the dogs to class. Sister Mary Margaret had encouraged her students to collect something from home that would be educational for the group. Max would show the dogs and prepare a short speech about their lineage.

"How do you plan on getting the dogs to and from school?" asked Ian.

"My class is at nine-thirty. Can one of you be just a little late to work?"

Blair explained that as much as they would like to help, they couldn't take an hour out of a Monday morning: dad had classes, and she always had a staff meeting at nine. Couldn't he find another exhibit that didn't require one of his parents?

"Sister said she'd like to meet our dogs, but someone would have to take them home afterward," whined Max. "I thought one of you would come and help."

Sister Mary Margaret was the fifth-grade science teacher at Saint Mark's Episcopal School, a K-8th grade school on West 113th Street, founded by Sister Bernice in 1945. Two years earlier, Sister Bernice had also established the

Women's Order of the Sacred Heart on twenty-five acres of woodland in Westchester County. The current faculty of St. Mark's was composed of a bushel of clerics from the Women's Order dressed in traditional, Catholic-style habits and a peck of civilians dressed in the livery of Ivied professors. Although not a denominational school, St. Mark's did offer Latin and a voluntary ecumenical service once a week.

The good sister was in her early twenties and brimming with enthusiasm for everything from the life of bees to why peaches didn't fall up. Once, while she and Ian rode the downtown subway together, she explained that she loved wearing the habit and felt that nuns of the Catholic Church looked at her with envy, as now one could hardly distinguish them from a waitress at Schrafft's. However, she did allow one break with tradition, as beneath her tunic poked a pair of black, high-top sneakers.

Glowering at his parents, Max said, "*Non placet.*"

"Aha," responded Ian, "using the Latin ploy?"

"What's that mean?" asked Blair.

"Max says he is 'not pleased.'" Ian paused and continued in kind, "*Non omnia possumus omnes*. Do you understand that one, my learned friend?" Max shook his head. "It means 'we can't all do everything.' But, given that you have applied your fledgling Latin to a good cause, I'll see what I can do to help solve your problem."

When the Kennedy boys were still young enough to be considered malleable, Ian and his brother were the recipients of what Mike called the "after dinner suffix," an hour each evening when the family patriarch would school his grudging scions in Latin and Greek prefixes and suffixes as well as common Latin phrases. English words were parsed prefix by suffix and then used in sentences and woe to the boy who had not reviewed the previous night's lessons.

Mr. Kennedy was a linguaphile, steeped in Greek and Latin and a love of Shakespeare, who put his expertise in the classics to work on Madison Avenue, dreaming up popular ad campaigns for toothpaste, breakfast cereals, toilet paper, and TV dinners. So it was no surprise to Mrs. Kennedy that Ian later chose to immerse himself in a language without an alphabet, much less a prefix, and Mike chose to skip Rome altogether, drifting through the ruins of the Etruscans and sharing wine from a goatskin with amiable Neapolitan Romani. Perhaps the resistance to these classes rendered the boys' adhesion to them inescapable—much like Br'er Fox tricking Br'er Rabbit into battling with the Tar Baby. Their lessons were gone but not forgotten.

Later that evening, Ian called his brother and made arrangements for show-and-tell. Mike's daughter, Esperanza, who everyone called Spira, was the same age as Max and was his classmate at St. Mark's. Each weekday morning, Mike drove Spira to the bookstore, where she would join Max and Logan to walk the last few blocks to school. Mike suggested they all meet at the store on Monday before Ian went to work. Mike would take the dogs, escort them to show-and-tell, and afterward, secure them in the bookstore basement, returning them to Blair at noon.

Monday arrived earlier than expected, finding Ian standing on a station platform watching steam hissing from the underbelly of an idling locomotive. As the train slowly began to exit the station, puffing and gasping, Ian realized he was dreaming, but he could still hear the rhythmic chug of the engine and feel the mist of its exhaust. Opening his eyes, he faced a large, wet nose, breathing heavily, only a finger's depth away. Behind it, two eyes bulged with the intensity of a Mongol Khan. Ian leaped from the bed, stumbled into his slippers, and raced with Zato to the foyer, where he attached the leash and threw open the door. Together they rushed through the lobby and across the sidewalk to the ill-fated tree. A trail of incontinence mapped their flight from the headwaters in the bedroom to the delta surrounding the long-suffering ginkgo. Lifting his leg, Zato looked over his shoulder in grateful apology while Ian stood by in his pajamas, chilled and humorless.

"I'm presuming this was another emergency," said Blair, as Ian entered the bedroom.

He nodded.

"Come back to bed; it's just six o'clock."

"I need to mop up the evidence before anyone else is out and about. There is some here, too," he said, pointing at the floor. "You don't need to be Sherlock Holmes to determine where the culprit lives."

As this was not the first time Zato had roused Ian with an urgent plea to pee, Ian had known better than to hesitate.

"At least he woke me up, so I guess it's an improvement, and I have developed a motto for living with this pet," he said with feigned gravity. "Always sleep in your pajamas."

Fully awake, Ian got dressed and took Bagel for a walk. Before exiting the apartment, he offered a rebuke to Zato, and ordered him to remain in bed.

As the sun rose over Harlem into a cloudless sky, a man in a business suit walked a black lab in their direction. The dogs exchanged pleasantries: no threats or growls, no spiked hair—just two dogs getting acquainted, and they went their separate ways.

"You are a pleasure to be with this morning, my friend," said Ian. "A pleasure."

Returning home, Ian prepared breakfast for the family. The smells of coffee, bacon, eggs, and toast preempted the need for alarm clocks, and everyone was soon readying themselves for breakfast, school, and work.

Ian, Max, Logan, and the dogs set out across campus a little before eight o'clock: Ian walking Zatc, Max nudging Bagel through the myriad of earthly bouquets that haunted her every step. Watson's Bookstore didn't open until nine, so Ian knocked on the store window as Uncle Mike's van was already parked in its usual spot. A moment later, the door opened; Spira and Mike greeted the quintet enthusiastically.

"Hello, brother *Mio*, I see the troops have arrived. *Per favore, entrate tutti*," said Mike as he ushered them inside, handing his brother a coffee, and locking the door behind them. "Come in, come in." The kids started chatting and playing with the dogs, who remained leashed, while Mike and Ian conferred on the logistics surrounding show-and-tell.

After a few minutes, Spira told her dad it was time for them to go to school.

"Okay, don't forget your case."

Spira picked up what looked like a battered trombone case boasting a faded travelogue of decals depicting exotic locations that stretched the length and breadth of the Italian peninsula.

Seeing the questioning looks of her uncle and cousins, she exchanged a conspiratorial look with her father and said, "It's a surprise for show-and-tell."

Esperanza was lithe and witty and had inherited something of her parents' love of the exotic. She had auburn hair with bands of yellow, not so fevered as her father's; brown eyes like her mother's; and a constant, impish smile. She hoisted the case, and Max volunteered to carry her knapsack. Then the kids pushed through the door and set out for school.

Ian watched them for a moment through the store window and inquired as to the contents of the trombone case.

"You'll find out from Max after school. It's a secret. Let's go downstairs; I want to show you something. Bring your coffee."

Mike took the leashes from Ian and unsnapped the dogs' collars. As Ian started to protest, Mike interrupted, "It's okay, Brother *Mio*, there is no one here and nowhere to run to. *Nessun problema.*" Ian followed Mike to the back of the store, dogs leading the way, noses to the floor.

"After I get back from show-and-tell, I'll work from the basement and keep the dogs with me until lunch."

The store's main floor displayed copies of new releases from the *Times'* "Best Seller" list. In addition, there were paperback titles covering everything from Hemingway to

Heidegger and a wide array of titles organized by subject. Dozens of required university textbooks stood in vertical stacks behind plywood counters.

Mike specialized in cultivating relationships with professors, often treating them to mugs of beer at the West End Bar and deep conversations about history, philosophy, and religion. Though he'd barely finished high school and had never set foot in a college classroom, he was well-read and could hold his own with students and faculty. As a result, Watson's became the recommended bookstore for all student needs. Under Michael's tutelage, Watson's also offered a unique collection of books for aficionados of the occult, resulting in frequent visitations by beings from other planets: Michael's favorite public.

The basement was a repository for a massive collection of paperback titles and overstock, arranged alphabetically by publisher and author on ceiling-to-floor metal shelves. As titles disappeared from displays on the main floor, replacements arrived by dumbwaiter from below. Titles in less demand were only in the basement stacks, and customers were often amazed at what was available if they asked. Word-of-mouth and the Manhattan Yellow Pages were Watson's only forms of advertising, and they worked well. Besides books, the basement's accouterments consisted only of a unisex toilet, a coffee maker, a small desk for paperwork, a couple of chairs, and a file cabinet.

Mike flipped the light at the top of the stairs leading to the basement. The dogs rushed down, their progress blocked by a closed door. Ian followed behind, noting a half-full jug of Paisano wine in its usual niche. He had worked for his brother many times during the fall "rush" and was familiar with Mike's predilection for wine—a habit developed while marinating in the produce of the

Amalfi coast. In recent years, the quality of the vintage was a minor concern, and Ian was uncertain if Paisano was indeed wine.

The group paused at the door. "When I open it, I'll turn on the lights. Then we'll see what happens."

Again, Ian started to protest, but his brother had already opened the door and flipped the switch.

Buildings in Manhattan have rats, especially older structures close to the rivers. Rats will eat almost anything, including the glue in book bindings, and they prefer to have their meals in the dark. The dogs bolted in with the light, sending rodents scampering across the walls like swallows, sliding through holes or large cracks in the brick foundation. Mike had done this trick with his dog, Isa, many times, as it was a fast way to keep the beasts at bay for days; the scent of dog was a warning to stay out.

Snorting as he went, Zato padded quickly up and down the aisles with the suspicious eye of a beat cop. Bagel, genetically suited to the hunt, attempted to climb the walls herself, knocking over stacks of books on a sorting table and barking frantically—her senses focused on an opening near the upper corner of a large metal door.

"They've gone into the rat room," yelled Ian. The rat room was an open space in the foundation, secured like Fort Knox. Once, Ian had looked behind the metal door with a flashlight. Once was enough. The open patch along the frame had been bricked and mortared many times, and a repair was long overdue.

Ian grabbed Bagel's leash from his brother, fastened it to her collar, and lifted her from the table. "Get Zato leashed up!" he shouted over Bagel's wild barking. "We're going upstairs. Bring Zato before he figures things out."

Immediately, Ian decided he would take the dogs to show-and-tell. He'd call Parker School with an excuse and go to work after lunch. He had planned to show a documentary later in the week that could be shown in his absence.

They returned the dogs to the relative tranquility of the main floor. Ian asked if there was rat poison in the basement, and Mike assured him there was not. Occasionally, rats died in the stacks without help from him, he explained, and the unsavory task of removing their decaying carcasses was his.

Ian often felt his brother was reckless, and he upbraided himself for allowing the dogs into the cellar. When he was sixteen, Mike had rolled a friend's car on a wet, country road; a year later, he lost control of his motorcycle—both mishaps resulting in broken bones. Luckily, the bones were only his. At nineteen, he'd set off for Italy on a Yugoslav freighter with only $300 in his pocket. He survived there for more than two years, doing odd jobs for farmers and posing for tourists' photographs. He had let his beard and hair run wild and was often found barefoot on the rock-strewn beaches of the Amalfi Coast in the company of a similarly coiffed American friend, both looking like descendants of the diaspora. A close-up photo of the two appeared in "Tempo," a popular magazine of the day, as part of a story on Positano. The caption read: "*I due Apostoli*" (The two Apostles). Tourists were fascinated with them, locals not so much.

Ian explained the change of heart to his brother. "I think Parker can do without me for a few hours. I have never no-showed before, and Max could use the support. Besides, I'm curious to see what's inside the trombone case. Hopefully, it's not alive."

With exaggerated gravity, Mike said, "I wouldn't get your hopes up."

-14-

Show & Tell

When the brothers arrived with the dogs, students were pouring into the science lab. The room had two sections: one containing lab-station sinks, Bunsen burners, test tubes, and microscopes; the other, individual desks and chairs. Max and Spira greeted their fathers in high spirits and thanked them for coming. A few other parents leaned idly against the walls. Ian and Mike stood to one side—the dogs wagging and straining at their leashes.Sister Mary Margaret started the class by welcoming the parents. She then called students alphabetically for their presentations. What followed was the St. Mark's fifth-grade vaudeville show, with everything but a dancing bear and a chorus line.

First up among the *A*'s, a pigtailed redhead showed replicas of coins dated 1776. In less than two minutes, she rattled off a short history of colonial coinage: metals used, the processes for coin striking, and the fact that Ben Franklin contributed the first design—all mind-boggling facts delivered without a stumble. Next, a student from the *D*'s had a turn-of-the-century, spring-wound music box with a half-dozen metal discs that played Strauss, Mozart, and others. Her explanation of its mechanics etherized the audience. Yet, consciousness returned when she placed a metal disc into the box, cranked the handle, and the "Blue Danube Waltz" played in full tintinnabulation. Not to be outdone, a bespectacled lass from the *G*'s with Harpo hair and a misbuttoned shirt pulled a stuffed squirrel from a burlap bag and told a Gothic tale of taxidermy, eliciting gasps and groans from her classmates.

Advancing to the *J*'s, a slender boy named Jenks, with protruding front teeth and an impeccably pressed uniform, presented what Ian thought would be the day's showstopper: ticket stubs from the Beatles 1965 concert at Shea Stadium and their *USA Tour* program. Such items were of only mild interest to the students, but the parents, including Mike and Ian, all stepped forward to have a look.

When Sister Mary Margaret arrived at the *K*s, it was Max's turn. Ian was already beginning to wonder if his son's presentation would equal those of his peers. Max asked his dad to bring the dogs forward. Ian obeyed, and Max introduced his exhibits. Picking Bagel up in his arms, he explained that there were many breeds and sizes of terrier, from the "little American hairless to the stately Airedale," and that all were bred to hunt vermin. Bagel was most likely a Rat terrier mix. Max extolled her ability to dig for field mice and leap tall buildings at a single bound. He had a notebook with photographs of all the terrier breeds and took a moment to share a photo of one of Bagel's pedigreed doppelgangers. Exchanging the dogs' leashes, he asked his dad to give Bagel a quick walkabout while he introduced her flatmate.

Here, too, Max had done his homework. He explained how the Malemiut Inupiaq people had developed the breed and used the dogs for hunting large prey, such as bears, and hauling heavy freight over long distances. "These brave Arctic dogs," said Max, adopting the gravity of a moon-landing narration, "left the comfort of their igloos, traveling more than 13,000 miles to accompany Admiral Byrd on his exploration of the South Pole in 1911."

Notwithstanding his devotion to the iron facts of science, Max showed that even he could stray from the Holy Writ as found in *The Complete Book of Dogs,* when he stated with the certitude of an Oxford don that the Malemute was a "bigger, stronger, tougher, and more intelligent breed than its smaller Russian cousin, the Siberian husky." He briefly described the circumstances of Zato's abandonment and heroic rescue by Uncle Mike, who stood like a Viking in a corner of the room.

Max concluded his presentation with two humorous anecdotes concerning Zato—which he called *the great escape* and *a case of the zoomies*. Then, after walking him up and down the aisles so students could have a pat, he returned him to Ian and took his seat.

Ian felt his son had performed well, giving him a nod and a smile while Sister Mary Margaret introduced the next student. "Esperanza has asked to present her exhibit last, so next up is Martin Liberman."

After explaining the origins, construction, and musical range of a palm-sized Jew's Harp, Martin gave a short concert of bone-rattling twangs to a tepid response, during which Ian felt his teeth begin to ache. Subsequent presentations were brief but instructive: a stone rubbing of a cuneiform inscription; a Constabulary helmet of a London policeman, replete with regal crest and star; and other curiosities plundered from ancestral vaults.

Finally, it was Spira's turn. She placed the trombone case on a table at the front of the room and opened it. "I have brought a pair of musical instruments you have probably never seen. The larger of the two," she said while removing what looked like a laundry bag and a bundle of kindling, "is made from sheepskin and wood. My father brought it back from Italy many years ago, and I will ask him to hold it."

Spira passed him the sheepskin and continued. "What my dad is holding is called a *zampogna*," which she pronounced in standard Italian. "It is a musical instrument that sounds like Scottish bagpipes. Do you all know the sound of bagpipes?" She was winding them up.

"Yes!" They replied in unison.

"Would you like to hear them?"

"Yes!" came an even more impassioned reply.

Spira smiled and continued. "The bag of the zampogna is made from a whole sheepskin, turned inside out, leg skins included. (Muffled gasps from the audience.) Three of its legs are tied off so that no air escapes. The leg that is not tied off is where the air goes in. The four wooden blowpipes you can see make the music. The two long ones are called *drones* and make a single sound, one octave apart. The two shorter ones, called *chanters*, are also of different lengths and tones, and each has finger holes: four for the right hand and four for the left. They are like the recorders we play in music class. So, there are four distinct pitches, and they harmonize."

As she spoke, her father indicated each location and fixture as if he were demonstrating the wonders of an Electrolux vacuum cleaner.

"I have a stand-alone chanter, too," she said as she reached back into the trombone case. "It is made of plastic and has three parts," she continued, holding up each piece as she named them so that all could gaze in wonder. "The mouthpiece, the base with eight finger holes, and a plastic reed to make the sound."

After a dramatic pause, she went on, "This kind of chanter is sometimes called a *piffero,* which is like the English word, *fife.*" She fastened the chanter together. "When I blow in the mouthpiece, the reed vibrates, making a high-pitched sound, something like Scottish bagpipes, or [pausing again for effect] a kazoo." At this point, she stopped speaking and demonstrated by blowing a few notes. The students laughed.

"Unlike my plastic chanter the reeds on the zampogna are made from plants," she added, "but they function in the same way. Would you like to hear it?"

The students clapped and drummed their desks in assent, and parents stopped looking at their watches.

Spira asked her dad to crank up the zampogna. As the sheepskin swelled under Mike's arm, the room filled with the medieval voicing of the drones, and, if you listened closely, you could hear the patter of olives falling from the trees.

Raising her chanter in both hands, Spira said they would now play an Italian folk song called a "tarantella," and eased into it with a lively, steady beat, swaying and tapping her foot to the rhythm. With a nod of her head, the students began to clap in time.

The whine of Spira's chanter and the hum of the zampogna thrummed Zato's tympanums and electrified his soul, moving him to throw back his head and join the performance with a series of long, baritone howls. Bagel, sensing the transcendence of the moment, joined the group with her crystalline soprano.

Ian was delighted with this ragtag troop of uptown gypsies and hoped Martin Liberman might amplify the rhythm with his Jew's Harp. However, Martin and the others continued clapping to keep time until the droning and howling subsided with a long sigh from the zampogna. Show-and-tell was not a competition, but there was no doubt the *K*'s had stolen the show.

-15-

What if My House Be Troubled with a Rat?

When Blair arrived home for lunch, she was surprised to find the dogs wagging a welcome at the door. A cryptic note from Ian only added to the mystery:

I went to show-and-tell. Quite fun. Much to tell you later
Love, Ian

Later that afternoon, while the spaghetti sauce simmered on the stove and the pasta was beginning to boil, Max clamored to tell his mother about the day's events, but she asked him to wait until dinner so everyone could hear his news at the same time. She might well have requested Niagara to stop falling. Max kept trying to tell his story, but Blair gently fended him off. Finally, when the family was seated around the dinner table, she opened the floodgates and asked Max for the full rundown.

"Dad was there," he said proudly. "He brought the dogs. Everyone loved them. I knew they would. And they sang a song!"

Max and Ian related the wonders of the day: Max's splendid speech, Spira's and Uncle Mike's bagpipe performance, and the dogs' musical triumph. As both dogs were under the table, stockinged feet nudged them affectionately.

"We could hear the bagpipes from down the hall," said Logan, "and when the dogs started singing, we stopped everything to listen. It was so funny."

Max and the dogs received high praise for their performance.

Addressing the group, Blair said, "I had no idea that Mike or Spira played those instruments. Did you?" No one did. "That family never ceases to amaze. I can only imagine that their practice sessions were not so enjoyable for the neighbors."

"I asked that question, too," said Ian. "It seems they practiced outdoors on Riverside Drive, by the bridge overlooking the Westside Highway. Hardly anyone walks along there, so they had free range to practice at full decibels."

"I'm happy you changed your mind about going to show-and-tell. What made you decide to go?"

Ian studied his dinner plate with renewed interest, then looked up. "Once we were all gathered at the bookstore, I saw Spira and Max were excited about their presentations, and I thought, why not? I've never been late for work or called in sick. I was at Parker by noon."

Blair smiled. "That's very nice."

Deftly shifting gears, Ian said, "So, Logan, besides the concert down the hall, any excitement in your day?"

*

The following morning, Logan was first to rise. Seeing no sign of Zato's morning wag, she called his name. Receiving no response, she walked to the foyer and, finding empty beds, continued to the kitchen.

"Zato, you are a very bad dog!"

"What now?" Blair called from down the hall.

Logan stepped into the hallway to answer. "He's chewed through the kitchen wall and has his nose halfway inside. Bagel is in here, too."

Upon entering the kitchen, Blair immediately thought of Pooh with his head stuck in a honey jar, an image that died quickly.

She grabbed Zato by his collars and pulled him away from the wall, exposing a hole the size of a grapefruit. Clearly, this excavation had been going on for hours, with possible subbing from an accomplice off the bench. Having observed a vacancy at the wall, Bagel plunged her snout into the hole just as Ian entered the kitchen and quickly pulled her back.

"What's this about?" Blair asked of the dogs.

"I think Zato must have heard something behind the drywall," said Ian while struggling to suppress yesterday's images of Watson's cellar.

Blair held Zato's muzzle so that they were nose-to-nose.

"You really try my patience, young man. I don't get it; you've had months to do something like this, and only now have you decided to open this vent into the underworld?"

Releasing him, she turned to Bagel. "Were you in on this, too? I thought you were better than this." The dogs were electrified—indifferent to their interrogation. There was something in the walls.

"I think I understand how this came about," said Ian, cautiously stepping onto thin ice. Blair looked at her husband, eyes narrowing.

"When we were at the bookstore yesterday, the dogs saw a couple of rats in the basement; that may have been the inspiration for burrowing into the wall."

The story poured forth in bits and spurts like curdled cream, with one significant omission: Uncle Mike's premeditation.

"Michael! I should have known when I came home and found the dogs."

As Max was still in the room, Ian said nothing more about his change of heart.

"Okay, let's get ready for school," said Ian. "I'll talk to the super before I go to work. Meanwhile, I'll patch the hole with cardboard and masking tape, and we can close off the kitchen to the dogs."

Ian dragged the offenders down the hall to the foyer. Retreating to their beds, the dogs exchanged furtive glances and assumed the posture of penitents.

"I can't take you guys anywhere," said Ian, exasperated. Then, lowering his voice to a whisper, "You two owe me—big time."

-16-

Canine Scruples

"Zato's under my bed again," shouted Logan from her doorway.

"Please check the hall and kitchen for crimes or misdemeanors," came a deflated reply from the bedroom.

Zato would often squeeze himself under Logan's bed if he felt he might be heading for the guillotine. Getting under the slats and turning to face the door was easier than getting out, often requiring Ian to lift the bed frame, allowing the perpetrator to make his *bad-dog-ridden-with-guilt* exit to his bed in the foyer.

Logan checked the bathroom and hallway for unwanted gifts; finding none, she proceeded to the kitchen, where a plastic Zabar's bag lay in tatters amid a liberal scattering of poppy seeds. A single salt bagel had been appraised and rejected, while the treasures reserved for the day's lunch were now grinding down Zato's alimentary canal.

Logan sang out her findings. "He's eaten all the bagels and most of the bag."

The family gathered in the doorway to Logan's room. A snout and the furtive eyes of the bagel snatcher were just visible under the bed. Ian crouched down on all fours. "Come out of there, Zato," he said sharply. "Or do I need to come in and get you?"

The scraping of nails on wood signaled he had run aground.

Ian stood and turned to Blair. "When I lift the bed, grab his collars. You may have to drag him."

As the bedframe rose, Blair hauled Zato, deadweight, before judge and jury, but the upbraid that followed only made him more inert. This crime required special handling.

Ian dragged the offending canine down the hall and into the kitchen like a bag of crushed stone. Then, lifting him to his feet, he directed the dog's muzzle to the crime scene. Unconsciously, Zato ran his tongue across his lips. The bagels had been delicious, and he could barely restrain himself from dispatching the last remnant of the plastic bag.

"You are incorrigible," said Blair as she picked up the spurned Bagel. "Naturally, you left the salt one, but only after sampling it. Maybe you'd like to give it one more shot?" she asked while pushing the salty side of the bread against the dog's clenched jaws.

Turning to the family, she groaned, "Now, what will we do about lunch? I bought everything we needed, the lox, cream cheese, cucumbers…." Her voice trailed off in uncharacteristic despair.

Ian almost joked about the Bagel having been "eschewed" but, noting the degree of Blair's irritation, quickly scuttled that idea and offered another.

"I'll take the subway down to Zabar's," he suggested. "I can be back in less than an hour. I'll take Logan with me while you and Max get everything else ready."

Blair's spirits immediately revived, and she assumed command. She assigned Max as sous-chef, in charge of mixing chives into the cream cheese, slicing vegetables, and feeding of Bagel. Zato, however, having forfeited his lunch, was condemned to watching his sanctimonious stepsister eat hers.

As father and daughter walked through the campus to catch the subway to 79th Street, Logan began an exposition on morality.

"We are reading the *Autobiography of Benjamin Franklin* in our literature seminar. Have you read it?"

"Yes, in high school. I enjoyed it. Franklin was a remarkable man. Is it difficult?"

"Not really; we read much of it in our lit seminar with Mr. Random. (Ian smiled at the man's name.) Franklin tried to live a good life by what he called 'virtues.' There were thirteen of them, things like 'justice,' 'temperance,' 'industry,' and 'sincerity.' We have also read the Ten Commandments for a comparison. Mr. Random asked us to think about our own moral code and write it down."

"That sounds like an interesting exercise. Have you started?"

"Yes, and I've been looking at our family—the codes we live by."

She paused as they bought tokens, passed through the turnstile, and descended the stairs to an empty bench.

"I can see there is certain behavior that we agree is good or bad," she continued. "There are obvious things like not lying or stealing. But there are more personal things, like you and mom not talking about money problems or even about Uncle Mike in front of us."

Ian looked at her closely, admiring her maturity and tact.

"As kids, we have codes, too. Trying to tell the truth, not be sneaky, and not talk bad behind each other's backs. We try to be a good friend and tolerate the opinions of others, even when we know they are *totally* stupid."

A train pulled into the station. As there were plenty of empty seats, they sat down, and Logan continued. "Some animals have codes: not birds or fish, or even cats. But dogs do, for sure.

"Zato's code around food is 'If you can eat it, eat it.' He knows when he shouldn't eat something, but *his* code says, 'eat it,' while our code says, 'If it is not in your bowl, don't!' Zato and Bagel both know that, and they also seem to know it's *our* code, not theirs. Zato hides under the bed because he knows he's violated *our* code. Do you see what I mean?"

"I do. So, there's more than one set of values at play?"

"Yes, the dogs' and ours, but we insist they play by our rules. Is that fair?"

"Well, we give them food and shelter," said her father. "Shouldn't that count for something?"

"I know we can't just allow them to act like barbarians," said Logan. "But I think dogs operate mostly on instinct and don't have much of what we call a conscience. When Bagel has done something bad, you can tell she knows, but she doesn't even fake guilt. On the other hand, Zato fakes it because he knows he's broken one of our codes.

"It must be how criminals make sense of things. They do it because they must or think they have a right. They know it's bad or a crime but by someone else's code. I believe there are different codes for different groups or even different people."

"I see your point. Your Uncle Mike told me that the Italian mafia has a code of silence. Their biggest sin against the group is to snitch on a fellow member. It's *different strokes for different folks*, even dogs. And I agree," her father said after a pregnant pause, "cats do not seem to give a damn."

They both laughed as the train pulled into the 96th Street station. Their car filled with passengers, and they rose, yielding their seats to an elderly couple.

As the train rattled out of the station, Ian and Logan held onto a pole. Nodding discretely toward the couple, Ian said to Logan, "Moral code. It's baked into our bones."

*

Mission accomplished. Lox and cream cheese joined in holy matrimony under the dome of an onion bagel. Cucumbers, tomatoes, capers, red onion, and dill were in attendance, and no one objected to the marriage (though one attendee looked on wistfully). Tranquility returned to the Kennedy clan, and Blair allotted Zato a mini biscuit which he ignored until Bagel gave it a sniff.

-17-

Never-befores

Summer officially began for the family in early June, when the Parker School, St. Mark's, and Columbia ended their classes for the year. Ian and the kids would bask in nearly three months of leisure, while Blair's reprieve came in sections: two weeks in June, then back on deck in July for the summer institute, followed by a month to use as she pleased.

City activities in the summer months provided a broad palate from which to plan. There were picnics and boating in Central Park; bike rides to the 79th Street Boat Basin (with a pit stop at Zabar's); museums of all kinds; the Staten Island Ferry with its stunning vistas of the Statue of Liberty and the Manhattan skyline, the Bronx Zoo, and scores of other possibilities. Often urban excursions included Bagel, who fit snugly in a bicycle basket, but with Zato's arrival came new restraints. His personality was not amenable to picnics in Central Park or bike rides along the Hudson; unfortunately, Bagel suffered the consequences. Ian reasoned if Zato were left alone, he might be prone to mischief. Even though Blair and the children thought this solution unjust, they unhappily agreed with the logic.

Over the last few years, excursions beyond Manhattan were taken in August and consisted of borrowing Mike's VW van for a week of camping in New Hampshire or Maine. Taking Bagel had not been a problem, as a trip into the forest had filled her nose with the worrisome smells of bears, coyotes, and mountain cats, so stepping away from the campsite was done with caution. Squirrels, however, could jumpstart her from a sound sleep.

This summer, the glories of carefree camping in the wilds had a Malamute problem. Earlier visits to the relatives in Connecticut had proved that such adventures would not be wise, as just the hopping of a robin would start Zato quivering with the intoxication of the hunt.

Realizing this summer's travels would be confined to the city, Ian and Blair created the "New York City Culture Tour" of off-the-path destinations for August, some of which would be dog friendly and all of which would remain classified. For the first tour, Uncle Mike volunteered his VW, and, after an early Sunday breakfast, the family and dogs, with a basket of provisions, walked across the campus, collected the keys from Uncle Mike, and piled them into the van: Mom, Dad, and Bagel seated in front, the kids on the bench seat behind them, with Zato allotted a spot by the window.

As Ian made a U-turn and headed uptown for parts unknown, the kids started speculating on possible destinations for the excursion.

"Coney Island," said Logan. "None of us have been there, except maybe Zato."

"Grand Canyon," offered Max.

Then a litany of alternatives:

"Mexico."

"Disneyland."

"Palisades Amusement Park."

"Sorry," replied Ian. It's lost and gone forever.

"West Point."

"Been there, done that," said Blair.

This exchange continued until they turned east on 125th Street and started across town. After crossing 8th Avenue, they passed under a colorful banner that read: "The All-New Apollo Grand Opening."

"I guess you are not taking us to the Apollo," said Logan, despondently, as the theater came into view. "Look, it has a new marquee."

"It's been closed for almost two years," explained Ian, "but it's a revered piece of Harlem history, and recent investment has resulted in a full renovation, top to bottom."

In brilliant illumination, the marquee read: *Jocko's Rocketship Show*, with names of the headliners in smaller print.

"Look," said Logan. It's *WAR*. I love that group, especially the 'Cisco Kid.'"

"I love that one too," her mother said, "and 'Why Can't We Be Friends.'"

"'Spill The Wine's' my favorite," said Ian. "Eric Burden."

"I don't know WAR," lamented Max. "So, who's Jocko?"

Ian, who was now in his element, said, "Jocko, my inquisitive young friend, is Douglas 'Jocko' Henderson, a popular New York disc jockey. I listened to him in high school every day. He played Rhythm and Blues and Rock and Roll on WOV, 1280 on your radio dial. Back in the 50s and 60s it was called *Jocko's Rocketship Show.*

"He had great style, and each of his shows began something like this." Ian cleared his throat for his performance.

> 'Greetings and salutations,
> oo-papa-doo, how do you do?
> 'Close the hatches, and
> Prepare to blast off!'

"Then he'd do a countdown from six to zero, followed by the sound of a rocket blasting off, and he'd say:

> 'Higher big rocket, Higher!
>
> 'Eee-tiddlee-yock, this is the Jock,
> and I'm back on the scene with the record machine,
> saying oo-papa-do, and how do you do?
>
> 'Mommy-o, daddy-o.
> Now we are gonna start the show,
> Great Gugga Mugga Shugga Bugga.'

and he'd play the next song.

"My high school buddies and I would often say 'Great Gugga Mugga' when expressing wonder or dispensing high praise for some crazy act of bravery."

Max put his arm around Zato and spoke into his ear. "Great Gugga Mugga Shugga Bugga," he said, receiving a bewildered look in return.

"Spoken like a pro," said his father.

As they crossed 5th Avenue, Ian said, "It was your Uncle Mike who first took me to the Apollo. We took the train down from Connecticut to the 125th Street station and got off just ahead. You see those stairs leading down from the trestle?" Ian pointed to a steep set of rusted steps descending from the platform to the street. "That's where we'd come down."

"At that time, many popular singing groups had animal names, like the Spaniels, the Flamingos, the Penguins, and the Crows. I remember seeing the Flamingos, Little Richard, and Fats Domino in the same show. They were big stars of the 50s. First, we saw a movie, usually a cowboy film, but no one was interested; flattened popcorn boxes flew every which way. When the final credits finished rolling, the theater went quiet until a spotlight made a circle on a red velvet curtain, and a deep, male voice came over the sound system, saying, 'Ladies and gentlemen, it's showtime at the Apollo.' Then all hell broke loose as the curtain lifted, revealing a twenty-piece band, playing some wild, upbeat music. It was electric, and fans of all ages went crazy."

"It sounds so fun," Logan said. "Will you take us there sometime?"

"That was nearly twenty years ago. Tensions between the races were high but not so stressed as now, and Harlem tolerated white kids from Connecticut. I think they found us amusing. But in the early sixties, it became unsafe for white kids to go there. In the summer of sixty-four, a white policeman shot a Black teenager, and a riot erupted. I had just come back from studying in Hong Kong. I remember standing on 116th Street and Morningside Drive—like we do every day—watching the buildings burning along the edge of the park and deep into Harlem. Many of those buildings had been abandoned for years and were gutted by fire. It went on for three or four days."

Max leaned forward and grasped the sides of his father's seat, "Is it safe here, now?"

"Yes, Max, don't worry. People get along, but racial tension is high. It's a long story we can talk about later, but Blacks in America have a tough time, and sometimes the pot boils over."

Max sat back and looked out the window, as did Blair, Logan, and the dogs.

They drove in silence for a few minutes. Ian turned on the radio to WWRL out of Harlem, and they listened to music as the van turned south on 1st Avenue and continued to 116th Street where it entered East River Drive. As they cruised south along the river, Ian pointed out Randall's Island, where he had attended a jazz festival in 1960, and the United Nations, where he heard Deng Xiaoping speak four years ago. Lesser sights and stories followed—all of which his passengers had seen or heard before. Finally, they turned onto the entrance to the Brooklyn Bridge. All but Zato had walked its boards the previous summer.

"This is not a repeat performance of last summer, but I looked up a few facts about the bridge you may not know. Remember, it took fourteen years to build: from 1869 to 1883, work started just three years after the Civil War ended."

"There's the Statue of Liberty," piped Max, pointing to the south.

"Within fifteen years of its completion, the population of Brooklyn had doubled from 500,000 to over a million."

"You can see the Staten Island Ferry, too!" added Logan.

"There was a panic when the bridge first opened up," continued Ian, attempting to rescue the narrative, "and people *died*." Now the kids were listening.

"In the first week, crowds of people walked the bridge, even more than you see now, but the technology of suspension bridge building was new, and several earlier attempts had failed. The story is that there were about 20,000 visitors on the bridge on opening day. One of them thought the bridge was falling and panicked, scaring the crowd into a stampede. Twelve people died, and dozens were injured."

"Was it falling?" asked Max, with tension in his voice.

"No, they had built the bridge to tolerate eight times the required stress levels. It was and still is perfectly safe, but people were afraid to use it until a clever man offered a solution to prove it."

"What solution?" asked Logan and Max simultaneously.

"Remember when we went to see the Ringling Brothers circus parade through Central Park a couple of years ago?" They all remembered it well. It was as if Noah's ark had finally sailed out of the Old Testament and up the Hudson, disgorging its cargo on 59th Street. Of course, a sighting of clowns on the streets of New York was not unusual, but in young Max's words, pachyderms gliding like honey through the park were no "simply heffalumpchuous."

"P.T. Barnum, who owned the circus when this bridge opened, arranged a full circus parade across it, from Manhattan to Brooklyn. Traveling in a long line were twenty-one elephants, seventeen camels, teams of horses pulling circus wagons, a gaggle of clowns, and a variety of colorfully costumed performers—all to demonstrate the stability of the new bridge—and it worked. Of course, it was also a fantastic advertisement for the circus."

As they passed under the second of the Neo-Gothic arches into Brooklyn and turned south onto Interstate 278, images of circus animals and gaily costumed performers paraded through the van.

They rumbled down the Interstate paralleling the East River. Gantry cranes moved containers on the Jersey-side dockyards.

"Can you tell us where we're going yet?" asked Logan. "It seems like we are leaving civilization altogether."

"You will know in about twenty minutes, but I'll give you a hint. There are two 'never-befores' on this trip."

Blair, who had been quiet, said, "Brooklyn has many places I've never been, with exotic names like Flatbush, Canarsie, Ozone Park, and Jamaica.

"I haven't been to any of those places either," responded Ian. "Maybe we should add some to our culture tours this summer." He paused, then added, "Jamaica and Ozone Park are technically in Queens, but we could include Little Caribbean; it's in Brooklyn."

"So where is the first never-before?" said an exasperated voice from the back seat. Max was getting impatient.

"Ten more minutes, and you will have your answer. Just relax and listen to the music. We are almost there."

Those ten minutes passed in agonizing boredom until Zato decided to join Bagel on Blair's lap. Leaping from his perch near the window, he clambered onto the cushion that separated the driver and neighboring passenger seat, causing Bagel to bite him on the cheek and the kids to pull him back by his hind legs and tumbling him to the floorboards. Jilted in his attempt, Zato spurned his assigned seating and retreated to the van's backmost bench to sulk.

As they rounded a sweep of the highway, the majestic arches of the Verrazzano Bridge rose before them like colossal tuning forks.

"Okay," announced Ian, "we have arrived at the first never-before. I typed up a bit of research on it, which your mom can read to you as we cross."

This revelation did not immediately galvanize the kids with enthusiasm, though it was a *first* and was indeed something. As they entered the long ramp leading onto the upper deck, Blair began disbursing some of the salient facts, piece-by-piece, so the kids would have time to digest them.

"In 1524, Giovanni da Verrazzano sailed into what is now the upper harbor of New York City, dropping anchor right about here. He was the first European explorer known to have done so. He was looking for a shortcut from Europe to China. Four hundred years later, the work began on this bridge, joining Brooklyn to Staten Island. It took five years to build—from 1959 to 1964. The central span is 4,260 feet, making this the world's longest suspension bridge—over fourteen football fields in length. You will be pleased to know that it is fifty-four feet longer than its closest rival, the pint-sized Golden Gate Bridge in San Francisco."

Max furrowed his brows in concentration. Logan stifled a yawn.

Blair continued. "Suspension bridges have supports or towers draping large cables from one structure to another. This one has four main cables, each one 36 inches in diameter, consisting of more than 26,000 steel strands wound together, totaling 143,000 miles of wire. That's six times the circumference of Earth.

"The vertical wires are attached to the deck from the draping cables to hold up the roadway we are traveling across. So it's all perfectly balanced."

Max's brow relaxed. "I get it," he said. "It's like the hammock at Grandpa's house."

"Exactly."

"When we get closer," his mother added, "you will be able to see all the rivets and bolts that hold the structure together. There are more than three million rivets and one million bolts in each tower: eight million altogether. That's the same number as the population of all five boroughs of New York City."

Interest was slowly building in the back seat. "The towers look like they come from a galaxy far, far away," said Max.

"Perhaps they have," responded Ian in a theatrical voice. "Let's boldly go where no Kennedy child has gone before."

Returning the group to reality, Blair asked, "Do you know how rivets differ from bolts?" The kids did not, so she added a few facts of her own.

"Bolts are fastened tight by nuts, like those on your bicycle baskets," she said, rotating her fingers to illustrate. "Rivets look like bolts but have no grooves or threads for a nut to turn on. They are heated until white-hot, then inserted through a hole that connects two pieces of iron or steel, where they are pounded on each end by hand-held machines to make those little caps you see on each one. The high heat allows a worker to hammer the metal down, so it will have a very tight fit when it cools."

The kids were now studying the bridge in earnest.

"These days, workers heat the rivets in small furnaces raised or lowered around the structure on hoists. Just thirty years ago, when building boats or bridges, workers would throw white-hot rivets to each other like baseballs—person-to-person from a furnace on the ground—throwing and catching them in metal scoops like first basemen. Very dangerous. Can you imagine?"

As the kids silently scanned the bridge for rivets, Ian stole an admiring look at his wife. This compelling explanation was her unsolicited contribution to the staccato statistics he'd supplied.

As they passed under the first tower, Logan asked, 'How high are they?"

"693 feet. That's roughly the height of a 60-story skyscraper."

After a pause, Blair asked, "How many gallons of paint do you think you'd need to cover it and keep it rust-free? All surfaces." The kids offered various underestimates. "11,530 gallons for each coat," she said. "It takes two coats, so about 23,000 gallons. A firetruck only carries 500 gallons of water, so that's about forty-five trucks full of paint. The workers stand on scaffolding and apply the paint with a spray machine."

"At least they don't have to use paintbrushes," said Max.

They passed under the second tower, and Blair concluded her presentation. "During the five-year construction, about 12,000 people worked on the bridge. Unfortunately, three died in falls, and workers went on strike for four days, demanding safety nets, which they got, saving the lives of three more workers who fell."

As the bridge slowly sank into the distance, Logan said, "I thought Henry Hudson was the first to explore the river. You'd think they would have named the bridge after him like they did with the river."

"Hudson's expedition was almost 100 years later," answered Blair, "so I guess that's why Verrazzano got dibs on the bridge. However, his name is not without controversy, as all the highway signs on both sides of the bridge have his name misspelled, there are two *Zs* in Verrazzano, but the signs show only one. Maybe in the future the city will set it right, and Giovanni can truly have his day."

"Ian laughed and, turning to his wife, said, "You are absolutely, positively amazing!"

"I did a little homework, too," she said.

On they rumbled toward never-before No. 2.

-18-

The Lighthouse

Fifteen minutes later, they left the interstate highway, passing through upscale, residential areas of Staten Island and miles of the protected Greenbelt Conservatory: a mermaid-shaped series of protected forests, wetlands, meadows, and hiking trails. There was even a sighting of Moses' Mountain, a well-regarded hiking spot.

"Not much of a mountain," commented Logan as she read the signs pointing to the trails.

"More like a molehill," added her brother.

Ian checked the time. "In preparation for our next never-before, I need to give you a little background on Buddhism. Do either of you know what that is?"

"We studied it a little in our religion class," answered Logan. "It is a religion from Asia, but that's all I can really remember."

Over the next twenty minutes, Ian provided his children with a simple outline of the fundamentals of Buddhism: life is suffering, but through mental and spiritual exercises [mediation], a person can achieve a sense of inner peace, free from the turmoil of everyday life. The kids listened and quietly wondered just how boring the next never-before would be.

"Is Buddha a god?" asked Max.

"No, a man like us. You could say he had a mystery to solve: how to eliminate suffering for his fellow man. He spent six days thinking about it, day and night, until he figured it out, then he spent the next fifty years teaching others how to relieve suffering for themselves. I think you will find that most religions share this same goal."

They dropped into a valley, then up a steep hill that opened into a residential area with well-tended streets and substantial homes, finally stopping before a seven-foot-high, hand-crafted stone wall with a red iron gate. A sign beside the entryway read: Jacques Marchais Museum of Tibetan Art.

"What's Tibetan Art?" asked Logan.

"Tibet is a large, semi-independent state, high in the mountains in between China and India," answered Ian. "They practice Buddhism there, and this museum has examples of their religious art. I'll tell you more about it later, but first, let's give the dogs some space and have lunch. There's a nice park nearby."

A few minutes later, the van pulled into a small parking area alongside one of the many entrances to Latourette Park. They found a space in the shade and unloaded themselves and their provisions. Before they had set sail for Staten Island, Michael had generously provided the van with bottled water, two metal bowls, and dry dog food, all sealed in a wooden box under the back bench seat.

They fed and watered the dogs on the asphalt beside the van, then all trooped into the park. Blair spread a blanket under the canopy of an old oak, laying out the food and drinks while the dogs and their keepers explored the park's periphery. Returning to the blanket, they ate sandwiches and drank Cokes while Zato and Bagel had biscuits.

Occasionally a dog walker came a little too close, providing Ian with a tug of war but, fortunately, pedestrians were not yet out in force.

"What's that?" asked Max, pointing to a structure that rose above the trees atop a hill opposite.

"It's a lighthouse," explained Ian. "It has been there since the turn of the century and is still operational. There are ten lighthouses on or around Staten Island. They help guide the ship traffic in New York Harbor."

"Can we see it?"

"Sure, why don't you take Bagel and have a look. It's outside the park, but it's less than half a mile's walk. Go through that path across the field. You can see the structure above the trees, so it's easy to find."

The kids and Bagel set out across the grass, causing Zato to strain at his leash, drop his ears, and look pathetic. "I brought Zato's rope leash," Ian told Blair. "It's in the car under the seat. We'll be back in a minute."

Blair watched Ian and Zato run back toward of the van and wondered if the kids would find this Tibetan never-before engaging. Museums were a bit hit-and-miss with the kids. Max loved science museums, and Logan gushed over the Impressionists at the Met, but they were so-so on the Museum of Modern Art and even less so on the Frick.

Blair shared Ian's appreciation of Buddhist sculpture. Still, her interest waned quickly on an overdose of bodhisattvas riding on clouds or oversized dogs fending off the monsters of lust and greed. Although Ian had been to this museum many times, it was a first for Blair, and she hoped it would hold the kids' interest. Ian had assured her that there was something for everyone—especially today.

While Blair settled into a book, Ian fastened Zato's rope leash, and they went for a jog along the tree-lined paths at the edge of the park. Half an hour later, the kids, Ian, and the dogs returned to the blanket to report on their adventures.

"We met a man at the lighthouse who told us all about it," sputtered Max. "It was built in 1912. Originally it had lamps that burned mineral oil, but now it has a 1,000-watt bulb, and it's all run electronically."

"It's closed to visitors but still cool," Logan said, obviously impressed. "It uses three kinds of prisms to focus all the light in one direction and is visible out at sea for over twenty miles."

Other bits of lighthouse lore were itemized enthusiastically, including details of the caretaker's adjacent quarters, the stone and brick construction of the lighthouse, and when it first lit its lamp. Blair was relieved they had run into someone who knew lighthouses and that this off-road excursion was a hit.

Ian informed the group they needed to pack up and return to the museum, as exhibitions would start shortly after lunch. Everyone wanted to know what to expect, but Ian told them to be patient as they would soon find out. Blair raised her eyes to the heavens and discreetly crossed her fingers.

-19-

Little *Tulku*

He parked the van in the shade on the street opposite the museum entrance, then cracked open the windows allowing air to circulate and keep the dogs comfortable.

The family entered the museum grounds. As they started along a flagstone path lined with Japanese maples and strings of colorful prayer flags, Ian explained a little of the museum's history.

"This museum is the creation of one person's love of Tibetan art and culture. For thirty years, an American woman named Jacque Marchais collected the treasures you will see inside. Most are from Tibet, but some are from other Asian countries. She created this museum to resemble a high-mountain monastery. She calls the central gallery a "chanting room," and there are numerous smaller rooms for quiet thought. Although Miss Marchais never traveled there, she created a glimpse into Tibet through this unique lens. She must have had quite an imagination."

As they approached the main building, a low murmur trembled through the leaves and along the flagstone walk.

"What's that noise?" asked Logan.

"It sounds like a foghorn," said Max.

"You'll see in just a minute."

The murmuring grew louder as they passed a small pond with a dozen lotus flowers floating in full bloom. Logan felt her ears hum.

Between the trees, they caught glimpses of a rustic, wood and stone building with muted purple trim. Log rafters projected from under the eaves, above trapezoidal-shaped windows. The roof swept up at the corners over a facade of rugged fieldstones harvested from local farmland and unwanted stone walls.

They entered a large room where a few dozen visitors gathered around eight monks dressed in saffron-colored robes. Four were standing, making deep murmuring sounds that filled the room with long singular notes punctuated by short breaths taken in unison. Another four monks sat at the cardinal points of a small table, carefully tapping colored sand from foot-long funnels onto the surface of an expanding mandala. Within the center ring, a white dove held an olive branch. The design radiated from there in concentric circles, each with its symbolism. The second circle contained the Tibetan word for *Ohm*, the four and eight-spoked wheels of Buddhism, the five-pointed star of Judaism, the Daoist yin-yang, and other symbols depicting the unity of all faiths. The third showed a string of male and female silhouettes holding hands. A fourth was in progress, with monks from each side of the table conjuring mountains, valleys, rivers, clouds, and forests.

Geometric lines laid out a plan for six circles to complete the mandala. However, from the pace of the work, it would take many more hours.

The questions and comments started as the family stepped away from the circle, allowing others to get a better view.

"What are the men doing?"

"It's beautiful, but it could all just blow away, couldn't it?"

"How do those men make that noise?

"It sounds like gargling."

As Ian was again in familiar territory, he began to fill the void.

"The sound they are making is called throat singing or overtone singing. It comes from deep in the throat. There is a central or fundamental note and a higher harmonic note, sometimes two or more, all sounding together. The placement of the tongue helps to produce the overtones. If you listen closely, you can hear them."

"Their singing makes my ears ring," said Logan.

"The human voice has overtones," continued Ian. "Each note or sound you make has about a dozen overtones or harmonics, like the color spectrum we see when white light passes through a prism."

"Is this singing hard to do?" asked Blair, knowing Ian had an answer.

"When I was in Hong Kong, I had a school friend from Mongolia. He knew how to do it and gave me lessons. So, I can do it a little. We can practice in the car on the way home." The kids were impressed and expressed interest in learning the technique.

"What are the monks doing at the table?" Blair asked, recentering the group's attention.

"They are making what is called a 'mandala.' The word comes from India, meaning 'circle.' It is a spiritual symbol representing something essential to think about or to concentrate on while creating it. This one has a goal of world peace, which you can see from the dove and the people holding hands."

"It looks like it will take them hours to finish it," said Logan.

"Yes, and this is a small one; some larger mandalas can take weeks, with a dozen monks working on it together."

Keeping the subject running, Blair asked, "What is the purpose of doing it?"

"Making a mandala requires intense concentration to get each grain of colored sand in the right place. It is a method of clearing the mind of distractions or thoughts of any kind. All toward the goal of achieving a sense of inner peace. The throat singing or chanting by the monks has the same purpose."

The children were listening, but Ian was not sure they were getting it.

"What do they do with the mandala when it's complete?" asked Logan. "It seems so fragile."

"First, there is a ceremony; then the sand is swept to the mandala's center, gathered up and taken to a nearby river to flow its spiritual message to the world."

"It seems sad to destroy such a beautiful thing."

"The Buddhist idea is that nothing lasts forever," said Ian, "and that becoming attached to things in life can only bring suffering. If you think about it, you can see the truth in that idea. You know how you feel when you have broken a favorite toy? Or when a friend moves away?" The children nodded in mute understanding, their expressions reflecting a connection to some past sorrow.

With a sudden change of tone, Ian continued. "I, however, prefer to remain attached and endure the suffering that comes with living a full life. What would be the fun of life without you, Max, Mom, and Bagel? And, yes, even Zato."

They all laughed and moved on, looking at other exhibits, with Ian helping where he could.

After a while, the chanting subsided, and the soft call of a Tibetan singing bowl rippled through the air: "gwong-ng-ng-ng."

"In ten minutes, there is another live exhibition," said Ian. "It's outside. We won't want to miss it."

The courtyard looked out over an expansive valley. Two of the chanters were now seated on small stools, each holding the mouthpiece of a Tibetan longhorn, their broad bells resting in semi-circular cutouts along the seatback of a wooden bench that faced the valley. The other two chanters stood to the side, while in the museum's main room, the mandala makers continued tapping out their colored sand, the absence of onlookers of no more significance than fallen leaves carried off by the wind.

A stately, white-haired woman in a tailored pink blouse and long blue skirt addressed the assemblage. First, she introduced herself and the four monks, explaining that these Tibetan guests were part of a cultural exchange program sponsored by the Gyutu Monastery and the Institute of Buddhist Dialectics in Dharamshala, India. She then acted as translator for Lama Lobsang, a diminutive man with a round, leathered face that radiated unrestrained joy.

The monk described the instrument and the music they would perform: "The longhorn is called a Dung-Chen and is a sacred musical instrument with a history of more than 1000 years. Traditionally, it is played in pairs for ceremonies and processions and as a daily call to prayer. These Dung-Chen horns are twelve feet long. They are made of brass and separated into five pieces for portability. Can you imagine airplane travel if we did not have a way to divide them into sections?" The monk laughed merrily and looked around at the crowd, his gaze settling on Max, who looked back intently.

As Lama Lopsang continued his explanation through the translator, he appeared to include the whole group, but Ian and Blair sensed he was addressing Max in particular. "The music we will play is a short version of a much longer musical prayer. It is called the *Longevity Dance of the Space Beings.* It has both vocal and instrumental sections, including cymbals, bells, and drums."

The monks rotated their stools and faced the valley while their colleagues chose from an array of musical instruments on a nearby table. One selected a pair of cymbals while the other chose a handbell and what resembled a child's double-sided rattle drum. Immediately they began with the deep guttural sounds of throat singing, accompanied by a cacophony of crashings, ringings, and a clattering drum.

Small chimes and a rasping, oboe-like horn contributed to the mix, and as the music grew louder, the longhorns joined in. Their initial pitch was high; then, dropping to a rumble, it traveled deep into the earth, trembling the roots of trees and vibrating matter. The calls were long, powerful, and majestic, as if some primordial behemoth was beckoning the herds of Earth to Staten Island.

The music ebbed, then stopped for a few beats, and the wailing of dogs echoed up from the valley below. Zato and Bagel had also heard the call of the longhorns and felt an overwhelming urge to answer. An elderly passer-by noted their efforts with applause and a cheer, "Bravo, bravo!" he said to the dogs through the crack in their window. Unnoticed, he continued on his way.

The prayer began again with the thrum of voices, followed by the clash of cymbals and the rattle of the drum. Finally, the longhorns grumbled onto center stage, evoking an even louder response from the backyards below. As the prayer ended, the voices and instruments muted, and only the clear ting-ting of the finger cymbals remained to purify the air, followed by a respectful silence and the slowing of hearts.

Lama Lopsang asked the audience through his interpreter if there were any questions or comments. Only one hand raised. Max.

"Yes?" asked Lama Lopsang in English, his cheeks glowing like polished brass, his eyes sparkling with interest.

"The horns sound like the voice of mountains."

"Yes," responded the monk, again in English, before his translator could open her mouth to speak. "They *are* the voice of the mountains. Would you like to try?"

With an open hand, Lama Lopsang gestured for Max to take his seat, and Max complied.

Lama Lopsang continued in English while holding the end of the longhorn in his hand. To Max, he said: "A short lesson before we start. First, close your mouth, then pucker your lips and blow like this."

The monk demonstrated the technique and laughed—Max laughing with him.

"The more the lips relax, the deeper the tone. You do it."

Max looked embarrassed but buzzed his lips in compliance.

"That is very good. Maybe you have done this before?"

"Playing with my sister, just for fun. We call it 'making horse lips.'"

"Ah, I see," said the monk, his burnished cheeks bulging at the edges of a broad smile. "Take the horn in your right hand," he said, handing it to Max. "Now, take a deep breath through your nose and make horse lips."

Max took a deep breath and blew as instructed. The first note was high pitched; then, as his lips relaxed, a low earthy tone emerged.

"Try again," said Lama Lopsang. "This time, put your lips to sleep."

Another breath and another deep rumble filled the valley. Cymbals clanged, bells rang, and valley dogs howled as Max made a third, even deeper tone.

"Excellent," said the monk when the boy had finished. "You have spoken to the mountains, and they have heard you."

Those assembled applauded his performance. Blushing, Max hastened to rejoin his family.

Blair beamed, and Ian ruffled the hair on his son's head. "Very nicely done."

"That was the best horse lips ever!" exclaimed Logan, patting him on the back.

As they started walking toward the exit, Lama Lopsang joined them.

"Thank you for visiting with us, and thank you, little *tulku,* for making horse lips. Today, you talked to the mountains." Lama Lopsang put his hands and fingers together in the Buddhist gesture of adoration, bowed slightly, and walked back through the trees.

"Little tulku?" asked Blair as she watched the monk move softly over the flagstones.

"It means 'little Buddha.'"

The dogs had been waiting. They barked and leaped from seat to seat as soon as they saw the family exit through the red gate.

Blair and Ian gave them a quick walk along the curb, accompanied by the kids who quizzed the dogs about the longhorns. "Did you hear them? Did you hear Max blow the horn? Did it make you howl?"

They decided not to try their luck with the ferry queue but to return to Manhattan across the bridges as they had come.

Blair provided bags of shelled peanuts and biscuits for the dogs, and, as the group settled into the rhythm of the road, the van rumbled north toward the Verrazzano Bridge.

After some time had passed, Ian asked Max, "What caused you to raise your hand and speak to the monk?"

"When I heard those low sounds, I thought that must be how mountains sound when talking, and for a moment, I thought I smelled snow."

Moses Mountain came and went without comment, and Ian asked if they would like to try throat singing. He had expected the monks would chant, so, in anticipation of the trip, he had been practicing while walking the dogs. He gave them a demonstration of his skill and some rudimentary instructions on technique. They all began to try it with varying degrees of success, and by the time they reached the bridge, even the dogs were singing.

Later that afternoon, as they walked across the campus toward home, Blair took Ian's hand. "That was a magical, never-before day. You done good, *myshka*. Very good."

Ian loved Blair's mysterious endearments. He pulled her closer, simultaneously tightening his grip on Zato's leash as he spotted a poodle, cut like a topiary, tiptoeing onto College Walk.

-20-

Izzat a Woof?

Ginkgo leaves fluttered in the November breeze as if migrating monarchs had come to winter in the trees of 116th Street. Some relaxed their grip, twirling freely. Others gathered in gutters or clustered on the street, swirling in golden confusion when cars passed through them.

After the trees had yellowed, Ian would often walk to the corner of Morningside Drive and position himself so the ginkgos of 116th Street lined up shoulder-to-shoulder like young ladies at a cotillion. He had studied the yellows of an artist's pallet but was now undecided as to ginkgo-leaf label, for each one was in continual change: the angle of the sun or a breeze ruffling through, morphed the colors like a snaking caterpillar: lighter here, darker there: the wheat fields of Van Gogh—amber, lemon, saffron, gold, all moving through the canvas like sea swells.

While Zato balanced on three legs beside his favorite tree, Ian plucked a leaf from its mooring, admiring its scalloped edges and vibrant color. Studying this small fan transported him back to Asia. Though he had stayed only a few days in Japan, he had visited Buddhist and Shinto shrines in Kyoto, Osaka, and Nara, where every twig or fading flower seemed placed in careless perfection, just like the leaf that blew from his hand.

"I heard from your cousin Sam today," said Blair as Ian walked into the kitchen. "She is coming to New York for Christmas and New Year's."

"She called from London?"

"No, she was in Inverness at some fancy hotel, arranging a malt whiskey tour for a group of American amateur golfers. They get to drink their way through Speyside and play a round of golf on the asphalt grasses of St. Andrews. As usual, she will be staying at the Plaza. I'm presuming her current sugar daddy is covering it."

Samantha McFarlane was Ian's third or fourth cousin; no one knew exactly how far removed. They had met at a family reunion near Mystic when they were teenagers and got along well. The McFarlanes lived in Greenwich, where Sam attended an all-girls private school and developed her love of everything English: literature, history, culture, and Winston Churchill. She spent two years at Smith College before heading out to London, where she'd landed a summer apprenticeship in the travel business. In short order, Sam proved herself invaluable and was sponsored to a work visa and then a permanent residence visa. Ultimately, she applied for and became a naturalized British citizen. After ten years of learning the ropes and rising through the ranks from working the tour bus mic to managing corporate sales, Sam left the relative security of an established business and started one of her own. Within five years, her client base had eclipsed that of her former employers.

Sam's love life was as eccentric as her professional life. She was unmarried but had no shortage of love affairs, almost all with older, married men—most were British. The first of these affairs was with Bertie Harris, the father of a high school classmate. Bertie was a pretentious thirty-year British ex-pat, sporting an accent layered with a crust so upper he might well have been speaking German. He was a child of storekeepers from the wrong end of Piccadilly, who found his way onto Madison Avenue as a copywriter, then, later, as an account executive. Bertie longed to wear a bowler and a bespoke suit from Savile Row but settled for a fedora and a pin-striped knock-off from Saks. He drank too much and drove a dated Rolls that he'd bought cheap at auction, but he had enough pizazz to knock Sam off her feet. Bertie and Sam secretly carried on their affair over her vacations from Smith, only cutting ties when Sam left the new England for the old.

"That should be fun; it's been nearly three years since her last visit. Is she coming with anyone?"

"Possibly, she didn't say. I doubt there is much business to do in New York over the holidays, so we should have some play time."

"I'll write her and work out the details," said Ian. "We could blow up the air mattress and put the kids together in Max's room, but she always chooses the Plaza."

"I would if I could. Wouldn't you?"

*

School chugged along for Ian and the kids. Blair finished her last course at the institute and turned in her thesis to Professor Belgrade three weeks before the winter holiday. Ian had proofed it. Though he was not well-read in Dostoyevsky and knew nothing about Anna Dostoevskaya, he thought Blair's analysis was brilliant and assured her that even Uncle Vanya would be wowed. Nevertheless, she was nervous about it and hoped to hear the result before everyone left to visit with family or rush to Florida to get a tan (an idea that made her laugh when thinking of Messrs. Belknap and Zaritsky).

December is a fickle month in New York, often coming in warm and threatening to anesthetize the holiday season or harsh, presaging the need for layers of wool and months of frigid dog walks in the early dark of an afternoon.

This first day of December should have been an omen: snow. It wasn't that heavy-gravity mush that splashes on windshields and is more like congealed rain. The TV weathermen had not predicted the cold front rushing down from Canada. It came in strong from across the Hudson under a light sky, whirling its small, dry flakes along the bricks and asphalt like grains of sand. It was hard to tell if it would last.

Squinting into the wind and snow while Zato and Bagel saw to their morning rituals, Ian thoughtfully critiqued the lack of moisture in these flakes, as he preferred a good "snowman snow," where above-ground traffic passed to the plows, schools closed, and children warred in the streets. He loved the sound of such snow: the crunch of boots and the heavy crush of tires moving slowly to maintain traction. At night after a good snowfall, when the city was deep in hibernation, he would look down Amsterdam Avenue and watch the street shift from red to yellow, then green—like strips of Christmas ribbon. Regrettably, today's desiccated pellets were more of a lash, punishing early risers for having defecating pets, than they were the hope of snowmen in the quad.

Ian and Bagel waited patiently for Zato to run dry; then, they started down 116th Street toward Morningside Park—the dogs idling over secret communications meant for their noses only. As they walked, a man and a small boy, age five or six, came out of the park, crossed Morningside Drive, and started up the street toward the university. They were both bundled for winter: the man, slightly stooped, was wrapped in a scarf and heavy overcoat with a cap pulled over his ears. His companion wore a padded coat, a wool hat tied under the chin, and an oversized scarf that showed beneath the hem of his coat. They were holding hands, and the boy was pointing with his mitten.

As they approached, the pair slowed, then stopped to admire the dogs. "Good morning," said Ian.

"Good morning," the man responded, smiling. "You have beautiful dogs. My grandson was excited to meet them."

Zato, already responding to friendly conversation, moved closer to sniff out the new arrivals.

"Izzat a woof?" asked the boy, taking a step back.

For just a moment, Ian thought of how he should answer. A "yes" might travel down through the park and ricochet through the nearby community, giving him an added sense of security when called to late-night canine duty. But such an answer carried a shame that he could already feel.

"No, he isn't," he said, easing up on Zato's leash. "He does kind of look like one, doesn't he? He is an Eskimo dog and loves the cold and snow. His name is Zato. His little friend is named Bagel. She would rather be home under a blanket."

Bagel inched into the conversation, and Ian coaxed the boy to give each a pat. The lad hesitated, then, after a nod from grandpa, removed a mitten and patted the malamute's head.

"He's soft," the child said, causing. Zato to wag his tail and move closer so the boy could rub behind his ears. "He likes me."

"He does," agreed Ian.

"We'd better get going, Nazim," said the man. "We must get to grandma's before nine, and I'm getting cold." Then, speaking to Ian, he added, "It was nice to meet you and the dogs." Turning to his grandson, he said, "Say goodbye, Nazim."

"Goodbye, Zato; goodbye, Bagel."

As Ian watched them walk to Amsterdam Avenue, hand in hand, and wait for the light to change, a sense of loss coupled with a deep longing caught him by surprise. "Where did that come from?" he asked of the dogs. Getting no answer, he set off through the gritty snow, hoping this would be a short walk.

-21-

The Summons

The first December snow had quickly come and gone, and within a few days, the skies had cleared, the temperature warmed to sweater wear, and clouds floated over Harlem like dolphins. A constant breeze had loosed the last remaining fans from the ginkgos, and sweeper trucks groomed the gutters as if readying them for guests.

One week before the university emptied for the holidays, Blair received a letter in her office inbox from Professor Belgrade summoning her to his office for an interview the following morning.

At home that evening, she showed the letter to her husband. "It seems so formal," she said. "It's not like I don't see him almost daily."

"He's simply following protocol," soothed Ian. "Remember, it's a bureaucracy, and they have their systems."

Professor Belgrade sported no semaphore to warn of possible mood swings. His expression was interested but otherwise enigmatic. He invited Blair to sit in one of the room's well-worn leather chairs. She chose one directly in front of the professor's desk and sat down. The deep chair enfolded her as if she'd thrown herself onto the feather bed at Nana's house in New Hope.

The professor opened a red plastic binder on his desk, his gaze lingering over the cover page, causing Blair's heart to race. She tried unsuccessfully to sit up but remained at a 45-degree angle.

Looking up from under extravagant eyebrows, he said,

"When you first proposed your thesis for acceptance, your reasoning worried me." He tapped his forefinger on the open binder. "I thought it bold, but there appeared to be reasonable avenues of pursuit, so I gave it a green light.

"Professor Zaritsky mentioned that you'd said, 'Fyodor would not have been Fyodor without Anna,' and, at the time, I laughed, thinking your remark glib, one-dimensional—which it may have been. I admit I was puzzled until I read your translation of Anna's letters and the sections from memoirs covering her 'diving into the trenches,' as you put it. The discussion of her intellect and independence, coupled with your description of Anna as a 'working-class feminist,' was compelling. In the final analysis, I understood and agreed that Fyodor's candle might well have burned out after *Crime and Punishment* had Anna not been there to protect and preserve."

Blair returned to her desk, elated. She could barely think about the work piled in her in-basket as she kept rewinding the tape of her interview with Professor Belgrade. By mid-afternoon, Uncle Vanya arrived wearing his usual uniform and a low-frequency bowtie: a good sign.

He stopped at Blair's desk and said in English, "Congratulations, *omnyashka*, I understand your thesis was accepted."

She blushed as this was the first time Uncle Vanya had used any intimate expression with her. Of course, calling her "clever one" was hardly an invitation to elope, but up to now, he had remained cordially dignified and always addressed her as Mrs. Kennedy.

"Professor Belgrade gave me your thesis to read," he said in Russian, "and we discussed it during lunch last week. I told him that you provided a unique perspective on the importance of Anna's contribution to Russian literature, and I hope that offering him my two kopeks of unsolicited opinion did you no harm. Perhaps you would consider continuing to a Ph.D.?"

Blair didn't know what to say, as she had not given this possibility serious thought. "Thank you, professor. Of course, that is something to consider."

He bowed slightly and retired to his office.

As the strains of Stravinsky's *Firebird* trembled from behind the door, Blair restrained herself from dancing a hornpipe and filling her office with unbridled sounds of joy.

-22-

The Duke & Duchess of Morningside Heights

In the 1970s, Morningside Heights was home to a gang of toughs. Longtime residents of the neighborhood thought the gang's territory stretched north-south from 125th Street to 110th Street and east-west from Morningside Park to Riverside Park. Veterans of this strictly canine crew were usually adults, but one or two pubescent pups always trailed along, largely ignored, at the back of the pack.

The undisputed leader of the gang was Duke. No one knew how the name was attributed, but seasoned residents of the Heights all used it, and it fit. Duke had earned his position and name the hard way. A diagonal scar cut across his eyebrow to the edge of his snout, rendering his right eye cloudy gray and useless. His genetic history was an olio of mutts and pedigrees dominated by a fearful combination of Boxer for height and Pitbull for full-jawed inaffability. A short-haired pelt, replete with knicks and tears, fit tight over well-defined muscles.

The amalgam of his genetic line had been simmering for generations, resulting in the ultimate reduction: Duke, the dog, Lord of Morningside Heights.

His posse's personnel varied daily, except for a svelte female greyhound with the curves and stature of a purebred. She was always by his side, slightly taller than

Duke, with protruding ribs, a long tail, and a gently pointed snout: an elegant counterpoint to her snub-nosed, battle-worn protector. Local dog walkers called her the Duchess.

Duke was street-smart, feral, and fearless. He was friendly with the butcher and knew all the restaurant back channels and deli bins in his territory. The alley behind the Moon Palace offered a mound of pork fried rice in a galvanized can, still warm, well after dark. One deft push served fare enough for all—provided the Duke and Duchess were allowed a few respectful moments to select their portions.

Generally, the troop roamed the Heights in the late afternoon and evening, with the Duke and Duchess in the lead. When encountering leashed members of their species, Duke would guide his followers into the street or the opposite sidewalk. He was not looking for trouble, but some pampered pets snarled and foamed under a false sense of security assumed by the presence of their omnipotent attendants. Duke paid little attention to petty ankle-biters, though he would turn his head and offer a toothy, one-eyed smile to frenzied Pekingese or Pomeranians.

If Ian saw them coming, he'd turn up a side street before Zato and Bagel caught sight or scent, but there were times the hounds appeared unexpectedly, and Ian would be forced to strap Zato to a signpost or the wrought iron railings along Morningside Drive. In these circumstances, Bagel would remain cautiously quiet while Zato fumed and sputtered from the sidelines.

Occasionally, such outbursts caused the Duke to turn and confront Ian and his companions. As there was no way to quiet Zato, Ian focused on the gang's leader instead.

"Get out of here, Duke," he'd yell, attempting to wave the group further down the street. "Go on! Get out of here!"

Sometimes Duke would growl and move a step closer, prompting Ian to yell even louder. He knew he would have to unsnap Zato's leash if the dog attacked. Zato might take Duke, but he would be no match if the posse got involved. Fortunately, Duke had never encroached further but seemed to take the trio's measure, then step back to the head of the gang and move on.

Returning from an early December walk, Ian mentioned he'd seen Duke and the gang approaching from 113th Street and managed to get the dogs home before they made eye contact. Blair said she had seen some strays near the law school while on her way to work the previous day, but campus police had chased them off. As the family often walked the dogs there in the evening, she cautioned that they should be more careful in the future.

The only way to be "more careful," thought Ian, would be to move to Alaska or carry a gun.

"[illegible] of the Bears" and [illegible] [illegible] was [illegible] further down [illegible] [illegible] Get out [illegible]"

Sometimes Duke would [illegible] [illegible] [illegible] [illegible] [illegible] [illegible] [illegible] [illegible] [illegible] [illegible] would [illegible] [illegible] [illegible] [illegible] [illegible] [illegible] [illegible] [illegible] [illegible] [illegible] [illegible] [illegible] [illegible] [illegible] [illegible] [illegible] [illegible] [illegible] Duke [illegible] [illegible] [illegible] [illegible] [illegible] [illegible] [illegible] [illegible] [illegible] [illegible] [illegible] of the gang [illegible] [illegible]

[illegible] [illegible] [illegible] [illegible] [illegible] Duke and [illegible] [illegible] [illegible] [illegible] [illegible] [illegible] [illegible] [illegible] [illegible] [illegible] [illegible] [illegible] [illegible] [illegible] [illegible] [illegible] [illegible] [illegible] while [illegible]

[illegible] [illegible] [illegible] [illegible] [illegible] [illegible] [illegible] Alaska [illegible] [illegible]

-23-

Spooning at the Plaza

After ten days of mild weather, winter slid in from Canada like a luge, toppling temperatures into the teens. The dolphins over Harlem had swum out to sea, leaving the sky a flawless, light blue. Midtown teamed with people bundled in warm coats, hats, and gloves. Window dressings glittered, strangers looked up from the sidewalk and smiled, some offering greetings or conversation.

"It seems winter has arrived ahead of schedule."

"Do you think it will snow?"

"It's certainly cold enough. But it's too dry."

"Hopefully, we'll get some by Christmas."

The first stop of the holiday season was always Macy's Department Store to experience the magic of their mechanical window displays. Once inside, Blair shopped for the children discreetly while Max lingered behind the fence surrounding Santa Claus, not daring to venture in lest his sister tease him irrepressibly. After Macy's, came the obligatory visit to Horn & Hardart's Automat on 42nd Street, where the kids enjoyed inspecting the chrome-plated walls of glass-encased compartments filled with individual servings of soup, sandwiches, cakes, and pies. For them, the sighting of a bodiless hand replenishing a tuna fish sandwich was akin to a sighting of the Virgin Mary. Then it was uptown to Bloomingdale's for more shopping, followed by a tour of FAO Schwarz—for viewing only, as the toys on display seemed more suited to children delivered by limousine than those disgorged by subway. On the Saturday before winter vacation officially got underway, Blair took the kids to Balanchine's Nutcracker (Max's squirming in Act II attracted an usher), and on Sunday everyone went ice skating at Wollman Rink in Central Park. With these seasonal peregrinations, the holiday season was getting underway.

*

Returning from a mission to Mama Joy's, Ian and Max hung their hats and coats on the rack, then chased the dogs down the hall into the kitchen where Blair was putting the final touches on an apple pie.

"Mama Joy's was out of meatballs," announced Ian, "so we got ham and cheese heroes and potato salad."

"That sounds good. Can you and Max set the table? I want to get this pie in the oven.'"

Max and his father did as requested; then returned to the kitchen to observe the magic of crust latticing.

"Sam called while you were out," reported Blair while mesmerizing the boys with the warp and weft of her dough strips. "She's back in London but getting ready to visit. She should be in New York in a few days, lounging in a plush robe and sipping champagne in her suite at the Plaza."

"Hardly a suite," responded Ian, "but sumptuous, I'm sure. Is there a sugar daddy in tow?"

"Yes. It's why I said 'suite.' His name, believe it or not," she said arching, an eyebrow at her husband, "is Reginald Spooning. Sam says it's an English name, derived from the profession of wooden shingle—or *spoon*—makers. She believes the 'ing' was the invention of a shingle-making poet, who thought the surname, Spoon, too utilitarian and lacked romance."

"You're joking, right?"

"No joke. From the lips of Sam. She is not sure if we will have a chance to meet Mr. Spooning, but if we do, she begs us not to make light of his name. It seems he's heard it all and is quite tired of what he calls," she paused, crooking her fingers into quotation marks, 'platitudinous pronouncements from the proletariat.' He works for Lloyd's of London, managing what she calls *syndicates*. It sounds like the Mafia, but Sam says he is a broker of some kind, specializing in high-risk clients needing insurance. All rather inscrutable. He's bought tickets for two Broadway shows, a concert at Lincoln Center, and they have reservations for dinner at Windows on the World. He's here for a week, but she's staying for two."

"Wow, lucky girl. What's the plan for getting together? Little Italy again?"

"After spending Christmas *spooning*," she said, smiling furtively, "Sam wants to go to the Puglia with your brother's family and all of us and suggested the 27th for dinner, followed by a visit to the Plaza so that she can distribute gifts."

"Our last visit to the Puglia was with Sam," said Ian, recalling the evening. "With that many people, I'd better make a reservation."

"And ask your brother if he will be ordering sheep's head again, as I'll need to prepare myself: plunging his spoon into brain matter, savoring an eyeball, and gnawing on the jawbone with bare hands are images impossible to forget."

-24-

Cream Cheese, Baseball, and Prokofiev

A few days later, the official vacation got underway: for the kids, the last day of classes was Thursday, December 14; for Ian and Blair, it was the Friday immediately following.

Parker School and Columbia started their holiday recesses at noon. So, before heading home, Ian and Blair decided to have lunch together at Chock full o' Nuts on the corner of Broadway and 116th Street: a cream cheese and walnut sandwich on dark raisin bread with a cup of coffee. Nearly fifteen years earlier, their first "date" was at the counter in this same restaurant, eating the same signature meal.

"I heard they are closing this place," said Ian wistfully. "Not just this one, but all of them. It will be a sad day, indeed, when they turn this into a bar or another sandwich shop. I'm sure this would never happen if Jackie Robinson were still swinging a bat for the brand."

A diehard Brooklyn Dodger fan, Ian had a strong affinity for Robinson, and when the Dodgers traded him to the Giants, he felt depressed and betrayed. "No! Not the Giants!" (Thank God he never played for them.) The following year, when the Dodgers had left Brooklyn for Los Angeles, Ian and two like-minded Dodger zealots made a pilgrimage to Brooklyn's Ebbets Field on a Saturday in mid-April—two days before the start of the new season. The ballpark was closed to visitors, but Doug Wunch—state champion of the Westbrook high school debate team—spun a tale of such betrayal and misery over management's sellout to the fat cats from Los Angeles that the stadium's security guard didn't stand a chance.

"O'Malley was bought and paid for by a bunch of Hollywood movie moguls," wailed Wunch to the guard. "The Bums had a home in Brooklyn since 1886, and here in Flatbush since 1913. O'Malley even convinced Horace Stoneham to move the Giants to San Francisco. Can you imagine? For owners like them, it's all about the greenback, not the fans or the players. This kind of betrayal makes the Rosenbergs look like pikers. L.A. is the place for Mantle or DiMaggio, not for Pee Wee, Zimmer, or Duke."

With the conclusion of Wunch's diatribe, the guard's objections slumped, and he allowed the boys fifteen minutes of unsupervised nostalgia inside the park.

Placing his right foot on second base, Ian imagined Robinson in full flight over that very bag of sand, throwing out a runner at first base or taunting pitchers to balk or grow weary trying to outwit him as he slipped from base to base. But the imminent closing of Chock full o'Nuts was a minor calamity compared to O'Malley's spitball thrown into the face of the Brooklyn faithful.

"Even if the doors close for good, I can still make cream cheese and nut sandwiches on Zabar's raisin-pumpernickel," soothed Blair. "It may help us in our recovery."

Half an hour later, they arrived home to a torrent of tears and a hail of bilateral recriminations.

"He threw my record player out the window into the alley," wailed Logan. "It's destroyed!"

"She wouldn't stop playing *Peter and the Wolf*—I told her to turn it down, but she wouldn't, and she went into my room and threw my dog encyclopedia out her window."

"I was in my room with the door closed. I should be able to play my music without burglars bursting in and destroying everything."

"She knows I hate that story," Max snarled, "and she plays it to get me mad. Well, I got mad! She had no right to throw my book out the window. It's ruined!

Tears flowed, and voices trembled as they elaborated and embellished the atrocities committed. Ian looked out the window into the alley. The record player was a small suitcase-style machine; its lid had broken off. Though intact, pages of Max's book were rippling in the wind, and the pink vinyl recording of Boris Karloff's reading of Prokefiev's *Peter and the Wolf* was in pieces.

The record was a Christmas present to Logan two years before. The family had gathered around the living room phonograph to listen to it on Christmas morning. Everyone enjoyed the music and the story until the wolf started chasing the duck. As the tempo raced faster and faster, the wolf got closer and closer. Flutes and violins screamed like the wail of a runaway train, and with one snap of his jaws, the duck was gone.

At this point, Max had covered his ears with the palms of his hands and burst into tears. His mother tried to comfort him, telling him that Peter and the hunters would catch the wolf and that the duck lived. Max bit his lip and did his best to brave it out, but he was not at all happy with the ending.

"The duck's alive," he'd said with anguish, "but he's still inside the wolf. How is that a happy ending? Why didn't it just fly out of reach? They should kill the wolf and save the duck, but . . ." More tears flowed.

"It's not fair," said Logan, "I should be able to play my record. It's a Christmas tradition for me. I play it every Christmas."

"It's a stupid story, and I hate it!" cried Max.

Blair employed a solution that had successfully resolved such heady conflicts. Max and Logan were to sit in chairs, knee to knee. They were to look at each other and take turns commenting on the room, using short declarative sentences: "There is a picture of Mom on the mantle." "There is a dog on the rug," etc. While commenting or listening to the other's comments, they were to maintain eye contact. No making faces, no wisecracks. This dialogue was to continue for ten minutes (supervised); only then would they be allowed to notice something innocuous about each other. "You have red hair." "Your shoes have laces." First one, then the other, until it sounded natural, not forced or fake. Finally, they would switch to finding something nice to say about the other person, back and forth, until it sounded sincere. Usually, by this time, they would start laughing.

Ian went into the alley and picked up the fallout from the argument. In fact, he shared both Logan's appreciation of Prokofiev and Max's view that the story did not have a happy ending. The duck's dubious fate had bothered Ian from childhood, as it seemed unlikely that after the hunters carried the wolf to the zoo, the keeper would choose to upset the balance of nature in favor of a half-digested duck.

Nevertheless, Ian would do his best to consult with the children on the merits of each point of view. Perhaps it was best to return the *Big Book of Dogs* to its shelf, repair the record player, and provide Logan with a different Prokofiev favorite. Hopefully, Max was not yet familiar with the tragedy of Romeo and Juliet.

-25-

And Did I Say Paris?

Six days remained until Christmas, and it was time for the Kennedys to put on their heavy coats and warm scarves and cross the campus to pick out a tree. Evergreens of various types and sizes stood side-by-side along a stretch of sidewalk on Broadway between 112th and 113th Streets. People roamed the tree line, removing a glove to test the tines for freshness and nose their boughs with the surety of sommeliers.

"The balsam fir is my favorite," said Blair, running a cupped hand along the needles of a branch as if stroking a cat's tail. "They have a nice smell and don't dry out quickly."

"I like the noble fir," said Ian. "But I'm happy with anything with full branches and rich scent."

Ian asked the kids to find the best of the balsam firs, something tall and full. After careful inspection and discussion, the children picked one out. Their parents confirmed its virtues, and the vendor began to tie it up.

"Look," said Max, pointing up Broadway. Twenty yards away, the Duke and Duchess intently sniffed the trunks along a line of nobles. Immediately, Max's call drew the attention of one of the vendors, who hastened to shoo the dogs away.

Ian and Max carried either end of a well-trussed tree, and the family started walking back up Broadway, Blair with her arm through a wreath; Logan shouldering her mother's bag.

"I'm glad we didn't have the dogs along," said Blair to Ian.

"This is the first time I've seen them on Broadway. I think they are stalking me."

"Perhaps the Duchess finds you attractive. She is a rather sensual-looking creature."

*

In the corner of the living room by the fireplace, Ian placed the tree in its stand, cut the twine, then gently bent the limbs, allowing everyone to admire the beauty of its boughs. With a small hatchet acquired for this purpose, he trimmed a few branches from the trunk base, making room for presents, long secreted in the top of closets or under the connubial bed. However, these gifts would only appear under the tree on Christmas morning, after Santa and his reindeer had sped off across the Hudson to Ho-Ho-Kus (aptly named) and westward to Pascagoula and Dubuque. Both Max and Logan had long since discovered the truth about St. Nick, but awakening Christmas morning to a mountain of gifts was still as magical for them as when they were toddlers.

Blair placed the cut boughs along the mantel, then broke out the ornaments, and the family set to work decorating the tree and hanging the wreath on the apartment door. The fireplace flue had long since been closed to fires, but when Blair hung the stockings from hooks below the mantelshelf, the living room looked perfect for a visit from

Santa. It was time to make some cocoa and tune the hi-fi to WQXR for the seasonal music of Handel and Bach.

The following morning, Ian and Max walked the dogs to the newsstand for the daily issue of the *Times* and checked in with Mike about dinner with Samantha McFarlane. Mike was at the cash register, so Ian knocked on the window and motioned him to come out.

"Our dinner date with Sam is the 27th", said Ian. "I made reservations at the Puglia for six-thirty. If you order brains again, I need to let them know."

"I've brains enough for now," said Mike. "This time, I'll stick to the house menu and have the tripe."

Ian's esophagus clenched in reflex to the image, but, as he'd eaten duck's blood soup and cicadas in Taiwan, he maintained an expression of respectful indifference.

"I can take us all in the van," said Mike.

"Sam wants to meet us at the restaurant and then go to the Plaza for drinks and gift giving, but the hotel has no parking facility."

"No worries, brother *mio*. There's a reasonably priced lot on West 56th, maybe a ten-minute walk. I can drop everyone off first."

As Max and Ian passed through the iron gates to College Walk, a crisp wind from across the Hudson caught their backs, rattling the last dry leaves from the maples that lined the walkway. Zato raised his head from the ambrosia of the bricks and hedges, taking in the air in long drafts. "I think Zato smells snow," said Max.

Ian and the dogs found Blair sitting in her corner of the couch wrapped in a blanket, holding a piece of blue stationery in her hand. "I received this letter from Sarah Reinhart today," said Blair. "Do you remember her? Brunette, shapely, emerald eyes." Ian nodded, perhaps remembering her too vividly.

"Didn't she marry an Italian law student she met in her senior year at Barnard?"

"It didn't last. She has since remarried, this time to another lawyer, a Frenchman, and for the last five years, they have been living in Paris, where she's teaching English lit at an International School—something like Parker."

"That sounds like a choice job."

"It does, and she's asking if we would consider joining her."

"Joining her? Where?"

"In Paris, teaching at her school—in Paris."

-26-

Looking with Eyes Closed

Sarah's letter provided details on the unsettling opportunity. Up to now, the Neuilly International School (NIS)—located just outside Paris—had offered French, English, Spanish, and German languages for middle and upper school students, but the board of directors wanted to add Chinese and include some Asian history. Ian's tenure with the Parker School was a strong selling point. Additionally, the assistant to the Headmistress was retiring after this school year. She had been among the school's founding staff since 1946. Blair's years as administrative assistant to the chairman of Columbia's Russian Institute, her handling of a faculty of diverse nationalities, her command of French, and the possibility of her teaching Russian, had given Sarah the idea that Ian and Blair would be a perfect match for NIS. Naturally, they would have to apply for the positions, but Sarah had spoken to the Headmistress of their qualifications and had been encouraged to contact them. As she was to spend Christmas with her parents in Baltimore, it was likely Sarah was already stateside. Her letter stated that she would call Blair from her parents' home to discuss details. But, of course, she understood this offer might be ill-timed.

Ian and Blair had not confronted a problem of this magnitude in close to fifteen years. Over time they had established roots, acquired good jobs, a great apartment at low cost, a good school for the kids, and their relatives were all within striking distance. Their lives were almost perfect. Life, however, does not seem to favor a constant.

To this proposal, Blair expressed interest, and Ian a quivering panic. "What about the kids and their friends, the dogs, the apartment, our families, general security—the Sunday *Times*?"

"Think of the opportunity," replied Blair. "A good international school, working together, bilingual children, an adventure—*La Monde*. Then, there is Paris and all of Europe—and did I mention Paris?"

They would certainly have to discuss it with the kids, but that could wait until after the phone call with Sarah and certainly until after Christmas. As so many unanswered questions remained, Ian did his best to move their focus from a European hegira to preparations for a holiday at home. It was customary for Mike and his family to come to them for dinner on Christmas day--Lizanne and Spira arriving in the late morning, with Mike following later in the day.

This year's main course was to be a goose—a suggestion of Lizanne's. A Cuban butcher shop on 160th Street would provide a fresh bird from a New Jersey farm. Lizanne had a recipe from her Spanish-born mother and assured Blair that even though goose was all dark meat, it was delicious—something like duck.

Blair was skeptical of culinary suggestions coming from the residents of 158th Street, as most of their recipes vulcanized the throat and belly, leaving both smoldering late into the night. However, a few years earlier, Blair had made duck à l'orange with a Grand Marnier sauce—a la

Julia Child. Oddly enough, even the kids liked it. So, after a discussion with the family, they agreed to give goose a try.

"After all," Blair offered hopefully, "perhaps the goose will have stuffing and cranberry sauce (would it be good with goose?), plus Lizanne's delicious mincemeat pie." As her contribution, Blair had been aging a Christmas pudding in a kitchen cabinet since Thanksgiving.

"Goose should be interesting," said Ian. "It sounds like we are receiving a visitation from the Ghost of Christmas Present: *there on the table sat a goose of universal admiration*," said Ian, expanding on an image from Dickens' *A Christmas Carol*.

"I hope it works out. Lizanne's mother spent a few years in London after the war, and the recipe came stateside along with one for steak and kidney pie, a dish I'm glad she is not suggesting. Lizanne has made goose a few times and claims it's wonderful, and that its fat dripped over what she calls 'beat up potatoes' is to die for."

Ian raised his eyebrows. "Hopefully, it won't come to that."

-27-

It's Snowing!

Sam was already ensconced at the Plaza when she called Ian to confirm the time and place of their rendezvous. Mr. Spooning had arrived a day earlier, having reserved them a "small suite." The couple had already seen a Broadway play and supped at Windows on the World. Sam explained it was unlikely they would have time to meet Mister Spooning, as their next few days were busy with shopping, seasonal entertainment, a quiet luncheon of prime rib at Joe & Rose's on Third Avenue, followed by dinner at the Four Seasons. Then, just in time for a short vacation in Spain, her clandestine inamorato would return to London (and his family) on the 26th. Ian warned that a winter storm was moving in from the Midwest and expected to arrive in the next couple of days, so Mr. Spooning might find it challenging to get a flight out of JFK on the 26th. But, with her usual blithe spirit, Sam said not to worry; it would all work out.

As predicted, the winter storm had steadily progressed across the Plains and Midwest. By December 23, it was dropping heavy snows in West Virginia and eastern Pennsylvania—moving steadily into New England. As a result, travel warnings were in effect from Washington to Boston. It was likely that New York City would receive a direct hit with the possibility of twelve inches of accumulation.

On Christmas Eve morning, snow started falling over Manhattan. At first, the flakes were fat and feathery, rocking gently through windless air. Max was first to rise and woke the family with high-pitched squeals: "It's snowing! It's snowing!"

Ian, Max, Logan, and the dogs were quickly out the door to have a look, Mom remaining behind to get breakfast in motion. It was 7:00 a.m., Sunday, with only intermittent signs of life visible on the avenue or College Walk. This snow looks good, thought Ian: moist, but not wet; no strong winds rushing it up the coast. Flakes are sticking. There would be a good accumulation within the hour. Logan and Max scraped together a few snowballs, including the dogs in their play.

The snow made Zato frisky, and, as Ian had neglected to make his usual trip to the newsstand the night before, they decided to walk across the campus and pick up the Sunday paper. Bagel attempted to hold her ground and return home, but Max insisted she tag along. Midway across College Walk, while the dogs hesitated at a hedge, Max looked skyward, opened his mouth, and extended his tongue. A gossamer flake touched down, and the tongue retracted. "Got it!" said Max.

Seeing his success, Ian and Logan followed suit. The trio dipped forward and back, following the fall of their individual flakes: mouths wide, tongues extended, like a group of sea lions at feeding time. Shortly, a young scholar approached the group, "That looks like fun," he said. "Mind if I join you?" And three became four. Had they not all begun to laugh, their small pod might have soon become a colony.

Back in the apartment, Blair had just finished frying a dozen strips of bacon and laying out the breakfast dishes. When she heard the door open and the kids rushing down the hallway, she dipped two slices of bread into an egg and cinnamon mixture and placed them in a frying pan. In addition to bacon, they would have freshly squeezed orange juice, hot chocolate, and French toast. It was a special day—Christmas was a-comin'.

Blair was as excited as the children, but she couldn't tell if her intoxication was due to the holiday or the whirl of Parisian images chasing her around the kitchen.

-28-

The Devil's in the Details

Later that afternoon, Sarah called. Ian and Blair took the call sitting side-by-side in the living room with the phone between them and asked the kids to play in their rooms while they handled some business.

"I'm sorry to call on Christmas Eve," said Sarah, "but this is the first time I've been free for any length of time—the place is screaming with relatives and children, but they are all out caroling for the next hour, so I thought I give you a call and see if you had time to talk."

Blair assured her this was a good time—though Ian rolled his eyes, and they hurried through the obligatory pleasantries.

Sarah repeated the general content of her letter, adding that the headmistress had been very encouraging and hoped to receive resumés in early January. News of the positions was already public knowledge, and applications would start arriving shortly after the holidays.

"What exactly are the administrative duties of the assistant to the headmistress?" asked Blair.

Sarah explained in detail, and it sounded much like those of Blair's current position with additional responsibilities of parental interaction. She would write much of the head's correspondence and act as a buffer with the public and faculty handling specific personnel or parental concerns that had somehow bypassed teachers or the personnel department.

It was also customary for faculty to assist in one of the many afternoon classes: debate, sports, music, etc. In the future, Blair might be asked to teach Russian in the upper school.

"That sounds like a full schedule. Does the current assistant have a foreign language or sports function?"

"She is an exceptional graphic artist," answered Sarah, "She has an afternoon class three days each week and designs most of the school's promotional materials. I'm unsure how they will replace her in that function, but almost everyone seems to have something extra. I assist the music director with the middle school choir."

Ian was listening silently. Finally, it was his turn, and the volcano erupted: "What about housing, the kids' education, salary, contracts, longevity of staff, moving expenses? We have two dogs."

Sarah hurried to answer, "Of course, of course, these are all important questions, and I'll do my best to tackle them one by one."

Her answers were detailed and, in many cases, sounded familiar, as his contracts and extra-curricular class responsibilities at Parker were similar. Salaries for families with school-age children were supplemented by tuition-free education—on a one-for-one basis (maximum of two). NIS owned two apartment buildings in Auteuil—a safe, old neighborhood in the 16th Arrondissement, just a twenty-minute drive from the school. These apartments were likely not so spacious as theirs at Columbia. A three-bedroom in either of the NIS buildings was adequate for a family of four, and the school rents were well below market. But, of course, one could choose to live elsewhere at greater expense.

The job description sounded comfortable enough, but what of all their furniture and possessions?

"There is a modest moving expense provided to foreign faculty," explained Sarah, "but it is not enough for a formal trans-Atlantic move. Large items like couches, chairs, beds, and tables would have to be rented or purchased. There is an allocation for rental furniture, which would be ready before your arrival."

As Sarah was married to a lawyer, she lived outside of school housing. However, she had visited the NIS accommodations in Auteuil. Each building appeared well cared for and safe, and the apartments were spacious enough for comfortable living.

From Sarah's description, the quality of the faculty at NIS seemed equal to—if not better than—those of Parker and St. Mark's, and graduates from the high school attended top universities in Europe and America.

Finally, there remained but one question: what of the dogs?

"The school's apartment buildings allow pets," said Sarah. "Dogs and cats are okay."

Before flying to the States, Sarah had posted school promotional materials and a copy of the faculty employment manual, all in English. It should come to them within a few days. There were photos of the school and its facilities, and she was sure they would be impressed, as, in the last thirty years, the generosity of alumni and their families had allowed for considerable improvements and expansion of the campus.

"Oh, Blair, I had almost forgotten. Another duty of the headmistress's assistant is to organize the yearly fundraising for the school's endowment."

"And the current assistant does this?"

"Sure."

*

When the call ended, Ian hurried the dogs and Max out for a walk. He was not ready for further discussion and needed a calming distraction which a dog walk might or might not provide.

"It's halfway up my boots," said Max, who was standing on a patch of pristine snow. Bagel stood to one side on a windswept stair, resisting stepping off. "It's at least eight inches deep!"

After dedicating a stream of appreciation to his favorite tree, Zato excitedly jumped into the berm left by the plows. It was surprisingly deep and impeded any sudden leaps toward freedom. Wistfully, he looked toward the park, then exited the snowbank pulling Ian toward Morningside Drive. Bagel, having attended to her duties, pulled for home.

"Why don't you take Bagel inside, Max? I'll take Zato down along the park and be in shortly."

Max agreed. He and Bagel entered the warmth of the lobby while Ian and Zato continued down 116th Street, snow blowing hard at their backs. As the sidewalks along Morningside were uncleared and there was no vehicle traffic, they started walking uptown in the middle of the street.

Buildings facing the park blocked the easterly flow of wind and snow, enhancing visibility. A man and his dog were walking toward them in the street two blocks away. Zato had been sniffing intently at a newly discovered attraction and had not noticed their approach, so Ian quickly turned toward home, pulling his disgruntled charge behind him.

They had walked only a few yards when a low growl trembled the leash. Ian felt the warning through his glove: three strays had emerged from 116th Street onto Morningside Drive, and each had seen the other. Plows had piled snow between the parked cars, making for a challenging escape to the safety of the iron fence along the park wall. From behind, the man and his dog continued their approach, oblivious to the developing dilemma before them.

The choices were three: scramble up the mountain of snow between cars (dubious!), push forward toward the strays (dangerous!), or retreat (chancy). Ian, choosing the latter, turned back, pulling hard on the leash. Zato resisted and, losing his footing, fell onto his side, pulling Ian down beside him. The dog quickly righted himself and, sighting the approaching canine and his walker, became instantly aggressive, moving forward, spinning Ian on his back like an overturned turtle. Malamutes have webbing between their toes to provide traction in snow and powerful hind legs and thighs, suitable for pulling sleds loaded with freight, or for dragging Ian supine, arms extended above his head, desperately clinging to the leash with both hands.

Digging his boot heels into the snow, Ian used all his strength to halt his forward progress, which provided some slack in the leash, allowing him to get to his knees and grab Zato's collar. Using the dog's body for leverage, Ian righted himself. To his surprise, found the street empty in both directions. So, rather than tempt fate, he chose to circle home, trudging uphill through the snow and headwinds of 117th Street.

"That was quite a walk," said Blair as Ian entered the kitchen. "Your cheeks look raw. Max said it was wicked out there. "

"Yes, wicked."

"I imagine Zato liked it," Blair said.

"He was in his element, for sure."

"I've made some hot tea for you. The paper is in the living room."

Ian carried his tea to the couch and opened the Arts & Leisure section of the *Times*. A few minutes later, Zato trotted in, nonchalant, tail wagging.

Lowering the paper, Ian said: "Zato, you are a lot of work." The wagging stopped, head dropped, ears folded back.

"Sometimes, I wonder if you are too much work. I was barely able to control you today. What if you'd gotten away? A fight? A brawl with the strays? Both? You are a lawsuit waiting to happen. I love you, but, my God, you are a pain in the butt."

"Zato! Bagel!" called Blair from the kitchen. "Come on! Dinner is ready!" Zato raised his head, perked his ears, and blithely retreated to the kitchen. Ian watched him go, lifted the paper, gave it a hard snap, and continued reading.

-29-

The Subject of Suet

For Christmas Eve dinner, Blair had prepared lasagna with extra mozzarella and parmesan, followed by a dish of chocolate ice cream floating in liberal swirls of Hershey's chocolate syrup. She called this her "Italian-American special." It was "special" because it was Christmas Eve and because the kids had requested it. The dogs received extra Milk-Bone treats.

When everyone was fully sated, Ian and the kids retreated to the living room, where Ian began reading from his cherished, clothbound copy of *The Hobbit.* Reading Ian's favorite childhood books to Max and Logan occurred three or four times each week, for half an hour to an hour, depending on the kids' interest. They all sat on the couch, Ian between the children so they could easily see each illustration as he turned the pages.

"Before we begin," said Ian in a theatrical voice, "I'd best see if you are prepared for a serious change of pace. Last week, we finished *Treasure Island*, a blood-soaked story of buried treasure and piracy on the high seas. In this book," he said, patting the dust jacket, "we will travel to a time long ago, far away from the sea to the forests, and mountains of Middle-earth, where elves, dwarves, trolls, giants, and goblins live and die, where wizards work wonders, and dragons cast terrifying shadows across the earth. Are you ready for a new adventure?"

"Yes!" came the answer in thunderous stereo.

As Ian began reading, the light faded from the room, replaced by the illumination of three individual but conjoined imaginations, each in its way, performing the alchemy of turning ink and sound into light and color. Traveling together, they passed through a small round door, down a labyrinth of corridors into well-appointed rooms so intimately described one could almost smell the smoke curling from a clay pipe. Then, in just a few short minutes, they were lost in the amiable, dwarf-like world of Bilbo Baggins.

The children studied the mysterious maps on the inside covers and lingered over the author's ink and watercolor illustrations, finding them acceptable but not so engaging as those of N.C. Wyeth, where the lifting of a tissue guard revealed the wild appearance of Ben Gunn in tattered clothes or peg-legged Long John Silver dragging young Jim Hawkins by a rope into a perilous future.

Over the next hour, Ian continued reading; while in the master bedroom Blair, surrounded by paper, ribbons, adhesive tape, and name cards, had pulled the last gifts from their hiding places to wrap for placement under the tree. Then she filled the stockings that would hang from hooks screwed into the mantlepiece. Each contained an apple, three or four glistening clementines, and a small box of mouth-watering confections from Mondel's Chocolates on 115th Street. Additionally, a tradition had developed over the last few Christmases where each child's stocking contained a glass jar of green olives with pimentos. Before any orange cream or black forest truffle passed their lips, Max and Logan would pop open the lid, pluck out an olive and suck the pimento from its hollow. They would then eat its crisp flesh and extract another, sipping the jar's salty brine between bites as if it were French champagne.

After reading two chapters of *The Hobbit*—the second delivered at the insistence of his audience—Ian put the children to bed. As they lay in the dark with their covers pulled close around their necks, the excitement of Christmas and the perils of hobbits and dwarves mixed and mingled in their heads, gradually dimming into sleep.

Stockings were hung and gifts placed around the tree, while uptown, where the snow surged relentlessly through the canyon of 158th Street, Lizanne Kennedy checked the glass jars packed with mincemeat she had placed in her refrigerator two weeks before. A thick layer of suet had congealed on the surface of each container, forming a seal that guaranteed the mystic melding of beef, candied fruits, apples, raisins, currents, and a potpourri of spices.

Earlier that day, she had checked the Christmas goose for unplucked quills (of which she found a few). It was then rinsed, dried, and scored to capture the bounty of fat that would later rain into the roasting pan. Finally, she rubbed it inside and out with her mother's prescribed spices from Asia and the Middle East—all hand-ground into a fine powder. She then sheathed the goose in Saran Wrap and placed it in the refrigerator, infusing the spices overnight. Stuffing with other herbs and fruit would wait until she arrived at her in-laws.

Lizanne was something of an urban pioneer when it came to cooking. She made her pasta from scratch and never threw out a chicken carcass or ham bone without making soup; she grew many herbs in pots on shelves stacked on the kitchen windowsill and always bought her meat fresh from the Cuban butcher. She followed a Victorian recipe for her mincemeat pies, as current formulations carrying the name were a far cry from those that appeared on the holiday tables of Victoria and Albert.

For Lizanne, modern mincemeat was an aberration, a mutation produced by mass production and propitiation of the great gods of the assembly line: Ransom Olds and Henry Ford. The Christmas pies of Sara Lee and her industrial clones, with their copious amounts of refined sugar, molasses, and corn syrup cloyed on the tongue. As with all conveyer-belt pies of this kind, there was no beef and, indeed, no suet—both absolute musts for traditional mincemeat. Directions for the 20th Century homemaker were brief and effortless: remove from the freezer; bake at 400 degrees for 60 minutes; allow to cool; and, voilà, mince (no meat) pie! Instead, Lizanne prepared her mincemeat two weeks before use—with beef, suet, fresh fruit, almonds, and homemade citrus peel—preserving the amalgam in two quart-sized Mason jars at the back of her refrigerator. She had asked Blair to have all the crust ingredients on hand, except for the suet; that she would bring from her Cuban butcher.

For weeks, Blair and Lizanne had been in conference over the preparations for Christmas dinner. They had anticipated everything down to the last peppercorn—everything but the logistical problems ensuant to the arrival of a winter storm: mainly the transporting of a fourteen-pound goose, two quarts of mincemeat in glass jars, and two bags of Christmas gifts—all by subway, then through deep snow. But, true to form, Michael Kennedy remained undaunted and resourceful. He had expected that snow accumulations could be a problem Christmas morning, so early the previous day, he parked his van on the street in front of his apartment, angling it between cars, allowing enough space from the curb and adjacent vehicles to shovel out with little difficulty.

He had also arranged with a security guard to park the van on Christmas day in a private garage on 115th Street and Broadway. The guard was an avid reader of mystery novels and had spent hours browsing them in Watson's. Mike often made and received recommendations for further genre reading, and the two had become friendly. So, he determined to load the car with people and provisions, drop them off at his brother's apartment, and safely secure the van just a few blocks away. An adventurous plan during a snowstorm, but Mike had a shovel, a sturdy set of chains, and a Sears Roebuck hand warmer running on lighter fluid he'd had since he was twelve.

-30-

It's Christmas Day Callooh! Callay!

Somewhere in the east, behind the low, gray clouds of morning, the sun had barely nudged the cusp of the horizon, but Christmas at the downtown Kennedys was already getting underway. Zato had been the first to rise, causing some concern by barking through the door at a group of early revelers exiting the elevator.

The clamor in the foyer roused Logan and Max, who quickly piled onto their parents' bed; Zato, abandoning sentry duty, immediately followed suit. While Bagel, from her nest at Blair's side, found Zato's incursion onto her turf an infraction of tacit agreements, so bit him on the cheek.

"Okay, okay," said Ian, trying to untangle himself from the bedclothes which now mummified him. "We will all get up and, like civilized people, proceed to the living room in due course, but first, please decamp from the bed so we can breathe."

"I have shut the living room doors and secured them with ribbon," said Blair. "I'm going to make coffee and hot chocolate while your dad takes the dogs for a short walk. You can look through the glass, but do *not* enter until we are all ready."

The kids and Zato dashed down the hallway, and stopping before the French doors, they pressed their noses to the glass panes. A pallid light entered through the alley window, but the lights on the tree had been left blazing.

While the children languished outside the French doors, Ian and the dogs exited the lobby into air so frigid it almost hurt to breathe. The snow had stopped but lay deep on the sidewalk, too early for the shovels and salt of building superintendents. The streets had been plowed but were covered with a layer of virgin crystals. No cars traveled along Amsterdam Avenue this Christmas morning. Zato found the cold and snow much to his liking, but Bagel needed to be carried to a more windswept location to perform her duties. Fortunately, both dogs executed their tasks quickly, allowing them to turn away from the bitter wind rushing along 116th Street and return to the warmth of home.

The odors of coffee and hot chocolate filled the kitchen while kids and dogs bumped and twirled in nervous anticipation. Finally, Blair loosened the ribbon, and the entire group rushed in. Ian and Blair officiated the selection of gifts, doling out treasures in a controlled crescendo. First, the needed upgrades in clothing: practical, even pleasing, but not inspiring; then books with hardcovers: *Woman Warrior* by Maxine Hong Kingston for Logan and Mark Twain's *Tom Sawyer* with original illustrations by True Williams for Max. Games followed: *Boggle* for Max (he had a knack for *Scrabble*, too) and *Rummikub* for Logan (who had mastered the art of the "poker face"); for Dad, a stereo turntable and speakers; and for Mom, a new watch and tickets to a revival of Bernard Shaw's *Man and Superman*. Even the dogs were in on the action, as their stockings contained rawhides, biscuits, and extra-hard rubber toys. Excitement was building as there were still two rather large presents under the tree with labels addressed to the kids from Santa.

Max received his gift first and tore into the wrapping like a lion at a wildebeest. Excited cries of "Wow! Fantastic!" and "It's just what I wanted!" filled the room as he examined the box and the description of its contents. It was a Logix Kosmos Optical Lab Kit (Model No. 29330)—deluxe edition.

Max read from the box, "I can build a microscope, periscope, telescope, and even a working 35-millimeter camera. This is amazing!" He removed the lid, and even the dogs admired the myriad of neatly packed parts.

Blair slid a square box across the rug to Logan. It was wreathed in red and tied with a white ribbon. With the sure hands of an archeologist unraveling a mummy, Logan slowly unfastened the wrapping, exposing a sky-blue, 3-speed RCA record player with built-in speakers. A vinyl record of orchestral selections from Prokofiev's *Romeo and Juliet* was in the same box.

The famed Suite No. 2, titled the "Montagues and Capulets," with its deep and pulsing brass, somber strings, and thundering kettle drums was soon to replace the agonies formerly produced by the plaintive cries of Prokofiev's star-crossed duck. Knowing a repeat performance would not be taken well, Max would later restrain himself from acts of mayhem when hearing this new bit of musical tragedy. While Logan, not wishing to see her treasure lying in pieces on the concrete of the alleyway, limited high-decibel performances to Max's absence.

After everyone had oohed and aahed over their gifts, the morning proceeded according to plan: eggs and bacon, waffles drowned in maple syrup, freshly squeezed orange juice, hot cocoa, and coffee.

-31-

So Fowl and Fair a Day

By noon, Uncle Mike had dropped off Lizanne and Spira, the goose, the mincemeat, two bars of suet wrapped in butcher paper, and a shopping bag filled with gifts. As arranged, Mike then secured his van in the parking garage on 115th Street and trudged through the unplowed snows of College Walk to his brother's apartment. After kicking the snow from his boots, he rang his usual Morse code greeting and listened through the door to the patter of feet and clatter of dogs. Logan, Max, Spira, and the dogs greeted him with enthusiasm.

"Do you want to see my new science kit, Uncle Mike?" said Max, jumping up and down in stocking feet. "I can make a telescope and even a 35-millimeter camera."

"Of course, I want to see it, Max," said his uncle, taking off his hat and coat, "but let me first say hello to everyone and get warmed up a bit. It's pretty harsh out there."

Uncle Mike proceeded to the kitchen while the kids and dogs retreated to Logan's room to continue their game of Rummikub.

The goose had already been stuffed with thick slices of orange, lemon, apple, and onion and sat fully trussed and placed on a rack in a deep roasting pan. While waiting for the oven to heat, Blair and Lizanne were busy making the crust for the mincemeat pie.

Mike and Ian opened beers and watched culinary history unfold.

"Here is where most people add butter," Lizanne said disdainfully to the group as she cut small, malleable pieces from a bar of cured beef fat and kneaded them into the dough. "Suet makes all the difference."

Early in December, Lizanne had bought a three-pound chunk of beef suet from her Cuban butcher—taken *only* from the kidneys—then, by hand, she had separated the connective tissue from the fat, which she rendered over a low flame in a small cast iron pot.

"This process," she told Blair, "separates the last of the tissue from the fat, and when strained, it hardens into this block of pure suet, which you can use in puddings, cookies, and preserving. I used it in the mincemeat, where besides adding a wonderful flavor, it naturally forms a protective seal on the top of the jars when stored."

Until now, Blair had never used or even seen suet; she thought Crisco was the same thing, only to hear from a horrified Lizanne that Crisco was hydrogenated cottonseed oil and not animal fat. In truth, Blair had used butter in making her Christmas pudding, not the suet that the recipe called for—a fact she dared not mention. Once again, Blair thought how fascinating these uptown Kennedys are.

Mike and Ian retreated to the living room, where a 14-inch TV was tuned to a basketball game between the Philadelphia 76ers and the New York Knicks. From the start, it looked like the Knicks' Earl the Pearl and Bob McAdoo were no match for the 76ers' Dr. J and Darryl Dawkins.

During halftime, while drinking a beer and dipping potato chips into a mixture of dried onions and sour cream, Ian mused aloud, "I wonder where the name McAdoo comes from?"

"I wondered the same thing," said brother Mike, "so I asked Samantha to look into it. The English have a solid system for keeping track of family lines, and, as she did such a good job tracing ours, I thought she might do the same with Mr. McAdoo. We correspond a few times a year, and, at the start of the basketball season, I asked her if she could look into it, and she did."

"Amazing. Great minds—so, what's the answer?"

"Sam was not able to trace Bob's particular lineage, but she did have some speculation on how the surname McAdoo might have ended up attached to a black man.

"The most likely story traces back to the Plantation of Ulster when in the early 1600s, thousands of English and Scot farmers were granted land rights in Ulster by King James VI. In addition to their religion, these Presbyterian migrants brought new surnames to Ireland, including McAdoo. However, less than a century later, these same Scots experienced a reversal of fortune when religious discrimination from Irish Anglicans forced them to migrate to the British colonies in America: one of their favored destinations being North Carolina.

"It just so happens that Mr. McAdoo was born, raised, and educated in North Carolina. As many of these migrant Scot farmers became slaveholders, Bob is probably an heir to early cross-pollination."

Ian smiled sardonically and was about to comment on his brother's flippant lack of compassion for the oppressed, but Mike was not quite finished.

"Coincidently," continued Mike, "the name McAdoo comes from 'Mc' or 'Mac,'" meaning 'son of,' and the near-impossible to pronounce place name, *Conduibh* [Mike pronouncing it *Con-doob*], meaning 'black hound.' So, putting them together, kinda-sorta, you get McCondoob or McAdoo: the son of a black hound—an interesting bit of irony."

"My God, Mike, even Bill Buckley would salute that display of callous rhetoric. Next, you'll be telling me you know how to turn lead into gold."

"Actually, Brother *Mio*, I do know something about that. In the early 1920s, a Japanese physicist bombarded some mercury with massive amounts of electricity. He was trying to split—"

"Gentleman, we need your help with the carving," came a voice from beyond the French doors.

The brothers entered the kitchen to find Lizanne and Blair, their aprons splattered with goose fat and flour, pulling a bubbling mincemeat pie from the oven and lifting a Christmas pudding from a steamer onto a plate. The goose lay on a large cutting board, bronzed and glistening. In a deep dish lay a scree of potatoes that had been partially cooked, then shaken in a covered pot and roasted in goose fat in the oven until they too boasted a crust of glimmering gold.

From their command post in the kitchen, the women assigned Mike to carve the goose and Ian to confiscate the children's card table and folding chairs and set them up next to the dinner table with additional settings for the kids. Mike carved the breast into thin slices, each surrounded by a fringe of crisply roasted skin. Legs, thighs, and portions of breast meat were arranged artfully on a large platter, surrounded by roasted carrots and beets. Lizette had made gravy from goose fat, wine, and giblets. Everything was as it should be, and the parade began from the kitchen to the table. The dogs, as usual, stationed themselves below decks.

Blair served the children first. For a time, little was said other than "Please pass the gravy" or "Potatoes please?" Soon followed the collective drone of satisfaction with eulogies to the goose and "Bravo!" to the crunch and creaminess of the potatoes. Then, as second helpings began distribution, a more general conversation ensued with Max posing a question.

"Did you know that Canada geese were hunted almost into extinction?" asked Max, addressing both tables, while popping a piece of goose flesh into his mouth. "These days you see them in Central Park, on golf courses, and even on the grass in front of Butler Library."

Sensing there was more to come, his audience gave him their silent, undivided attention.

"In 1918," he continued in his most professorial style, "the United States and Great Britain signed the Migratory Bird Treaty Act which protected all migratory birds in Britain, Canada and the United States. Some worried bird lovers helped to increase the numbers of Canada geese by raising them on farms, then setting them free. There are now over one million in the United States alone, and you can only kill them with a special license. Some like it here so much that they no longer migrate."

"Interesting, Max," said Uncle Mike. "Where did you come across such an abundance of fascinating facts?"

"I researched it at the library and wrote a report on it for Sister Mary Margaret's science class. We were studying endangered species."

"Ah," his uncle replied, "I guess they have long since shed that label."

"My research," continued Max, "showed that their numbers are rising each year. Every time a golf course opens, a new flock flies in. Many people consider them pests and would prefer they went the way of the dodo."

Assuming a similar scholarly tone, Lizanne interjected, "Lest anyone be concerned about the genealogy of this bird, our goose is an American Emden, not an illegal immigrant from Canada raised on golf balls, but a New Jersey-bred bird allowed to run free to eat succulent clover and fresh green grass.

"And, my dear Max, as your plate appears nearly cleaned of this fowl serving,' she said with a wry smile, "can I assume you approve both of the eating and the taste of this American citizen?"

Accustomed to this kind of banter with adult family members, Max replied, "I approve of both and hope to receive another slice if I haven't already cooked my goose."

Max's dissertation and clever repartee were rewarded with laughter and another slice of meat. However, Ian, not to be outdone by a recently minted eleven-year-old, removed a piece of paper from his breast pocket and cleared his throat.

"Last week, while waiting impatiently to be ushered into surgery for the pleasure of having a tooth pulled, I penned a short Christmas poem and would like to read it to you in honor of the season and this esteemed gathering of the Kennedy clan. It is called 'A Querulous Creature.' But, first, I should clarify the meaning of a few unfamiliar words in deference to the kids." This he did, then read the poem as follows:

A Querulous Creature
A poem by Dr. Spoof

A goose is a querulous creature
It's true,
Complaining of everything
Within her milieu

It grumbles at grass
That is coarse as a thorn,
And honks impolitely
When not given corn

By the chickens and ducks
She struts like a queen,
Distaining to chat
Preferring to preen

Outraged by the rooster
Who calls her to muster,
She ignores his commands
With indignance and bluster

She's proud of her eggs
For their size and their tint,
And her gaggle of goslings
Who she can imprint

The gaggle of goslings to
Carry the line,
To rant and complain
To the fringes of time

But she does have a purpose
Of that be assured,
That is found on the menu
Of each epicure

When singing the birth
Of the babe in the stable,
We can do it with wine
And a goose on the table.

His audience clapped and cheered.

Spira clasped her hands together and said, "That is positively-ozitively the best poem I have ever heard." Ian recognized with admiration that her exclamation was an offhand parody of a line spoken by the goose in *Charlotte's Web*, a book he and the children had read together just a few months back.

As the food disappeared from the serving dishes, the conversation at both tables grew even merrier. Mike and Ian raised their glasses, offering more toasts to the cooks and the wonders of the meal. Logan toasted the Christmas season, Max blessed the potatoes, and Spira raised her milk glass to the Kennedy families and their beloved dogs. Before long, the topic naturally turned to dessert and, as Blair pushed her chair back to attend to the next course, there was a crash from the kitchen.

Blair moved quickly through the French doors while the others remained seated, waiting for the news, though all knew what was coming.

"It's Zato!" shouted Blair. "He's got hold of the goose carcass, and he's not giving it up."

Everyone rushed into the kitchen, where Blair was close to losing a tug of war with the dog who was aggressively asserting his rights in the *finders keepers* game. Commands to "drop it" were ignored, and Zato had started to growl.

"Lift him by the tail," said Lizanne. "Or twist a wooden spoon through his collar."

Zato backed up against a cabinet, so his tail was not available for lifting, and, as the shaking of his head was becoming more extreme, Mike stepped forward and calmly placed his hand across Zato's upper muzzle. Then, putting a thumb on one side and four fingers on the other, he pressed hard against the gums.

"Let go, Zato, or I am going to squeeze harder."

Blair held her end of the carcass as Mike applied more pressure, and the dog released his grip.

"There you go, boy," said Mike. "Good fight, but that's all for now."

Ian took the dog by his collar and escorted him to his bed in the foyer. "Bad dog! Stay here!"

Zato looked at the floor and then at Ian, giving his tail a slight supplicative wag.

"Forget it! Stay here!"

While Blair and Lizanne plated dessert, the men and children cleared the table and piled dishes in and around the kitchen sink. A twenty-minute steaming had resurrected the Christmas pudding from a month of hibernation in the cupboard, which, with the mincemeat pie, would be served warm and topped with a cream sauce—brandied for adults.

Each supplicant received a plate and a slice of pie. "We are leaving space on your plates for the pudding, as I am serving that at the table," explained Blair.

When all were seated, Blair carried in her magnum opus—a mottled parabola of rich, dark succulents, held together by love and butter. She placed it in the center of the table, christening it with a bath of brandy poured from a copper ibrik she had warmed over a low flame.

"British chefs warm the brandy in the bowl of a metal ladle until it catches fire," commented Blair, "then, flaming, they pour it over the pudding. But tonight, with so many innocent lives at stake, I have chosen a less dangerous method. So, if you value your eyebrows, please lean back in your chairs."

Having poured the brandy, she struck a match. Flames flared for a few moments, then died away. Applause followed, and the pudding was sliced and distributed.

Spira, while helping herself, to a generous pouring of cream sauce, raised her hand like a schoolgirl and asked: "Why is this cake called a pudding?"

"That is an excellent question," responded Blair, "and, as I have served this dessert before, perhaps one of the kids can answer. Logan?"

"I think it is because cakes are baked, and this one is steamed."

"Yes, but there is more. Max?"

"It's got something to do with being steamed in a pig's intestine."

All forks paused above their puddings, awaiting clarification.

"More or less," said Blair. "It's thought that the word comes from Old English 'pud', which was a kind of sausage: a combination of meat, raisins, and spices stuffed into a pig's intestine and then steamed in a cloth until hardened. Over time, the word changed to 'pudding' and now describes anything cooked this way. But worry not, no pig intestines were used in the making of this pud."

Lizanne Kennedy thought to herself, what wondrous people these downtown Kennedys are.

After an all-hands effort to clean and put away the dishes, the evening ended with an exchange of gifts between the families. Aside from the Battle of the Bones, the day had gone well, and it was time for the uptown Kennedys to run the Broadway gauntlet back home. Mike left first to retrieve the van.

As the goose had been picked clean and slobbered on by Zato, leftovers were mainly desserts. They were packaged in plastic containers and divided evenly between the families. Presents for Mike's family were returned to their boxes and bagged. After ensuring there was no food within striking distance of any unscrupulous jaws, the assembly of Kennedys put on their coats, hats, and boots and went out to wait for Uncle Mike in the warmth of the building's lobby.

Though not yet six o'clock, it had been dark for more than two hours; finally, the sky was beginning to clear, with stars glistening between clouds like shards of ice. Before long, the van pulled alongside the curb, which plows had buried under three feet of packed snow. Consequently, as the group exited the lobby, Mike leaned over and rolled down the window, yelling that he needed to turn around and pick them up on Amsterdam, where the building supers had cleared the sidewalk. The flock followed when the van turned, all pushing against the wind that blew like it always did in winter along 116th Street. It was bracing and helped counteract the lethargy that comes after a day of grazing in the deep grass.

Spira and Lizanne, with their bags of presents and containers of leftovers, piled into the hippy bus while Ian and Mike agreed on a pick-up time for Tuesday's date with Samantha McFarlane. They said their goodbyes, and the van door slid closed. The uptown Kennedys turned cautiously onto a deserted Amsterdam Avenue, and Mike beeped a farewell Christmas message in Morse code.

-32-

Showdown

On entering the building, Ian suggested they burn off some dinner calories by taking the dogs to the upper campus behind the law school for some exercise. But, of course, this meant activity only for Zato and the family, as Bagel would require carrying through the deeper snow.

The dogs began prancing in the foyer when the key turned in the door lock. However, when Ian entered and took the leashes from the coat rack, Bagel retreated to her sanctuary in the master bedroom while Zato continued to wag his enthusiasm for an evening walk. Blair coaxed her reluctant charge into a resigned agreement, then dressed her in a sweater used for long walks in cold weather. As they tethered the dogs, Ian slung his brother's rope leash over his neck and shoulder, and the group set out.

Groundskeepers had plowed College Walk, allowing the dogs to stake out new territory along the snowbanks. In addition, small, gasoline-powered plows had cleared a section of stairs and narrow pathways between buildings on the upper campus, including one across the pedestrian bridge that passed over Amsterdam Avenue, leading to the steps of the law school, but no further.

As the group approached the bridge, a colossus of mythical proportions loomed into view: Jacques Lipchitz's massive bronze: *Bellerophon Taming Pegasus*. Over the holidays, the campus was lifeless and lightless, but for this five-story, twenty-three-ton behemoth, lit like the Parthenon, frozen in space in front of the law school. A single path through the snow beckoned pilgrims to stand in awe at the foot of its spike-shaped plinth.

The group stopped to study its complex asymmetry: man and monster locked in battle; legs splayed with terrifying hooves; wings tilted, almost vertical; and, with its neck and head twisted in the powerful grip of Bellerophon, the beast screams as it fights off the golden bridle that allows a mere mortal to capture him, tame him, and ride him into battle.

The assembled spectators submitted their critiques:

"It looked like such a jumble from a distance."

"Where is Bellerophon? Oh, I see him now, under the horse's belly. He looks like a cellist, sitting without a chair, playing a horse's head."

"I think Blar-o-fon looks like Gumby."

"It's hard to argue with that, but if you look closely," came the sweet voice of reason, "everything is in motion except Bellerophon. Perhaps it is meant to show man bringing order to chaos."

"Perhaps," said Ian, attempting to bring this audit to a close, "but I believe this sculpture was placed here intentionally as a tribute to my efforts to corral the mighty malamute. Zato cannot fly, but he comes close, as even with three choke collars and a thick leather leash, I am often no match for him. If only I had a magic bridle to help me tame this crazy canine."

He paused and tightened his scarf. "But enough of standing here in the open; let's get out of the wind and give the hound some running room."

Blair picked up Bagel and tucked her inside her coat, and they stepped away from the myth and its players and trudged off into the snow along the edge of the open courtyard that paralleled Amsterdam Avenue. They turned and passed through a gap between buildings onto a spacious plaza. It was a cul-de-sac, walled by buildings on three sides, allowing a dog to get up a head of steam on a long leash.

It was darker here, with the only light emanating through metal gratings that lined the base of a building, below which hummed the sound of powerful turbines that sent a warm breeze steadily upward through the grate. A narrow terrace extended from the building, four feet above the metal mesh, protecting the generators from rain and snow, and making an ideal refuge for four-legged creatures seeking relief from the elements.

Everyone noticed the signs of recent visitors: trampled snow from creatures seeking the warmth that wafted from below. Strays. The crisscross of the mesh was small enough to allow even Bagel to walk across it, though she wouldn't dare. Zato, however, patrolled the surface, probing and analyzing the scents of previous visitors.

"Come on, Zato, let's give you a workout." Ian pulled the dog back into the snow and walked him to the center of the plaza. Taking the rope from his shoulder, he knotted one end to the loop of the leash and wound the other fast around a gloved hand. Then, with the rope secured, he asked the kids and Blair to take their positions at the cardinal points along the lead's radius. They had done this before in the daylight of late summer and knew their stations.

"Okay, Max, call him!

Max patted his thighs and called. The snow reached a few inches above the dog's elbows, providing resistance when bounding from person to person. As Zato sprang forward, Ian dealt out more leash. Arriving at Max, the dog received playful roughhousing until the boy fell back in the snow, laughing.

"Zato, come," called Logan, causing him to break free from Max and porpoise over to her and then to Blair, receiving hugs and praise for his strength and athleticism at each stop.

Anchored at the hub, Ian kept tension on the rope as if lunging a horse in a training circle. At the end of his second revolution, Zato was visibly tired. However, halfway between Blair and Max, he stopped, although not from fatigue. The Duke and Duchess had entered the plaza. Ian immediately tightened the line to Zato, pulling him back and folding the rope hand-over-hand.

"You all come and stand by me," Ian yelled to the family. 'I'm going to chase these two out of here."

Ian hauled in the last bit of rope as the group closed ranks. Zato was snarling and straining toward the intruders—hackles up, tail erect.

The light from the grating cast disquieting shadows across Duke's muzzle. He was leaning forward with his ears erect, his dead eye a misty blue. The Duchess stood back a few feet, stiff, looking on.

Ian turned to Blair. "I'll pass you the lead; you'll need to hold him tight against your thigh," he cautioned. "I'm going to step forward and order them out of here. If Duke charges us, let Zato go, but only if you must—I'll tell you when."

Blair passed Bagel to Logan, who, unhappy with the transfer, tried to wriggle loose, but Logan wrapped her inside her coat, holding her tight. Duke advanced a few steps and stopped, causing Zato to buck and bark viciously.

Stepping away from his family and the dogs, Ian took off his gloves and put them in his coat pocket.

"Get out of here, Duke!" he yelled, clapping his hands loudly. "Get out!"

The strays did not move.

Ian continued forward, yelling and clapping, but the pair stood firm, and Duke began to snarl.

Ian was uncertain if Zato would have an advantage in a fight. Duke was not tall, closer to a pit bull than a boxer in stature, the snow reaching his belly. He was muscled and wiry, forty pounds at most; Zato was more than double Duke's weight. The Dutchess, taller than her man, was leaner and lighter, and she held back. Although Duke was blind in one eye and considerably older and more worn than his prospective young and vibrant opponent, Zato was inexperienced in combat and knew nothing of strategy should Duke decide to engage him (or Ian) in a fight.

Again, Ian moved toward the strays, clapping his hands and commanding the strays to leave, but Duke pushed nearer, paused briefly, then advanced. In response, Zato sprang forward with all his weight, breaking loose from Blair's grip. She scrambled to find the rope as it uncurled at her feet, but it had disappeared into the snow. Zato surged toward Ian and Duke, picking up speed, bounding higher with each thrust. Ten thousand years of domestication had done little to dilute this malamute's kinship to the wolf.

Adrenaline surged, and the primal commands of genetics took charge, transforming him into a feral, Arctic beast.

The Duchess was first to react. She turned and fled. Duke stopped suddenly, and Ian could see the whirr of his calculations: realizing he was outgunned, the old soldier turned and slugged hard in retreat through the deep snow. As Zato bounded by, Ian made a desperate dive into his wake and, finding the trailing rope, squeezed it with his bare hands until it stopped sliding, and he could halt the dog's progress.

The Duke and Duchess were gone. Zato was spent and lay panting in the snow some yards from Ian. Blair and the kids rushed forward.

"Are you okay?

"My god! I thought Duke was going to attack you. I couldn't hold Zato, but I was about to let him go anyway. He saved the day."

"I'm okay," said Ian, his heart hammering against his ribs. "That was a close call."

Ian righted himself, and they all shuffled over to Zato, still lying in the snow, breathing heavily, tongue lolling.

"Bagel was going nuts, and I had to hide her in my coat," Logan said, unzipping it enough to let the dog's head peek out.

"You're our hero," said Max to Zato, and they all knelt in the snow to hug him and thank him for his bravery.

Handing the leash to Blair, Ian stood up and looked at his hands. Despite the cold, they were red hot, and, even in the dark, a burn had left a visible trail across each palm.

He untied the rope from the leash, wound it into a circle, and slung it over his shoulder. Putting on his gloves, he said: "I think it's safe to head out now. Let's go home and get warm."

Blair slid her arm under Ian's and pulled him close. "*You* are *my* hero," she whispered.

As they passed the grating where the strays went in and out, Zato paused and lifted his leg for a long and purposeful pee.

-33-

Pushmi-Pullyu

Ian's return from a deli run galvanized the dogs. Flanking him on either side as he walked down the hallway, they raised their noses, tracking the aromas that oozed from the paper bag filled with four six-inch meatball heroes from Mama Joy's deli.

"It's wicked out there," Ian reported to Blair as he pulled the sandwiches from the paper bag. "The temperature is in the teens, and the wind is fierce in the cross streets. Fortunately, Mama Joy's was open, and there was no line."

"Thank you, Sir Hillary, for braving the elements once again," said Blair. "I've made a pot of tea if you're interested."

"That should warm you up. Oh, the materials from Neuilly International School arrived in the mail just after you left. They are on the coffee table, but let's eat before you start grumbling over them."

After plating the heroes, Blair summoned the kids. The sandwiches were still warm, and Max and Logan gushed over how this was their favorite lunch.

Wiping tomato sauce from her chin, Blair said, "Sam called. She was checking the time to meet us at the Puglia tomorrow night. Unfortunately, Mr. Spooning is leaving for his home and family today, so we will have Sam all to ourselves tomorrow. I would like to have met him, though."

"Me too," said Ian. "He might have sprung for the meal."

Blair sensed Ian's mood had soured when he heard that the school materials had arrived. He had been happy to set the subject of Paris aside, hoping not to revisit it until after the new year. However, with the arrival of the brochures and faculty information, it was sure to be a topic after lunch. He felt his stomach churn and his chest tighten in anticipation.

After lunch, the kids retreated to their rooms, and as predicted, Blair invited Ian to sit with her on the couch and look over the Paris school brochures. As he flipped through a magazine-sized brochure glancing at artful photographs of the school and students, Blair read aloud from Sarah Reinhart's accompanying letter.

Dear Blair and Ian,

I have sent you everything I could lay my hands on, including the Faculty Handbook. That, along with the school's brochures and a sample contract, should provide a good idea of faculty requirements and perquisites.

"She sounds like a lawyer," said Ian.

"She is a lawyer," responded Blair, matching her husband's edgy tone, then continued reading:

"I think starting with a bit of history may be helpful, then let the accompanying documents speak for themselves. In 1945, American families began moving to Paris to fill diplomatic positions and serve in public and private businesses. Economic recovery in Europe was just underway, and the war had taken a heavy toll on qualified teaching personnel. It was clear that

Americans working in Europe needed a school to care for the growing numbers of their children.

The older building that you see in the photographs wasn't built until the early 1880s but still has the Haussmann stamp: a broad mansard roof resting on four stories of Lutetian limestone, giving it that warm, chanterelle beige you see in so much of Paris. The house and grounds came on the market soon after the war, and my understanding is that a small group of American businessmen purchased the property in a fire sale and gifted it to the school in a trust.

The mansion has been fully remodeled and is quite beautiful, currently housing school administration and some upper-school classrooms. In the three decades following its purchase, management of this ten-acre property removed the old stables and most of the gardens, replacing them with five modern facilities: a three-story building for classrooms (including a science lab and art studio), a full-sized gymnasium, an auditorium for dramatic arts and assemblies, a soccer field, and four tennis courts. In addition, fundraising is nearly complete for a new middle and elementary school building, which should break ground next year. NIS has a waiting list, and the new facility will allow us to expand the student body from 450 to 600 students, but that's a good two or three years off. The school is ten miles from central Paris (a 15-20 minute drive) and about the same distance to the NIS apartments in Auteuil.

I am sure you will have questions after looking this over. I will be at my parents' home in Baltimore until January 6th; please feel free to call me. Weekday mornings are best: 301-228-9901.

I look forward to talking with you.

All the best,

Sarah

"That was informative," said Ian, meaning it, "and no actual sales pitch. NIS is about the same age as St. Mark's, so it's a relative baby, but it certainly has done well for itself in thirty years."

Blair moved closer to her husband to examine the brochure.

"We have two good schools to compare it to, so let's both try and keep an open mind and see what it has to offer."

Ian's objections were practical: they had stable employment, doing things they both enjoyed; a spacious apartment on the Columbia campus at an unbeatable rate; the kids were doing well at St. Mark's, and Logan had been accepted at an excellent public high school. It would likely not be easy for them to uproot and move to another country. Plus, working at Columbia, it was easy for Blair to care for the dogs over lunch and handle domestic emergencies.

Blair did not dispute these objections but felt the benefits of NIS outweighed the risks. She listed out her litany of positives: Logan already had three years of French, Max had one, and not only would they live in the most beautiful city in Europe, but the family would have easy access to travel and the experience of other cultures. In the same amount of time it takes to drive from New York to Boston, they could go from Paris to Frankfurt, even to Brussels or Luxembourg. The kids would have friends from different countries and cultures, learn to speak French like natives, and have the cultural amenities of Paris and all of Europe at their fingertips. Although she had no experience teaching, she had always wanted to and felt she would be good at it. Finally, she had never been out of the country, not even to Canada, and she longed to travel.

For Ian, problems with the move were those of stability and predictability, which conflicted with Blair's sudden wanderlust. For her, not moving was a problem of inertia. Was it so bad to be carefree, to loosen oneself from the hypnotic grip of a metronomic life, to want to expand one's interests and challenges, to take the road less traveled?

"How did you feel when you set out for Taiwan by yourself, with a strict budget, knowing no one, and not having a place to live?"

"A bit like diving into the ocean in the dead of night."

"So, amid all those uncertainties. How could you do it?"

"I guess it was the game I'd chosen. If I wanted to play it, I'd have to take the plunge and figure it out on the fly. It was exciting, challenging, new."

"And with all those reasons not to do it, you did it. I feel the same way now. We know all the reasons not to do it, but taking this plunge has fewer variables than when you set out for Taiwan—we would have jobs, a decent income, a home, and a good school for the kids. We could even bring the dogs."

"The dogs, yes. That is a subject," Ian said.

After a pause, Blair added, "I've been thinking about them, too."

At that moment, the kids bounded into the living room, dogs in their wake. Logan placed a game box on the dining room table and began unpacking tiles.

"It's time for Rummikub," she said. "Come on over."

The subject of Paris and the dogs would have to wait.

-34-

Chow Yuk Crosses the Rubicon

Chinatown and Little Italy resembled city-states on the shores of two continents separated only by a narrow river. Denizens of each could look across the divide and see a somewhat familiar form, but the effect was like giraffes contemplating zebras at a shared waterhole. The Chinese, drained of vital juices at the mines and the railroad, arrived from the west—spat out like bitter pits. Italians came from the east with nothing but hope in their pockets, escaping drought, cholera, corruption, and a crumbling economy. Despite their shared hardships of language, xenophobia, or outright racism, these cultures kept to their side of the river: Canal Street—the border. No man's land.

Ian began frequenting Chinatown during his first year at Columbia. He desired to get away from the fare of local restaurants with menus claiming a spurious Chinese provenance—dishes like chicken chow mein, chop suey, and pork fried rice struck him as American mutations, lacking in authenticity. So, with a few other wannabe Sinophiles, he would take the subway to Chinatown and challenge their grass-fed palates by ordering Cantonese dishes with exotic ingredients. These included chicken feet, fish lips, bird's nest soup, fish maw, and barbequed snake. Granted, these dishes were not all immediately awarded with Michelin constellations, but the students found many of them delicious.

Often, after a filling meal on Mott Street, when Ian and friends were feeling particularly ambitious, they would dare to cross the continental divide still smelling of fish lips and take a long stroll up Mulberry Street to Ferrara's Bakery for an espresso and a chocolate cannoli. Two blocks before reaching their destination, they would pass the Ristorante Puglia on Hester Street, always full, always boisterous, with accordion and vocal music spilling out into the street.

Ian decided that once he had fully gratified his Cantonese palate, he would refocus his gastronomic interests on Little Italy and place Ristorante Puglia at the top of his "eat-Italian" list. However, that resolution would remain dormant until his junior year, when brother Mike returned from his Italian odyssey. Within a month of his repatriation, Mike took his brother to dinner at what he claimed was "the best Italian restaurant in New York"—Ristorante Puglia. To Ian, the food was good; however, the wine (no labels on the bottles), the music, and the constant celebration of patrons lifted the intensity of flavors from merely good to sublime.

As Mike now spoke Italian with the ease of a Neapolitan fishmonger and had traveled through Italy's Puglia region, visiting cities along the Adriatic from Bari to Brindisi, he was quickly embraced by the Garofolo family who had captained this emporium of Italian delights since 1919. For the initiated, there were off-menu items that one could order ahead of time: *orecchiette* (pasta shaped like little ears), *pettole* (a kind of Italian donut), *caciocavallo* (cheese in the shape of a wine gourd), or the *piatto principale*: *capuzzella d'agnello*, a lamb's head cloven in two and baked. The latter was one of Mike's favorites, and when served with a long spoon to a freckle-faced, red-bearded American, it caused quite a stir.

In the nearly two decades following Ian's first visit to Ristorante Puglia, the uptown and downtown Kennedys had visited the restaurant dozens of times. First, they had gone with friends, then with children, nieces, nephews, and cousins. When Samantha McFarlane was in town, she insisted they break bread there, even if their conversation was swallowed up in the din like Jonah. So, it was arranged.

*

It had not snowed since Christmas morning, but temperatures had remained in the teens for the last few days leaving the asphalt of side streets under a layer of packed ice and snow. Berms left by occasional plows had buried the cars parked along the major arteries of Manhattan. As a result, curbside parking was available only in clumsy half-excavated igloos left by resolute drivers carrying shovels. Finding parking spaces along the narrow streets of Little Italy was rare, even in good weather. However, Mike had a seventh sense for ferreting out such locations, and after loading the van with his relatives and wending his way downtown, he found a plowed lot on Baxter Street, one long block from the Puglia.

Concentrating on keeping balance on the icy sidewalk, the group trooped along two-by-two, stopping at the intersection of Hester and Mulberry Streets to let a car pass. On the opposite corner, the Ristorante Puglia glowed like a warm beacon of hope. But as they were about to cross the street, Mike cried out in despair, "This was not here in August!" He was looking up and to his right at the signage of a Chinese restaurant: The Golden Pavilion.

"That name sounds like a Chinese porn film and is a bad omen," he said. "The end is near."

Ian stepped closer to the restaurant window to read a menu taped to the inside glass. It had all the usual dishes of southern China as well as two geared to an American palate: *moo gu gai pan* and *pork chow yuk*. The restaurant was a large square, starkly lit, its inside blurred with condensation and cigarette smoke. Simple aluminum tables and chairs with Formica tops accommodated several generations of Chinese: toddlers ran unchecked while grandmas calmly fed babies in highchairs with chopsticks. Waiters darted between tables like swallows, snatching empty plates and bowls and carrying mounds of glistening vegetables, cauldrons of soup, stacks of palm-sized river crabs, and platters of whole fish. The murmur from behind the glass was of migrating geese. Mike was right; these were likely just the first few foot soldiers of a legion to follow.

"Well, at least the Puglia is still here beckoning us back to our roots," said Mike in resignation. "I hope Sam's here. Because it's time to party!"

-35-

A Little Night Music

Dinner hour at the Puglia was underway, and the restaurant was already boisterous with patrons. A diminutive man with furrowed cheeks and a solemn expression sat in a chair behind an enormous accordion strapped between his shoulders. Peering over the top of his instrument, he pulsated the bellows with the ease of a maestro swelling the cellos, filling the room with a familiar Italian melody. Some patrons were clapping in time, while others rhythmically waved their wine glasses. "He's playing a tarantella," Spira said to her father. "I know this one," she added, wishing she had brought her chanter.

Standing in the restaurant's warmth, they scanned the room for Samantha McFarlane, but she had yet to arrive. Soon a waiter in a crisp white jacket and green bow tie ushered them to a table set for eight. They hung their coats on their seatbacks and sat down. Water, warm bread, and a bottle of unsolicited and unlabeled wine arrived, and the families settled in to wait for Sam.

Sam's arrival might have drawn little attention at the Four Seasons but not at the Puglia. She was wearing a long, silky, brown mink, topped with a Russian-style, blue fox hat the size of a pumpkin, and just visible below the hem of her coat showed a pair of red high-heeled boots. She had only walked a few steps from the cab, but her cheeks were flushed from the cold, and she looked like a movie star expecting to find Marcello Mastroianni looking up expectantly from his tortellini.

Except for the accordion, the room fell silent for just a moment as Sam swept through the door; however, quickly realizing that they could put away their autograph books, the crowd returned to their wine, food, and friends. Mike waved Sam over, and the two families scrambled from their chairs to welcome her with hugs and kisses and to smell and feel the cool silk of her fur. Mike deftly handled Sam's indecision of where to put her sumptuous hat by stuffing it unceremoniously into a sleeve of his heavy military coat.

Wine was poured, and menu items discussed—with Mike making suggestions. They selected a multi-course, family-style array of dishes. The *antipasto* was an olio of seafood, stuffed mushrooms, fried zucchini, and bruschetta. Mike asked for and was accommodated with an off-menu item reserved for locals from the motherland, *mozzarella di bufala*, served in thick slices over tomatoes, covered in olive oil, and strips of basil. Only at the Puglia could you find this cheese made from the milk of water buffalo raised on the sweet grasses of Campania. Ian was relieved that tripe was not on the menu and that Mike had limited his off-menu indulgence to the buffalo's milk and not its stomach.

For their *primi*, they ordered manicotti, lasagna, and spaghetti with meatballs, followed by a two-part *secondi*, a platter of scampi swimming in garlic butter and two plates of veal: parmigiana and marsala.

While the kids sat at the end of the table, near the wall, laughing and fighting over meatballs, Samantha McFarlane held court at the other end of the table. Sam tried to elicit family updates covering the three years since their last dinner together but received only pro forma answers from her cousins, such as they might provide to their parents when asked about work. Conversely, the cousins wanted to know about her, as they were confident that life in London must be more glamorous and exciting than theirs. As it turned out, they were right.

Raising her voice above the din, Sam did her best to respond to the fusillade of questions without informing the patrons at neighboring tables, much less the children at the far end of hers. Yes, Reggie had left for London that morning. Yes, he works for Lloyd's as a mathematician, conducting high-level actuarial analysis for member syndicates. I know; it sounds like the Mafia, but he acts as a broker between interested parties. All very legal. Yes, his wife knows about us, but she's French, so she is rather French about it. Occasionally she even invites me to dinner. Reggie has a small chalet in Anzère, Switzerland, where we go skiing in winter and hiking in summer. He is very generous, and I love his kids.

Eventually, her inquisitors exhausted their curiosity, and it looked like Sam could resume eating in relative peace when an older woman of generous proportions wearing a floor-length, black-sequined dress came in from the kitchen and stepped up to a microphone placed alongside the accordionist. Her face was thickly powdered; her lips broadened and brightened with an electric rouge, applied as if by paintbrush; her hair, dyed black, flowed in curls over her shoulders.

"*Buonasera*, everyone!" she said, opening her arms wide and holding a long red handkerchief in her right hand.

"*Buonasera*," responded the crowd.

"Are you enjoying your dinner?" she asked.

"Yes!" they replied.

"Are you happy?"

"Yes!"

"Fantastica. Tonight, I am going to teach you a little *Italiano*. If you want to say, 'I am happy,' you say, *'Sono felice.'* Now, repeat after me, *sono felice.*"

A wave of *sono felice* swept the room.

"When I say, *Se felice*? It means 'Are you happy?' And you answer?"

"*Sono felice*!"

"Eccellente!" she responded. "*Se felice*?"

"*Sono felice*!" they answered.

"*Magnifico*! Would you like to sing with me—a song you all know?

The room roared in agreement.

"Do you all know *funiculi, funicula*?" There was a mixed reaction from the audience.

"Some yes, some no?" She turned to her accompanist, "Paolo, can you help?"

Expressionless, Paolo played the chorus.

"Do you know it now?"

"Yes!" thundered the room.

"In this song, a young man invites his sweetheart to ride with him on the new tram, the funicular, to the top of

Vesuvio. Funiculi, funicula, means going up and going down on the tram. That is your part. Can you do it?"

"Yes!" they replied, trembling the photo of the restaurant's founder on its nail.

"Sometimes I will sing a part and ask you to sing the same back to me. If you don't remember the Italian, you can just sing, la-la-la. It's easy. Are you ready?"

A plate-rattling response signaled their readiness.

Paolo played a short introductory melody, and the diva began her spirited performance. When she wanted her guests to repeat a line just sung, she would wave her handkerchief like Toscanini's baton, with the room responding la-la-la like a chorus of La Scala professionals.

She continued in Italian with the patrons serving in their role enthusiastically, if not accurately. Then, each time the refrain approached, she unhooked her mic from the stand and moved among the patrons, thus amplifying one or more of the congregants.

Ultimately, she came to Mike, who was sitting at the end of the table, nearest the center of the room. He rendered the refrain in perfect Italian, without recourse to la-la-la.

Impressed, the songstress joined him for another exchange, and, as the song closed, all those present gave both singers a riotous round of applause. Mike sat back and saluted the crowd, basking in the accolade.

Finally, the veal arrived, accompanied by another bottle of anonymous wine. By now, the room had filled, and there was more singing at higher and higher decibels until it was impossible to have any meaningful conversation. A dessert menu appeared but was voted down in favor of a refreshing walk up Mulberry Street to Ferrara's Bakery for an espresso and a cannoli.

Pooling their money, the Kennedys treated Cousin Sam to dinner, then readied themselves for stepping into the cold. As they wound through the crowd toward the door, Mike went to the tip jar and put in a bill. As the diva was between songs, she thanked him, and, after exchanging goodbyes in Italian, she blew Mike a kiss, with Paolo giving him a friendly wink.

Outside, the temperature had fallen precipitously, and the group watched impatiently through the window as Mike finished his farewells. Lizanne, who had been nursing a single glass of wine all evening, offered to get the van and join them at Ferrara's. She would be the driver tonight. She set out for the parking lot on Baker Street while the rest of the troop huddled in twos and threes, scuttling up the long block to Ferrara's. Fortunately for Sam in her high-heeled boots, the sidewalks along Mulberry Street had been cleared and salted by shop keepers along the way.

"You have quite a rapport with that singer. Do you know her?" asked Sam, hanging onto Mike's arm for balance.

"I have gotten to know the family just a bit," he said. "Her name is Paloma, and I think she is a cousin of the owners. It's hard to tell. Paulo, her accompanist, is also her husband. Paulo and Paloma."

"It sounds like the name of a Fellini movie," said Sam.

-36-

La Questione dei Cannoli

As the group rounded the corner at Grand Street, the light from Ferrara's neon marquee and the warm glow of its windows caused a glandular eruption in this group of wayfarers. Since the turn of the century, Ferrara's bakers were the high priests of the New York cannoli: a crispy, blistered shell stuffed with ricotta cream, blended with sugar, citrus, and chocolate chips, with a splash of marsala wine. Of course, they offered a cornucopia of other delicacies, but cannoli were the cornerstone of their fame and continued success.

Over the years, those few remaining generational purveyors of authentic Italian foods like the Puglia and Ferrara's became the glue binding together those few remaining blocks of Little Italy. They also helped to fend off the total appropriation of the neighborhood by ersatz Italian lookalikes and Chinese invaders.

Ian and Blair were first to arrive and inspect the scene. "It looks like there's no line," said Ian as he held open the door and waved them in, out of the cold.

The dining room was narrow and offered limited space on the ground floor, with tables for two or four along the walls and a few larger tables at the back. There was additional seating on the floor above, but it lacked panache and was too quiet and far from the din of business, the calming Tuscan lighting, and the polychrome of the display cases.

A waiter approached, announcing there was a table for four in the back and another for two along the wall, but if they wanted to sit together, it would be a fifteen to twenty-minute wait.

After a quick discussion, they agreed to order their pastries to go.

Two clerks were busy plating delights behind the counter, so while waiting to be served, the group spread out along the display cases to agonize over their choices. Ian and Blair's palates were easily satisfied: vanilla cannoli dipped in chocolate on each end. At the same time, a few feet down the counter, Max and Logan discussed the subtleties of cannoli variants: yellow peanut butter or green pistachio. Sam was busy reimagining the flavor of a crisp, flakey lobster tail stuffed with Bavarian cream, while Mike—ever the iconoclast—considered the alternative of a rum-filled *baba*. Ultimately, they all backed away from reckless adventurism and chose the traditional vanilla or chocolate-dipped cannoli flaked with chocolate chips. In addition, Mike ordered the mandatory *sfogliatella* for Lizanne and for himself a boozy box of babas and a rum-soaked tiramisu, all to be consumed over the next few days with an espresso and a Dominican cigar.

Mike and Ian moved near the cash register to watch the simple magic of the string machine. To its manufacturers, it was known as a Bunn Package Tying Machine; however, for the mesmerized visitors to Ferrara's, it was simply the string machine. This very device had been in use since the twenties, and all that had changed in over fifty years of tying packages was the spool of twine. Operated by a pump motion of the foot, it was like kick-starting a motorcycle. With each pump, a line of cord encircled a cardboard box: two pumps and one rotation—*voilà*, the package is tied.

As the brothers succumbed to the rhythmic thump of the metal and the hiss of the milk steamer, Mike turned his head and spoke in a low voice to his brother.

"Did you notice that the Golden Pavilion was still going strong? People were waiting to be seated."

"Yes, I noticed."

"Should we be worried?"

"Yes, we should."

Orders placed and boxes strung, the group exited the bakery into a chilling wind. Lizanne had double-parked in front of Ferrara's—motor running—and the group hurried into the warmth of its cabin.

"How wonderful!" said Blair. "You arrived just when we needed you."

"I thought you might have a wait," explained Lizanne, "so I watched to see if you would be seated before finding somewhere to park. Mike knows I always have the *sfogliatella*, so I knew it was win-win either way."

"The what?" asked Sam from the bench seat behind Lizanne.

"The sfogliatella. It's a crisp, flakey pastry filled with smooth Bavarian cream. To die for or, even better, to live for."

Bavarian cream, mused Sam, wondering if she shouldn't have ordered the lobster tail.

-37-

Elysium

As the van rocked uptown over the ruts of ice and snow, the group drifted into the quiet of their thoughts, and the kids quickly fell asleep. When they joined the uptown traffic on 6th Avenue, the road smoothed out, and they traveled unimpeded to 59th Street; then, crossing to 5th Avenue, they turned right and pulled into the semi-circle in front of the east entrance to the Plaza Hotel. In the summer, horse-drawn carriages lined up here, but the space was empty tonight.

"Let's not wake the kids," said Sam softly. "I can run in and get your gifts. They are already wrapped and clearly labeled. So, it's no problem at all."

Blair reached under her seat to retrieve a large shopping bag. "I'll go up and help," she said. "Plus, we have a few gifts here for you."

It was not just a desire to be of assistance that motivated Blair's offer. She wanted to see what a posh room in the Plaza looked like.

A liveried doorman approached the van, no doubt with some trepidation, but as soon as Sam stepped out from the sliding door, it became clear that he was dealing with the appropriate level of patron, and he offered her his gloved hand in assistance.

Mike had rolled down his window to chat with Sam and Blair as they arranged themselves at the bottom of a long flight of red-carpeted stairs under the Plaza's marquee. "Don't forget to come back," he said to Blair.

"If I'm not back in ten, you all can go on without me," she answered.

Side-by-side, they ascended the middle of three equally heroic entrances. At the top of the carpeted stairs, gilt candelabras illuminated a black-lacquer doorway trimmed with decorative brass and topped with an elliptical, stained-glass lunette.

"It feels like I've been summoned to an audience with Zeus," said Blair, as the pair pushed against a revolving door.

Passing through the lobby was like a stroll through the Parthenon: inlaid marble floors and walls reflected the light from a thousand suns; round marble columns with Corinthian capitals supported coffered ceilings, nearly lost in the clouds. Here, the temple statues wore no togas, but men in long wool coats and women wrapped in furs glided through the lobby as if Zeus had breathed life into the flawless marble of this lesser pantheon.

Tables strained under the weight of elaborate bouquets: red and white poinsettias, pink amaryllis, and fragrant lilies abounded, but a perfectly tapered, twenty-foot fir stood at center stage, supporting a galaxy of half-carat lights. Beyond the tree, a bank of four mirrored elevators rimmed in gleaming brass floated the consecrated to the luxury of their private chambers.

Sam summoned a "lift," and they soared as if through velvet to the twelfth floor. Then, while stepping along a plush runner, Blair sighed, "I could curl up and fall asleep right here, on this carpet."

At the end of a long corridor, Sam unlocked the last door and turned on the lights, exposing an entryway of closets and a spacious living room with a parquet floor. The walls were light gray, with darker accents. A carpet of soft blue with gold flowers in low relief covered the sitting area, where a steel-gray couch and matching chairs allowed for comfortable relaxation. There was a coffee table, writing desk, a television, and a wet bar with a marble sink.

Blair allowed the room to marinate her senses while Sam passed through sliding doors into the bedroom to collect the gifts. "Keep your coat on and come in here," called Sam. "It will just take a minute."

When they had first entered the suite, the bedroom doors were closed, but now, they revealed an equally large room with its array of living room furniture and a bed the size of a concert grand. Its head and footboards would no doubt have pleased the gaggle of interior designers who once ran wild in Versailles.

"When did you arrive here?" asked Blair, taking in the sumptuousness of the room.

"I came on the twenty-second, Reggie the day before," Sam said while she sorted through exquisitely wrapped gifts on the bed.

"He left this morning, but I'll be here through January third. It's amazing, isn't it?" she said, indicating the suite with a sweep of her hand. "The room even comes with butler service. Imagine."

"Does a Llyod's mathematician make this much money? I'm sorry if that is too rude a question, but all this must cost a fortune."

Sam looked up from checking a name tag. "Reggie has a special function at Lloyd's. The simple explanation is that he connects individuals or corporations with high-risk activities to groups of investors called 'syndicates' who underwrite the policy. Part of his job is to assess the risk involved, finding the best match and recommending the premium."

"He deals mainly with international shipping: cargo ships and oil tankers: problems involving acts of God or man—even piracy. At times he seems to have almost diplomatic as well as financial functions. I have not told Michael this, but he used to work for the International Monetary Fund. You know what that is?"

"Yes, a little," said Blair. "The Bretton Woods agreement at the end of the war, formed the IMF and the World Bank. Central banks pooled resources that could be borrowed against by member countries—provided they agreed to specific economic policies that may or may not be all that beneficial to the borrower."

"That sounds about right," agreed Sam. "It's a bit convoluted for me. Reggie didn't see eye to eye with the board of directors, and, after five years there, he left to join Lloyd's. However, he is still well known in those circles, and various contacts from his IMF days help him obtain what he calls 'discrete information.'"

Sam continued sorting gifts into bags. "Reggie has investments of various kinds, and he is a shareholder in my agency." She hesitated and looked at Blair, "Please don't relate his IMF history to Michael, as he gets so worked up over politics and real or imagined injustices, and, frankly, I don't know enough about those organizations to have a reasoned opinion."

"Of course, mum's the word. There is no purpose in passing that along. I only asked as this suite is amazing. Even a view of Central Park. You are a lucky lady to have such a generous friend."

"Yes, I am, but it's not without its downside." Sam paused for a moment, looking inward, then continued buoyantly. "Let's bag these gifts and get you all on your way. The Bergdorf bag has a few things for you and the kids, but don't get your hopes up; only the bag has the label. The one from Bloomies's is for Michael's family."

"We have a few things for you as well," said Blair. "It's all from Zabar's, even the bag. I put it on the sofa in the living room. I know you love Zabar's goodies, so Lizanne and I put together quite an assortment."

"I *was* hoping it wasn't just the bag," said Sam.

They each took a sack by the handles and exited the suite. As they walked toward the elevator, Blair said, "I have something to tell you that I'd like your opinion about."

"Sure."

"Ian and I have a possible job offer at an international school outside Paris. It's a K through twelfth-grade day school. I would assist the headmistress with administrative work and possibly teach Russian; Ian would teach Chinese and Asian history as he does now. It comes with free tuition for the kids and a low-cost apartment. We're still talking about it, as it's a huge change for us and the kids. Ian is not all that keen on it, but—"

"What's not to be keen about?" interrupted Sam. "It sounds wonderful for you and the kids. So, what's Ian's worry?"

"It's mainly job security. We both have solid jobs here, a lovely apartment, and a good school for the kids. Logan has applied to Stuyvesant—a public school downtown; tough to get in, but her school counselor is confident she will. It's a big deal for her, and Logan may be unhappy about not attending."

They arrived at the elevator, and Sam pressed the button. "The kids don't know about it yet?"

"Not yet. We don't want to get them riled up if we are still undecided. We haven't told Michael and Lizanne either, and Ian's been avoiding talking about it altogether. Anyway, we still need to apply for the positions; it's not a done deal by any means."

Once inside the elevator, Sam put down her shopping bag and checked her reflection in a mirrored wall panel. She arranged her hair and adjusted her hat. "How soon do you have to apply?" she asked.

"Right after the new year."

The elevator cabin door opened, and they stepped into the hum and bustle of the lobby.

"That is a big decision; I can see that," said Sam. "Maybe I can help. What if I take the kids on Thursday? I was planning on taking them to Rumpelmayer's for lunch and ice cream sundaes. Then, we can go skating at Rockefeller Center or see a movie. I'd have them all day, and you and Ian would have time to talk. What do you think?"

"I'd love it. We could use the time alone. We might even begin writing our resumés—if we get that far."

"Okay then. We can deal with the logistics tomorrow by phone."

They pushed through the revolving door and stood under the hotel marquee, looking for the van. The doorman recognized Sam and pointed to the right of the entrance, where the van idled in the shadows.

Ian slid open the door and took the gift bags. "It was delightful seeing you all," Sam said in hushed tones. "Hopefully, we can get together one more time before I fly home. Blair knows whose bag is whose."

"What about your cannoli?" asked Ian. "I can open the box. We have napkins."

"No, no. You can give mine to the kids. I think it's best if I wind down my holiday indulgences, as they have been challenging the seams of my slacks ever since I arrived in New York."

As Blair watched Sam ascend the stairs to the hotel with the help of the doorman—he in his red coat with gold epaulets and brass buttons and she in her polished red boots, fur coat, and hat—images from *Anna Karenina* bubbled forth. Ian, however, absently began to hum the theme from *Sgt. Pepper's Lonely Hearts Club Band.*

*

On the corner of 116th Street, the van unloaded the downtown Kennedys with their box of cannolis and their bag of gifts. After brief farewells, the van turned down Amsterdam Avenue and drove off into the night with a beep of Morse code.

They walked the half block to their building with their backs to the wind. Inside, as they approached their apartment door, the sound of dog nails on hardwood and the banging of bicycles announced their arrival.

Cannolis were offered to the children but postponed to the next day as both were tired and longed for bed. Their parents bid them goodnight and withdrew to the kitchen to brew some instant decaf and open the pastry box. As it happened, Uncle Mike had mistakenly given them his singular selection of rum-soaked babas and an equally dissolute tiramisu. Humm, what to do?

Ian inspected the box. "There is little chance that these will retain their quality overnight," he said.

"Certainly not the tiramisu," confirmed Blair. "No doubt Mike and Lizanne are saying the same thing about our box right now."

"No doubt," said Ian. "And alcohol-laden pastries would not be appropriate for the children.

"I agree," said Blair. "The kids don't know it yet, but Sam is inviting them to Rumpelmayer's for lunch and ice cream sundaes on Thursday, so I think we are safe here."

Ian poured boiling water into two cups and stirred in instant coffee.

"Fortunately, for Mike," he said, "Lizanne's 'to die for' pastry is not in our box, or the police may have found him floating in the Hudson tomorrow morning."

And, in this way, the night's festivities drew to a rum-soaked close.

-38-

The Reprieve

"He's eaten the cannolis and half the box they came in," shouted Logan.

"Who?" asked a sleepy voice from down the hall.

"Who do you think?"

As the absence of the anticipated cannolis was a subject of considerable gravity, the family assembled in the kitchen to discuss the whos, whats, and wherefores of this catastrophe.

Ian assured the children that Zato was not responsible for the missing cannolis, only for the mutilated pastry box. With a slight flush of guilt, he explained the consequences of Uncle Mike's errant hand-off as they had exited the van the night before.

"And our cannolis?" pined Max.

"In all likelihood, what happened here also happened there," said Blair. "But there is a silver lining."

The children looked at her suspiciously.

"Samantha has invited you and Spira to Rumpelmayer's tomorrow for lunch and sundaes, followed by a day of ice skating or movies or some other exciting adventure."

As the children had been to Rumpelmayer's in the past, they accepted the plan as an adequate swap of confections. They then retreated to their rooms to conjure images of glass gondolas glutted with mountains of ice cream, drenched in warm sauces, under a cloud of whipped cream and a glistening cherry.

In the ensuing silence, Blair broached the subject of the Paris school. "The kids will be with Sam almost all day," she said. "It will give us time to talk about the Paris idea. Then, if we want, we can call Sarah in Baltimore and ask any remaining questions—even start our resumés if we're up to it."

Ian picked up the mutilated pastry box and pushed it into the kitchen trash can. "I guess we can do that, but it seems a shame to waste a day off."

"If you don't want to consider it," said Blair trying to restrain her irritation, "then we can let Sarah know we are happy where we are." She wanted to add, "living our uninspired, button-down lives." But she remained silent, allowing her words to work their way into Ian's brain cells and propagate like a virus.

"It's not that I don't want to consider it," he said. "I am considering it, but it's a whole life upheaval and yet it feels like it's moving along like a bullet train."

"I agree," said Blair. "We have a very narrow window in which to act, one way or the other, and it makes me uncomfortable, too. But it's a rare opportunity for us and the kids, should we dare to take it. But, of course, there is no guarantee we will even get it."

Reluctantly, Ian agreed to spend the following day confronting the pros and cons of this offer, including a call to Sarah Reinhart. Later, while walking the dogs, he realized that his reluctance was not to the opportunity *per se* but to starting over: needing to prove himself in a new environment. What if he was not as hot a prospect as Sarah thought? Factually, Blair had more to offer the school than he. Not only was she fluent in Russian and almost as good in French, but she was a skilled administrator, something he was not; Ian felt one-dimensional in comparison.

The following day, Blair, Sam, and Lizanne conversed by phone and worked out the logistics for the kids' journey to Rumpelmayer's. She and Ian would walk the kids to the bookstore, where they would meet Spira and see them all off on the downtown 104 bus at Broadway and 116th Street.

It would be the first "solo" excursion for Max and Spira, whereas Logan had ridden the bus a few times with school friends to performances at Lincoln Center, so she knew the route. Logan refused to ride the subway without her parents.

She felt it too enclosed, too dark, and a little scary.

However, it was safe on a bus with ladies and their shopping bags, men in work clothes or uniforms, and even some in suits. There were also college students absorbed in their books; and, most welcome, a complete lack of inappropriate smells. She could see the driver, and he could see her.

Logan would be the commander of this voyage and pull the cord at Broadway and 63rd Street, where Samantha McFarlane would await them. The way home would run in reverse.

Both sets of Kennedys agreed it was time for the kids to enjoy this bit of freedom, especially as Logan was a seasoned traveler. At the same time, Max and Spira considered the prospect of such adult activity thrilling.

*

Mid-morning, the doorbell rang. It was Spira, holding a Ferrara's box in her outstretched hands. "I brought your cannolis," she said happily, "but I'm afraid the shells got soggy. So, this morning when I had mine, I just ate the filling." Blair accepted the box, which was soggy on the bottom.

Today, Spira had come to work with her parents. While her dad helped customers on the main floor, Lizanne balanced the accounts and checked invoices in her basement "office." Generally, she did this work from home, but Lizanne spent a day at the store twice a month, keeping filing up to date and, if time allowed, helping her husband with the inventory, often assisted by Spira.

Addressing Aunt and Uncle, Spira raised her chin, squared her shoulders, and like a seasoned soldier, said, "I have a message from Dad, and I quote, 'I know you ate my babas and tiramisu, so we ate your cannolis; however, out of kindness to the children, we spared Max and Logan's. So, we are even, but I know you got the better deal. *Mazel tov* and happy new year.'"

"Well," said Ian, laughing, "I must confess, we did eat the babas and tiramisu, and they were quite tasty. Thank you, Spira, for bringing the cannolis. I'm sure the kids will be happy with them, soggy or not."

"Would you like to visit for a while?" asked Blair, handing the box to Ian and taking a step back into the foyer. Logan and Max seconded the motion. "I would, but today I'm helping with inventory. I just came to deliver the cannolis, and Dad wanted to know if Max and Logan might like to come to the store and help."

The kids asserted their willingness to do so, and as they prepared for the walk across campus, Blair asked Spira if she knew that Samantha was taking them all to Rumpelmayer's the next day.

"Oh, yes. I love that place. Even its name is magical," she said.

"It truly is," agreed Blair. "We will meet you at the store tomorrow morning at 10:45, so you can all catch the Broadway bus downtown."

"I know, Mom told me. It's really cool!"

"Logan has taken that bus many times," said Blair reassuringly, "so she will be the guide. Okay?"

"Sure. It sounds so fun!"

Logan and Max had donned their winter clothing, and the three set out across the campus to the bookstore.

As the apartment door closed, Blair said, "Well, it looks like we're getting a twofer."

Ian thought about it for a moment, then realized they now had twice as much time to devote to the Paris plan. "Yes, lucky us," he grumbled.

Realizing that her husband had only agreed to one day of Paris talk, Blair thought it best to propose a less contentious use of their unexpected freedom. "Why don't we go to the Richard Avedon exhibit at the Met?" she asked. "I think it's in its last week. It should be fun."

Ian was quick to agree. As both admired Avedon's photography, they decided to take the afternoon off and devote themselves to the arts. Uncle Mike offered to treat the kids to lunch and keep them productive until their parents returned from their foray into the monochrome world of Richard Avedon.

They took the subway to 79th Street, then hailed a crosstown cab to 5th Avenue. From there, it was only a three-block walk to the Met. The exhibit's fashion element was a windswept display of long legs in off-kilter postures, with bodies and clothes moving in balanced perfection. In contrast, the photographs in the portrait galleries were mostly motionless, stark, and unflattering: those of Audrey Hepburn being an especially welcome exception. Ian thought Avedon might have been in love with her, as there were dozens of portraits and fashion shots of the actress, lithe and winsome, even one with Fred Astaire down on one knee as if proposing, offering her not a ring but a camera. Ian suggested this was an example of Freudian sublimation: the moonstruck Avedon replacing himself with Astaire. He commented to Blair that given the opportunity, he too might get down on one devotional knee and offer the porcelain-skinned beauty not a camera or a ring but an ambrosial plate of tender, soy-soaked chicken feet.

They stood for some time before an image titled *Dovima with the Elephants*: the model, Dovima, leaning back in imperial serenity with one hand on an elephant's trunk, the other reaching out as if to beckon her butler.

"There is something beautiful yet heartbreaking about this photo," said Blair. "The woman is elegant, with her long, sweeping lines, seemingly in control of these ponderous pachyderms, but the chains around their ankles belie the fact of their enslavement. It's sad, don't you think?"

"It does have a distasteful, antebellum flavor," Ian said. But this was not the only picture that struck them as sad. There were portraits of coal miners without coal or chimney sweeps without chimneys; a shirtless, hairless man covered in bees; there were faces frightened, angry, or pained; only two or three were elegant or thoughtful, plus a series with Janice Joplin hanging on only by a thread.

These images were haunting but not pleasing. So, to take the edge off, they made their obligatory museum side-trips: a stroll through the collection of 8th-century Chinese ceramics, then through the galleries bursting with a kaleidoscope of Impressionist color. Sweet relief.

Outside, hot dog and hot nut vendors had fired up their propane and opened their umbrellas, so Ian invited his wife to lunch on the town, sitting on the swept but frozen steps of the Met.

*

A college student was working the register as they entered the bookstore to retrieve the children.

"Hi, Fumiko," said Blair, "are the kids here?"

"They're in the basement helping Lizanne. Mike's in the back buying books."

As they passed through the aisles to the top of the cellar stairs, Mike called out over his shoulder, "How was the exhibit?"

"Curious," answered Blair.

"Curious good or curious bad?"

"Curious both," answered Ian.

When they entered the cellar, Lizanne was busy with a stack of invoices at her desk while the kids sat in chairs around the sorting table adjacent to the rat room. Fortunately, only Ian made that association. "How's it going?" he asked.

The kids looked up from their tally sheets and stacks of books. "We're doing great," answered Logan. "We've made good progress today."

The children had experienced a day of adult work. Conducting an inventory of hundreds of paperback books arranged alphabetically by publisher and author was tedious; yet, working from a master list of required basic stock, they could easily see that what they were doing was valued. Lizanne double-checked their results, publisher by publisher, and praised them for their precision. Rewards had included lunch at Chock full o'Nuts and a trip to Mondel's for dark chocolate truffles.

"How was your trip to the museum?" Lizanne inquired.

"Good. A nice little outing."

"We have accomplished a lot," Max burst in, "and have finished the inventory for Ace, Anchor, Avon, Bantam, Ballantine, Dover, Free Press, and Grosset, and we have almost finished with Grove; but there's much more to do."

"They have been wonderful," added Lizanne, "and have enabled me to get the invoices sorted out. Each June and December, we do a full inventory of all the books on the floor as well as the paperback overstock. It's a long process, but many hands make short work, and they performed like seasoned staff."

Blair walked to the sorting table and placed her hands on Logan's shoulders. "I'm glad to hear you have all been productive professionals," she said. Then, addressing her children, she added, "It's getting close to dinner time. I've got cooking to do, and Dad needs to walk the dogs. Will you be able to wrap this up soon?"

"We're nearly finished, Aunt Blair," said Spira. "Just another minute."

While the kids tallied Grove Press title by title and placed them back in the stacks, Lizanne and Blair confirmed the timing for the kid's expedition to mid-town with Samantha McFarlane.

Later, while Ian walked the dogs and the marinara sauce simmered on the stove, Blair called Sarah Reinhart and arranged a call for eleven forty-five the following day.

Sarah asked how Ian was doing with the idea. "I think he's a bit frightened by it," Blair said, "but truthfully, so am I."

Plum walked to the awning and placed her hand on Lorcan's shoulders. "I'm glad to meet you. I have [illegible] professionally," she said. Then, addressing [illegible] Phillip, she added, "It's getting close to dinner time. I've [illegible] to do, and Dad needs to walk the dogs. [illegible] outside to wrap this up soon?"

"We'd really like to," Aunt [illegible] "[illegible] time."

While the kids [illegible] through the [illegible] Brock, [illegible] and Kamelle, and Plum [illegible] for the kids [illegible] Montana.

[illegible]

[illegible] thanked how [illegible] with [illegible]

-39-

On the Bus

Inexorably, the next day came and, with it, the Paris talk. However, the first order of business was to accompany the kids to the bookstore, pick up Spira, and send the group off on their adventure. After a leisurely breakfast, a dog walk, and a weather report, the children dressed for any off-road eventualities with Sam. Lizanne had double-checked the schedule for the 104 buses, and, as Broadway was now mostly clear of snow and ice, they expected an on-time arrival.

Both families gathered inside the entrance to the bookstore. Ian and Mike presented the kids with bus money, plus a little extra for emergencies, including loose change in case they needed to call home for any reason.

Samantha was to call the bookstore and Blair from a phone booth after the kids boarded the uptown bus so their parents could meet them at the 116th Street stop. A half-empty bus arrived on schedule; the kids got on and, kneeling side-by-side on their seats, waved goodbye to their parents as the bus pulled away from the curb.

Being an old hand at bus travel, Logan turned around in her seat and surveyed her fellow travelers. The 104 launched from 129th Street and Convent Avenue (the street name being the only vestige of a convent long gone), then traveled south to 125th Street, where it turned west for two long blocks, then south again down Broadway to

41st Street. Logan felt comfortable with its collection of humanity: a mix of ethnicities, ages, and genders from various regional haunts: Blacks and some Hispanics from "uptown," mainly sober-faced women, neatly dressed, carrying shopping bags, some empty, some not. A smattering of students from college row (Manhattan School of Music, Union Theological Seminary, Teachers College, Barnard and Columbia—all looking a bit unkempt) were buried in their textbooks or squeezing musical instrument cases between their knees. A brown-skinned woman sat immediately behind the driver, twin toddlers to her right and left, both surprisingly content. A big man in an army coat, wearing a hard hat and holding a lunch box on his lap, sat across from Logan, smiling at Max and Spira as they looked out the window, mesmerized. Broadway, below 110th Street, was a foreign country to Max and Spira—accessible only during chaperoned bike rides in Riverside Park, where access to Broadway came by the back door of 79th Street, and only then when on safari hoping to bag the odd bagel or bialy.

Logan enjoyed providing a back story for bus riders. In one scenario, the woman with twins was a Brazilian opera singer traveling to a rehearsal at Lincoln Center. Her governess had called in sick, so the children accompanied her to work. In another, a girl sitting in the back with long, black hair and a slim instrument case resting on her knees was a flute player returning from an audition at the music school. Judging from her expression, it had not gone well. What will she tell her parents? The man in the hard hat was en route to an unfinished skyscraper, where he would laze with fellow workers on iron girders a thousand feet above 6th Avenue, legs dangling, and eat a sandwich from his lunch box (she had once seen a photo of just such a scene).

From his perch at the window, Max was amazed and pleased that so many people walking on the sidewalks had dogs. There were canines of all sizes and breeds, most of which he knew immediately: a Pekinese, a poodle, a dachshund, two Jack Russell terriers, and even a brown-and-white Newfoundland that looked remarkably like a Giant Panda. There were so many people walking dogs that Max decided to try and predict the type of dog based on the appearance of the person walking it. He and his father had played this game with people not walking dogs, so this would be even more fun.

Max placed his hand against the window, shielding a dog from its walker—hitting the mark in his first attempt: a portly man with triple chins, dressed in a heavy winter coat and long woolen scarf, slid into view, arching his back and pulling on the leash as if reeling in a marlin. Max guessed his dog would be either a Shar-pei or a bulldog—hoping for the former but getting the latter. Unfortunately for Mister Triple Chins, the bulldog was on strike, sitting sidesaddle on the sidewalk, an immovable lump, apparently waiting for his companion to hail a cab or commandeer a baby carriage. Max laughed, but by the time he got Spira's attention, the bus had moved on, so Max continued his game with new players.

Still kneeling at her window on the other side of Logan, Spira was busy measuring and calculating—so many stores selling so many things: hardware, vacuums, clothes, appliances, shoes, wedding dresses, liquor, butchered meats, and fruits and vegetables. Squeezed between larger stores, slivers of truncated food counters with only three or four stools, sold pizza, while others offered items she had never tried: knishes, falafel, shawarma, blintzes. Above the stores were apartments—each building pressed against the next like slices of Swiss cheese; the only thing distinguishing one from another was the color of the brick, an additional floor, or a different decorative cornice. But where were the apartment doors, she wondered? How did people get in and out? Oh, there's a door. I see now: a dark notch, almost invisible between storefronts. Were there elevators, or did people trudge up five or six flights carrying babies with strollers, then race back for bags of groceries left inside the door? Did people like living above the honking horns and bus exhaust? Perhaps it was convenient if you needed a vacuum cleaner or a falafel. But were the stores too few or too many for people on the street and in the buildings? She was chewing it over as the scene sped by like a film running sideways.

Max and Spira elbowed Logan's shoulders at the same time. "There's Zabar's," they chimed.

"Only twenty blocks to go," answered the indifferent old pro of the 104.

Then, after another fifteen blocks, another nudge of elbows: "There's Lincoln Center."

Logan turned, looked, confirmed, and stood. "Get ready." She told her companions. "Two more blocks, and we get out. "

"Can I pull the cord?" asked Max.

"Sure, I'll tell you when."

Samantha McFarlane greeted them at the 63rd Street stop in full Doctor Zhivago regalia. In contrast, the children tumbled from the bus like a trio of Fagan's orphans come to pick her pockets.

-40-

Coming of Age

Eleven-thirty: witching hour. Blair dialed Sarah's number in Baltimore and held the phone sidewise to her ear so both she and Ian could hear.

Sarah answered, and a light-hearted catch-up commenced while Ian absently flipped through pages of the Neuilly school brochure.

Though Blair motioned to him many times to join in, Ian continued to browse the brochure. Finally, he spoke up and did his best to be interested and cordial, even humorous, and they got down to business. Blair thanked Sarah for sending the brochure and accompanying documents. Ian said the contracts were much the same as Parker's. He, too, had extra duties, as he ran an after-school writing club for high school students twice a week.

Blair asked about the nationalities of the staff and faculty. Sarah explained that all teachers were American, born and raised, except for the foreign language teachers. A Parisian taught French. Imports from across their respective borders taught German and Spanish. Americans taught intermediate and advanced English as a Second Language to those needing it, and some French locals worked as administrative and maintenance staff.

The headmistress, Madam Chevalier, was from Lyon and had been an administrator at an all-girls school there before the war.

In the initial establishment of the Neuilly school, only a French national could have dealt with the complexities of the town's bureaucracy and sophisticated Parisian families. Now in her early sixties, Madam Chevalier has been headmistress for over thirty years.

"You might not know," added Sarah, "Neuilly is primarily residential and is the wealthiest and most expensive suburb of Paris. As I recall, you are movie buffs, so it might be interesting to know that Jean-Paul Belmondo, Francois Truffaut, and Vittorio De Sica live in Neuilly. Jacques Prévert, too, but sadly, he died last year."

"Jacques Prévert?" questioned Blair. "The name is so familiar, but—"

"*Les Enfants du Paradis*, I'm sure you remember that beautiful tragedy."

"It is one of our favorite movies," piped up Ian, suddenly interested.

"I only mention it," continued Sarah, "to help give the flavor of the place. There are private homes, embassies, and an excellent American hospital."

"What about the academic background of the teaching staff?" asked Ian. "Are they fresh from university, or do some have former teaching experience?" He was finally getting down to his real concerns.

Sarah explained that of the forty-some-odd teachers, most held university diplomas, and of those, nearly half had master's degrees. But there were also those without formal university backgrounds who had professional abilities in specialized fields: art, music, drama, microcomputers, sports. Some of the latter were part-time locals, providing extension classes for students needing to stay until late afternoon.

"Attrition is glacial," she said, "and many teachers have been there for more than ten years. Faculty openings are rare."

"The board of directors stresses the employment of Americans for most teaching positions," said Sarah, attempting to allay Ian's concerns, "although there is some talk about becoming more diverse. Of the students, half are American, with the rest coming from more than fifteen countries. Many of their parents have diplomatic jobs or work for international companies, so they are generally an interesting lot."

Ian continued to press. "You said that the foreign language teachers are not Americans, so I am presuming they are native speakers?"

"Yes."

"Then why would NIS want to hire a white American to teach Chinese?"

The conversation had finally reached the bedrock of Ian's concerns. Blair flushed as she realized she had failed to let her husband fully air his hesitance. His argument was valid, and she should have thought of it.

"That is a good question," answered Sarah, "and I asked Madam Chevalier about it. It concerns current politics: French, American, Chinese, and a cold war mentality among the American board members. Frankly, I don't know all the ins and outs of the board's politics. Still, NIS is an American international school and wants to reflect American culture and values by hiring US nationals.

"You and Blair bring much to the table that others would not. Some American-born Chinese may apply for this position, but I doubt any would equal your experience. Furthermore, as your role would include teaching Asian history, you are uniquely qualified. Both you and Blair are talented and practiced in what you do, and I hope you will consider sending in your CVs."

Curricula Vitae thought Blair, I have not written one since graduating college. Bragging without bragging. My last effort required only academic accomplishments; now, they expect me to create something riveting from fifteen years as a departmental secretary. No rockets going off here. Ian's CV is dynamic, with years of teaching Chinese and Asian history. He built Parker's Asian program from scratch and could do it again. He's a shoo-in. What if only one of us is wanted?

Blair asked for more clarification as to the academic pedigrees of the faculty and was pleased to hear there were only three from Ivy League schools. Perhaps that would weigh in their favor. Ian asked if anyone was teaching creative writing, as he enjoyed doing this at Parker. Over the last few years, he had repeatedly started and stopped writing a novel about China during the Japanese occupation of Shanghai. He considered writing to be a hobby, but he'd like to devote more time to it.

"At present there is no one teaching creative writing," she said.

Sarah introduced one last subject for consideration but was unsure if it might be disquieting. Teachers, she said, were not micromanaged. On the contrary, NIS prided itself on giving teachers the latitude to innovate and create their curriculum. Often students worked collaboratively or independently. Many classes were not lecture-based but were discussion groups led by students. It was rare to have a timed test. In history teaching, the influence of ideas was more important than the strict memorization of wars and their dates.

Both Ian and Blair were pleased to hear this. Ian felt that the teaching of high school history often consisted of a linear serving of dates, stressing conflicts and shifting borders rather than the ideas which shaped these events. He often strayed from strict historical chronology to introduce poems, readings from historical novels, and even films to help breathe life and humanity into the past. It was high school, and rather than provide his students with a glut of vacuous facts, Ian wanted to whet their appetites, not blunt their nascent interests. He felt he often walked a fine line with Parker's administrators, as more than once, the Dean of Studies had asked that he provide less improvision and pay more attention to historical timelines and the facts of their development.

Blair knew of this situation at Parker and would often offer Ian suggestions on how he might deal with any efforts to control his unique approach to teaching. But, despite management's concerns over Ian's unorthodox style, his classes were always full; students and parents sang his praises. Over the last decade, he inspired many of Parker's graduates to continue Oriental studies at university.

"This is music to my ears," said Ian.

"And to mine," said Blair.

"All right," said Sarah, happily closing the discussion. "Why don't you send me your CVs in the next day or two. If you send them special delivery on Tuesday, I will have them in time. I leave on January 6th and can take them with me."

The call ended with Blair and Ian agreeing to get them done and send them by fast mail.

After the call, Blair apologized to Ian for not having gotten to the bottom of his concerns and assured him that, as, and if, things moved forward, she would own his concerns as her own. Ian agreed not to be such a schlub.

*

The phone rang about four-thirty that afternoon. Samantha McFarlane checking in. Five minutes earlier, she had seen the kids off on the uptown 104. They would be arriving at 116th Street in twenty minutes. She reported that they had a great time together: first at Rumpelmayer's for lunch and a trio of "absolutely Byzantine sundaes," then Rockefeller Center for ice skating, and, finally, tea and a bit of relaxation in Sam's suite. Altogether, the kids were delightful and kept her laughing from start to stop.

Blair asked if Sam had plans for New Year's Eve. "Well, partially," she said. "Reggie knows I'm resourceful, but he didn't want me to get bored, so he bought me tickets to a matinee performance of a Eugene O'Neill revival at Lincoln Center, but I've no plans for the evening."

That being the case, they decided to spend it together uptown, dining on a menu of wine and pizza, and as Mike and his family were visiting Lizanne's parents in New Jersey for the evening, it would just be the five of them.

Immediately after the call, Ian assembled the dogs, and he and Blair set out across campus to meet the kids. Lizanne was waiting at the bus stop, drinking coffee, and smoking a cigarette. They greeted each other, messed with the dogs, and the 104 pulled up at the appointed time.

The kids bounced out and, speaking all at once, regaled their parents with the day's wonders. It had indeed been a success, with the unexpected highlight being Sam's suite at the Plaza.

"It was so cool," said Logan. "Aunt Sam's windows look out on Central Park. You can see pathways winding through the snow and trees and people walking their dogs. It looked like a painting."

"There were gold faucets in the bathroom," added Max.

"And the most comfortable chairs," said Spira. "I felt like taking a nap."

They continued to rhapsodize about the suite, then the glamor of ice skating beneath the colossal statue of Atlas. Rumpelmayer's, though magical, seemed to come in a surprising third.

"And the bus ride? How did that go?" asked Lizanne.

All agreed it went smooth as glass. Sam was there to greet them at 63rd Street and, later, saw them off as planned.

A productive day for one and all: the kids had ridden the bus without incident, and Blair and Ian had conducted themselves like grown-ups. Another page had turned in the lives of the downtown Kennedys.

-41-

Code Red

A breeze rustled through the palm fronds while soft waves fanned along the shoreline and frothed around his ankles. Surprised by his nakedness, Ian worried that someone might notice. Where were his clothes? Were those voices? Should he run into the sea or turn back among the palms? He tried to move, but wet sand mired his feet. It had started to rain.

The images faded as he pulled himself from sleep, and for a moment, his anxiety eased. Ian opened one eye, saw the silhouette of a large head, and felt a misty breath exhaling from a nose only inches from his own. Throwing aside the bedclothes, he leaped into his slippers and rushed to the foyer. Grabbing the leash from the rack, he fastened it with one hand and struggled into his coat with the other. The two dashed across the lobby—a trail of incontinence following them across the tiles into a deep freeze. Zato lifted his leg near a snowbank, arcing a stream toward his favorite tree, while his companion looked over the flats of Harlem for signs of dawn, but there were none.

Only then did Ian become aware that there was new snow on the sidewalk, some touching his ankles and dropping into his slippers. A few flakes, defying gravity, moved through the darkness like moths. He couldn't tell if this was the beginning or end of a snowfall, but he knew he was cold and his pajamas porous. It was time to go home.

Zato resisted the pull on the leash and jumped into deeper snow, straining toward Morningside Drive, but at this early hour, Ian had no tolerance for self-indulgent canines who couldn't tell time.

"No!" he commanded, yanking the leash hard. "Inside!" The dog lowered his ears, then his head, and complied.

*

"I gather Zato gave you some heavy breathing last night?" Blair said a few hours later while snuggling with Ian beneath the padded quilt.

"Yes, heavy and wet. Thoroughly unenjoyable."

"What time did you come to bed?"

"I'm not sure, maybe four or four-thirty. Zato must have been drinking from the toilet. Bagel had the good sense to play dead; she must have known it was snowing again."

"It's still snowing. Look out the window."

Ian rolled over and saw snowflakes drifting gently between buildings. Ordinarily, when tucked beneath the warmth of bedclothes, he found this sight welcome and calming, and, when outside, he loved to follow the slow turn of crystalline goose down until it rested on his glove like a fossil. But not today.

Woken from a sound sleep and an anxiety-producing dream, then racing against the tidal surge of an unbridled bladder—wearing only slippers, pajamas, and an unbuttoned coat—had chilled Ian's sense of winter aesthetics. Conversely, these urgent calls to nature only served to fan an already smoldering annoyance with Zato's many eccentricities.

"You know, I love that hairy beast," he said, "but I worry that one day he will drag me out in traffic on my back, or worse, swallow some old lady's Chihuahua like a sausage. I'm thinking of getting a muzzle for him to wear on walks, but I worry Duke's posse might decide to take him on, leaving him defenseless."

"I wish I could be more help," Blair responded sympathetically, "but I can barely handle lunchtime duties to the tree and back. I don't know what I'd do if you decided to go on walkabout."

"If I do, I'll take Zato with me. You'll be free at last."

-42-

Epiphany

After breakfast--followed by an uneventful dog walk and a game of Rummikub--the family donned their snowsuits. Then, leaving the dogs pining in the foyer, they trekked across campus in light snow for lunch at the West End Bar.

Since college, the West End Bar on Broadway had been a hangout for Ian and Blair. Early in their marriage—she a few months pregnant—they had even spent a couple of hours there during the '65 blackout, sitting in a booth, drinking beer, and eating fries by candlelight. Fortunately for beer drinkers, the taps ran on CO2, not electricity. As a result, it was one of their most romantic dates. So now, nearly fourteen years later, here they sat with two kids and two dogs, living two very comfortable New York lives.

Amid the din of the bar, Ian sipped his beer and looked at the kids as they tried talking to each other with mouths stuffed like squirrels: cheerful, bright faces, loving life with family, friends, and school—all here, in a neatly strung package, like a box of Ferrara's cannoli.

It's true, he thought. I traveled to Taiwan on a cloud. By chance, a Taiwanese clerk from the commie bookstore on 107th Street had given me the name, address, and phone number of one of his old professors. He wrote it on a notepad and suggested calling him when I landed. So, I did, and it worked out. Things just fell into place for the next two years and have fallen into place ever since.

"What are you thinking about?" asked Blair. "You look distracted."

"Remember being here in the blackout? Maybe this very booth. Candles everywhere, me drinking stout. I felt like I was living a chapter from *Tom Jones*. You, sitting across from me looking luscious, me feeling lucky."

Blair touched Ian's hand under the table. "Yes, I remember—people in the street, carrying candles and lanterns, greeting strangers like old friends. And you directing traffic on 110th Street with a candle in your hand."

"I took it from the bar to light our way home."

"And you guided me by the hand up five flights of pitch-black stairs."

"I've been thinking about Paris," said Ian softly, out of the kids' earshot. "After lunch, let's write our CVs and see what happens."

"O-kay," answered Blair pumping the breaks just a little. "I still have my keys to the building and the office, and I can format them tomorrow if we are happy with them."

"I think it's time we broached this subject with the kids," said Ian. "Maybe tomorrow, before Sam shows up."

"Sure," said Blair, uncertain of what else to say. Ian's sudden reversal of polarity had transposed everything. Across the table, the kids sat in their manicured world, playfully fighting over the last few fries, unconscious of the tectonic shifts moving the earth beneath their feet.

*

The family trudged back through the thickening snow. The kids had a snowball fight at the foot of Alma Mater, which inevitably involved their parents. The battle raged briefly, then eased as they approached Amsterdam Avenue. As no cars traveled in either direction, they stopped in the middle of the street and looked downhill. The Kennedys loved these fleeting winter moments, where everything was mute except the shush of falling snow. The contrast of the buildings and skeletal trees against the untraveled streets produced an antique, almost daguerreotype picture of New York. There was something spiritual about it—a city absolved of sin, at least for the day.

Max and Logan called the O'Reilly kids down from the third floor to join them for a snowball fight. There were four O'Reillys, but as two were "just squirts," Max declared the odds fair. With the kids thus occupied, Blair and Ian took to their legal pads and began gilding their lilies.

"Use declarative sentences," said Blair. "They should be unadorned, spare of adjectives. Pure Hemingway."

"The naked, rarified truth should give them nosebleeds," added Ian.

An hour later, with CVs completed, they examined each other's carefully worded bits of narcissism. Then, smiling, Blair placed Ian's CV on the coffee table and looked up.

"This is good," she said. "I'd hire you in an instant. But, at the risk of suffocating your new interest, may I ask what's caused this change of heart?"

"I was going to tell you earlier," said Ian, "but breakfast, dogs, and hamburgers got in the way. I had a kind of epiphany this morning when I was in the shower. The water was almost scalding, and rather than adjusting the faucets,

I simply changed my mind and decided the temperature was just right, and it was. It was merely a difference in consideration that changed pain to pleasure. I then thought about Paris, and my worries about starting over kicked up again: the kids, the dogs, money, family, success, or failure. It was like a mental Maginot Line, keeping me out of Paris. I'd constructed quite a fortification: cement walls backed by heavy artillery, but with only one soldier to defend the ramparts. So, I decided to change my mind again, and the barriers to Paris fell away, opening the playing field to an exciting new game. So, here I am, ready to play."

Blair had seen Ian change on a dime before. It didn't happen often, but when it did, it was startling. At first, he would appear trapped in the binds of cautious reasoning—stalled, immovable—then he'd suddenly break loose and change direction as if a Zen master had whacked him with a stick.

Blair looked puzzled but pleased. "Well, I don't know what to say."

Ian raised his eyebrows and looked at her expectantly; then, lifting his legal pad, he asked: "Can you get this typed up?"

There was bustling at the front door, barking and crashing of dogs against bicycles, and the noise of the kids taking off their coats and boots. Then, finally, they all tumbled into the living room, the kids raw and pink-cheeked, the dogs trying to engage them in play. Max immediately took up the narration, providing the blow-by-blow that had taken place on the battlefield in front of Butler Library. There were forays and retreats; ricochets and direct hits; it was touch and go; but finally, the last remaining warriors of the Kennedy clan filled their coat pockets with ammo and leaped bravely from the trenches amid a hail of enemy fire. According to General Max and his trusty aide-de-camp, the Kennedys prevailed over the O'Reillys, despite being heavily outnumbered.

After such a vigorous battle, it was apparent the troops needed sustenance, so Blair heated some cocoa and leftover macaroni and cheese. The kids plowed into their snacks like Zato at his kibble bowl. When their plates had been scraped as clean as mirrors, and they leaned back in their chairs fully sated, Ian suggested they settle in for a few chapters of *The Hobbit.*

"While you read to the kids," said Blair, "I have an errand to run. I'll be back in half an hour."

As Mom and the dogs retreated down the hallway, the kids happily took their places on the couch beside Ian, and the door to Middle-earth creaked open. Before long, Ian, Max, and Logan—together with Bilbo and the dwarfs—had left the comforts of Hobbit Hill to reclaim the kingdom of Erebor.

Blair bundled up for the trek across campus and slid the CVs into a slim briefcase. The dogs pleaded to accompany her—even Bagel had come to the door from her nest on the bed and put her front paws on Blair's leg. "Sorry, guys, this is a one-person mission. No dogs allowed." Then, carefully squeezing through the door, she made her escape.

The snow was lighter now, just a few meandering flakes. There was even some blue sky showing over New Jersey: a good omen for turning a leap of faith into an act of will.

-43-

Pazzo's

New Year's Eve day arrived without any unwanted assistance from over-hydrated dogs. The snow had stopped, and the clouds had scudded out to sea, leaving flawless indigo skies. The thermometer outside the kitchen window read ten degrees, assuring it would be arctic in Times Square that evening. Early in their marriage, Blair and Ian had reveled with the Times Square masses, but it was not something they wished to repeat. Watching Dick Clark bring in the new year on TV from their living room was good enough and certainly warm enough.

After breakfast, Blair called Sam to arrange the details for dinner. "The snowbanks are high in front of our apartment building, so have the cabbie drop you on Amsterdam and 116th. They should have salted the sidewalk by then."

"Don't worry," replied Sam. "I'll manage just fine. I believe the play gets out at four-thirty, so I should arrive around five o'clock."

"Perfect timing. We are having pizza for dinner," added Blair, somewhat apologetically. "Plain and simple. I hope you don't mind."

"I don't mind at all. Pizza is one of my many addictions."

"I'm afraid we'll have to reheat it," Blair said, "so we'll see how it goes. But I am also making a Greek salad and a chocolate *pot de crème* for dessert. Very decadent."

"The more wanton, the better," replied Sam. "Especially considering I forfeited my cannoli for the greater good. It fits in perfectly with my vacation diet."

"Okay then, we'll see you tonight."

Pizza was the promised repast to bring in the New Year; however, no one had thought through the likelihood that vendors might be home warming their hands over their radiators, not tending the fires of their pizza ovens. The urgency of the situation called for a volunteer. Ian stepped forward but could persuade no one to accompany him other than Zato. So, shortly after lunch, the two set forth onto the frozen plateau of Morningside Heights.

The air was frigid, and the sidewalks not yet shoveled. The plows were ringing their chains up and down Amsterdam Avenue. It wasn't exactly the nuance of a horse and carriage, but it was a pleasant sound during winter snows in the city. Ian thought V & T's Pizzeria might be open, just three blocks down Amsterdam. The pair crossed the street at St. John's Cathedral, but V&T's was closed, and the ice on the windows gave him pause.

They crossed 110th Street and walked to Broadway, where unknown philanthropists had cleared narrow pathways for pedestrians and small dogs.

Bigger dogs like Zato walked in the deep snow, closer to the street, so it was slow going and challenging, as Zato wanted to mush. Finally, at 106th Street, Ian spotted a small man opening the door to a slender, three-stool pizzeria called Pazzo's. Brother Mike was constantly interjecting Italian into English conversations, so Ian had long since mastered the art of translation through context, but in this case, without context, he nevertheless recognized the word: *pazzo* meant "crazy." Something to think about.

Ian paused before approaching the diminutive man who appeared to be readying his store for business on the second most unlikely day of the year.

"Good morning," said Ian. "Are you opening?"

The man wore a heavy winter coat, a wool hat pulled low over his ears, and a scarf wrapped around his neck and chin. He was unshaven, appeared well past fifty, and seemed shriveled inside his wrappings.

"Yes," he said gruffly, looking at Zato, then at Ian. "In half-hour. Come back then."

Ian thought waiting another ten minutes, much less thirty was not a good plan in this temperature. No coffee shops were open; if they were, none would allow a dog inside. But, of course, he could always hook Zato to a parking meter and keep an eye on him.

"I've just walked from 116th Street, and nothing's open," said Ian. "You seem to be the only one in New York who has dared to brave the elements."

The man keyed a padlock and raised the roller shutter covering the store window, then another covering the doorway.

"Would you mind if I came in and waited?" asked Ian.

"OK, but leave the dog outside."

Ian stepped through the berm at the edge of the sidewalk, looked up and down Broadway for dog walkers, and, seeing none, looped Zato's leash around a parking meter and went inside the pizzeria to get warm and to wait. Zato stood by the meter, looking through the door pane at Ian.

The chef, or pizzaiolo, had removed his coat and boots but retained his wool hat. He now wore a clean apron over a sleeveless T-shirt. He was slightly hunched but built like a welterweight, all muscle and sinew.

The gauges on the two gas ovens showed they were still hot from the day before. Ian wondered if they retained heat or were left on a low flame overnight. However, starting a conversation about the vagaries of gas ovens seemed an unlikely icebreaker.

The chef dialed up the heat and asked for Ian's order: one extra-large New York pie (just cheese) and one extra-large three-cheese with pepperoni and black olives. "Extra-large" guaranteed a pie of eight slices, eighteen to twenty inches across. These two pies should easily provide for the night's dinner and possibly lunch the next day.

The chef washed his hands and pulled two large dough balls from a refrigerator in the back. Setting one aside, he sprinkled cornmeal on a marble slab and more on a large pizza peel and got to work.

Ian watched silently as bony, veined hands worked the dough over the marble. His left hand provided a wall, against which he flattened the dough with his right. Then, continually turning and pressing with outstretched fingers, he formed a rim or cornice in a circle that widened with each turn.

After flipping the dough from palm to palm several times, he tucked his hands under it, making a fist of his left and an open palm of his right; then, twisting his body inward like a discus thrower, he unwound and spun the pie into the air with both hands. It rose above them like a harvest moon. The pizzaiolo caught it the same way he had released it and threw it repeatedly until satisfied with its size and shape. Finally, he eased it onto a wooden pizza peel sprinkled with cornmeal, then ladled on the marinara sauce and placed mozzarella around the pie, adding a few strategically placed drops of olive oil.

At last, he looked at Ian but said only: "The oven ain't ready." So, he put that pizza aside and began work on the next.

No word was spoken until he had thrown the second pizza, ladled the marinara sauce, added the cheese, and artfully arranged the olives and pepperoni.

"Oven's ready now," he said; "Eight minutes."

Ian stood transfixed by the performance and, for a few minutes, watched the pizzaiolo shifting the pies in the oven and checking the temperature until he realized he had forgotten about Zato. Looking out the window, he saw the dog straining at his leash, running around the parking meter in circles. Ian told the chef he'd be right back and rushed out the door.

A stray moved up Broadway, sniffing along the sidewalk's narrow path. Zato was did to spring loose from his collars, but they held firm as he circled the meter, making a trough in the snow. Ian realized the stray had spotted Zato as it shifted from idle sniffing to a trot. Quickly, Ian lifted the leash over the meter and considered his alternatives, but there was only one safe solution. He pulled Zato from the berm and dragged him across the icy path into Pazzo's.

"No dogs! No dogs!" shouted the pizza man.

"There's a stray off the leash out there," said Ian pulling Zato tight against his thigh. I'll take him out as soon as it's gone."

Zato was straining at his leash and growling when the stray stopped in front of the pizzeria.

"I don't want no dogs in here!" shouted the pizzaiolo. "People eat here. It's against the law."

The stray approached, looked through the glass door, and bared its teeth. It was a mixed breed of no apparent pedigree. It stood about the same height as Zato but was far leaner, with ribs showing. Its coat was dirty and mottled, but its teeth looked quite serviceable. Ian pulled Zato further back into the shop, next to a door.

"Is that a bathroom?" he asked.

"It ain't public," replied the man.

Ian opened the door and put Zato inside. "I'm sorry," he said. "It's better if they can't see each other."

As the stray continued to look through the window, growling and showing his teeth, the pizza man grabbed a broom from a corner and came around the counter. He opened the door and swung at the stray, who jumped back. After another swing, the dog sped off toward 106th Street. The man paused to ensure the dog was not coming back, then returned to his shop and placed the broom in the corner.

"Sit down," he said. "Five minutes."

He then took two large pizza boxes from above the oven and readied them for the pies, saying nothing more about the lamentations from the bathroom.

The pies came bubbling from the oven, and the chef cut them into slices, placing them into extra-large boxes. Ian realized that the cartons were more extensive than the pies they housed and carrying them ten blocks home while tied to a straining Zato would be challenging.

"Sixteen," said the pizza man.

Ian looked surprised. "The sign says two extra-large are fourteen."

Pointing to another sign to the bathroom's right, the pizza man said, "That sign says, 'No Dogs.' So, sixteen."

Mumbling a half-hearted apology, Ian paid for the pizzas and retrieved Zato from the bathroom. Then pushing the loop of the leash over his coat sleeve to his elbow, he lifted the pizza boxes with two hands, carrying them like a cigarette girl.

The chef opened the door for them, and, as they stepped into the cold, he shrugged, "Like I said, no dogs." Then he flipped the sign on the door from Closed to Open.

The trip home was uphill and with Amsterdam's sidewalks still deep with snow and Zato continually pulling him off course, Ian had a couple of falls, but he treated the pizzas like fine china—the boxes never touching the ground. Finally, at home, still wearing his gloves, boots, and heavy coat, he placed the pizzas on the kitchen counter. Blair was at the sink washing dishes and, failing to notice the condition of her man, asked him why it had taken so long.

Restraining himself from making an indelicate comment, Ian said only, "Traffic."

-44-

Pandora's Box

As Ian retreated down the hall, pulling off his coat and hat, Blair realized she should have thanked him for braving the elements. Putting the dishes aside, she followed and found him sitting at the foot of their bed, changing his socks, which were wet with snow.

"We should have planned better," he said, shaking caked snow onto the bedroom rug.

Ian had considered not mentioning the incident with the menacing stray, as Zato's rap sheet was already long, but he thought it best, given the direction things were heading with the dog, that she had all the details.

"Just finding an open pizzeria in Siberia was quite a trial in itself," he said, "but throw in a run-in with a stray and a shakedown from the pizza man and you have all the ingredients for an epic but unpleasant story." Ian went on to provide her with the blow-by-blow.

Blair sat beside her husband, hearing him out, and, with warm hands, turned his chapped face toward hers. "Your face is frozen. I'm sorry you had to pick up the slack. Let me make you some coffee or pour you a whisky if you'd prefer."

"Yes, whisky. Two inches, no ice. That will help."

After providing her champion with a draft of Jim Beam, she rewarded him further with his favorite comfort food: peanut butter and jelly on white bread and a bowl of Campbell's chicken noodle soup.

As Ian slurped the last few noodles from his bowl, Blair could see his feathers had settled, so she asked if it was a good time to talk to the kids about Paris as they had planned.

"Yes, let's do it," he responded. "We'll keep it low-key, stressing that this move is far from certain."

The kids trooped into the living room and sat down, waiting uneasily for the conversation to begin. The school brochure lay closed on the coffee table.

Blair began by telling them about the letter from Sarah Reinhart, the job openings at the Paris school, and Sarah's recommendation that they apply for the positions.

Immediately, the kids interrupted with questions and comments.

"Will we go forever?" asked Max.

"Then I wouldn't go to Stuyvesant?" anguished Logan.

"What about Spira, Uncle Mike, and Aunt Lizanne?"

"I don't speak French."

"What kind of school is it?"

"I'll miss my friends."

On and on, with each question answered in caring detail. Then came the inevitable.

"What about the dogs?" asked Max.

Ian explained that dogs were allowed. "Just like here," he said, feeling like he was skating onto thin ice.

They walked the kids through the school brochure, which they all agreed was impressive. Blair talked about the various plusses of living in Europe, especially in Paris, how they could travel and easily visit many other countries, make new friends, and best of all, be together in the same school.

"Would we ever come home—to America?" asked Max.

"Of course, dear," said Blair. "We could visit our relatives, and you could see your friends. We might even have them visit us."

"Yes, but if we came back here to visit, who would take care of the dogs?"

"We would work it out, Max," answered Ian. "Friends or even a kennel for a week or two. We did that for a few days with Bagel when we went to D. C. and Williamsburg—remember?"

Afterward, the kids retreated to their rooms—emotions and worries in a swirl. Logan fretted over friends and the possible loss of Stuyvesant, while Max thought about snowball fights with the O'Reillys, biking with his family in Riverside Park, and getting bagels at Zabar's. Then there was the Columbia campus with all the locations that fixed his world as solidly as the caissons that anchored the Brooklyn Bridge. It was like a picture on a puzzle box that had collapsed into a jumble of disconnected pieces.

*

Sam arrived as expected, a little before five. While she stood outside the apartment adjusting her hat and coat, the dogs must have heard the rustle of mink as they rushed down the hallway to see what exotic animal had arrived at the door. Before sounding the bell, the door opened--the children and dogs were there to welcome her.

Logan held Zato back, and Max called to his parents. "Aunt Sam is here!"

Blair and Ian arrived to take her coat and hat and escort her to the living room. Sam had been to their apartment before but still marveled at its abundance of space. It was at least one-third larger than her ground-level duplex in Hempstead. Even the refrigerator and stove were twice the size of those in her home. She had almost forgotten how "exponential" everything was in America.

"The kids got off the bus in a tizzy yesterday," said Blair. "Like they had seen a troop of Oompa Loompas walking down 5th Avenue. Truly, you spoiled them."

"Well, what are Aunties for if not to pave the streets with Curly Wurlies and Maltesers?" she said, affecting a strong British accent.

Blair presumed these were delicacies sold only along the cobbled streets of Dickensville by the Thames.

Sam passed Blair a shopping bag containing two bottles of wine, then settled into a living room chair while Max and Logan extolled the wonders of the previous day. The pictures they painted were larger than life, and Sam was pleased they had enjoyed it so much.

While the pizzas warmed in the oven and Ian took the dogs outside for a brief but necessary walk. Blair invited Sam to join her in the kitchen to help with the salad.

"How is the Paris idea coming along?" Sam whispered conspiratorially.

"There has been a breakthrough," Blair responded. "Ian has come around; he even initiated a talk with the kids. We made it clear that it could all go nowhere, but it's rough on them, especially Max. Still, we're moving forward and have written our resumés to send off on Tuesday by fast mail."

"That sounds like progress. But how are *you* doing on it? Are you still willing to pull up stakes and take the plunge?"

"I admit I'm scared of so much change," confided Blair, "especially for the kids. But, if the school feels we are the right choice, I think it will be good for all of us. You know, Ian created a curriculum from scratch at Parker. So he won't need to reinvent the wheel. He'll fit right in, and my job sounds quite like what I have been doing for almost fifteen years."

"If you think it would help," said Sam, "I could talk to the kids about my experience—leaving everything behind and traveling alone to London to find work, barely out of my teens, and how it turned out for me."

"If you can make it sound like I didn't send you to talk to them, I think it could be helpful. The kids love you."

"Good. I'll find a way to be discreet."

-45-

Damage Control

The dinner table was minimalist with everyday cutlery, paper cups for the beer and Cokes, and paper plates for the main course. Blair dished out the salad and placed the pizzas on the table, still in their cardboard boxes.

"I thought beer might go best with pizza," explained Ian while punching open a Rheingold and pouring it into Sam's cup. "We can save the wine you brought for properly bringing in the New Year."

They agreed that was a good plan and serious eating began.

Wiping marinara sauce from her mouth, Blair asked, "What was the play you saw earlier today? Some Eugene O'Neil, right?"

"Long Day's Journey—and a long day it was," answered Sam. "It's a day in the life of depressed, self-absorbed family members that argue constantly but who seem to love each other despite insufferable flaws and addictions to booze or morphine."

"Well, Happy New Year!" said Ian raising his paper cup in ironic good cheer. "May we all be granted immunity from depressing lives!"

Together they raised their cups of beer and soda, followed by cheers of "Hear, hear!"

While the pizza and salad disappeared amid grunts of satisfaction, Ian regaled his family and guest with the story of the afternoon's pizza expedition. Although the tale necessitated no embellishments, Ian couldn't help but drop the temperature below zero and ascribe to himself the heroic attributes of Antarctic explorer Ernest Shackleton rescuing the frozen crew of the ship *Endurance*.

Ending his story with a flourish, he said:

"Fraught with the perils of ice and snow, my faithful companion and I braved the elements. We pushed on despite the howling of angry curs, the extortion exacted by a grizzled Mafioso, and crosswinds that threatened to carry the pizzas to the rooftops—all to bring sustenance to the beleaguered troops of 116th Street—struggling uphill both ways."

"You are our hero, Daddy," said Logan.

"A true Olympian!" added Sam.

"A colossus!" said Blair.

"A mahatma!" cried Max, causing the hurrahs to stop in surprise and Ian to ask: "Where did that one come from?"

"From Mahatma Gandhi, the 'great soul.' You know about him."

"We do indeed," said Ian, giving Max a respectful nod.

While the children cleared the table, Blair removed five ramekins and a bowl of whipped cream from the refrigerator. She plumped a dollop of perfectly whipped, slightly sweet cream on top of each dessert and carried them on a tray to the table, along with five small spoons.

"We have the French to thank for many things," said Blair, pausing her spoon above her ramekin, "there are the grand architectural achievements like the Eiffel Tower, the Louvre, Versailles, and Notre Dame, to name a few; there are scores of French artists, writers, composers, and filmmakers who have beautified the world with the fruits of their imaginations, and restaurants with chefs famous for the subtleties of their cuisine, but in my opinion, it is the simple foods that are their transcendent contributions to the good life: pommes frites, a panoply of cheeses, onion soup, foie gras, croissants, crepes, baguettes, and this little pot of velvet, the *pot de crème*. But much as I would like to include French toast, it is not French but rather the creation of an American innkeeper by that name."

The kids seemed somewhat bewildered by this flowery homage to a pudding, but Sam and Ian laughed heartily.

"I hope you enjoy it," continued Blair, "the recipe comes from the Belgian mother of my college roommate. I believe it goes with anything, even pizza. *Bon Appétit*!"

After dessert, Max suggested playing a game while watching crazy people on TV try to keep warm in Times Square.

"We have all kinds of games, Aunt Sam," said Logan. "Why don't you come and choose one?"

All agreed that a game would be fun because it was still early in the evening. "So long as it's not Monopoly," said Ian.

The kids, dogs, and Sam went down the hall to Max's room, where board games were stacked on his closet floor. Logan, Sam, and the dogs sat on the bed while Max set the boxes on the rug.

"Well," he said, pointing to each box in turn, "I have Risk, Stratego, Battleship, Clue, Parcheesi, Sorry, and playing cards. Logan has Rummikub. Of course, we also have Monopoly," he added, flashing his eyebrows in the manner of Groucho.

"Ah," said Sam, "but much as I'd like to see you and Logan bankrupt and in jail, I think we'd best choose another. I like Parcheesi, and I enjoy playing Gin Rummy. Is Rummykub something like that?"

"I think it is," said Logan, "but it only allows four players. It's the same with Parcheesi, and there are five of us. But Clue can take six."

"Okay then, how about we play Clue?"

The kids agreed that Clue would be fun, and Max began sorting through its pieces to be sure the box contained all the necessary murder weapons.

"I understand your parents are considering a pretty big change," Samantha said cautiously. "What do you think?"

The children answered simultaneously: Max, in protest, with Logan slightly less adamant in expressing her disagreements.

"I can understand this is a lot to swallow," said Sam. "Tell me, Max, what is your main concern? A new school? New country? French? Friends?"

"I like it here," he said plaintively. "Everything I like is here. Our apartment, my school, friends, Spira, Uncle Mike and Aunt Lizanne. New York is home."

Max wiped a tear from his cheek.

"Of course it is," said Sam compassionately. "You have lived here all your life. You know what's coming tomorrow, the next day, and the next."

"Logan, how about you? What are your concerns?"

"Similar to Max, I guess. New York is home for me, too. I love it here. I hope to go to Stuyvesant for high school in September, and I've been looking forward to it for months."

"I understand. You have your immediate future mapped out. All the bricks are in place. Your road is clear."

The kids nodded in anxious agreement.

"Is there anything you like about the idea? A new country? Paris? Seeing Europe?"

Max shook his head. Logan looked away thoughtfully, then said, "I have always wanted to *visit* Paris. I've had French class for almost four years, starting in fifth grade. I love the language, and sometimes Mom and I will speak it together; she is super good at it. I want to visit the impressionist museum and the Louvre." Then, after a short pause, she added, "But I could never eat snails."

Sam laughed. "Did you know that I grew up in Connecticut? I lived in the same house for eighteen years until I went to college a couple hours' drive from Boston. Before that, my only travels were visiting relatives in Rhode Island and summer camp in New Hampshire. Beyond that, I'd only traveled through books.

"But then, in college, I was introduced to British writers and poets. I studied English history with its 1200 years of kings and queens and fell in love with the country and its literature. I even had a crush on Winston Churchill. Do you know who he is?" Both the kids nodded yes.

"He was eighty years old and married for almost fifty years when I landed at London airport. So, there was little hope for me, a child from Connecticut!" She laughed to make sure the kids knew she was joking.

"But what do you think I did then, Max? Just twenty and having completed only two years of college?"

"Did you run away from home?" he asked.

"Good guess, but not exactly. I found a summer job in London through my college and served as an apprentice in a travel agency specializing in tours of Great Britain, mainly England and Scotland. So, I set off alone, never having traveled outside New England. My parents gave me airfare and five-hundred dollars, and the agency gave me the use of a one-bedroom apartment. It was a four-story walk-up, and I worked six days a week for almost nothing."

"Weren't you scared to be alone in a new place without your parents or friends?" asked Logan.

"Of course I was," Sam answered gently. "But it was thrilling at the same time. Everything was new to me, though, in fact, the environment was often quite old. There was history everywhere, from Buckingham Palace to the Parliament buildings to Big Ben chiming on the hour with a bell weighing thirteen tons."

She paused momentarily and looked at Max. "That's twelve times the weight of the Liberty Bell. You can hear it all over London. It would be like ringing it in Times Square and hearing it through your bedroom window."

The children were following her story attentively, so she continued. "I'm sure if I'd had my parents with me, it would have been much easier, but I wanted to challenge myself, to see if I could handle living on my own, somewhere completely new. So, I made friends at work and with young people at the local pub. They all helped me to get used to living in London. It was a kind of game for me. I'd explore the city by bus and walk the streets using maps on my days off. It was great fun.

"By summer's end, the agency had offered me a full-time job, and within a year, I was a London guide on an open-top tour bus."

Raising her chin and throwing back her shoulders, Sam placed the fist of her right hand before her mouth as if it were a microphone and, adopting a posh London accent, said, "On your left is the infamous Tower of London or the White Tower. It was built in 1078 by William the Conqueror and was long resented as a symbol of oppression inflicted upon Londoners by the Norman invaders. It served as a prison from the 11th century until 1952."

She dropped her imaginary mic, and they all laughed. "I can still recite it, word for word, from Marble Arch to Victoria Station."

"Was it fun doing that," asked Max, "being a tour guide on the bus?"

"I loved it, except when it rained or on bitter-cold winter days, but even that was part of the fun."

"Did you ever go home and back to college?" asked Logan.

"I went home, of course, but only to settle things with my family. Fortunately, they supported my decision to take the job in London, and, as time went on, I became a British citizen. Formal college ended then, although I took courses at a London university on and off for years."

"So, you aren't an American anymore?" asked Max, worried that her conversion had taken away something sacred.

"I've always considered myself an American, Max, born and raised. But as I had decided to live and work in England, I wanted to have all the rights and responsibilities of a citizen, so I thought it best to apply for British citizenship."

"Do you travel much, Aunt Sam?" asked Logan.

"All the time, both for business and fun. Of course, I come back to the States a few times each year to see my parents and meet with clients and friends, but my business takes me all over. In addition to England and America, I have clients in Germany, France, and Italy. And, for fun, I have traveled to almost every country in Western Europe, and, of course, I could easily visit you if you were in Paris. I know Paris almost as well as I know London."

It looked like the right moment to end the conversation, so Sam suggested they take the board game into the living room and find out who killed whom with what and where.

-46-

Popcorn, Paris, Cats & Dogs

As the evening progressed, Blair made popcorn, and Ian opened a bottle of Sam's wine, pouring it into fresh paper cups. While at the game board, various false accusations were made, including one by Ian, who, affecting a rather poor Belgian accent, declared in the manner of Hercule Poirot, "There are some who call me the greatest detective of all time, a description with which I find it difficult to quarrel. The murderer is Miss Scarlet in the kitchen with a lead pipe." [In the 1970 version of the game—Miss Scarlett was an Asian *femme fatal*, hence Ian's particular but fatally flawed deduction.]

The game concluded with Blair delivering an eloquent summation of all the clues leading to her well-reasoned and accurate accusation. Thus, with the murder solved, the kids moved their chairs and popcorn closer to the T.V. to watch Dick Clark marvel at the crowds in Times Square and count down the hours and minutes until midnight.

Ian moved the wingback chair closer to the coffee table while Blair and Sam made themselves comfortable at either end of the couch. Bagel assumed her usual place on Blair's lap while Zato, following suit, attempted the same maneuver with Sam.

"Zato, get down!" commanded Blair, giving him a rap on the haunches.

"It's okay, I don't mind," said Sam.

"He's not allowed on the furniture, and he knows it," said Blair. "He's always trying his luck with guests."

Zato decamped but remained stationed between the coffee table and the couch, placing his chin on Sam's knee, gratefully accepting a scratch behind his ears. "It seems unfair to provide Bagel with lap privileges while confining Zato to the floor," said Sam in a haughty English accent.

Ian immediately picked up the gauntlet. "We have worked incessantly, if unsuccessfully, to ingrain in the kids and the dogs the motto 'Life is unfair, so get over it!' A lesson Zato seems incapable of understanding."

Sam smiled and ruffled the dog's ears. "Poor boy," she said. "I love dogs, but fundamentally, I am a cat person. I have two Siamese at home, Nefertiti and Bastet. They are brilliant and entirely self-sufficient. I'm sure you know the ancient Egyptians worshiped cats. Bastet, the cat goddess, was the daughter of Ra and Isis. It's like being a Kennedy; I mean, of course, the Jack and Jackie variety."

"I would submit that dogs have more to offer than cats," rebutted Ian. "Dogs are respected for their observable abilities, not worshiped for some vaporous virtue. Unlike the cat, which offers no utilitarian function, many canines provide valued services: shepherds depend on their talents to keep sheep from straying; hunters value the retriever, bloodhound and beagle for their olfactory skills; just as Italian and French chefs rely on the nose of a certain dog to locate the truffles used to amplify the flavor of pasta and soup. Peoples from the Arctic to the tropics appreciate canines of all shapes and sizes for their affinity, empathy, and bold devotion to their adoptive family members. These are material powers, born not of myth and superstition but from everyday life."

"I can see some modicum of truth there," responded Sam in kind, "but all of that is created from a dependence, if not outright subservience to man, whereas cats can fend for themselves, surviving on rodents and birds. They were not domesticated until the 7th century B.C., whereas the dog was doing man's bidding thousands of years before that. Cats come when called, only if they feel like it, and, usually, they don't. They don't chase balls or sticks for hours on end, and they will leave home for days or weeks, having adventures we can only imagine."

"I don't disagree that a cat has many laudable attributes," said Ian, continuing the argument, "but a dog is man's best friend not because he will purr on your lap or bring home donations of half-devoured fauna, but because he will give succor if you are sad and protect you if attacked. He contributes to family life with affection and a spirit of play; he understands English, French, even Japanese, and stars in dozens of movies. You may recall his roles in Rin Tin Tin and Lassie, where a dog saves the day repeatedly. Sargent Preston of the Mounties had his trusty dog King, who sniffed out criminals and protected children from wild animals in the Yukon. However, you can look high and low and find nary a heroic tale of a cat—if anything, they are the antagonist in the story: two cases in point: there's Tom and Jerry, not to mention Sylvester and Tweety Bird. No one is rooting for the cat!"

Even the children laughed at this exchange; a clear indication that they'd lost interest in Dick Clark's New Year's show.

Soon afterward, the children retired to Max's room to play Parcheesi. But, before abandoning the TV to the adults, Max had to agree not to hold blockades for more than two minutes, as this habit of his tended to stop the game's flow to the extreme irritation of opponents.

Now left to their popcorn, wine, and the drone from Times Square, the adults turned from the high drama of cats and dogs to the low comedy of American and British politics. Sam was hoping for a Thatcher victory in the May elections, while Ian and Blair were holding out for the reincarnation of Gandhi to shepherd the United States.

Inevitably the conversation turned to Paris, and Sam recounted her chat with the kids, describing their reactions in full. There was no earth-shattering revelation, but Blair and Ian were thankful Sam had broached the subject with the kids and that she had put some positive perspective on it.

Ian opened the second bottle of wine.

When Blair began to talk of what it might be like to live and work in Paris, Sam offered some surprising context to their prospective living environment.

"I have been to Auteuil a few times," she said. "This past June, Reggie and I had a few glasses of wine courtside at Roland-Garros when Bjorn Borg defeated Guillermo Vilas, and the June before that, I saw Vilas destroy Jimmy Conners in just three sets. I love tennis, and Roland-Garros is in Auteuil. It's in a section of Paris called Passy-Auteuil, which, along with Neuilly, is among the most expensive areas in the city to live. So, you, my friends, have lucked out."

She described Auteuil as sedate but quaint, tucked away like a bun in a breadbasket, adding it had been a country retreat for the ruling class during the 18th century. But when she said it was the birthplace of Marcel Proust and Baudelaire and the former home of Victor Hugo and Molière, Blair sighed audibly.

"It is not an area famous for shops or restaurants," Sam added, "but it is safe and has all the amenities you need for daily life. In addition, it is an easy walk to a beautiful botanical garden and many other attractions of the *Bois de Boulogne*."

As the hour moved closer to midnight, the kids returned for more popcorn and gathered around the TV with the family to watch the last thirty minutes of 1978 drain through the narrows of the hourglass.

In a manner to which the family had become accustomed, Ian offered some historical context to Dick Clark's New Year's show: "That ball of lights is the second or third version to descend the flagpole," he said, "but before establishing this tradition in Times Square to bring in the new year, it was literally rung in by the bells of Trinity Church."

Addressing the kids, he said, "I don't know if you remember, but we made a 'never-before' trip to Wall Street a couple of years ago and visited that church."

The kids nodded solemnly, expecting a repeat of an already ingested historical monologue.

"Two Trinity churches had either burned down or collapsed near that spot," said Ian, ignoring the leaden stares of the kids, "so another was built nearby on Broadway, just a block from Wall Street. In 1846 it opened its doors, but unlike any other church of its day, Trinity's bells spanned a full octave allowing a skilled bell ringer to chime well-known hymns or even *Yankee Doodle Dandy*. Over the following decades, people came from as far away as New Jersey and Connecticut to ring out the old and ring in the new. As time went on, crowds amped up the excitement by blowing tin horns sold in the streets, and it got quite raucous."

As if on cue, Max asked with surprising interest, "So, when did it start being held in Times Square?"

"I'm glad you asked, my dear Max. In 1904 the newly built offices of the *New York Times* opened at Number One Times Square. Curiously, its owner celebrated its opening its opening and the new year by igniting dynamite from the building's roof. This explosive celebration and its rain of smoldering embers continued for a couple of years until banned by the police. Thus began the tradition of dropping a ball of electrified lights."

"How do you know this stuff?" asked Sam, shaking her head in disbelief.

"As punishment for many incidents of bad behavior as a boy," responded Ian, "I was confined to my room with only a child's encyclopedia and my dad's stack of pre-war copies of *Popular Mechanics* for entertainment. Max seems to have inherited my interest in useful trivia without the need for involuntary confinement," he concluded, winking at Max.

Minutes later, the ball dropped, and the room erupted in cheers of "Happy New Year!" Logan beat a small drum; Max blew a kazoo; Zato sat up and howled.

Ian raised his paper cup. "Here's to a new year filled with just enough adventure and more than enough happiness and joy!"

"Hear, hear! Hear, hear!"

-47-

Unjust Deserts

When the last of the confetti had fallen into Times Square and the crowd was beginning to thin, it was time for Sam to return to her plush carpets and her 800 thread-count sheets. The family, plus dogs, would accompany her across campus to Broadway as, at this hour, there was a better chance of catching a cab there than on Amsterdam.

All donned their heavy coats, boots, hats, and gloves, with Bagel particularly fashionable in a new Christmas sweater. As they exited the building, Zato raced to the edge of the snowbank to relieve himself while his admirers patiently waited in the still, frigid air until waiting in the still, frigid air until he finished and jumped into the deep snow.

"Let me walk him for a bit," Sam said to Ian as they started moving toward the campus. "He's up to his chest in snow, so he's not rushing off to Alaska."

"It's not a good idea, Sam. He can easily pull you right off your feet."

"Just to the end of the block," she pleaded. "I'll give you the reins before he hits dry land."

Ian reluctantly agreed and passed Sam the lead. "I'll be right beside you," he said, "so, if he starts pulling too hard, just hand him over."

The group walked together over the well-salted sidewalk, chatting amiably and remarking on the snow-laden beauty of the campus ahead. Zato was making easy bounds through the snowbank but was gradually increasing his pace.

"Okay, Sam, pass me the leash. He's getting a little too energetic."

As Ian reached over to take the dog's lead, Zato sprang forward, increasing the length of his leap, jerking Sam's hand out in front of her. She tried to keep up while pulling back on the leash but was no match for the dog's acceleration.

"Don't let go!" yelled Ian, trotting beside her.

He lunged for the leash just as Sam lost her footing, released her grip and pitched forward into the snow. Sensing the absence of tension on his collar, Zato pushed on with increased effort and bounding from the piled snow, raced across Amsterdam Avenue onto College Walk, heading full speed across campus.

Hastily, Ian helped Sam to her feet.

"Are you okay?" he asked, brushing snow from her errant hat and handing it to her.

"I'm so sorry," she said, "I lost my footing, and he pulled the leash right out of my hand."

"I know; it's my fault," said Ian, speaking quickly. "It's happened to me, too. But, if you are okay, we need to get after him before he runs into the subway or gets into a fight with other dogs. He's not friendly out here like he is inside."

Columbia's quad is in the shape of a simple Latin cross. Libraries anchor the vertical line to the north and south, while College Walk forms its east-west axis with its ends split like a tuning fork: trees and shrubs in the hollow space between, and brick walkways to either side.

Ian quickly led the group onto the campus. They had not gone far before he realized the futility of pursuit. The dog was well past the open section of the quad and less than a hundred yards from passing through the gates onto Broadway.

"It's a game!" Ian shouted. "That damn dog loves games." Then to the group, he said, "We need to play it, or we'll lose him. So, you turn back and start walking quickly toward home. I'll whistle and try to get his attention. Hopefully, he'll see that we've changed course, and he'll come charging back. I'll move among the trees and grab him as he runs by."

The group reversed direction. Ian put his pinky fingers into either side of his mouth, producing an undulating whistle that carried across the still air of the campus. But the dog kept running, now only a black mass rushing toward the gate. Another long undulating whistle followed, and the mass stopped. Then, a few anxious breaths later, it started moving again, in reverse, toward the receding group.

Ian stepped back into the shadows cast through the trees by campus lamps and watched Zato approach, eyes sparkling with crazed excitement. His strides were long and powerful, head bent, ears taut, tongue lolling, and his tail plume furling and unfurling with each bound.

Ian and Mike had played tackle football with friends on the playground after school, but that was scrawny kids in sneakers and sweatshirts, not snow boots and padded winter coats. That was sandlot, and this was the pros. He would have to time his leap flawlessly, like a tight end led cross-field by a perfect spiral.

When Zato was five yards away, breathing steam like a Percheron, Ian stepped from the shadows and threw himself headlong into space, grasping the dog's collars as it passed between his arms, and the two went down hard onto the packed snow. Both lay still, Ian on top, Zato panting heavily.

They remained in that position until the family ran up.

"Are you alright?"

"Are you hurt?

"Is Zato okay?"

The questions poured forth as Ian got to his knees. Zato remained on the ground, gasping.

"This is the second time I've had to tackle this guy in a few days," said Ian in exasperation while Blair helped him to his feet. "It's getting to be too much for me."

A prolonged silence followed, broken by Max. "We could see everything! You were like a rodeo cowboy." High praise continued, attempting to buoy Ian's mood, but without success.

"Okay, said Ian, brushing off his coat and pants, "let's get Sam to a taxi before there are none to get."

Giving the leash a yank, he said, "Get up, Zato; you can recover when we get home."

As they passed through the college gates to Broadway, a cab pulled up, disgorging four inebriated passengers: two couples still winding down from the evening's revelry. One turned to the Kennedy group. "Your chariot awaits, my friends, but I fear your coachman caters only to humans."

Ignoring the man and leaning into an open door, Ian said, "It's a human party of one, going to the Plaza Hotel on 59th Street." Then, as the driver may have been at the end of his shift, he asked, "Are you okay with going downtown?" The cabbie nodded his approval, and the Kennedys, Sam, and dogs all said their farewells. Sam rolled down her window, offering one more apology as the cab rolled away.

The family trundled back across campus, with Max and Logan walking ahead, following Bagel's erratic lead.

"This has been quite a New Year's Eve," said Blair. "All quite delightful until the last twenty minutes. I do hope it's not an omen for the coming year."

Ian frowned. "No omens. We are not living a Greek tragedy. But these last twenty minutes have helped me make up my mind," he said softly. "Paris or no Paris, we need to rethink Zato."

"I know," said Blair. "I've been wrestling with that thought as well."

She slid her hand under her husband's arm. "Thank you, Mr. Kennedy, for your quick thinking and derring-do," she said. "You done good, *myshka*, very good.

-48-

Irritable Conscience Syndrome

Sarah Reinhart and Samantha McFarland returned to their respective countries while the downtown Kennedys played out the last few days of the winter break. The topic of Paris was put on hold for now, and life at home resumed its usual rhythm.

Blair and Ian returned to work a few days before the children returned to school, quickly finding that maintaining a secret of this kind from one's fellows is burdensome, especially when one is not just a cog in the machine. Answers to casual questions about the future caused anxiety and introversion.

"Do they know? No, they couldn't. But could they?"

A secret soon becomes a distraction, stealing valued attention from routine actions, resulting in forgetfulness and mistakes. Moreover, it acts as a sponge absorbing thought and can make one appear furtive to others. Worst of all, both Ian and Blair began to feel that abandoning their posts was somehow dishonorable.

The children, however, did not have a secret, so they discussed it freely with friends. The first to get the news was Spira while accompanying her cousins to school the first day after winter break.

"For real?" she asked.

"For real," said Max.

"Forever?" she asked.

"Forever," said Max.

"It is not so bad as that," said Logan, seeing Spira on the verge of tears. "Dad says we would come back to visit often, and if we do move, you could come and visit us."

"I'd like that, but I would miss you guys."

"We'd miss you, too."

*

Over the lunch break, Ian phoned Blair from his office, reaching her at home. "I imagine the kids have reported the news to Spira and their friends by now. I'd better brief Mike before the kids get out of school."

"I'll call Lizanne as soon as I walk the dogs," said Blair. "Then let's regroup if there's time."

The calls were made, with Mike and Lizanne expressing their full support. They understood Max and Logan might not be thrilled about uprooting to live in a foreign country, and they would check with Spira after school to see how she was taking it. If Ian and Blair did get the positions, it would take some getting used to by everyone.

A week went by, then another, with no word from either Sarah or the school, causing second thoughts. Was this the right move when everything was going so smoothly in New York? Would the kids have trouble adjusting? Sam said apartments in Europe were small. How small? What if NIS didn't renew their contracts after two years? And what about the elephant in the room wagging its tail? The whirr of doubts was nearly audible, but they did their best to keep the kids from noticing.

Mike and Lizanne continued to encourage, and they assured their disconsolate daughter that they would all continue to see one another despite the distance. Spira could even visit her cousins in Paris.

*

"Sam called over lunch," said Blair when Ian came home from work the following Friday. "She asked if we had any news. I told her it had only been two weeks but that we were already in a bit of a spin waiting for word."

"Hopefully, we will hear something next week," said Ian. "I imagine there are many applicants to consider, and this is a pretty good deal for whomever gets it."

Then, quickly shifting the topic, he said, "Let's all go to the West End for burgers and fries."

*

On the third Monday of the new year a letter arrived from NIS by fast mail. Blair retrieved it from the mailbox over lunch and immediately called Ian at Parker, but he was not available, so she left a message for him to call her. The letter was on school stationery and read as follows:

January 15, 1979

Dear Mr. and Mrs. Kennedy,

Sarah was kind enough to deliver your curricula vitae, which were well received. The board of directors has reviewed them and agrees that your credentials and experience are exceptional; therefore, we hope you will confirm acceptance of the positions offered as staff and faculty at NIS beginning in September of 1979.

I know Sarah has done her best to provide details regarding your appointments, responsibilities, salary, and accommodations, but I imagine many questions remain. Given the impact on your family that such a change entails, I strongly recommend a visit. It can be as short or as long as you would like. Unfortunately, we are not at liberty to provide airfare for visits, but we can provide you with accommodation at the apartment in Auteuil. It is only partially furnished at the moment but should allow you to judge its suitability for your family. In addition, we would provide for all your transportation needs once here.

My assistant, Mme Clément, will contact you by telephone to discuss details regarding contracts, transportation, etc. She will try and reach you after 6:00 PM on either Saturday (1/20) or Sunday (1/21). However, you may wish to hold your final decision until after a visit. If so, it would be best to make travel arrangements as soon as possible.

Thank you also for the school records from St. Mark's. I am sure Logan and Max will make a valuable contribution to the student body.

I am happy to welcome you and your children to the NIS family, and it is my hope you will find our community agreeable.

Please accept my best regards,

Directeur, Corentine Chevalier

Ecole Internationale de Neuilly

cc Mme Clément

Ian received the message to call Blair after finishing his second afternoon class. But, still having a writing seminar to run, he decided to return home immediately afterward rather than call now.

Only the dogs greeted him at the door, as Blair was still at work and the children had not yet returned from after-school activities. Entering the kitchen to search for a snack, he saw a manilla envelope with his name on it taped to the refrigerator. Inside was the letter from NIS. Ian read it twice to ensure he had not misunderstood anything, then called Blair.

"I read the letter," he said. "Sorry I didn't call sooner. It looks like we have some logistics to work out."

"It does, but I can't talk right now. I'll be home in twenty minutes, and we can discuss it."

Once home, the floodgates opened, ideas began to flow, and, finally, after the children went to bed, Ian and Blair worked out a step-by-step plan.

1. Arrange a school visit by either Blair or Ian
2. Inform the children
3. Discuss the visit and any other pending questions with Madam Clément
4. Arrange time away from work for either Blair or Ian (six days, including flights each way)
5. Make the final decision

The fact of the offer had brought them back to ground zero. The move was no longer just an idea. It now had form and substance. As a result, they revisited the familiar pros and cons of the situation, but for Blair, the prospect of submitting her resignation to the institute was particularly agonizing.

"We are not vassals," said Ian. "My contract was up last year, but no one took the time to renew it, and you don't even have one. I feel a twinge walking around the halls at Parker, too. But no employer expects infinite loyalty. Staff come and go. People move on, retire."

"I know," said Blair, "but I feel a sense of loyalty. It's hard to imagine someone replacing me fully. It took me years to learn how to satisfy each faculty member's unique needs and wants. Not to mention, I just finished my Master's in December, and that was made possible only through special arrangements with the department. I feel I owe them."

"You've held that position for nearly fifteen years," countered Ian. "I think you have overbalanced the scales by far. You owe them nothing but gratitude, as they do you."

Blair did not reply, so Ian continued. "If we accept the offer, I imagine we will be here into the August break, allowing you a few months to train a replacement. As always, life will proceed with us or without us."

"What about you?" rejoined Blair after a pause. "Don't you feel some obligation to Parker? Who could pick up all your duties?"

"I expect they will easily find someone to take the Chinese classes. I have complete lesson plans for each class throughout the year, so no one will have to reinvent the wheel. The history classes would likely just be dropped. Things like that happen. Remember Parker's Latin class?" Blair nodded. "Dropped after a year."

As Ian had come to terms with his misgivings, he was surprised at Blair's continued back-peddling. So, he decided to change direction.

"The best way to handle this is for you to make the trip. You speak French much better than I do, and, as you would be working for the Director, you could get to know her, understand your responsibilities, and meet some of the faculty. You can confirm whether the school allows its teachers as much flexibility as Sarah claims. Then, you'll know if it's right for the kids and us. I'm sure of it."

Even though Blair seemed the obvious choice, she was startled by Ian's suggestion.

"I'll stay here and mind the store," he added, "and we can communicate by phone and fax."

Reluctantly, Blair agreed this was the best plan, and after reviewing the calendar, they selected a date just a month away. Blair would immediately apply for a passport and inform the institute that she required time off—something she'd never done. Ian would see to the ticket:

- A departure on February 15th
- Returning five days later—Washington's birthday
- Requiring only three days of leave of absence

This schedule would allow two full days at the school and two days to explore Paris—an itinerary that quickly dissipated any reticence clouding the room.

The next day, Blair left work early to visit the U.S. Passport Agency in Rockefeller Center, where she submitted her application and paid for expedited service. Ian booked a direct flight for her from JFK to Charles de Gaulle Airport and sent a letter covering flight details to Madam Chevalier. When Blair's request for time off encountered no resistance, there was no turning back.

That evening the children were briefed on the plan. There was little comment except from Max, who doubted his father's ability to look after them.

"Does Dad know how to cook?" he asked his mother.

"You've had his scrambled eggs and bacon many times. He makes a suitably soggy French toast and a good hamburger. So, with that and some frozen vegetables, buckets of popcorn, and ice cream for dessert, you should all survive for five days."

-49-

Leaving and Leaves

The call from Paris came late Saturday afternoon. Blair and Ian took up their positions on the couch with the phone held between them. Madam Clément was friendly and business-like, speaking English with a thick accent. She covered much the same ground as Sarah Reinhart, then discussed Blair's trip to Paris. Ian apologized for not waiting to hear if the visit dates they had selected were convenient for the school, explaining he had to act quickly to take advantage of the American holiday. Madam Clément was pleased they had gone ahead with the scheduling and understood they would want to visit before making a final decision. She assured Blair that she would personally meet her at the airport and take her to the apartment in Auteuil. When she heard Blair had never been to Paris, she offered to be her guide over the weekend.

The next four weeks passed quickly. Ian picked up Blair's ticket from the travel agency and, ten days later, her passport arrived. Sarah Reinhart called, excited about Blair's visit. She warned that the weather in February could be cold and wet and possibly even snow. She recommended suitable clothing for the school visit and the weekend, suggesting—much to Blair's relief—that she replace Madam Clément as the weekend guide.

As the date for her departure approached, Blair became more and more uncomfortable at work. No one said anything about her upcoming leave except to assure her they could get along well without her for a few days. But, of course, this made it more difficult as she wanted desperately to prostrate herself before Professor Zaritsky and confess: "Forgive me, Father, for I have sinned."

Despite the haunting presence of guilt, Blair was excited. This trip was to be her first venture outside the country and to a city she had longed to visit since high school. She looked forward to testing her French, seeing the school, meeting its faculty, and especially having a few days to enjoy Paris.

Everything was arranged: Ian would take the morning off and borrow his brother's van to take Blair to the airport. Mike would walk the dogs over lunch.

The evening before her departure, they had a conversation with the children. Blair asked, "What questions should I be sure to ask for you? I'll make a list."

Logan: "Will I have my own room?
"Do we have to wear uniforms?""
"Will we have to ride the subway?"

Max: "Is the apartment big enough for the dogs?"
"Do they teach Latin?"
"Do we have to go?"

A little before eight a.m., Mike arrived with the van. He double-parked in front of the apartment and handed Ian the keys.

Knowing his brother had a pair of traffic cones, Ian said, "Save me a space in front of the store. I should have the van back by noon."

"Wish Blair good luck for me," Mike said. "But I doubt she'll need it. They are going to love you guys." He gave his brother a pinch on both cheeks and set out for work.

Blair rolled her suitcase into the foyer and made sure she had her passport and money belt stuffed with francs, as Ian had warned her that "pickpockets abound in Paris."

She took only one medium-sized suitcase packed with Sarah's recommendations for dress and an oversized shoulder bag.

"Don't forget to do the dishes and leave water for the dogs," she said, then hugged and kissed the children goodbye, reminding them to be kind to their father and lock up after themselves when they left for school. She would talk to them by phone and would be back on Monday.

Logan remained stoic, but Max teared up, holding his hug longer than usual. The door closed, and they were gone.

Logan finished washing the breakfast dishes while Max poured water into the dogs' bowls. After gathering their homework into their briefcases, they put on their coats and hats and prepared to leave. Max cracked open the front door, so he and Logan could make their escape, one at a time. Not realizing that Zato had inserted his snout in the gap, Max opened the door wider to squeeze himself through. Simultaneously, Zato muscled his head and shoulders forward, pushing Max aside, and bolted into the foyer.

"He's out!" shouted Max, "And running for the doors."

Max and Logan tore out of the apartment and ran toward Zato, who, seeing an opening, dogged them like a seasoned halfback and headed up the stairs.

"Take the elevator up to the sixth floor and chase him down the stairs," instructed Logan. "I'll wait here to make sure no one lets him out and try and grab him as he comes down."

As the elevator car groaned slowly up the shaft, Logan opened their apartment door, took Zato's leash, and readied herself at the base of the stairway. Bagel stood bewildered beside the bicycles.

Max exited on the sixth floor and began descending the stairs. Two flights down, he spotted Zato, who quickly turned and raced ahead. "He's coming!" shouted Max. "Get ready!"

When Max reached the second-floor landing, Zato was waiting for him, eyes glistening, tail moving slowly. Max stopped, thinking the escapee was turning himself in, so with an outstretched hand, he called him.

The dog took two cautious steps forward, then dropped to his elbows, rear in the air, tail furled. Max lunged for the collars, but the dog faked right, turned left, and dashed off.

"Here he comes!" shouted Max.

Recalling her father's heroic tackle in the snow on New Year's Eve, Logan braced herself for impact just as Zato, half a flight up, bounced off a corner wall coming her way. Still trying to regain balance, the dog charged down the stairway but fell sideways over the last few steps, taking Logan down with him.

She squeezed him tight around the waist as they tumbled together across the tiles. Skidding to a stop, Logan pulled herself on top, pinning him with her body weight.

Max arrived a moment later, took the leash from her hand, and fastened it to one of the choke collars. "We've got you!" he cried.

Logan scrambled to her feet, took the leash from her brother, and dragged the delinquent into the apartment. Bagel greeted the escapee with disdain and then watched with interest from behind a bicycle as her flatmate received a vigorous dressing-down.

Later, as the children entered Campus Walk, Max said: "I don't know what we would have done if he'd gotten out."

"I don't either," said Logan. "He'd have gotten into trouble for sure, and I think that would have been the last of him."

Max's expression darkened. "I know," he said. "Do we have to tell dad?"

"I don't want to, but I think we have to."

-50-

The Red Balloon

With the time difference between New York and Paris and Blair arriving at her flat sometime after midnight, she had scheduled no call that first day. So, after dinner, Ian drilled the children on how to enter and exit the apartment without misadventure. The drill was declared a "pass" after a few unassisted exits and entrances.

The following morning as Ian was preparing breakfast, the phone rang. Max answered and, before he heard the voice on the other end of the line, said, "Mom? It's me. Dad's cooking bacon and eggs. We're having hamburgers and peas for dinner and chocolate ice cream for dessert."

"Well, Max," said his mother calmly, "I guess our plans for your survival have worked well. How's school going?"

Max briefed his mother, leaving out the previous day's near disaster with Zato. "Are you coming home soon?" he asked.

"I'll be home on Monday. Maybe you can come and pick me up at the airport with Dad. It's a holiday."

"Sure," he said. Will you call tomorrow?"

"Yes, I should be able to call around this time. It's lunchtime here, and I'm using the school's phone. There's no phone in the apartment, so I am not sure if I can call over the weekend."

Omitting to ask her anything about Paris, Max said, "Okay, Mom, I love you. Logan wants to say hello," and passed the phone to his sister.

"*Bonsoir maman, comment ça va*? asked Logan.

"*Je vais bien, merci, ma petite chérie*," answered Blair. Then, switching from French, said, "But, so far, my conversations here have been largely in English."

"How's the apartment?" asked Logan. "Will I have my own room?"

"It's not so large as ours, but it's comfortable, and, yes, you would have your own room *if* we came to Paris."

They chatted a bit longer, and Blair explained that she'd only been at the school for a few hours, so she was still getting oriented. It was as picturesque as in the brochure; the kids were friendly—all wearing uniforms—and the staff she had met were welcoming. She'd have more to report on Friday. But with no working phone in the apartment, she would have to keep it brief. Logan sent kisses and passed the phone to her dad.

"I'm sorry, but I'll have to keep it short, as this call is on the school's dime. But how's it going? Max sounded a little distant."

"Yes, that's true, but there's nothing to worry about. I've got the wheel. What's your first impression of everything?"

"All positive. The campus is beautiful, and they are mid an expansion for the middle and elementary schools. Quite amazing what they have done with less than ten acres: an auditorium, tennis courts, a full gymnasium, a playground for the younger students, and flower gardens that should be lovely in spring and summer.

"Madam Chevalier is very nice. Occasionally we spoke in French, as I suspect she was testing me a bit to see how I'd deal with the locals. Tomorrow I will get to sit in on a couple of classes. I'll have my choice."

"And the apartment?" asked Ian.

"It has three bedrooms, one bath, a kitchen with a gas stove, and, surprisingly, a full-sized refrigerator. The dining area is next to the living room. It's much like ours but more compact and with a bit less square footage. We'd be comfortable there. Oh, the bathroom has a separate bidet. It's optional, so the kids needn't worry."

"Nor I," joked Ian.

"I've tried it out. It takes some getting used to."

"I can only imagine."

"The apartment's on the third floor, accessible by stairs or a tiny elevator for two—quite intimate. The building was constructed in the 1870s, but it's in excellent shape, and the neighborhood is picturesque and quiet. I'm taking lots of photos with that little camera you gave me, so you should get a good idea of everything."

"That all sounds good. How's the weather?"

"Cold and clear. Hopefully, that will hold through the weekend. Sarah is going to show me around."

"I wish I could have been with you on your maiden voyage," said Ian.

"Me too. That would have been perfect. Madam Clément picked me up and drove me directly to the apartment. It was nearly midnight, so I didn't see anything I recognized. The apartment and the school feel like they are in the suburbs, especially the school. There is a uniformity of building design everywhere, and I've seen no high rises. I guess it's the Haussmann influence. Auteuil is like Morningside Heights but prettier.

"I'm looking forward to the weekend," she continued. "Sarah has a car and is going to chauffeur me around. We are going to the *Jeu de Paume* to see the Impressionists on Saturday. She said it's not far from the *Louvre*, so, if there is time, we'll go there too. But frankly, I've been to the Met so often the idea of seeing more Old-World pilferage is not at the top of my list for Paris, and, if you promise not to let it slip, the *Mona Lisa* has never awed me—does that make me a philistine?"

"I hope not, as they would throw me into the Bastille for cultural turpitude right next to you."

"I'd rather spend the day walking down the Champs-Elysees to the Tuileries or sipping wine on the Left Bank," said Blair. "Probably Sarah would prefer that as well, but I'll leave it up to her, as we've only got two days."

"What a problem to solve," moaned Ian in mock dismay. "But I'm sure you and Sarah will make the best use of your time."

"I'm sorry, dear, I'd better go now. This is probably costing the school a fortune. I'll call again tomorrow with much more news. Hug and kiss the kids for me and don't spoil them…too much."

*

The following morning during breakfast, Blair called as promised, and again, Max was the first to answer the phone. "Hi, Mom, Bagel is here to say hello."

"How nice, but let's start with you. How are you surviving without me? Is Daddy burning the toast?"

"No, he's making hot cereal right now, with maple syrup."

"Do you guys have plans for the weekend? I understand it's getting warmer in New York. Unfortunately, it's cold here, and we had a little rain this morning."

"Dad wants to take Spira and us to the Seaport Museum near the Brooklyn Bridge tomorrow. You can go on a real schooner and maybe a tugboat, too, and he wants to take us to a fish market."

"That sounds like fun," said his mother. "I know that fish market. It's huge with all kinds of strange sea creatures. I hope you can handle the smell."

"I hadn't thought about that," said Max thoughtfully. "Dad said Logan and I could come to pick you up on Monday, and we can bring the dogs. They really miss you. Do you want to say hello to Bagel?"

"Sure, Max, put the phone to her ear."

Max did as instructed. Blair said her hellos, causing Bagel to perk her ears and wag a questioning tail.

"She knows it's you, Mom," said Max. "She is all excited. But Logan wants to talk to you now, okay?"

Blair said her goodbyes, and Max passed the phone to his sister.

"Hi, Mom. Have you seen the Eiffel Tower yet?"

"Not yet, but I'm going sightseeing over the weekend. I hope to see it on the way to the impressionist museum tomorrow. I'm quite excited about it."

"I'm so jealous," moaned Logan. "I bet it will be amazing." Then, after a pause, "So, what do you think of the school?"

Blair tried to sound upbeat but not enthralled, as she was trying not to stir things up over a long distance. "It's very nice and surprisingly modern," she said. "The science lab is beautiful, and the classes are small, with less than twenty students each. The student body is quite a melting pot, with kids coming from more than a dozen countries. They travel to and from the school by private bus," she added, recalling Logan's issues with public transportation.

"What about your job? Would you be happy there?"

Blair shouldn't have been surprised by the question, as Logan was mature and genuinely cared about the feelings of others, but for a moment, she was tongue-tied.

"The headmistress is cordial and businesslike," she answered haltingly, "but I'm used to that at the Institute. My duties would be somewhat like what I do now, but with much more contact with students and parents. Of course, all the students are younger than what I'm accustomed to, but that's part of the charm."

Instantly, Blair regretted saying "charm," as it seemed too rhapsodic. There were so many other words she could have used but didn't.

Logan was narrowing her focus. "And what about Dad? What about his work?"

"It's hard to say," replied Blair. "I sat in on a German class yesterday afternoon; it was traditional, like French at St. Mark's. And, as you know, Dad's teaching style is anything but traditional. However, the headmistress assured me that she is open to innovation and thought Dad's fresh approach to teaching might be inspirational for others."

Now Blair was sure she'd put her foot in it, sensing she sounded swayed and reaching for reasons to uproot.

Logan thought about asking the obvious question but said, "I see. It all sounds good. I know this is an expensive call, and Dad's signaling me to wrap it up, so I'd better give him the phone.

"We are all coming to pick you up on Monday, dogs too. Love you." Logan passed the phone to her dad.

As both kids were still in the living room, Ian censored his questions and answers.

"How are you doing?"

"I got the third degree. Did you hear it?"

"Yes. So how was it?"

"If by 'it' you mean my answers to Logan, I think I could have done better. I was trying not to weigh in on this yet, but I don't think I succeeded."

"And have you?"

"What? Weighed in?"

"Yes. Have you?

"It all looks good. I had a long talk with Madam Chevalier this morning. She is in her 60s but progressive in her thinking. She thinks you will be what she calls '*un stimulant pour l'innovation*' to teaching foreign language and history. She was quite spirited when talking about you."

"And when talking about you?"

"Less so, but then mine is not a glamor job. It's in the trenches, handling the palpitations of parents, students, and even staff. It reminds me of the institute in many ways. I'd have the full aide-de-camp portfolio: correspondence secretary, second to the last line of defense, keeper of the calendar, fire chief. This posting also has fundraising responsibilities: planning and managing two events for this purpose each year. It's a lot of work. Quite challenging to juggle all those balls, and Madam Clément spent an hour convincing me how I'd make a perfect replacement for her. There is also the chance I could offer beginning Russian in a year or two, but that's in the future."

"So, do you think Madam Clément is right?" asked Ian.

"You mean, perfect for the job? Yes, I guess I do."

"Well, that all sounds like progress. The weekend should provide you with some space to mull things over."

"Perhaps, but I'll be pretty busy. I'm going to Sarah's apartment for lunch on Sunday. I'll get to meet her husband, and she said I could use their phone to call home."

Blair described her schedule for the remainder of the day and that she was to have dinner that evening with Mesdames Chevalier and Clément.

"Lucky girl," said Ian. "I hope they take you somewhere special; perhaps you can taste your first *foie gras*." Then he briefed her on the upcoming excursion to the Seaport

Museum and the fish market and assured her that he and the kids were managing well on hamburgers and milkshakes."

"I know you're not joking," she said. "Hopefully, I can call you Sunday from Sarah's, but if not, I'll see you all Monday."

Max retreated to his room as the call ended, but Logan remained idly flipping pages of a *New Yorker* magazine.

"How's Mom doing?" she asked, turning another page.

Ian wanted to be honest but not sound committed, as there was still much to discuss with Blair. "It sounds like her visit is going well," he said. "She'll be at the school for the rest of the afternoon, sitting in on a couple of classes in the high school. After that, she has dinner with the headmistress; then she's free for the weekend to tour Paris with her friend from college. Lucky girl."

Looking up from her magazine, Logan said, "I think Mom likes the school and the apartment. Tomorrow, she'll be out on her own, like that little boy followed by a red balloon through the streets of Paris. Except, in Mom's case, all of Paris will be flirting with her coattails."

Ian had forgotten that Blair had taken Logan to Lincoln Center for a French film festival last year where that magical short film, *The Red Balloon*, was among those presented. "Yes," he said, marveling at his daughter's insight, "I expect it will be just like that."

-51-

The Mice Will Play

The following morning, after breakfast, Ian and the kids crossed the campus to pick up Spira and to commandeer Uncle Mike's van. Mike provided his daughter with pocket money, and as they drove off, he placed a pair of traffic cones in the parking place to hold it for later.

The trip to the Seaport Museum lived up to Ian's hype, especially for Max. In addition to many interesting shops along the riverfront, one of the historic sailing ships was open for visitors. *The Peking*, a four-masted bark constructed in 1911, was a new arrival to the shores of Manhattan, having been privately purchased and brought from its home in Hamburg, Germany, to her berth in the East River at Pier 19. Max was particularly excited to board her and see the captain's cabin, the galley, bunk beds for the crew, and peek into the cargo hold, where he was sure he could still smell traces of some foul-smelling cargo that the ship's docent called "saltpeter."

Max was unfamiliar with this word, so he asked his father for clarification. As the docent spoke, Ian bent down and whispered, "It means guano or bird poop, used as fertilizer. Men mined it like coal from islands off the coast of Peru. Millions of sea birds left their deposits over thousands of years, and so in the eighteen hundreds, these deposits were more than 200 feet deep."

Max held his nose and left the ship's hold to join his sister and Spira, who were up on deck repelling pirates.

Topside, after hearing the docent's explanation of "square-rigged" and other terminology related to setting the sails and running the ship, Max had dozens of questions. The docent was a retired ship's mate who, as a young man, had crewed aboard a bark of this kind in the North Sea. He was patient with the interruptions, providing answers to the many questions from this inquisitive boy.

"Could the braces move the yardarms from side to side so the ship could turn?"

"Can this ship move faster than the wind speed?"

"How did they stop the ship?"

"Did it carry animals?"

"What was the age of the youngest crew member?"

And, of course,

"Did people die in the storms?"

The man realized these were not just idle questions, so, at the end of the tour, he closed with a dramatic eulogy that seemed spontaneous.

"Men and boys who worried about danger were not aboard these ships, nor were they wanted. It was a rough life, but it was beautiful and fulfilling. There were many dangers. Gales and hurricanes tore the sails from the yards. Furled sails would come loose in a storm, forcing men to climb the shrouds and step out along the yards to rope them down while the ship heeled from side to side like the pendulum of a great clock. Waves as tall as buildings would lift the ship like a cork, taking four men on the wheel to keep her windward while breakers washed and foamed over the main deck. Of course, there were casualties. Sometimes whole ships and crews were lost in storms in the North Sea or along the coal-black coast of Cape Horn. Men were washed overboard or caught in the rigging. However, before sailing into a storm, nets were strung along the port and starboard bulwarks to catch a man. Many a life was saved in this way, and it was a life worth saving, where boys soon became men, men became a team, and everyone had value."

*

Back along the wharf, the Kennedys wandered in and out of stores. Ian bought the girls captain's caps in the museum store, which they wore at jaunty angles, while Max selected a model kit of the schooner, *Albatross*. Thus equipped, they continued up South Street to the edge of the fish market, piloting themselves through a labyrinth of boxes, barrels, baskets, wooden crates, and moving handcarts—some empty, some filled with ice and shimmering fish.

"The smells are strong," said Ian, "but there are sights here you will not soon forget."

They passed under the broad canopy of the Tin Building into a noisy open-air market filled with the motion of men and carts, carrying with them the fetid smells of decaying organic matter. Working men wearing waders or boots and denim overalls smoked cigars and cigarettes as they gutted, boned, and fileted their wares under the stuttering hum of fluorescent lights.

Max tugged his father's coat sleeve. "It stinks in here."

"You'll get used to it. Give it a moment. Follow me."

The children followed Ian, passing bin after bin of crabs, lobsters, mussels, and spiny, black sea urchins that Spira said they looked like thistles. At the end of the aisle, a grizzled man in a rubber apron and tall boots noted the weight of a six-foot tuna hanging from a hook attached to a rust-encrusted scale.

"Wow," said Logan and Spira simultaneously.

The worker pulled a cigar from the corner of his mouth and addressed the group, "This is a bluefin tuna, a young one, maybe four or five years old. They can get to be three times this size, some twelve feet or more, weighing over 1000 pounds."

Max got busy doing mental calculations. "How much is a big fish like this worth?"

"Some this size sell for five thousand at the dock, even more in Japan. Did you want to buy it?"

"No, thank you," answered Max, unsure if the man was serious.

"They are cutting one up three aisles over if you want to watch."

Ian was uncertain if that much reality would sit well with the kids. "It might be a bit gruesome for you," he said to the group, "so how about we walk back through the shellfish and see what else is on display."

"I'd like to see it," said Max. 'It can't be worse than the butcher shop, can it?"

The girls expressed nervy support for the idea, and they all trooped off in search of the butchery.

Along the way, they stopped and marveled at the shapes and sizes of other sea and river creatures: flat, thin, broad, droop-bellied, tubular, some with eyes atop their heads or long-bodied with stiff pectoral fins like glider wings; tails were forked, rounded, crescent-like, or truncated; two had dorsal fins that leaned forward above their eyes like Presley pompadours; still others lay in their bins like strands of black licorice or piles of small, silver pens; some wielded spears or readied themselves for battle behind spikes or armor plate. A few had the faces of old men who'd lost their teeth, all sadly frowning. One muddy mass with a broad tail resembled an inflated pollywog, and when passing a case of deep-river catfish, Max remarked, "That one looks like Snidely Whiplash."

Finally, they arrived at a space between displays where an eight-foot tuna lay on an orange tarp next to a drain that was covered by a steel grate. A man in shorts and rubber boots stood over the fish wielding a blade resembling a Medieval battle-ax.

He attacked the head with a series of well-placed blows and, pulling it back from the body, exposed its gills, which unfolded like the bellows of an accordion. After a few deft chops, he set the head aside, as an assistant swept its blood into the drain.

Having already dispatched the tail and fins, the butcher began to section the body: first incisions were long and lateral, followed by transverse cuts. The blade of his tool slid through flesh like a ship through a calm sea, thus enabling the man to peel away slabs of meat which he divided into yard-long pieces. As he dismantled the tuna, his assistant hefted the cuttings and arranged them on a marble-topped table for fileting.

"Have you seen enough?" asked Ian, sensing they had all experienced more than they had expected. "It may seem an odd question to ask now, but are you interested in lunch?"

The kids groaned in response, and they moved together toward the exit.

"There is a good Italian restaurant just a block away," said Ian as they passed from under the canopy. "And you will not have to eat fish."

*

It was not quite noon, but Carmine's Seafood Restaurant was already busy with tourists and workers from the fish market. Coming into Carmine's from the bright sun was like entering a roadhouse before the advent of electricity. As their eyes adjusted to the gloom, a friendly waiter greeted them and showed them to a booth at the back. Dark wooden walls carelessly hung with fishnets and ropes, faded lifebuoys, and glass fishing floats gave the small dining room an unkempt but nautical flavor. In keeping with the derelict look of the place, their table was scarred, the leatherette seats had taped-over tears, and it was almost impossible to read the menus in the low light.

"The sign said this is a seafood restaurant," commented Max dolefully.

"Fear not, my young friend. They have spaghetti, lasagna, and other finless dishes. If I could read the menu, I could tell you more."

The waiter arrived to clarify the day's specials, and they all decided to jettison seafood in favor of a large order of garlic bread coupled with spaghetti and meatballs for the table. Soon the bread arrived, redolent with garlic; the eating of which stimulated conversation about the fish market.

"I had no idea a tuna could get that big. We only eat it from cans at home," said Spira, forming a small circle with her hands in illustration.

"I have never seen fish gills before," said Logan. "They looked like piano strings with little mushrooms at the end. And they're so much bigger than I thought."

"For such a huge fish," said Max assuming his professorial tone, "gills need to be big to absorb enough oxygen into the blood. They have thousands of tiny blood vessels to take oxygen from the water. It was so cool to see that."

As the kids shared their fascination with the morning's sights, Ian felt gratified that this never-before had turned out so well. Come Blair's arrival on Monday, he hoped his report card would have all A's.

*

Sunday morning came and went with no call. Ian explained to the children that their mother was likely out with Sarah Reinhart enjoying her last day in Paris with no way to call home, but that they would see her the following afternoon and hear all her adventures. In the meantime, he suggested they go for a bike ride in Riverside Park. It was a balmy day for mid-February, and the diehard handball players might be having a game.

After breakfast, they took leave of the dogs, rolled their bikes through the lobby, and set out for the park. New York's "big-league" handball courts were in Greenwich Village and Brooklyn, but where Riverside Park possessed solid walls, there were a few makeshift courts. For more than thirty blocks, the ground level of the park was as much as forty feet below the traffic lanes of Riverside Drive, and retaining walls stood at the backside of many playgrounds. Some had painted lines extending from the wall base onto the asphalt, marking the boundaries of handball courts. These crude quadrangles allowed locals of all ages to work on their technique before heading downtown to try their luck with the "pros." All they needed at this time of year was a handball and a stiff broom to remove the leaves and sweep away the puddles.

First stop for the trio was Chock full o'Nuts to get cream cheese sandwiches on date-nut bread, which Logan tucked under a blanket in her basket, should they wish to stop and picnic.

Entering the park at 116th Street, they headed south into a chill, easterly breeze, which made them happy that they had worn hats and gloves.

The courts at 110th and 103rd Streets were crude and empty, but at 97th Street at the back of the Dinosaur Playground, two players were warming up, so the travelers stopped to watch. One was black, tall, and muscular, the other a wiry, brown bantamweight. The tall one looked in his twenties, his opponent twice that, and despite the chill air, both had set aside their sweatsuits and wore only T-shirts, shorts, and leather gloves.

The court was in fair condition, with clearly defined lines, but still wet from a recent clearing of water and debris. A twelve-foot chain link fence surrounded it, behind which a wooden bench provided the Kennedys with a seat from which to watch safely.

The men finished warming up and began play. It was fast, with bodies moving quickly, side to side, from front to back, and back to front, almost touching, exchanging positions with the intimacy and controlled aggression of a tango. Serves were high or low, some cutting sharp, cross-court angles, others hugging the sidelines. Returns came dangerously close to heads and backs. One strike came back between the legs of the server and was returned the way it came.

"That's amazing!" said Max. "Did you see that?"

They soon found themselves cheering and clapping for both players as the game progressed. The younger man served first, taking an 8 to 0 lead. His opponent came back with ten straight service wins, after which the game tightened with the lead changing back and forth every two or three points. Finally, at 20-20, the older man served, giving his opponent a low ball which he returned from beyond the sideline, hitting the wall just an inch above the junction, then dribbling off.

The two men slapped hands in appreciation of the competition and resumed positions for the start of a second game. The Kennedys agreed they had had enough spectator excitement; it was time for lunch.

On a bench back in Dinosaur Park, they chatted about the game, and Max provided the names and attributes of the two fiberglass dinosaurs that foraged for acorns among the slides and climbers: a triceratops and a hadrosaur. They ate their sandwiches and shared a bottle of water, which Ian had extracted from his coat pocket.

"Mom will be home tomorrow," said Logan. "I can't wait to hear about Paris—especially the Louvre and the Impressionists."

"Bagel really misses mom," said Max. "She's gonna go crazy."

-52-

Back to the Future

When the Kennedys arrived at the airport the next morning, the International Arrivals Building at JFK was already disembarking passengers from Europe. Blair's Air France flight was not due until 10:40, but the Kennedys arrived at ten o'clock in case of an early arrival. Additionally, Ian wanted the kids to have a chance to look around the airport and hoped the exposure to air travel would give Max something to look forward to if Paris got the green light.

They parked the car in a short-term lot along the Van Wyck Expressway, about a mile from the airport. On such excursions, the dogs remained in the car with two bowls of water and windows cracked for good circulation. They would only be gone an hour. Ten minutes later, an airport bus took them from the lot to the arrival terminal, which was expansive with an east and west wing providing thirty-five gates servicing more than thirty different airlines.

In the center of the lobby, a large, brightly colored mobile dangled from the ceiling, and along the walls, below a viewing gallery, hung flags representing each of the nations served by the airport. Max did his best to identify them but soon realized he had more work to do before he could claim mastery of the world's colors. A sign pointing to the observation deck got the kids running in that direction, with Ian walking fast to keep up.

The deck had changed since Ian had stood on it more than fifteen years earlier. It was no longer open to the skies but was enclosed in glass with a limited view. For the kids, however, it was perfect. They could see aircraft hit the ground on a distant runway and hear the roar of the thrust reversers working to slow the plane's forward motion.

Carriers from various airlines were taxiing slowly along pathways toward their gates.

"What's BIWA?" asked Max.

"It's an airline from the British West Indies," answered Ian. Then pointing to others, he added, "The one to the left is Sabina—it's from Belgium; Avianca is the Columbian Airline, and El Al is from Israel. Those are national airlines, unlike TWA or Pan Am, which are private American companies."

"So, each plane has people from Israel or Belgium or somewhere?"

"Sure. Maybe some are tourists or are coming here on business or to family members. Some, like your mom, might be returning home from somewhere."

"Where are the American planes?"

"I'm sure they'll be along."

Logan had been off surveying the narrow viewing walk that oversaw the terminal lobby. She returned to tell them they could also look down into the customs area where they might see their mom come through.

Ian checked his watch. "Her plane should land in five minutes," he said, "but it will take at least fifteen for her to pick up her luggage and get to customs."

They walked to the gallery and watched people showing their passports and opening their luggage for inspection by customs officers. The flow was steady, and the number of travelers was thinning out. After a few minutes, they turned away to look down into the terminal and at the colorful sculpture hanging from the ceiling.

"That's an Alexander Calder mobile," said Ian. "I think he invented the art form. He's done thousands of them, large and small. This one has been here for twenty years."

"It looks like a gigantic bird," said Logan, somewhat in awe, "in so many colorful pieces, and it seems to be moving."

"It is moving," said Ian. "It's called *Flight*. I guess with doors opening and closing and people moving around, it changes daily or even hour to hour. A few years ago, Calder painted two jet aircraft in bright colors like these. They're quite beautiful. Both display his signature and are like traveling exhibitions shown only at airports."

"This is so cool," Logan said. "A sculpture that moves through space and is never quite the same. It's like something alive."

"Yes, it is."

"More people are entering customs now," shouted Max, who had been monitoring pedestrian traffic through the window behind them. "Mom could be coming through any minute."

They took positions alongside Max and studied the flow of travelers stepping into lines for luggage inspection. Some men wore suits and ties like they were going to work; old and young stood patiently, inching along in their line; there were families with children, even infants, held in arms; and an older woman in a wheelchair holding a pillow was pushed by a uniformed attendant. Lines were lengthening as more passengers streamed into the customs space.

Max was the first to notice her. "There's Mom!" he shouted. "Back by the row of carts, to the right of the entrance. Do you see her? She's in her blue coat, pulling her suitcase."

The gallery was filling fast with others looking for friends or family members. They waved and called greetings, inaudible through the thick glass. Max waved and shouted, trying to catch his mother's attention as she stepped into line.

Blair began scanning the gallery from the floor, looking for familiar faces. Finally finding her small complement of greeters, she waved back.

"She sees us!" shouted Max.

Ian signaled that they would meet her at the exit gate, then shepherded the kids away from the window and down the escalator to the fenced-off area outside customs. Fifteen minutes later, Blair emerged, pulling her bag and smiling at her welcoming committee. She felt she had been gone for weeks.

As she rounded the far edge of a metal fence, the family embraced her like a warrior, home from the war.

"I missed you all so much," said Blair kissing her children's heads.

"We missed you, too."

"Are you exhausted from the flight?"

"No, I'm so happy to be home."

"Because it wasn't fun?"

"No, Max, it was fun, I just missed you all, and I'm so looking forward to sleeping in my own bed."

"Wait until Bagel sees you, Mom; she's gonna' go crazy."

There was much kerfuffle back in the van with dogs leaping over seats, bodies bumping bodies, the spilling of water bowls, and Bagel madly licking Blair's face. But after the excitement ebbed and they got underway, the conversation naturally shifted to Paris. Logan peppered her mother with questions about the Louvre and the impressionist museum. As for Max, the subject was more about mechanics than aesthetics:

"Does the Eiffel Tower have elevators?"

"How tall is it?"

"Can you go all the way to the top?"

"Are there really open toilettes on the sidewalks?"

Not having seen one, Blair could provide no detail about the once common *pissoirs* of Paris, and, as she had seen the Eiffel Tower only at a distance, she had little to say about its design or internal organs. However, she could feel Ian was about to offer a history of its construction and subsequent aesthetic controversy, so she squeezed his leg, hoping he'd let it drop for now.

Finally, as they approached the Queensboro Bridge, Logan broached the subject of the school.

"It was impressive," said Blair flatly. "The headmistress and staff were very nice to me, and the classroom instruction looks as good, if not better, than St. Mark's. The apartment is slightly smaller than ours, in a nice area that looks like Morningside Heights, but without the university. We would be comfortable there."

Silence followed as the group marinated in Blair's answer.

Uneasy in the burgeoning quiet, Ian said: "And Paris overall, how was it? Romantic? Or overblown by the likes of Gertrude Stein, Hemingway, and the hype of travel agents?"

"I loved it, and you would too," said Blair, no longer able to suppress her emotions. "It's everything I expected and more. I loved the architecture, the wide wooden doors to apartment buildings and their wrought-iron balconies; the abundance of parks; the small, all-purpose neighborhood stores run by colonial immigrants; the bakeries; cafes; and wine—even the cobblestones on the streets. There must be fifty museums in addition to the Louvre: there's one for the Middle Ages, another just for the sculpture of Rodin, and still another devoted to Monet, and of course, there is the *Jeu de Paume*—a cornucopia of Impressionists. It was fantastic, and I only visited two."

"Which was your favorite?" asked Logan.

"I guess the *Jeu de Paume*, as I love the Impressionists, but the Louvre has pictures by Rembrandt, da Vinci, Raphel, and a host of other Renaissance painters and sculptors. It's hard to have a favorite among so many masters."

"Did you see the *Mona Lisa*?" asked Logan.

"Kind of. The *Mona Lisa* is like a Venus flytrap, enticing you to step into the crowd of onlookers, but I fear you will never get out once you have dared to place your foot into the crowd. People stand transfixed, seemingly for hours, inching forward. I jumped up and caught a fleeting glimpse, but I had to keep moving, as I had limited time in the Louvre.

"However, the *Jeu de Paume*," she continued passionately, "though a shoebox in comparison, possessed a broad gallery of vibrating color and a few magical rooms. One, no bigger than our living room, had a dozen of Gauguin's Tahitian paintings. These have darker hues and a flatter perspective than the Monet's or Van Gogh's but are quite beautiful, though my favorites were the Renoirs with groups of people enjoying each other in the parks or by a lake. The colors are soft; sunlight filters through the trees, dappling the ladies' dresses and the men's straw hats; and the people are so engaged, you can almost hear their conversations.

"Of course, there are the little things," Blair said, finally slowing her pace. "You would not believe the quality of the croissants or pastries. The *croque madam* is a delicious ham and Gruyere cheese sandwich covered in a creamy bechamel sauce and served with a fried egg; sublime. And the hot chocolate, *miam miam*! It pours like honey into a well of whipped cream that rises around it like a cloud."

"Did you see any French Poodles?" asked Max trying to find traction in the conversation.

"I did see one prancing down the Champs-Élysées—that's the 5th Avenue of Paris—she looked like a ballerina in a tutu."

Max laughed. "My book says they are originally from Germany, not France. They bred them as water dogs, and their name meant 'puddle.' They even have webbed feet and clipping their fur close helps them swim."

The conversation flowed back and forth until Blair felt entirely sapped of commentary, and the group fell silent. They had been traveling west along East 60th Street and were approaching Central Park when Max spoke, "So, are we moving?"

Blair had rehearsed an answer to this question, although she hadn't expected it to come from Max, as he seemed to avoid the subject.

"Well, there is still much to discuss, but the headmistress thinks we are a good match, and they were impressed with both of your school reports. She thinks you and Logan will contribute much to the student body. Unfortunately, they don't teach Latin, but they do offer Spanish, French, and German, and, if we accept their offer, you could even study Chinese."

"Do *you* think we are a good match, Mom?" he asked.

"Yes, I do," she said frankly, "and not just for the school. Paris has many things to offer us. There are dozens of parks; a large zoo—many times the size of the one in Central Park; there are bicycle tours of the city at night; you can sail boats in the pond at Luxembourg Gardens or visit the Natural History Museum to see the dinosaurs. Many of the parks have merry-go-rounds and marionette shows. I saw a mime entertaining people in front of a hotel and a man sitting cross-legged as if suspended in air, three feet off the ground. I think you and Logan would find it magical."

"It does sound cool," said Logan.

"Did the mime have a striped shirt and a painted face?" asked Max.

"Yes, with a red beret and black gloves. He opened invisible doors and windows, bumped into invisible people with whom he shook hands, and held their invisible baby until he tripped over an invisible stone and almost dropped it. It was horrible but hilarious at the same time."

"It sounds like fun," said Max.

"Yes, there is a lot we could do in Paris, and there's much to see and do outside of the city as well."

Ian turned from 59th Street onto Broadway and headed uptown.

"Can we make a pit stop at Zabar's?" Blair asked. "I've been thinking about making bagels and cream cheese for lunch. Interested?"

Half an hour later, Blair threw her coat and suitcase onto her bed and went to the kitchen to prepare lunch. The smell of the bagels warming in the oven permeated the kitchen, and the kids looked on with unmasked admiration as their mom scooped a mixture of cream cheese and herbs into the blender.

"It's nice to have you home again, Mom," said Logan.

"I can only imagine," she said, glancing mischievously at Ian.

Later, after a family dinner of Italian heroes from Mama Joys and a large glass of wine for Blair, the time difference between Paris and New York took its toll, and shortly after sunset, she fell into bed.

As the rest of the family had woken early on this President's Day, they, too, were tired. So, after a mesmerizing chapter of *The Hobbit* and a short dog walk, the remaining Kennedys turned off the lights and snuggled under their bedclothes, each imagining their lives in a land far, far away.

-53-

Barely a Ripple

Tuesday morning, the family set out for work and school as on any other day, but for Ian and Blair, the world of work had changed. Although they had not put a final seal of approval on the Paris arrangement, both knew it was now only a formality, and conversations with employers about the future would be necessary in the next few days. Over the years, Ian had written scrupulous lesson plans to guide his students' history and language classes, so he felt that passing the torch would be relatively painless for all concerned. Blair, on the other hand, was not so self-assured.

Upon returning to work after her short vacation, no one asked for a travelog. Naturally, her inbox was deeper than usual, but there was nothing out of the ordinary beyond that. Professor Zaritsky was cordial, proceeding with the day's agenda without comment. Blair was relieved but surprised that her absence seemed to have gone unnoticed, and she wondered if her resignation would be received with equal indifference.

The children, however, had correctly read the tea leaves, telling Spira and their close friends they would be moving to Paris sometime in the summer. The prospect of this change ruffled the sensibilities of some, especially Spira's.

At dinner, Spira reported the news to her parents. Subsequently, Mike called his brother to voice his support, preempting the actual discussion of the matter between Ian and Blair. Ian asked Mike to hold the farewells as Logan and Max had gotten ahead of their parents, and there were still a few steps to iron out.

Finally, when the kids were in bed for the night, Ian received a full debrief of the Paris trip. As expected, Blair gave a favorable report which included details regarding salaries paid in French Francs and reimbursement for shipping.

Blair had been thorough and felt there were only upsides to the proposal. Ian was satisfied with her judgment, and they agreed to tell the children at breakfast. Blair had returned home with new contracts, which would be signed and mailed in the next twenty-four hours. They would submit written resignations to their respective employers by Monday. Ian's tenure would terminate at the end of the school year, Blair's no later than August 1st. The dye was cast.

*

Breaking the news to the children produced no marked change in their demeanor, as they had already preempted the announcement of their parents' decision by telling their friends it had been decided. So, for the moment, there were no tears or barrage of questions other than those concerning their departure date.

Ian was the first to break the news to his employers. Parker's headmistress was only in the third year of her tenure, but she had developed a good relationship with Ian. From her perspective, the prospect of replacing him was not as simple as Ian had thought. She didn't want to discontinue either the Chinese or the Asian history component of their curriculum. She felt it was a strong selling point with many of her parents, and she doubted she could find a substitute who could handle both subjects. Ian explained that he had drafted thorough lesson plans for all his classes, and until someone learned the ropes and personalized their approach, these notes should provide good continuity for the transition. Sensing her disappointment, he volunteered to check with the Chinese department at Columbia for possible candidates, and he could post a job offer on the university's student bulletin board. Reluctantly, she accepted the news and wished him well in his new venture.

Blair, however, waited until the following Monday. Professor Zaritsky arrived at the office, fortuitously sporting a low-frequency, red bowtie. He appeared cheerful, offering a warm "Good morning, Mrs. Kennedy" in Russian as he passed into his office.

The professor drank only English tea, so she prepared a cup with a teaspoon of sugar and a slice of lemon (always kept fresh in a small refrigerator) and carried it into his office.

Professor Zaritsky looked up from his papers and thanked Blair for the tea. She took a seat and said she would like to talk to him. He smiled, stroked his goatee, and waited.

Nervously, Blair began the careful narration of her story. She started with the letter from her Barnard classmate and the nature of the positions available at NIS. She then provided chronological details leading up to her short leave of absence and the decision to accept the offer.

Professor Zaritsky listened quietly, occasionally stroking his goatee, asking only a few questions to clarify some detail. When she had finished, he smiled broadly. "This is quite a change for you and your family. How are your children handling it?"

He spoke in English, and she was surprised by the intimacy of the question, as the subject of her children had rarely come up.

"Pretty well," she answered. "Max, my youngest, was upset about leaving family and friends, but I think he's coming around. Logan is almost fourteen and is mature for her age. She is warming up to the cultural advantages of living in Europe."

"I can see there would be many," said the professor, folding his hands under his chin and leaning forward on his elbows. "Of course, you know your work is appreciated here, and, speaking frankly, I've come to regard you almost as a daughter."

He spoke earnestly, catching Blair off guard. She had never imagined he'd considered her as anything other than a competent secretary. He knew almost nothing about her personal life, and since the beginning of her tenure, he had only addressed her as Mrs. Kennedy. Ian and the kids had met him several times at departmental functions, but never outside the office. She would talk about the children if they were ill, and needed to attend to them, but nothing more. She'd gleaned the little she knew of his life from copies of his CV, personal letters he had asked her to type, honors he'd received, or over coffee with office staff, but his history was skeletal, and he'd never discussed it with her.

As Blair said nothing in return, the professor continued. "You may not realize it, but you have been the co-pilot of this ship, and as I am often asleep at the helm, your hand has always been there to steady things. Where I am forgetful, you are not. Where I am neglectful, you are not.

You are like a seer, perceiving through the mist what is coming so we may prepare."

Blair sensed that he was about to ask her to stay. She started to speak in her defense, but the professor raised a finger to allow him to continue.

"Of course, we will have to find someone, and I am confident we will, and with your help, train them to carry on. Despite the difficulties such a transition will present to me and others, I am happy for you, and I am happy for your family. You deserve to leave your desk and the narrow confines of the university. I felt you were a bit of a caged bird here, but I had not the nerve to throw open the door and encourage you to take flight. I didn't want you to misunderstand. But this is God-sent, and I am happy for you, *moya dorogaya*."

It was only the second time in fifteen years that Professor Zaritsky had used a term of endearment with her, and it was the first time he called her "my dear." Blair was momentarily flustered but thanked him for his understanding and assured him she would do all she could to train her replacement.

The meeting ended quickly with Professor Zaritsky saying, "*Udachi, moya dorogaya devochka.*" Good luck, my dear girl.

Not a believer in Russian fatalism, Blair excited the room, relieved at the professor's calm and caring demeanor, but vowed never to put her trust in luck.

-54-

The Verdict

Over the next month, the wheels of progress moved into high gear. Parker and Columbia started a formal search for replacements, and the Kennedys began to tackle the long list of personal logistics with NIS in Paris and with family and friends at home. Fortunately, the arrival of spring break allowed them to deal with the burgeoning details almost full-time.

Michael solved the problem of abandoned family furniture by volunteering to rent a U-Haul and truck it to his cabin in upstate New York. The property had a metal barn where he stored essentials, as "you never know when you might need 'em."

Blair handled details of their working visas with Madam Clément in Paris and the French Consulate on 5th Avenue. Then she met with the headmistress at St. Mark's School regarding forwarding school records and to thank her for all they had done for Max and Logan.

Everything was falling into place, except for one wagging omission.

Ian volunteered to handle the Zato problem, which meant finding a good home for him—one that could deal with his many eccentricities. Zato's readoption and the expected fallout from the children seemed the most problematic of all the issues needing attention. Still, even that soon fell into place, shortly before the spring holiday.

For the last ten years, Marian Santora had been the business manager for Parker School. Each morning she rode the subway into Manhattan from the Forest Hills section of Queens, where she lived in a two-story, four-bedroom home with her husband, a daughter in middle school, and a live-in mother-in-law. A doghouse stood empty in a fully fenced-in backyard. Her husband was a contractor with a penchant for big dogs. To that end, they had raised 140-pound Newfoundland, but it had passed away six months earlier from heart disease at age nine. So, they were in the market for a dog, a big dog, and when she heard the Kennedys were moving and could not take their malamute, she discussed it with her husband. She had laughed at and admired Ian's stories of the malamute's bravery and buffoonery. However, she had seen photos of the fabled canine, and, despite his quirks and "diminutive size," she thought he was beautiful and asked Ian to arrange an introduction.

"Are we really doing this?" Blair asked rhetorically. "I know we must, but it's tearing me up. God knows what it will do to the kids."

Ian knew he would need to be the family's emotional mainstay in negotiating any readoption. "Marion has a strong personality," he said confidently, "and will be good for Zato. She was an athlete in high school and college; she's tough and feels up to the challenge. They have a fenced-in backyard with a large doghouse, so Zato could spend plenty of time outside. Their Nuffy spent most of his time in the house, so I'm sure Zato would have lots of love time with the family."

"When does she want to visit?"

"Over a weekend when it's convenient for us. We can do a test run. Marion would likely bring her husband and possibly her daughter. I think it's important that the kids get to meet them and feel assured that Zato's new family will provide him with enough love and care. But they wouldn't be taking him until we were on the verge of moving."

"Do you think she can walk him? I know I can't," said Blair.

"I guess we'll see. Marion referred to her husband as a 'large man,' and she's confident they can handle him."

"Well, I'm glad she's so optimistic."

*

A few days later, Ian arranged for the Santoras to visit on the last Sunday of spring break, thus requiring a sit-down with the kids. Informing them was bound to be heartbreaking, so Blair decided to tell them after a good night's sleep and a hearty breakfast. However, there was palpable tension as soon as the family assembled in the living room for the news. The kids knew what was coming. Ian and Blair reviewed the challenges of parenting Zato, and although there was no mention of his near escape from the apartment, the kids knew how close they had come to disaster.

Ian explained that even if they were not moving to Paris, the subject of Zato's adoption by another family would still have become necessary. Some dogs were good city dogs, and some were not. Zato was not. He was a dog needing open spaces or a yard to run around. Being so confined was not fair to him, especially in summer.

Surprisingly, Zato's defense had no arguments, only questions about who, when, and where. Ian provided some background on the Santoras, their home in the suburbs, and how their Newfoundland had recently passed away. They missed their big, wooly dog, and wanted to meet Zato to see if they might make a good home for him.

The kids had met Marion Santora a few times when visiting Parker School with their dad. She seemed nice, but was that enough?

"Do they know how he is?" asked Max.

"Yes, and despite all the issues, they are still interested," Ian said with a laugh. "I've shown Marion pictures of him; she thinks he is beautiful."

"Newfoundlands are very loving," said Max. "They shed a lot and love the snow. They can even swim underwater, but they drool like St. Bernard's."

"How old is their daughter?" queried Logan.

"Twelve or thirteen. I'm sure she will love Zato as much as you do, as much as we all do."

Zato was lying on the rug in the middle of the living room, looking up now and then, perking his ears when he heard his name.

Max had begun to tear. "But we are taking Bagel, right?" he asked.

"Of course, dear," said his mother.

The kids left the couch and joined Zato on the rug. They hugged him and rubbed his ears, causing him to roll over and beg for a tummy scratch.

-55-

Road Test

Saturday was a grooming day for Zato. After a bath and a thorough brushing from his chest to the tip of his tail, followed by an exuberant bout of the zoomies, he was prepared to meet guests on the following day. His fur was silky, and he looked like a man in a new suit.

After breakfast Sunday morning, the apartment was readied for guests: the rugs and hallways vacuumed, pillows plumped, human beds made, and dog beds deboned. The visit would begin at 2:00 PM with a chat in the living room to get acquainted with one another and with Zato—to whom Ian had provided detailed instructions on deportment. Afterward, the two families and dogs would go for a walk together. Ian expected there would be more than one encounter to check the mettle of these prospective parents.

The conversation before lunch was uneasy in anticipation.

"They'll be here in three hours."

"Do you think they will like Zato? He is very likable."

"They will love him. How could they not?"

"What if he jumps on the couch or their laps?"

"He won't. He's been warned."

"What if he goes crazy outside when he sees another dog?"

"I've explained everything to Marion and what to do if it happens. It's partly why we arranged this meeting."

"What if Zato doesn't like them? He must like them, too, right?"

"When has he ever not liked someone?"

"What if he gets excited and pees in the hall, or worse?"

"I'm giving him a good walk after lunch. He'll be fine."

"He's not a big, slobbering, over-stuffed Nuffy," moaned Max. "They may be expecting a teddy bear. What then? We'd have to find someone else to take him, which might be impossible."

"He is a teddy bear: handsome and lovable. The fact that he doesn't slobber might be a good thing, don't you think?"

As the children expressed their concerns, their parents offered comforting replies, but as the conversation progressed, the emphasis shifted.

"They will never find a better friend than Zato."

"He loves everyone—indoors!"

"There is no dog braver."

"And there is no dog funnier."

"I hope they have a long hallway for him practice his flip turns."

"And a comfortable bed in his doghouse."

*

The doorbell rang just a little after 2:00 PM. The dogs raced down the hall, Bagel yapping loudly. The family assembled in the foyer and corralled the dogs. Ian and Blair welcomed the Santoras warmly and invited them inside. Marion introduced her husband, Victor, and her daughter, Chiara. Victor stood well over six feet, was broad-shouldered, and the curl in his black hair made Ian think of Superman. Chiara resembled her mother: black hair, intelligent blue eyes, and olive skin.

Ian introduced his brood, moving along by age and seniority, with Zato bringing up the rear. He then released his grip on Zato's collar, allowing him to move forward for a more intimate greeting. His tail had been wagging from the start, and as he moved closer to Chiara, she held out her hand for him to sniff, which he did. Then she patted his head warily.

"He's friendly, isn't he?" she asked.

"He loves people," responded Logan.

Chiara bent down to stroke his cheeks, receiving a lick in return.

"He's a purebred malamute," said Max authoritatively. "My Uncle Mike found him lost in a snowstorm last year and brought him to us. We named him after Zatoichi, a famous Japanese movie hero, but we call him Zato."

"Zato," said Chiara, addressing her new friend. "You are very handsome."

Blair placed Bagel on the floor, introduced her to the guests and ushered them into the living room for a chat and soft drinks.

The Santoras sat together on the couch. Blair and Bagel took the wingback, and Ian moved a chair from the dining room for himself. Max and Logan sat with Zato on the rug, stroking him jealously.

Victor talked about their dog, Nuffy, and what a joy he had been for them, but it seemed that he, too, had had his downside.

"Marion told me Zato is not friendly with other dogs," said Victor. "We are familiar with that trait, too. Nuffy had a big problem with male dogs, large or small. At 140 pounds, he could be tough to manage when walking in the neighborhood. Females were fine, but male dogs and cats of any kind were on his hit list. So, we always wore sneakers when walking him and often changed direction to avoid skirmishes or wrapped his leash around a street sign to keep balance when other dogs passed by."

"We're familiar with that M.O.," said Ian laughing.

Marion rose quickly to Nuffy's defense. "But he was friendly to lady dogs and playful and loving at home. He liked having a yard to run around in, especially in summer, and enjoyed having a doghouse with a comfy bed in bad weather. But he was most happy in the house."

"Nuffy sounds much like Zato," said Ian. "But Zato is fixed and so does not share an interest in females. So, I, too, dodge up side streets or wrap his leash around signposts. I've learned to keep him out of chomping distance the hard way. Frankly, Blair's walks with Zato are limited to necessary ones at a nearby tree once or twice each day, but long walks fall to me."

Again, Marion jumped in. "I could handle Nuffy," she said. "He was big, but I could deal with him. I'm sure I could handle Zato. He's lighter than Nuffy, although he looks considerably more athletic," she said, smiling.

"It's true," said Victor. "Marion is very strong; I'm sure she can handle him."

They talked more about each dog's habits and eccentricities, and the children of both families gushed about their dog's sterling qualities. Marion explained how they would care for Zato and how he might enjoy being outside for part of the day.

"Mom, show them the pictures of Nuffy in his doghouse," said Chiara. "And show them his favorite tree."

Marion gave her daughter a look of mild disapproval and took a spiral-bound, 5x7-inch photo album from her purse.

"There are many photos of Nuffy in the yard," she said, passing the album to Blair. "So, you can get an idea of his play area."

Blair turned the pages, commenting on how comfortable Nuffy looked in his supersized doghouse, munching his supersized bone. She noticed the yard near the doghouse was dirt, but that there was also a grassy area and a small flower garden alongside the house. A sturdy, six-foot picket fence enclosed the entire space. There was no looking in or out.

"It looks nice and secure," Blair said, then passed the album to Max and Logan.

"Only the birds and occasional squirrels got him going," said Victor, "but they were always too fast for him."

Chiara moved to the floor beside Max and Logan. "That's Nuffy's doghouse," she said, pointing to a photograph. "And there in the corner is his favorite tree."

"For peeing?" asked Max.

Chiara laughed and nodded.

"Zato's favorite is out front, and he can pee for hours."

To keep the conversation from running wild, Victor stood up and suggested they go outside and give Zato a test run. "Let's see how much of a battler this pooch is," he said.

The weather was clear and crisp, so the Kennedys donned light sweaters or jackets, linked up the dogs, and led the way: first stop, Zato's favorite tree.

"I told you," said Max.

Ian handed Zato's reins to Marion. As she had heard the New Year's Eve escape story, she kept a solid grip, impressed by the three choke collars and the sturdy leather leash. The kids brought up the rear with Bagel.

"I'm sorry to hear about Nuffy," Logan said to Chiara as the group turned onto Morningside Drive, "He looks so cuddly. I bet he was loving."

"He was very loving," said Chiara. "Mom called him 'her little bear.'"

The three children walked on in silence while observing Marion keep her charge in check.

Just before they reached 117th Street, Zato began straining at his leash and growling. The Duke, the Duchess, and one of their minions approached in the middle of the street. Ian had warned them of this possibility and pointed them out.

"We can change direction and go up 117th Street or tie up against the posts," said Ian, indicating the wrought iron railings that lined the retaining wall of Morningside Park. Marion chose the latter and wound the leash around one of the decorative posts, pulling Zato's muzzle close to the wall.

The trio paused mid-street, and their leader faced his sputtering adversary. Bagel remained silent. Duke tilted his head, appearing to recall something, then looked away and slowly led his posse down the street. Zato's frothing abated, and the group turned up 117th Street toward the campus.

Victor asked to take over as they passed onto College Walk, and Marion passed him the leash. Immediately, Zato sensed a firmer hand, stopped straining, and slowed his pace. The walk to Broadway was uneventful, allowing for casual conversation.

"I hope your visit hasn't seemed like an inspection from Social Services," said Ian. "Of course, we want Zato to have a good home, but we are more concerned with him not disrupting yours. He's loving and often hilarious, but he's rambunctious to an extreme and is not a good listener."

Victor smiled. "We had many near disasters with Nuffy, so we're not rookies when handling a trust of this kind."

"I guess not," responded Ian affably. "I didn't know Newfoundlands had an aggressive bone in their body. Zato loves people to a fault: babies can crawl on him, gouge his eyes, and pull his ears; guests love to scratch him and encourage his affection which can end up with an 80-pound malamute perched on their lap; and, because of his people-friendliness, he is *not* a watchdog. He may bark viciously at almost anything on four legs—horses being the one exception—but strangers at the door receive only a welcoming wag. Bagel has tried to teach him otherwise, but to no avail."

At that moment, Ian spotted a pug approaching them in a bicycle basket. "Hold on tight," said Ian. "Incoming, at twelve o'clock. Riding in the basket."

Zato crossed in front of Vincent directly into the bike's path as the cyclist approached. He strained to get traction, but Vincent pulled him back, pressing the dog's head firmly against his knee. The cyclist put a steadying hand on the pug, and the two dogs exchanged insults. As the bicycle turned and disappeared down Broadway, Zato soon redirected his attention to the anonymous ciphers left on the shrubbery.

"He's got quite an antenna," said Vincent.

"Sometimes he sees the enemy before I have a chance to steady myself," said Ian. "But I have learned to expand my attention during walks, and I usually see them coming before he does."

They continued across campus without incident and returned to the apartment to talk things over.

Blair suggested the kids take the dogs and show Chiara their rooms so the adults could discuss the day's experience.

When the kids were out of earshot, Vincent said: "I think we are up to the task." Then turning to his wife, he asked, "Do you?"

"I feel we are a good match and would give him a good home," answered Marion. "I know Chiara would love him like she did Nuffy."

"It wouldn't be for a few months yet," said Blair. "I may have to work through July. So, if that works for you," she said, looking at her husband for agreement, "it works for us."

Ian called the children into the living room and provided the details of their arrangement. Blair ensured that Logan and Max understood Zato would remain with them until they had to leave for France.

"I promise to take good care of him," said Chiara to her new friends. "He was very friendly to me just now. I think he likes me."

"He does like you," said Logan. Then after a pause, said, "And he likes lots of hugs."

"And tummy scratches," added Max, eyes glistening. "He needs lots of tummy scratches.

*

The following weekend, Ian and the kids procured a dozen collapsed boxes from the bookstore, and family packing got underway. Upon their departure for France, the furniture would go to Mike's barn in upstate New York, while essential household goods would travel to Paris by boat a month before. Finally, essentials would go by air, together with the family and their luggage.

Blair had found a freight forwarding company specializing in transporting small lots or personal items by container ship. The company provided everything from pickup in Manhattan to delivery at the port of arrival, followed by customs clearance and transfer to the destination city. They could cope for a few weeks if they arrived ahead of their shipment.

Ian and Blair labeled each box for air or sea, placing a complete packing list inside. They were sealed and stacked along the foyer walls and at either end of the hallway, thoroughly deconstructing Zato's racing lanes for his occasional bouts of the zoomies.

In the weeks following, the children spent even more time playing and roughhousing with Zato. He enjoyed the additional attention and would moan loudly for more when the kids had had enough. However, Bagel was not accustomed to sharing the children's beds with Zato and seemed confused about her role. When Zato moaned, she would too, but more to harmonize than sympathize.

"Bagel cries for Zato," Logan said to her mother one afternoon in late April. "I think she knows something is going to happen. I saw her sleeping in Zato's bed this morning when he was in the kitchen."

"She's very sensitive," consoled Blair. "The first few weeks without Zato will be hard. But, once she is out of quarantine, we can go for long walks and get acquainted with the new neighborhood. It should be therapeutic for all of us, but it might take a little time."

Yes, it might take a little time, thought Logan.

-56-

Curtain Calls

On the first Saturday in June, St. Mark's concluded its school year with a graduation ceremony in the gymnasium. Ian and Blair applauded vigorously when the headmistress awarded certificates to Max and Logan for their achievements. Max received acknowledgment in Latin, math, and science, while his sister earned recognition in French, literature, and composition. There was a special fanfare for those moving on to either of New York's premier public high schools. Logan's acceptance to Stuyvesant had arrived in March like a bad penny. Now, as Sister Bernice called her name to join the ranks of the consecrated, Logan stood, stone-faced, to receive the hollow honor of that achievement. Blair bit her lip and squeezed her husband's hand.

Later, on the walk home, Logan was quiet while her brother expounded on his accomplishments. "I think I got the science award for my research on how even Pekinese and Dachshunds evolved from wolves." While Max recounted the salient points of his analysis, Logan dropped back a few steps.

Blair slowed her pace, linking arms with her daughter.

"I really wanted to go to Stuyvesant, Mom."

"I know, dear. I wanted it for you, too."

"With so many smart kids—it would have been challenging."

Blair pulled Logan close. "I had lunch with a few Neuilly students during my visit there, as I wanted to get a sense of their interests and how they felt about the school's program and their teachers. I was impressed with their enthusiasm. They seemed to genuinely like the variety of teaching methods there and spoke freely about how their personal interests can be met by these variations. Not all classes are lecture-style, which allows them to move through some subjects quickly, or, if needed, take more time to understand something fully. There are many hands-on projects, and, for juniors and seniors, the school arranges apprenticeships in career interests with various professionals in Paris. It's unique and may take some getting used to."

"That sounds a little scary, but cool," responded Logan.

"One of the girls even asked about you."

"Really, how?"

"I think her family is from Munich. She's in ninth grade, and she asked about your interests. I told her that you were creative, a good writer, and enjoyed acting and singing in the choir. Hearing that, she bubbled on about how NIS was strong in the arts, that she was in the choir and had been in several school plays. She was certain you'd love it and said she looked forward to meeting you."

"That's nice. She sounds friendly."

"All the kids I met were friendly. I even spoke to parents who were picking their kids up after school. One was Swiss, and another Spanish. Very nice people who spoke English beautifully."

Logan continued walking, now quiet and reflective.

"There are going to be challenges for all of us," said Blair. "But we Kennedys are a tough lot, and I think we are up to it."

"I guess we'll have to be," said Logan, forcing a smile.

*

To help find his replacement at Parker School, Ian posted a job notice on the student bulletin board outside Columbia's Asian Library and met with two of his former professors for suggestions regarding local talent. However, it was the announcement faxed from Parker's personnel director to Asian Studies departments around the country that resulted in inquiries. Most were from students at Ivy League schools, but one from the University of Wisconsin was the most inspiring: a twenty-four-year-old woman of Indian parentage with a B.A. in East Asian Languages and Culture and an M.A. in Chinese Language and Culture. Born and raised in San Jose, Sahara Dash was the child of immigrants: two professionals—a pediatrician and a neurologist. In addition to speaking Chinese, she was fluent in Hindi and a student of Indian culture.

Ian could not believe the school's good fortune when he shook her hand and was able to conduct the interview entirely in Chinese. In addition to spending two years in Taiwan, she had lived for six months in Japan and spent numerous summers with relatives in Northern India. Ian reluctantly conceded—but only to himself—that she might well bring new life and a fresh perspective to Asian studies at Parker.

Meanwhile, "Position available" adverts set in motion by the Russian Institute before spring break resulted in a flurry of resumés. The professor expected the search would take some time, so he asked Blair to "find the needle in the haystack." To his surprise, the needle appeared after only a half-dozen interviews.

The chosen replacement was the youngest daughter of a family of Polish immigrants who arrived in Manhattan from Warsaw in 1952. Ziva Musial—sorry, no relation to Stan—was twenty-eight, spoke Polish fluently, and had studied Russian as an undergraduate at New York University. She was bright and cheerful and lived with her parents in an apartment above their pharmacy in the East Village.

Blair had trained Zeva Musial for nearly three months, and she was proving a worthy replacement. Professor Zaritsky spoke highly of her and often chatted with her in Polish, a language Blair had never heard him speak. Was she jealous? A little, she confessed to her husband, but she was happy that the professor was pleased with her choice and that the administrative management of the department was in good hands.

There was a small "retirement" party in the institute's main office with coffee, tea, and Polish babkas from Zabar's. The summer staff and faculty were present. Professor Zaritsky, wearing a low-frequency, orange bowtie, stroked his goatee and made a short speech commending "Mrs. Kennedy" for fifteen years of exceptional service to the institute and to him personally. It ended with a firm handshake and a light pat on her shoulder.

In contrast, the headmistress and senior faculty celebrated Ian's departure from Parker over dinner and wine at a midtown Italian restaurant. Blair was at Ian's side, and there was much playful taunting, attributing

Ian's departure to Paris as him having a midlife crisis, and "pulling a Hemingway," a literary allusion that neither Ian nor Blair understood.

The kids' departure party was with Spira and her parents, who took them all to see the movie *Grease*, followed by sundaes at Rumpelemeyer's. All did their best not to talk about Paris, but, despite heroic efforts, youthful tears lightly salted the fudge sauce.

A week before the family took flight for France, it was Zato's turn for a formal sendoff. The Santoras had arranged to pick up their adoptee on Saturday afternoon, so a party was held for the family foundling after dinner the night before. There were milk bones for the dogs and an empty bag of bagels for Zato to deconstruct. Blair had made a beautifully bronzed New York-style cheesecake and filled paper cups with beer or Coke for toasting. In the cake's center stood a small candle and a message piped in a pink script:

For Our Loving Palamute

Forever in Our Hearts

Logan supplied the music, feeling it appropriate to play "Linus and Lucy" from her *Charlie Brown Christmas* album.

The dogs were at their places under the dinner table, and while Linus and Lucy frolicked in the background, Blair lit the candle, and, in unison, they blew it out.

Cheers for Zato followed, rousing the dogs from underfoot. Blair carried the cake into the kitchen for distribution. She cut four thick slices for the family and two slim ones for the dogs, placing them all on paper plates. In the spirit of the moment, Zato and Bagel expressed their enthusiasm by gulping their slices almost before they hit the floor. As neither dog had paused to chew, Ian poured a few ounces of beer into their water bowls to clear their palates, then raised his cup.

"A toast to Zato! Our merry, beautiful, hilarious, and very exasperating malamute. May he have a long and happy life with his new family."

"Here, here!" responded the group.

The object of the accolades, hearing his name, glanced up momentarily from his beer.

Other toasts followed.

"To Zato, for all the love and laughs you gave us."

"To Zato, for protecting us from the Duke and his gang of thugs."

"To Bagel's best friend, live long and prosper!"

Zato looked up again, licked beer suds from his muzzle, then moved to Bagel's untouched bowl and set to work.

-57-

The Passing of the Leash

On Saturday, the Kennedys' emotional flags were all at half-mast, except for Zato's, who, in his usual carefree manner, reveled in renewed attention, happy to be mauled, scratched, and hugged. When Logan wrapped her arms around his neck and sobbed, he howled in a descending scale of sympathy. Then, sensing something was wrong, Bagel added her soulful soprano, which, in turn, infected the remaining family, who soon found themselves piled on Logan's bed in a mournful scrum.

The Santoras arrived on time, double parking in the street. All parties had agreed on a fast in and out for everyone's sake. The Kennedys did their best to smile and be welcoming. Stacked in the foyer were all Zato's possessions: a large bag of dog food, a box of giant Milk-Bones, his bed, a bag of half-chewed rubber toys, and two metal bowls.

"We put all of Zato's things together for you," said Blair. "We can help take them to your car."

"Thank you," said Marion. "That was very thoughtful of you."

Ian leashed Zato and, picking up his doggie bed, led the way out of the apartment. Blair and the kids each carried what remained.

"Bagel needs to come too," said Max, noticing she was standing at the back of the foyer looking puzzled. "I'll get her leash."

They walked through the lobby in single file, like a group of refugees fleeing a warzone. The Santora's car was a late model station wagon. Wire mesh separated the passenger seats from the far back, allowing ample space for a big dog to move about without interfering with passengers. Victor opened the tailgate, and Ian encouraged Zato to jump in, which he did eagerly. Bagel hopped in behind him as Max had relaxed his grip on her leash.

Blair handed Marion the bag of bowls and toys, then extracted the confused Bagel from the back of the car, gathering her in her arms and stepping back to allow Ian to arrange Zato's bed. The Kennedy clan (including Bagel) all stood quietly beside the open tailgate, Zato in the car, wagging, excited to be going for a ride.

Finally, Ian said, "You have been a great friend, Zato. We will miss you. But we have found a perfect family who will love you as we have. So be good to them, and don't give them too hard a time."

Ian turned to his children, "Say goodbye, kids."

Blair and the children stroked Zato's cheeks and rubbed his chest as they said their tearful goodbyes. Ian closed the tailgate and pulled a handwritten list from his back pocket titled: *Zato's Needs and Idiosyncrasies*, which he handed to Marion.

"This has our address in Paris and some tips on keeping yourselves and Zato happy. Please write and tell us how he's getting on, as he will constantly be on our minds, and we will need to reassure the kids and Bagel that he's okay."

"Of course. We will," said Marion.

Chiara took Logan and Max by their hands. "I will write you and tell you all the funny stories. I'm sure there will be many. Don't worry. I'll give him lots of hugs and tummy scratches."

The Santoras got into their car, and the Kennedys stepped back from the tailgate, looking at Zato, who was looking at them. Victor made a slow U-turn, stopping for a moment so everyone could wave goodbye, then eased to the corner and waited for the light to turn. Zato, wagging slowly, looked back at his family, who waved until the car turned and headed uptown.

Ian turned to the kids, "Alright, let's go to the movies," he said, clearly ending the moment and intending to begin another that would take their minds off Zato. "*King Kong* is playing at the Plaza on 58th Street. It starts in an hour."

"We've seen it," said Max.

"I know, but let's see it again. Will it be popcorn, chocolate mints, or Good & Plenty?"

"All three," said Blair.

-58-

Doing What Dogs Do

After more than two hours of watching an edgy version of the beauty and the beast fantasy, the family went to Carnegie Deli on 54th Street for dinner. The conversation wandered between Jessica Lange's scanty costume and how best to divvy up the deli's elephantine sandwiches.

"King Kong's a pervert," said Logan, in disgust, "poking around at the girl's clothes and messing with her hair. I don't remember that from the last time we saw it. He was gross, and I'm glad he got shot."

"Yes, that moment was…disquieting," said Blair. "I'd forgotten about that too."

"Her top almost came off," added Max. "You could see her bosom."

"Terrible, terrible," said Ian feigning outrage and concentrating on the menu. "How are we going to handle these sandwiches? One is enough for two of us, so what will it be, corned beef and pastrami on rye or the classic Reuben?"

They ordered one of each, followed by slices of the deli's much-vaunted New York cheesecake. As they ate, Blair and Ian filled any conversational vacuums with comments or questions about the film or the food, and they completed their meal without drifting into melancholy.

Later, after exiting the subway and walking across the campus, the group fell silent, and, when turning the key in the door lock produced no scratching of toenails or bumping against bicycles, four hearts sank.

When they had set out for the movies, the door to the master bedroom had been left ajar for the first time in more than a year, so it was unexpected to find Bagel curled behind the bike tires. The entrance now seemed out of proportion with just Bagel and her small bed and the absence of a large body getting in the way, jostling against legs and sniffing hands and shoes as if to discover what he'd missed.

Bagel slunk out from behind the tires. "She doesn't know what to do with herself," said Logan. "Her world is out of kilter."

Blair scooped the dog into her arms. "It's okay, my little friend," she cooed. "We understand. Let's get you a snack."

*

The day before departure: boxes destined for Paris had long since been packed and carted to a container ship in Brooklyn that would carry them to Europe—leaving only essentials stacked in the foyer that the family would bring with them by air. Suitcases were three-quarters packed and open on their respective beds. Bagel's travel carrier stood in the hallway with her documentation attached. After landing in Paris, she would require one month of quarantine—a bitter but necessary pill to swallow for everyone.

As passengers, luggage, and boxes of household essentials exceeded the capacity of Mike's van, Ian arranged for a six-passenger limo to take them to the airport. Mike and his family would come to see them off and, later, with the help of two clerks from the bookstore, load boxes and furniture from the apartment into a U-Haul for the trip upstate.

What remained in the apartment stood barren and inert: side tables without lamps; bare ceiling lightbulbs; rugs rolled side-by-side like unbaked pastries; while four sets of paper plates, cups, bowls, and plastic cutlery lingered on the dining room table.

"It looks like a graveyard," Max said to his sister. "I feel like Bagel. Everything is disappearing."

"I felt the same way until I tried one of Dad's tricks."

"What trick is that?"

"The one where he just changes his mind about something."

"I can't just change my mind," said Max. "I'm stuck with it."

"It's a process," said his sister. "You have to work at it. I've been practicing." Logan pulled her bike away from the wall. "Let's go for a ride. I'll show you."

She told her mother they were going out and would be back in an hour, then walked her bike out and onto the sidewalk and waited. When Max came alongside, she explained.

"I realized how to do this by watching Bagel. She places droplets of pee everywhere. Other dogs may have peed there before, but she puts her mark on top, making it her space. It's like saying, 'I own this spot.' Then she leaves her mark on other spots, all over the campus or the park, wherever we are. She is marking her territory, her space."

"I know," said Max, not getting the connection to his current feelings of loss.

"We need to think like Bagel—do like dogs," she said. "Leave our marks everywhere we want. Claim our territory; make it our space, now and forever. So, when we leave, it's not gone at all; we can step back into it from anywhere. I do it by touch."

Logan got on her bike and started forward. "Follow me and do what I do."

They crossed Amsterdam Avenue, and Logan stopped by the east gate. Touching it, she said emphatically, "You are mine."

Max had pulled up behind her. "Try it," she said. "Be forceful. Leave your mark forever."

"But you've already left yours."

"It doesn't matter, you'll see. So, leave yours, too, or leave it somewhere else."

Max touched the gate and said firmly, "My gate."

"Perfect," said Logan. "Now, let's ride around the campus and leave our marks."

They rode together, touching and marking spots: the brass robe of Alma Mater; the corner bricks of Hamilton Hall; the steps to the library and its colonnades; the bricks of College Walk; the sundial in the center of the campus; and on and on. They moved quickly, taking different paths, joining and separating again, leaving their marks, finally coming together at the campus west gate.

"Now Chock Full o'Nuts and the bookstore," said Logan as she walked her bike across Broadway. Placing her hand on the restaurant window, she said, "Mine." Max grasped the rubber of the revolving door and squeezed. "My door."

At the bookstore, they put down their kickstands, placing their palms against the display window, and moved along, putting their hands high, then low, like mimes looking for a door, repeating "my store" as they traveled its length.

They continued down Broadway, "doing what dogs do" to the steps of a church, the door to St. Mark's, windows of delis and bars, a shoe store, a pharmacy, and even a phone booth. Mondel's Chocolates got special attention as they left their bikes and subtly marked the display counter inside while ordering raspberry truffles.

They crossed 110th Street and began moving uptown, tagging a vegetable stand, another bar, Mama Joys (where they paused, inhaling deeply), and a subway exit.

When they reached 116th Street, Max suggested they go into Riverside Park, where they bounced down the steps and rolled to a stop. Max looked down the asphalt pathway and across the Hudson River to the Jersey Palisades and smiled.

"I don't think you have to touch it to mark it. You just need to..." He cupped his hands to either side of his mouth and yelled, "This river is mine! Those cliffs are mine!" Then, looking upriver, he cried, "That bridge is mine!"

Logan laughed and followed suit, claiming the trees, the walking path, the river, the bridge, and the clouds in the sky.

Their return home turned many heads as the two rode through the campus, exclaiming ownership of fountains, hedges, and pathways, even the grass in front of Butler Library.

"Where have you two been?" asked Blair as the kids leaned their bikes against the foyer wall.

"Just riding around doing what dogs do," said Max.

Blair was not sure what her son meant, but the sparkle in the eyes of her children gave her hope.

-59-

Bon Voyage

The following morning, Logan was the first to rise. The clock on her dresser read six-thirty. On the building opposite her window, a dim light crept along the bricks. Moving day had arrived. She turned on her light and started down the hall toward the bathroom. Passing the foyer, she thought she saw an odd bundle on Bagel's bed. Stepping around luggage and boxes in the foyer, she turned on the light for a better look. Bagel was asleep, wrapped in one of Zato's old blankets. How sweet, she thought, and how sad, then turned off the light and stepped away.

A minute later, the alarm went off in her parents' bedroom, followed by a call to wake up and get moving. They had a lot to do in the next two hours.

Everyone had showered the night before, so the line to the bathroom moved quickly. Blair went to the kitchen to start breakfast while the family got dressed, but in the early hour and semi-comatose states of mind, the fact that Bagel was not underfoot had gone unnoticed for a while.

Where's Bagel?" shouted Blair as she poured milk into a bowl of Cheerios.

"She's in the foyer," answered Logan from down the hall. "Take a look."

Blair put aside the milk carton and went to find her. At first, she saw only the silhouettes of the boxes, so she stepped around the dog bed and turned on the light. Tucked between the folds of one of Zato's blankets, Bagel looked up but didn't move.

"Hi honey, wouldn't you like some breakfast?" Blair asked her forlorn friend. "We have a lot to do today, so we'd better get started." She lifted Bagel from the blanket and nestled her in her arms. "Where did you find that blanket? Well, don't worry. If it comforts you, we'll take it with us."

"I found Bagel wrapped in Zato's old blanket," said Blair to her husband as she placed the dog on a pillow next to Ian's open suitcase. "It almost made me cry. I know our ship has sailed, but are we sure we're doing the right thing? I feel like I did after Logan was born."

Ian had been quietly grappling with the same question for a few days but knew there was nothing gained by confessing it. "It's certainly daunting, but it's right for all of us. We've covered our bases many times over. There may be a steep learning curve, but we'll do fine. All of us."

*

After breakfast, the final packing got underway, and orders rang out from the bedroom and kitchen:

"Make sure to pack your PJs and toothbrushes."

"Wear your most comfortable clothes and shoes for the flight. It's long, more than seven hours."

"Bring a book or two. They usually show a couple of movies, but you might have seen them already."

"It gets cold in the plane. Bring a sweater."

"Please put Zato's blanket into Bagel's carrying case. She's going to need it."

At eight a.m., the doorbell rang: Uncle Mike, Lizanne, and Spira were there to say goodbye and to begin loading the U-Haul with things going into storage at the cabin. The truck was parked at the curb, as some early risers had already left for work, leaving space enough to pull it in at an angle.

"I have two clerks from the store coming at eight-thirty to help," said Mike. "We should be out of here by eleven, but we can get started now."

Ian explained that the boxes in the foyer were going with them to the airport, but everything else should go in the truck. So, the move began box by box, then small tables and chairs with Ian and the kids helping while Blair took inventory of all their travel needs: passports (those for Ian and the kids had arrived two weeks earlier), tickets, snacks, books, sweaters, etc.

Half an hour later, the limo arrived like a blue whale. Mike and Ian started by putting the luggage and boxes in the trunk. Then the family and Bagel piled in. The limo could fit everything except one long box stuffed with sheets, pillows, and blankets. So Mike organized a complete reshuffle with two small bags going on the laps of the travelers next to Bagel's carrying case and another in the front seat beside the driver. It was clear that getting them all from the limo to check-in would require a legion of porters and a caravan of luggage carts.

Finally, everything and everyone was situated and immobilized. The tone in the back seats was somber. Mike told the driver to wait while he went to the truck bed and removed his trombone case. He set it on the sidewalk, snapped open the locks, and extracted the sheepskin zampogna and Spira's plastic chanter. Lizanne stood to the side, holding a lamp.

Mike blew some air into the instrument's mouthpiece, causing it to drone, then leaning into the open window, said, "Darest thou leave with so many so aggrieved?"

Ian forced a smile and answered in his most theatrical voice, "Please, my dear brother, give us now leave to leave thee. We must away."

"Alas, then, my blooded friends," Mike continued, "if ye must go, we will nurse our wounded hearts with this gay tune. Spira and I have been practicing it to festoon your departure."

He stepped back beside Spira and blew more air into the sheepskin, infusing the limo with the whine of the drones. Then with a nod, he and Spira began a tarantella. It started slowly with just the thrum of the zampogna and gradually picked up speed with Spira taking the melody.

Lizanne placed the lamp on the sidewalk and clapped in time to the music.

Spira picked up the tempo, playing with fervor. But, before long, tears began flowing down her cheeks, causing her mother to stop clapping. Leaning down, Lizanne blew a kiss through the window and waved at the driver to pull away.

The limo was too long to manage a U-turn, so it moved off toward Morningside Drive—the band still playing—

then, turning uptown with arms waving out of windows, disappeared.

Mike let the sheepskin deflate with a long sorrowful note.

"Here come the boys," he said, pointing to his clerks waiting for the light to change across Amsterdam Avenue. "Let's pack up the instruments and move everything into the truck. Then we'll pick up Isa and spend a week in the country. How's that sound?"

"It sounds good," said Spira, "but I miss them already. Zato too."

Lizanne placed her hand on her daughter's shoulder. "Me too," she said.

Mike squeezed the last of the air from the zampogna and folded it into the trombone case along with Spira's chanter. "Me too," he said, snapping the case closed. "Let's get to work."

Epilogue

August 11, 1979

From our Cabin in the woods

Dear Logan and Max,

I miss you!!!

I guess you are now in your new home in Paris. It must be very beautiful there. You have to send me pictures of everything.

We are at the cabin, and all your furniture is safe in the barn. We packed it up right after you left for the airport and drove it here. Sometimes I go in and sit on your couch. It smells like your apartment.

We are driving to Montreal next week and staying for a few days in a hotel that allows dogs. Dad says it's very French, so I can get used to saying "La plume de ma tante" to everyone. I will be ready to wow your friends next summer if I come to visit. No! When I come visit!

Mom said Bagel was still in the kennel. I wonder what she is thinking. She will be so happy to see you. I'm sending you a picture of Isa and me at the cabin. She can run free up here and is happy chasing everything.

I'm afraid to ask about Zato, but if you know how he's doing, please let me know. I miss him, too. I'm sure his new family loves him like we all do. He is such a clown.

I worry the city will feel empty without you guys. School is going to be terrible. I can't wait until next summer. Don't forget to send photos.

I miss you,

Spira

August 22, 1979

Dear Spira,

Max and I miss you, too!!

All our stuff arrived by boat two days after we arrived here, and we are still unpacking boxes. Bagel is in quarantine for two more weeks, and we all miss her very much. She must think we have abandoned her. She is probably frightened and lonely. Poor girl. At least Zato has a family who loves him.

Our apartment is nice but smaller than our old one. Max and I each have our own room, so it's good. The neighborhood is quiet, not at all like 116th Street. I think mainly retired people live in this part of the city. I haven't seen a stroller yet.

We took some bus rides, and I saw the Eiffel Tower, but only from the window. Tomorrow we are taking a tourist boat down the river Seine. It runs through the center of Paris, so it should be fun. I have begged Mom to take us to the impressionist museum, and she promised to do it before school starts in September. I wonder how different the paintings will be from the picture books. I can't wait!

I'll send you postcards so you can see where we go. I have tried my French in some small restaurants (Bistros) and the grocery store. People understand me, but I don't always understand them.

They don't let you touch the fruit here. I don't know how anyone knows if the clerk's selection is any good. We went to a cheese store a few days ago. Max and I had to wait outside as it smelled worse than Max's sneakers. Mom bought a book about French cheeses, and is trying out different kinds. Thank God our market has peanut butter and jelly!

We visited the new school. It's in a kind of suburb, near lots of fancy homes. The headmistress showed us around. She is very nice, and she even complimented my French. It's still summer vacation here so we didn't meet any students or teachers. The school grounds have four tennis courts, many trees, and a few flower gardens. There are offices and a few classrooms in a beautiful building that must have once been a private home. It's 100 years old, but you would never know it,

Paris is hot and humid, but I think New York is worse. We have fans running in every room.

Max is going stir-crazy. The teachers who live in this building and work at the school are all on vacation. So there are no kids to play with. He is looking forward to seventh grade, especially after seeing the science lab. It's twice the size of St. Mark's with all modern equipment. But I'm a little anxious. I didn't feel this way about going to Stuyvesant, but I do here. I'm worried I won't fit in.

Half of these kids come from cities like Paris, Rome, Madrid or London. Even though I'm from New York, they may think of me as a hayseed.

I loved the music you and Uncle Mike played for us before the limo pulled away. I can still hear it. If Zato had been with us, he and Bagel would have joined in for sure. Max and I cried all the way to the airport.

That's all for now. Don't stop writing to us.

See you soon.

Love,
Logan

Here's a note from Max:

> **Hi, come visit us. We miss you. Really! We will go out for hot chocolate, then eat elephant ears in the park. People speak French here. Did you know that? So strange.**
>
> **Max**

September 15, 1979

Dear Logan and Max,

Please don't worry, Zato is doing well. I am sure you miss him very much. I know he misses you. Sometimes he sits in the backyard and either sings or howls, it is hard to tell which. So I go out and hug and kiss him, and he quiets down. He seems happy in the yard, but he also likes to be inside where the action is (the kitchen).

I've tried to teach him to fetch. I guess you know what that's like—KEEP AWAY! He loves to play, but not the game I'm trying to teach him.

Zato likes the same tree that Nuffy did. I feel sorry for that tree. But if it survived Nuffy for 9 years, it should survive Zato.

I play the guitar and he often sings along with me. He's very funny, and he has a nice voice.

Max, I am giving him lots of tummy scratches. Sometimes I use Nuffy's old wire brush to scratch his back, and he really likes it—especially right above his tail.

I hope you like your new home in Paris. Mom and I have been looking at pictures of your city in her "I Love Paris" book. I hope to visit there some day. It seems so romantic. Maybe we can meet under the "eyefull" tower.

I will write again and tell you what Zato has been up to.

Your friend,

Chiara

P.S. I have attached a photo of Zato sleeping outside his doghouse. So far, he doesn't use it much.

September 25, 1979

Dear Chiara,

Thank you for your letter. Max and I are glad you and Zato are doing well. Believe me—I know all about Keep Away! That and "Escape" are his favorite games. Hopefully, you will never see him play "Escape," as that game is fun only for him!

I think he will get used to the doghouse in time. Maybe when it's raining, he will figure it out. Thank you for the picture. He looks happy.

We have started school here. It's a little scary for me—so many new faces and people from dozens of countries. That's the cool part, but making new friends is not so easy for me, although I have met a nice girl from Germany, and she is introducing me to other kids.

Bagel just came out of quarantine. She sure was happy to see us. I think she'd given up. Now she is a bit jumpy when we leave her in the apartment, but we take her on lots of walks and it's helping to settle her down. Everything is so new. Not just for her.

Max sends Zato his love. Me too. We thank you for taking such good care of him.

Write back soon,
Logan (& Max)

September 18, 1979

Dear Ian, Blair, Logan, Max, and Bagel,

Hello from New York. I imagine you are all moved in by now. Hopefully, you are not still waiting for your boxes to come by ship.

Classes have started at Parker, and Ian's replacement is learning the ropes quickly. She has often told me how grateful she is that he left such thorough lesson plans. She struggles a bit, but I'm sure she will get through it. Everyone likes her. They have decided to have her teach the history class after the new year. For now, it's just Chinese. She started a class with kindergarten children, and they are having a blast.

Zato is a handful, as you predicted. But he shares many of Nuffy's characteristics—both good and bad—so no real surprises. The walks in the neighborhood have been "interesting," and our neighbors now know we have a new dog. Those with females have had some "come to Jesus" moments. Strangely, our neighbors now prefer to walk their ladies on the other side of the street with the boys. So much for the society of one's peers.

At first, Zato seemed confused about everything. We showed him the doghouse and put a comfortable bed inside, but it took him almost two weeks to use it. We put bowls of food and water there, but he would only go in to eat or drink, then he'd rest under the big oak tree. In the last few days, he has started using the doghouse, and yesterday I saw him sleeping there. At night he sleeps in his old bed in our bedroom, just like Nuffy used to. He snores a little, but so did Nuffy. We close the kitchen and bathroom as you suggested, so he stays out of trouble. He's in the house about half the time.

Chiara loves him, and he loves her. They spend a lot of time together. She is trying to teach him new tricks, but you know the adage. It's been fun to watch the two of them. Chiara plays the guitar, and they sit together on her bed while she plays. Zato sings along with her either out of sympathy or to get her to stop. I'm not sure which. She loves getting him to do it.

Vic is the alpha male in the house. Zato listens to him more than to Chiara or me. I do the morning walk, but Vic does the long evening walks, and we do the weekends together. We have taken him for rides in the car. Of course, he loves to put his head out the window. Thank you for the tip regarding giving him little headroom. He goes crazy when he sees another dog in the street or in another car. If we tire of it, we put him in the back of the station wagon, as he is much quieter there.

I know he misses you all, but he is doing well, and we are giving him oodles of love. We are grateful to be his adoptive parents. It is working well.

Love to you all,
Marion, Vic, Chiara & Zato

September 26, 1979

Dear Marion,

Thank you for your letter and the update on Zato. We couldn't have found better parents for him, and we admire your taking him on. We had a good laugh about Chiara trying to teach him to fetch. Zato and Bagel think fetching is for the lower classes, perhaps Labradors or Beagles. It sounds like he and Chiara are hitting it off. Their duets sound lovely.

Bagel spent almost a month in quarantine and was ecstatic to see us. She is still getting used to the neighborhood sights and smells. Strangely, Parisians don't clean up after their dogs; perhaps there is no city ordinance requiring it, or maybe they don't care, but we seem to be the only ones doing it. Bagel, however, doesn't mind as it adds adventure to her walks.

Each night she sleeps cuddled in Zato's old blanket. That seems to help.

Ian is getting Chinese classes off the ground. Currently, he is teaching only the language but will be offering a history class after the new year. He was glad to hear that Miss Dash was doing well. He thinks she's a gem.

Fortunately, our furniture arrived a few days after we did. We still have two boxes to unpack but have already run out of places to put things—so they may remain that way.

The kids appear to like the school. Surprisingly, Max is settling in more easily than Logan, but she has made a friend from Germany and is coming along.

My responsibilities here resemble those I had at Columbia, but there are numerous functions my predecessor neglected to communicate. I knew I'd be busy, but there is more to it than I'd imagined. Fortunately for Ian and me, the wine here is cheaper than Coca-Cola.

Give our best to your family and our love to Zato, and please remind our young friend that we expect him to behave.

All the best,

Blair, Ian, Max, Logan, and Bagel

September 22, 1979

Dear Wumpling,

Greetings on the Autumnal Equinox.

You've been gone only a month, but you are dearly missed. Even Isa wonders where you've been. In truth, Spira is a bit out of sorts over your departure. These cousins are like siblings, and it's been tough for her. Hopefully, we can send her to you for a couple of weeks next summer. It will be good for her to know there is life beyond New Jersey.

We may all descend on you like locusts one of these days--sleeping bags in the living room for them, as I have dibs on the bathtub.

After your limo drifted out of sight, it took us just an hour to load the truck, and we moved all the furniture to the barn that same day. It's dry there and, at least for the moment, free of critters, but I'll keep an eye on it for you. Of course, if it looks like you will never return, we can always have what the locals call a "barn sale."

Liz and I saw Pepper Adams at the Village Gate last week. Roland Hanna on piano. Adams was surprisingly avant-garde, a bit too avant for us, but there were some elegant moments. You would have liked it--some of it.

If the Yankees end up playing the Los Angeles Dodgers (what a ridiculous name) in the World Series, I'm rooting for the Yankees. It's a first for me, but there are some things you can't forget--or forgive.

Tuo fratello maggiore,
Michael

P.S. Please let me know if the French indeed wear berets. I once had one in Positano. It may be in a box somewhere. If I find it, I will send it to you so that you blend in.

October 1, 1979

Dearest Gollum, Lizanne, Spira, and Isa,

It seems like a year has passed since we reveled in the ear-rattling thrum of your musical sendoff. That was quite a moment. Thank you! Please tell Spira how much we loved it. Thank you also for dealing with our furniture. That was above and beyond the call. We will return from France one day, open the barn door, and laugh at what vulgarians we once were.

We are mostly settled now--living with rented, rather ornate, furniture. The school is covering the first year, but I expect we will replace beds, tables, etc., with a more pedestrian taste in furnishings as finances allow. The apartment is comfortable, and we'd love to have Spira visit--or all of you; and, yes, you can have the bathtub.

Bagel spent a month in quarantine and was happy to learn we had not exiled her to Elba. She is still getting used to the ambiance of a new city and has met a few French canines, but they are a snooty lot and do not deign to speak Dog. I imagine that is because they are primarily German immigrants (Dachshunds, Shepards, Weimaraners, Schnauzers, etc.) who, having lost the war, spitefully leave their hunderhaufen all over the sidewalks of Paris.

Work at the school is challenging. I have middle school and high school Chinese classes and a writing class in the late afternoon. There are students from more than a dozen countries. It's like working at the U.N. Fortunately, there are no Russians banging their shoes on the tables protesting my inadequacies. I keep wondering when the management will discover I'm a fraud and transfer my contract to the Foreign Legion.

The parents of students are polite, cultivated, and dressed in custom-made suits and dresses (against which Blair and I resemble Georgia sharecroppers). The kids wear uniforms, so they don't have that problem.

Max has made a few friends among the scientists and brain surgeons here. Logan clings to one cute German girl a grade ahead of her. Strangely, it's been tough on her, but she is gradually coming out of her shell. Blair is working wonders already, as I predicted. She is like Atlas, holding the pillars of administration on her shoulders. People think she's French.

Sarah Reinhart, a Barnard schoolmate of Blair's and English teacher at the Neuilly school, had us to lunch. She has a six-year-old son who also attends school here. I'm sure we told you about her. We met her husband: a corporate lawyer who relaxes in a three-piece suit. Nice guy, despite looking like he might accuse me of having unmatched socks. Their apartment is spacious with polished parquet floors, furniture from Versailles, and a romantic city view. A class above.

There are many things to love here. One example: the parent/teacher orientation in early September consisted of hors d'oeuvres from around the world made by polyglot parents from half a dozen countries and excellent wine served in plastic cups. As I recall, St. Mark's offered only whine—in the form of parents arguing about a math grade.

Blair and I ride with the kids together on the same bus to and from school. These are not the yellow clunkers of our childhood but are European tour buses, air-conditioned with comfortable seats. For

Our school is different from what Max and I are used to. Some classes don't have lectures. Instead, we study independently, as fast or as slowly as we want. There are lots of projects that you do in teams of two or more. Last week, three of us built an electromagnet from wires wrapped around an iron rod. Next week we are building a gyroscope, and I don't even know what that is!! And I used to think science was boring. I'm getting to know more kids at school, but sometimes I feel a little out of place--like I have to act worldly when I'm not.

Bagel seems happy now, and sleeps with Zato's blanket every night. So we are afraid to wash it. It may just fall apart one day, and you might have to send us one from his doghouse.

I guess that's all the news. I wish you, your family, and Zato a merry Christmas in advance.

All the best,

Logan, Max and Bagel, Mom and Dad

P.S. Please tell Zato that I sniffed his old blanket yesterday, and I thought I could still smell him. Maybe I should sleep with it too. Please kiss him for me.

November 30, 1978

Dear Ian and Family,

I guess Chiara told you about Zato's misadventure on Thanksgiving morning. He got his teeth stuck in the turkey's plastic wrapping. Vic had to lift him by his collars to make him open his mouth so I could wriggle the bird free. Fortunately, it wasn't mauled, so we still had a successful Thanksgiving dinner. Zato received quite a lecture and pouted for the remainder of the day.

We also witnessed the zoomies. I had forgotten your warning that Zato might go crazy after a bath. But other than the loss of a small table lamp, there was no serious damage.

Beyond that, Zato has been delightful. He has fully settled into family life and seems to appreciate his doghouse, the freedom of the yard, his new beachball, his bones, and us. Perhaps we indulge him too much.

Miss Dash is doing well, and though she is not you, Ian, she is the best possible replacement. The students and their parents like her, and she is following your lesson plans to the letter, making the transition seamless.

That's about it. If you need updates, let me know, but we are finally all in a groove. Of course, the needle jumps out occasionally, and we must reset, but that's just part of canine parenting.

I hope your Thanksgiving was enjoyable despite not having the day off. Please give my love to Blair, the kids, and Bagel. We wish you a happy Christmas future.

Much love,
Marion and family

December 11, 1978

Dear Marion, Vic, Chiara, & Zato:

I'm glad to hear things have smoothed out with Zato. We were sorry but not too surprised to hear about the turkey in the sink. As you know, we had a similar event with a Christmas goose.

One experience with the zoomies should be enough to put in place the necessary safeguards to keep beds from traveling through walls. After that, the spectacle is a lot of fun to watch run its course.

I'm glad to hear about Miss Dash. I'm sure she is more than up to the task and will bring new life to the school in many ways. I'm not so sure that is what's happening here, as my presentation is more a vaudeville act than what they (management and students) are accustomed to seeing. The headmistress told me she was "excited" about my "teaching style." I worry about that a little, as my French is not great, and I may be mistranslating "agitated" for "excited."

I agree there is no need to drag the Zato correspondence out infinitely. We need to let go, and we are finally ready. We have wept, reminisced, and laughed. The topic of Zato still comes up, but emotions have settled out, and we are no longer sitting shiva. Please let us know if he runs off to Alaska for some decent weather or attempts to snack on the unsuspecting. Contact me if you are desperate for advice, need a posse, or just miss me. I am always available.

Good luck,
Merry Christmas and have a wonderful New Year.

Ian and family

Postscript

"I hear knocking at the door. Can someone get it?"

Logan and Bagel ran down the hallway. Bagel barking frantically.

Scooping the dog into her arms, Logan opened the door to a visitor clomping snow from her red leather boots. "Hi Logan," said the visitor. "Are your parents home?"

"Who is it?" floated a voice from the living room.

"It's Aunt Sam," Logan yelled back. "She has a dog with her, and it looks like a baby Zato!"